THE SPECTACLE

THE SPECTACLE

A NOVEL

ANNA BARRINGTON

UNION
SQUARE
& CO.

NEW YORK

**UNION
SQUARE
&CO.**

NEW YORK

ISBN 978-1-4549-6048-5 (paperback)
ISBN 978-1-4549-6049-2 (e-book)

Library of Congress Control Number is available upon request.

Union Square & Co. books may be purchased in bulk for business, educational, or
promotional use. For more information, please contact your local bookseller or the
Hachette Book Group's Special Markets department at special.markets@hbgusa.com.

Printed in the United States of America

2 4 6 8 10 9 7 5 3 1

unionsquareandco.com

Cover design by Patrick Sullivan
Cover image by JJs/Alamy Stock Photo (frame)
Interior design by Kevin Ullrich

To my mother, Deborah Scroggins.

"The spectacle is the flip side of money."

—Guy Debord, *The Society of the Spectacle*, 1967

DIVING OFF THE BOAT, RUDOLPH THOUGHT OF HER.

He'd expected the water to be cold, ice-cold, like it was on the Cape, but to his surprise the tropical ocean felt warm and forgiving on his raw skin. He opened his eyes underwater, precious bubbles escaping his lips. It was so beautiful down here in the bright deep blue, with the pink and gold fish swimming past him and something ominously darker flashing below. He remembered that sense of opulence then, of nervous self-invention in the city that was no longer his.

It was the nature of the terrain, the FBI agents said, that his body hadn't yet been recovered. What does that mean? Ingrid asked, and someone coughed. A long silence unspooled over the metal table.

Sharks, the woman said delicately.

Ingrid felt their probing eyes on her, waiting for her to cry.

It was funny. No one even suggested that he had been killed, though considering all the people who'd hated his guts, they probably thought he deserved it.

I'm going to die here, he realized in the water, and maybe it was for the best.

Let the salt flood his throat.

White sea frothed under his tongue, cool and crisp as chardonnay, and it reminded him of the money, the money lost and won and stolen,

1

the taste of money, trailing crimson like blood in clean water, on that frozen November night when he first met Ingrid Groenfeld.

Suddenly an instinct, a desire to survive, kicked in his chest. He refused to die. He absolutely refused to die, no, not like this.

Thrashing his legs, he fought his way upward, desperately seeking the glinting white sun. Don't choke, Rudolph begged himself, don't choke, and in a way, it was the motto of his lifetime. Don't you dare fucking choke.

RISE

I

ALL POWERFUL MARRIAGES INVOLVE A DEAL WITH A DEVIL, PAUL
Bernot was always saying, whether both parties know it or not.
Paul, who prided himself on going into things with his eyes wide
open, had known it—even if his own powerful marriage had
ended in failure because he was unwilling or unable to pay that
price. (His ex-wife said it was because he couldn't stop fucking
twenty-two-year-olds.)

Watching him stride about the gallery office, going on about deals
and devils, Ingrid had a moment of pity for him. Talking, talking,
talking. It was like, Ingrid thought, he expected her to write down
what he was saying, to record it for posterity. As though he considered
himself the center of a history instead of the footnote in someone
else's, as she secretly knew him to be.

But earlier tonight, when they'd been going over the numbers, Paul's
mouth had twisted into a sullen pout. He'd put his head in his hands. For
a moment, he had looked almost tragic, like he was about to cry.

No more Mommy, Ingrid had thought.

"We need new artists, fast," he had said. "This Dermott Dermott
Critchley—I want you to go to his opening tonight. Find me people of
value. Is there hard money behind the guy? Enough for us to bother
poaching him off Duma?"

Cut off from his ex-wife's inheritance, Paul was alone, and his
hands on the beautiful desk were bunched up with veins. The cold
November sun slid slowly down, flashing over the signet ring on his
pinky finger. That was the business.

* * *

By evening a brown fog had wrapped itself around Manhattan, hiding the cantilevered sparkle of the Jenga Building behind a dank drizzle. Hurrying down Walker Street, Ingrid felt a thrill go up her spine. Value, value. Paul was always searching for people of value, but this was the first time he'd ever trusted his twenty-five-year-old assistant with the task. It seemed proof that something important was about to happen, something that would justify her entire life so far. She wove in and out of the traffic, marching behind the commuters with a feeling of vague importance in her step. Nobody else seemed to notice. Everyone kept their faces muzzled, in black coats and scarves, with their eyes glued to their devices. Nothing visible but an abstract pattern of tiny squares in the dark, a Mondrian painting of cell phones, glowing smokily through the twilight.

Duma Gallery was newish, owned by a pair of promiscuous Israelis rumored to be linked to the mob, and it operated like a club right down to its tight security and drug-fueled after-parties. From the frozen street where Ingrid stood shivering, her nose pressed up to the rain-spattered glass, the gallery seemed to cast a shifting underwater light. She gave her name to the boy intern at the door, whose eyes ran doubtfully over her wet clothes.

"That name isn't on our RSVP list."

"It's Groenfeld, Ingrid Groenfeld." She started to spell it. "I-N-G—" He cut her off.

"Yeah, and as I told you, it's just not on the list."

"Well, it should be."

"Well, it isn't," the boy mimicked, imitating her voice.

Ingrid looked at him. He had on a wool sweater that looked as though it had been ravaged by a pack of angry house cats and then sold for six hundred dollars, which was probably the case. Beneath it his skin was the color of sour milk, concave.

Why wasn't she on the list?

Ingrid breathed out. The money required to play in the art world had recently reached new heights, new levels, though when you were riding high off the chem trails of other people's jets, there always was another level. But Paul had reached that level, a long time ago. Unless. Unless he was slipping.

The boy gave her a sympathetic little half-smile.

"I'm here on behalf of Paul Bernot Gallery," she said, louder. "Check the list."

He blinked, twice.

"Oh," he said. "I see."

And reluctantly he lifted the velvet rope.

Inside, beautiful people in pleated Japanese silks drifted among the waiters, who were offering out semolina cakes and champagne. Only a few graying critics bucked the trend, announcing to the world with their messy tufts of hair and square-framed black glasses that they were far too cerebral to care about such petty vanities. They stuck their faces up to the walls, moving with the natural arrogance of the tastemakers of a modern empire at the apogee of its powers.

Tonight, Dermott Dermott Critchley was their man. Enormous canvases stretched along the vast white walls. Acrobats, abstract splashes, the odd Freudian symbol—a parsnip, a couple of vulvic flowers—whirled across the paintings. To Ingrid, they looked as though someone had thrown hair at the canvas and snipped haphazardly with a pair of garden shears, but what did she know? Ugliness. The art world loved ugliness. Pretty was so boring to look at, and everyone here hated to be bored.

December 2016. The defiant mood vaguely surprised Ingrid. Election night: people had been crying, screaming. What the hell was going on? Everyone they knew had voted for Hillary, so who was out there clapping for the loudmouth?

Somehow the other side of the country had become a shadow, a black outline. People were still wandering the streets of New York with dazed and confused faces, stunned by the extent of their collective misjudgment. So Ingrid might be forgiven for expecting to see fear, sadness, maybe even impotent guilt, in this room full of liberals in the weeks post-election. Or maybe that just showed how little she still knew about the art world, even after two years as Paul's assistant—because by the week after Thanksgiving, its denizens had already begun to flicker onward, like snakes shedding their scales.

"It's no wonder they can't understand the benefits of a progressive culture, you know?" a sleek PR woman in a white pantsuit wondered aloud. She was sipping a glass of the free Cristal provided by the German bank that was the evening's sponsor. Now she winced. "Ugh. I hate champagne. Do you hate champagne?"

"It always makes my breath stink," her friend agreed. "But to your point. It's so important to empathize. Can you imagine the conditions his voters live in? You really can't blame them for not being able to identify their own interests."

"No. No, I'm just disappointed. I mean, they live in fucking food deserts, just imagine like, buying from Walmart all the time. Zero access to high-quality produce, let alone fresh pasta."

"No Dean and DeLuca." White Pantsuit rolled *DeLuca* deliciously over her tongue.

"No Citarella either," the friend giggled. "Ugh, I feel so bad for them."

"Me too. Just so guilty!" cried White Pantsuit. "But can't they see that it's their own tired values holding them back?"

She gestured with her flute at the window, as though this block of polished glass was the only thing stopping the unwashed masses from storming in and joyously partaking in the champagne.

"What I really can't believe are the prices at this show." The friend spoke out of one corner of her mouth, while attempting to remove with a cocktail napkin an errant blob of goat cheese encrusted to her chin.

"So inflated! Forty thousand here, a million at auction—"

"Soon I won't be able to afford art at all!"

Laughter. She had one of those voices cultivated to sparkle like sugarplums, rich and weighty. Ingrid noticed that the room was barely half full. As usual, there had been no need for an exclusive guest list.

Ingrid saw Dermott's lowered head from a distance, surrounded by an older couple in furs. Wearing the paint-stained overalls he liked to bring out for these occasions, he'd affected a pensive expression and was stroking the goatee he'd grown to look more intellectual.

"Tell us," the woman said in a hushed tone. "These paintings. They're so genius. Can you talk a little bit more about your process?"

Dermott sighed. Ingrid could feel anxiety radiating off him in waves. *Lights, camera, action*—the moment that every artist longs for. After all those years of struggle and self-doubt, finally, *finally* the Establishment sees you, wants you, is desperate to eat up a slice of your heart and soul. It's classic transference: they hope to swallow you up to prove they're more amusing, charming, cooler, and more sophisticated than all the other bankers and CEOs and partners in their boring Excel-based lives. Tonight, they're not just paying for paintings; they're paying for you. What to say?

"The impetus behind these paintings was my connection to Picasso. You know, I've always been fascinated by certain motifs, like the head. Or like a woman's breasts."

The man and woman nodded.

"And then one day I just had this bolt of, like, lightning. I thought, how crazy would it be if I reinvented these motifs for the twenty-first century? Reflect the grittiness of the city, the chaos of the street. Picasso did it his way, I'm gonna do it mine."

"Well, we think they're incredible. Just incredible."

Dermott let out a self-deprecating little laugh: aw, shucks, me?

"I struggled. Truly I struggled. It was a long way toward finding a signature style." He paused, readying himself to launch a new line. With gravity, he said: "My work is a punch in the face. It's almost like being mugged, it's so intense—so—so against the grain."

Had it landed? Hopeful, Dermott checked for signs of a successful sound bite. The banker shrank back into his glossy snow jacket with a vague look of alarm, but his wife leaned in. Her cheeks were flushed, eyes alive.

"It's like how the cavemen used to paint with blood," the woman said, "at the caves of Lascaux. So primal, so—so *raw*. Isn't it, sweetie?"

"But the references you use," the man wanted to know, "how does all that data stick in your head?"

"Um?"

"The references," the man persisted. "Chinese gymnasts, Picasso, the political whatever . . . I just wondered how you manage to bring out all that data in the paintings? Do you use a spreadsheet?"

Uncertainty flickered across Dermott's face.

"Um, it just comes out. It's like all the things you've ever seen are locked inside you, waiting. Your memories, feelings—they're alive, they're part of you, but you don't know what they mean until you start painting. In some ways you never know."

The collector nodded unhappily. Christ, for forty thousand dollars you'd think an artist would come up with better than that. Calculation, forethought, planning, these were the methods he knew of justifying a price. Art should be like sustainable yoga pants: a beautiful palliative for a dying world.

When a silence fell, Ingrid took the opportunity to congratulate Dermott. "The show's incredible," she said, watching the collector steer his wife away. Was there jealousy in her voice? She squelched it. The woman kept glancing behind her husband's shoulder, her eyes searching for Dermott, desperate to soak up the juices of his celebrity.

"You think so?"

"Yeah. I love the references to Mayan art."

Dermott's face darkened with blood.

"Hey, don't mention that to anyone," he whispered, his hand closing tight on her arm. "The absolute last thing I need right now is to get accused of cultural appropriation. It's hard enough being a white male artist these days. I'm really trying to emphasize that this is one hundred percent original, all right?"

"Oh, got it. I mean, I totally get that," Ingrid stumbled. "Sorry, I didn't mean to say anything wrong."

Seconds later, Dermott's black expression vanished: he'd spotted a silverback collector lumbering off behind Ingrid's shoulder. He put on a large artificial smile. "It's an easy mistake to make! What must you think of me, this crazy neurotic artist? Though it kinda comes with the territory, right? So, where's Paul, eh?" he asked, scanning the room rapidly. "Is he here?"

"Paul couldn't make it," she explained, wincing a little. It was insulting, no doubt, that Paul had decided to go see *Hamilton* and ditch the exhibition, sending a lowly minion like herself instead. She bumbled on: "He had a dinner at the Whitney. Guest of honor, unfortunately—"

"Cool, cool," Dermott said, losing interest. "Sorry, I just—I have to go talk to that woman over there. She's on the board of the MoMA— you understand?"

* * *

Left alone, Ingrid decided to wander off. Dermott had been spoken to, and the rest of the evening could be whatever she wanted it to be. She walked slowly toward the strange blue glow. Originally, she'd thought it was the spotlights, but the light appeared to thicken behind a partition about forty feet away. At the back of the room, Ingrid found herself staring at a tank. It was filled with gel. Within the tank floated an enormous brown cow, spotted white. Its eyes were wide open in death, staring accusingly at Ingrid as if to express a general astonishment at the banal disappointments of the afterlife. Eternity frozen inside a shitty two-bit gallery. What a fucking nightmare.

"These things are so passé," said a bored voice behind her.

A shadow had appeared in the glass. His accent was nationless, those flat unplaceable tones of an international school, and she peered around the glass to find its source.

A tall slim man was leaning insolently against the tank. He had auburn hair, a jaw like cut glass, and cool green eyes the palest shade of malachite. She had a confused but immediate impression of a wolf in human clothing. Then her gaze dropped down over his suit: expensive, meant to tailor over sharp shoulders and terminate on witty orange socks, and it clicked. The socks. Yes, it was the socks that marked him out to her as a member of the culture industry: that carefully crafted flash of eccentricity you wouldn't get in just a regular finance guy.

Vain eyes, she thought, looking at him. Eyes that knew exactly how beautiful he was.

"Rudolph," he said, offering his hand.

"Ingrid." She took it.

"You work for Paul Bernot?"

"Yeah. How'd you know?"

"I was in line behind you at the door," he explained. "The guy was a dick."

She nodded, shrugged to show she didn't care.

"So what do you make of all this?"

He smiled at her. In the silence, she stared into his eyes, feeling the impulse for speech leave her body. Later she'd realize it was his greatest gift—the way his attention crystallized on you, as if there was nothing he wanted to know more than what you were about to say— because who really listens to us, who really cares? But tonight, she was simply tongue-tied.

"I thought the market for Hirsts totally crashed, anyway," she said vaguely. "And isn't it supposed to be a shark?"

He snorted. "Well, yeah. But you know they have to replace these things?"

"Really?"

"Of course. The skin's drilled with formaldehyde, but they still rot. They replace them every five years when the old corpses disintegrate, make the collectors pay for it. But what happened was, the owner was some hedge funder who got nailed by the SEC. He was too cheap to buy a new twelve-thousand-dollar shark—hedge funders are the cheapest guys you'll ever meet, believe me—so he replaced it with a cow to advertise his Wagyu beef farm. Two birds one stone, you get me? Anyway, he's in jail now, so they're trying to flog it off to some gullible fuck as a limited-edition piece, and God knows they'll manage."

"A match made in heaven. Dermott Dermott Critchley and a sacrificial cow."

Ingrid was red with embarrassment before she had even finished, hating the artifice, hating the low-hanging fruit of her lame joke, but no, he was laughing with her.

"I take it you don't like his stuff."

Ingrid shrugged. She'd meant how the collectors swarmed over Dermott, but she felt pierced by a sudden desire to act rebellious, to impress him with her irony, her contempt. Maybe it was the white wine, but she was feeling much more confident than usual, much more alive, and she finally got up the nerve to ask him if he wanted a cigarette.

"Oh God no, I don't smoke. Quit years ago."

He hesitated. In that moment a well-heeled man came up and tapped him on the shoulder, and she could see that he was about to leave her behind. Her stomach burned.

"Rudolph! We've been trying to get you round to our place for weeks now."

But he surprised her by saying a few brief words to the man and turning back to her. The ghost of a smile drifted over his face.

"Well—maybe just this once."

Outside, they smoked and watched the trail of visitors ebb and flow, trading commentary on the people they recognized. Ingrid barely knew anyone. She had never been very good at the oozing and schmoozing she should be doing. But Rudolph seemed to know everybody worth knowing.

"So, I'm sorry. You know I work for Paul, but what are you doing here? Just taking in our great city's rich cultural offerings?" she asked.

"I'm a dealer." He laughed.

"That's funny?"

"I guess I just thought you'd already figured it out."

"Was I supposed to?" She blinked innocently at him. "I'm way too jejune to know the ins and outs of the art world."

"Think you're some kind of child bride?" He slowly picked a stray thread off her elbow. Feeling his hand graze her inner arm, she tensed—it was that little shock of someone else entering her periphery without permission. She hoped he wouldn't smell her coat. It was thrift-store Margiela, not half-bad either, if you ignored the lingering odor of mothballs. "Anyway," he continued, "seems like you'd be good at that kind of thing."

"What kind of thing?"

"Sussing people out."

"Me?" She laughed. "Oh, no. I'm on the wrong side of the business. I actually tried to be an artist for a few years—selling paintings on the street, that sort of thing. But, uh, it didn't work out," she said.

He smiled. "So here you are."

"Here I am," Ingrid said dryly.

"That the chip on your shoulder, huh? Daddy's not a close personal friend of the boss?" He took a drag of one of her American Spirits. "Let me tell you something. *Everybody* thinks they're an outsider. You're on the inside, trust me."

Ingrid's heart buzzed. The wine was rambling about in her stomach, making it harder and harder to repress a dark, familiar echo: Simone's voice on that nightmarish day two years ago Ingrid had packed up and left. *There's nothing wrong. I just want to be alone now.*

Behind her a famous art dealer said comfortably, "Geffen has exquisite taste. Real connoisseurs are now being born in Los Angeles."

"I just think there's something sick about it all, don't you think?" She nodded at the dealer. "Look at all these people, heaped with praise for buying things, as if blind consumption gives you some kind of profound sensitivity to the world. As if anyone from West Virginia or Indiana who'll never be in anything but alien abduction tabloids couldn't have great taste, too, if only they had the stylists and PR people and decorators to buy it for them."

Ingrid stopped; Rudolph was staring at her. Out loud her voice sounded pissed off, maybe a little drunk, and she cringed at herself while trying to smile. Playing the awkward, bitter naïf? She wished she could melt into the ground. But Rudolph simply changed the subject, flicking a hand at her cigarette.

"Why do you smoke? Everybody's cut it out since I moved back from London."

"You're from London?"

She couldn't tell. He shook his head, still gazing at her, but didn't clarify where he was from or what he had been doing in London.

"Well, I don't know," she said. "I guess it started in art school. But then—it sounds stupid—but as a woman you're inundated with products. Magazines and wellness ads and gummy vitamins trying to whip you up in a frenzy of fear, make you feel so fat and old and ugly you'll do almost anything to make it go away. That's what it means to be a woman, isn't it? But I hate that. I don't care about fighting some battle to stay young and attractive." She waved her cigarette, its embers singeing the air. "Bodies age. Life ends. Let me be free to just live it."

"You say that now, because you are young and attractive."

Ingrid ducked her head. Her face felt feverish under his laughing green eyes. Rudolph dropped his cigarette, which sizzled on the dull ice before he crushed it out with one polished loafer.

"Hey," he said, and hesitated. "Do you want to come to a party tomorrow night?"

"A party on a Thursday?" she said without thinking.

He smiled at her, two dimples appearing in his cheeks.

"Worried about school the next day?"

Ingrid's heart fell.

"Sure, whatever," she said quickly, trying to regain her previous froideur. "As long as you're not, like, a serial killer or something."

"You don't trust me?"

"You could be anyone." She eyed him coolly. "Patrick Bateman, not even trying for a disguise."

He winced. "That bad, huh?"

When he asked for her number she raised her eyebrows, a rush of confidence fueling her on until he began to shuffle around the frozen pavement with visible awkwardness. Finally she relented and typed it into his phone.

Bashfully he said, "I hope that you'll answer."

Ingrid walked over to MacIntyre's, a lit cigarette in hand. A nervous excitement was bubbling up in her lungs—a crush, a weak-at-the-knees kind of crush, the kind that didn't happen very often these days. *You're on the inside*, the man had said. *Trust me.* But she didn't. Perhaps that was part of the excitement: his foreignness. It was the type of encounter she had always wanted to have in New York, but it had never happened until now.

MacIntyre's was a low-lit Irish pub chain with shuddering windows and bad drinks, nearly deserted but for a few grizzled old regulars. She and Richard had started coming here during college, on day trips to New York City—half because they were too broke and intimidated by the roaring concrete jungle to go elsewhere, half because they didn't know any better. What brilliant successes they'd planned of their lives! And they'd always said it just like that: *New York City.* With a radiant faith they had hoped would pay off into the future.

Richard was waiting for her in a torn leather booth. Olives beaded his empty martini. Seeing Ingrid's sweaty face, he widened his eyes.

"Were you just running?" he asked. "Your face is so red."

"It's freezing outside," she said, embarrassed, and sat down. She recalled something an ex-boyfriend had once said: *Your feelings are always written all over your face.* No knack for mystery, for dissimulation and fantasy: honesty could be so distinctively unsexy.

"Did you order me a drink?"

"The service is terrible, you know that. How else can you explain the existence of the last dive bar in this shitty overpriced neighborhood?" But he generously slid over a glass. "How was the opening?"

"Oh, just the usual inane bullshitting."

Ingrid picked at a dried-out bowl of nuts on the table. Richard was talking, talking, about his boyfriend and why he didn't like him so much anymore, while Ingrid drifted into space. She was remembering this hysterical Reagan-era propaganda novel that she'd once read in high school about a girl who accidentally ate a bowl of peanuts covered in acid. Later, locked in a closet by some concerned friends and family members, she had torn out her own hair and nails scratching at the door. Which reminded her of something. Seeing Dermott's anxious expression tonight, when he'd struggled to answer the collectors' question—*why do you throw yourself at the canvas, day after day after day?*—Ingrid had kept up the polite smile that her job now required. Inside, though, she had been seething. She'd wanted to grab his hand, to cry out, *I know!*

Only once, in the false dawn of a cheap studio, had she ever come close to what Dermott had described. Swirling the colors over the canvas, she had felt the city's undercurrents channeling down through each brushstroke, so fast her hands could barely keep up with the urge to paint. There had been a force, a force and a power in her inner mind. But never again had she heard it, this secret scream pitched to the ultrasonic soul of New York, no matter how hard she sought it out.

". . . and I just want to shake him sometimes!" Richard was saying. "I want to scream at him. He literally sits there smiling at me like a big hot lump, like a big old Ken doll while I'm wallowing in a pool of wine and self-pity. It's just not *enough*, you know? And his friends, I hate his friends. Did you hate Brian's friends? They're so shallow and self-absorbed. Like, they'll say, Oh, I have the *best* apartment in Tribeca and I go to the *best* parties at Art Basel—when, dude, they barely even got into the general section at Art Basel—not even asking you a word about yourself for hours—"

"Yeah."

"What's wrong?" Richard poked her arm accusingly. "Are you hungover or what? You're not listening to my story."

"What? Yes I am." Ingrid was fiddling with her straw, folding its tiny squares into one clenched palm. "I just, uh, I met this really hot guy."

"Really? Who?"

"An art dealer, I guess. Not really sure where from."

"Art dealer?" he repeated in surprise. "Hmm. But what about . . ."

"Brian?" Contemplative, she ate a peanut under his gaze. "Oh, horrible. Absolutely vile. I loathe him and we're done, completely done. But this guy, this guy . . ." She couldn't say his name yet; it felt too intimate. Instead she told Richard about the party tomorrow. "Want to come?"

"Sure!" Richard said brightly. "Maybe let's wait, though? See what he texts you?"

"I just thought there was a vibe."

"Of course there was," Richard reassured her. "I just don't want you to ride off into the sunset looking like a bunny boiler." And he began singing out a twangy Shania Twain song about a lover gone bad.

Reluctantly Ingrid laughed. It was offensive that Richard thought she was so ready to drop everything for this stranger, albeit a stranger whose voice still murmured in her ears. But when she looked up, Richard was still gazing at her. He had the far-off stare of a chess player, gaming out the scenarios of love in his mind. She watched him raise a finger. Testing the winds, he rotated it slowly in the air. Ingrid felt breathless. She prepared herself, body and mind, to receive his advice, this shaman, a divine prophecy from the gods of dating. Then he blinked: the answer had come.

"Play it cool," Richard said finally.

2

IT WAS A COMMON ENOUGH THING IN SALES TO FUCK YOUR WAY TO THE middle and stay there. But Rudolph Sullivan was proud to say that he had never participated in such desperate, muddy slithering—or at least, no more than was strictly necessary.

One o'clock on Thursday afternoon. Rudolph stood over his brand-new (antique) Bauhaus desk, searching its polished surface for flaws. He lifted a magnifying glass. Examined the wood for chips, dents, scratches, before moving his eye down over his own suit. It was beautiful, tailored, English, flannel, perfectly matching the chestnut suede loafers from a niche Florentine tannery. Stray hairs? There were none.

Satisfied, he replaced the glass in its drawer and stood up. The desk had been shipped overnight from Sweden for today's meeting with the German investors, which had obviously cost a fucking fortune. But when the meeting you'd been waiting your whole life for dropped into your lap with a jingle of coins, you leapt up in the air to grab them. You couldn't expect to be taken seriously in this business without the necessary expenses—the coldly beautiful girl casting vicious glances at frightened tourists over the front desk; the light-filled gallery in the heart of Chelsea; the library of dusty-looking academic tomes to indicate one's belonging to an elite historical tradition that *you* (you hopeless rube!) could never even aspire to understand.

Rudolph snatched up the phone and dialed Madison, the hot new Barnard grad he'd recently hired as eye candy for collectors. Not for Rudolph, though—first rule of business: don't shit where you eat.

"The investors here yet?" he demanded.

"Uh, no, sorry, Rudolph. But the accountant did say it's pretty urgent you call him back."

Rudolph exhaled. There was a sudden tight pressure in his chest. He wanted to call the accountant like he wanted to fuck a chicken.

"Just let me know when the Germans arrive," he said.

Slowly, reluctantly, Rudolph dialed voicemail. The accountant's quivering tones rang out: *Uh, hi Rudolph, I don't want to bore you, but we do need to talk about—*

When someone prefaces a statement with *I don't want to bore you*, chances that you will be bored suddenly leap into the ninetieth percentile.

He paced the vast concrete halls of his gallery—adjusting a painting hanging slightly off-center, brushing a grain of dust off an El Anatsui tapestry—before stopping to admire the jewel in his collection: the 1981 Bélizaire.

A frisson of satisfaction ran down Rudolph's spine. Taking in its enormity, he allowed the calm of possession to wash slowly over him. It was big—at least five feet tall by four feet across, and abattoir red with impasto. Slick, almost violet in its globs of encrusted paint, like a prime rib leaking blood onto a clean white plate.

The Bélizaire had come into his hands in 2015, around the same time he'd left the gallery empire of his old mentor Harry Olbrich in London to spread his own wings, here in New York. It had taken a decade for his dreams to match the reality—hurtling forcefully upward, from intern to sales director to operating rinky-dink temporary spaces on the Upper East Side—but finally, *finally* he'd opened his own grand new space on West 25th Street. Massive profits, a square footage to rival Olbrich's, and a whirling dervish of a PR agent to shout out the great news: Rudolph Sullivan had arrived.

Of course, it's not really your painting, he reminded himself.

If he was honest, Rudolph often had trouble remembering this fact. He'd first heard about the painting while holidaying in St. Tropez; another dealer had run into him at the beach club and later called him to sniff around. Might he be interested in an eight-figure Bélizaire, painted at the height of the artist's fame? Condition *fantastisch*. From a significant private collection (Rockefeller, but keep it under wraps). In short, everything you could ask of a museum-quality Bélizaire.

Perfect, Rudolph had said. I've got just the guy in mind.

He phoned Frederick Asaka, one of his biggest clients, who happened to be yachting nearby in Antibes. Asaka'd promptly turned the boat around just to come and take a look at the painting. Rich people lived differently, that was for sure.

Picture this: An evening spent walking around the swaying deck, Asaka blowing fierce white crumbs of cigar ash across the oiled walnut prow. Rudolph had come aboard with a couple of muscled-up security men carrying the painting behind him. (Was it difficult to find last-minute security guys? You bet. But that, too, was part of his particular set of skills.)

Of all Rudolph's clients, Asaka was by far the most cryptic. Though he claimed to be a French-Japanese investor, he spoke in the smooth, monotone LA drawl so popular within their circle, meant to mask your emotions from the listener. The lips barely moved. People used it to make themselves sound like celebrities, fending off the paparazzi, discreetly important. But Frederick Asaka was unusual in that Rudolph thought he did actually have things to hide. He was one of those ambiguously rootless people who seemed to have no real resting place or origin—multilingual, multinational, denizen of everywhere and nowhere. There was some kind of connection to Russia, something about the dark web—nothing you could pin down for sure—since anything on the internet seemed to have been scrubbed off, or perhaps it had never existed at all. Suffice to say that he owned countless passports and houses, and the origins of his money remained mysterious to Rudolph. Ultimately, though, the specifics of Frederick's job weren't Rudolph's problem to solve. This business was teeming with wizards trying to magic ill-begotten gains into clean, shiny art. If he wasn't selling to Frederick Asaka, someone else would be.

"Should we go out?" Rudolph had suggested with a smile, stretching his arms languidly over his head as if he'd completely forgotten about the painting.

In tacit agreement, they'd sat through an eye-wateringly dull dinner with Asaka's family, ignoring the way the Bélizaire loomed like a ghost under its plastic veil in the stateroom. He and Asaka were both a little drunk, drawn to the shouts of young people in the glittering harbor, trying to ignore the cries of the children urgently hushed by their nannies. Asaka toted around his family like prize horses, though no one had ever seemed less like a family man. But Asaka only waved him toward the painting, a king's brusque command:

"No, no. Show me the Bélizaire, Sullivan. Don't be a tease."

Rudolph had laughed, though his ears had bristled with resentment.

"I do have to say," he said casually, "that the owner's very attached to it. I can't guarantee he'd be willing to sell."

"Stop dicking me around," Asaka snarled. "I came all the way to see the goddamn thing. I've got over two thousand paintings in my collection, all right? I don't need to start at the bottom, I start at the top."

"All right, all right."

Rudolph had sighed, knowing he'd inadvertently crossed the Rubicon, and this client was the kind of guy you didn't really want to piss off. Asaka scowled over the polished walnut table until Rudolph got up and whisked the long white cloth away.

Asaka's face rippled in surprise. His eyes traversed the canvas: there was a pulpy human heart in flames, a jagged spear on blood-colored ground, a skirmish of color. Rudolph watched him. Every line burned with talent, but if you knew what you were looking at, something else burned harder. The painting was money, pure money.

"Nice, isn't it?" Rudolph said, in the same casual tone. "Only twenty-one when he painted it. That was the year he got discovered uptown. Went from being a grubby little street kid to Michelangelo and Mick Jagger and Jesus Christ all wrapped into one in about sixty seconds or less."

"An enfant terrible, no? He really went against the grain."

Rudolph smiled to hide his derision. What an amateur! It made him laugh to watch these puddle-bellied tech titans try to buy street cred by purchasing artists they considered edgy proles. Extra points if the artist was Black—they thought it made them seem less bourgeois.

Everyone in the art world knew that Adrien Bélizaire hadn't really gone against the grain. He'd just had the right story: dated a couple celebrities, made friends with the right people, overdosed on barbiturates early enough to fly out in flames, the lucky asshole! Sure he was okay with a paintbrush, but what really made you was the man, the myth, the charisma. That blazing mirage of sex and drama and story, impossible to re-create.

"That's right," he said, keeping his voice honeyed. "You're well-read on his history, I can see. So you'll notice the symbols, the color, the size—it's peak Bélizaire, teetering on the razor's edge of self-destruction," he added, gearing himself up for a sales pitch.

"It was the year his talents crystallized, literally minutes before he spiraled too deep into his addiction to get out. Some artists are destined for torment, you know. To disappear into the grunge of madness and to leave us their life story, and Bélizaire? He was like Jesus Christ. Born to die. He had a legendary habit, I've heard—he'd spend twenty, thirty grand on a bag in a single night at the Mudd Club. But he was a genius to the end. See the gesturalism of Abstract Expressionism, here? The connections to Frankenthaler, Twombly, Rauschenberg..." He stopped. Pointed to a figure in the middle of the painting. "See that? That's Booker Little, the jazz guy."

"Oh, I *love* jazz," Asaka breathed.

"No way. Seriously?" Obviously, Rudolph had known this.

"You know I even used to think of being a pianist? My first wife and I used to go to jazz bars, back when we were students—Ronnie Scott's in London . . . fell in love there . . ."

Abruptly his dangerous mood had mellowed, shifting as quickly as the winds keening against the deck of the boat.

"Anyway. Please continue."

"Bélizaire painted this in a fury after seeing Goya's Black Paintings in Madrid. The link has never been proven with such specificity, but I'm in close contact with some historians who are about to release a groundbreaking study in the definitive new Bélizaire book. See, Frederick, this painting may be *the* most important work of the artist's career. I've already committed it to a major new exhibition in Japan, just major, absolutely transformative scientific research behind it— and as for the value added to the painting?" He shook his head slowly. "Well, I don't need to tell a guy as sophisticated as you."

"But," Asaka said. "If you were to tell me?"

That was the thing, Rudolph thought. They brought it on themselves.

"Well," Rudolph said, and paused. He allowed a smile to cross his lips. "It would be—colossal. Simply colossal."

"I see," Asaka said.

Alcohol had slipped the careful mask. Asaka wore an expression that Rudolph had come to recognize in his line of work: a look of cowed astonishment, the unmistakable blend of greed and awe that accompanied the translation of hieroglyphs into a celestial alphabet of meaning, a subculture possessed only by the elite. They, too, could access a vivid new language of images and symbols, something impervious to the world of cash and corporate boardrooms in which they lived every waking minute. What he dangled before their eyes was more rarefied than even the most exclusive club, the silvery reward for their blood and sweat and tears—and by now they really fucking wanted it.

"Will you send me that book? I'd like to read it myself."

"It's not published yet," Rudolph said smoothly, "but of course, I have an advance copy. I'll have it couriered over tomorrow."

With a sudden flash of suspicion Asaka asked: "You're sure about this museum thing? The investment potential, I mean?"

A measured nod, signaling scholarly expertise:

"I'd buy it myself if I could."

He had him then, he just knew it. Asaka's eyes were still fixated on the thick, bruise-colored brushstrokes. But then:

"I'm not interested in paying sales tax," he said. His stiff fingers brushed the painting carefully—almost longingly—before turning back to Rudolph with effort. "Keep the painting in your gallery for me, all right? Just like the last one I bought. Keep it under your name, and if this Japanese show really does make the price shoot up, I'll flip it."

Rudolph was surprised, he really was. Obscurely disappointed, even. He could've sworn the guy loved the painting the way he loved it himself, for its radiant history and beauty. But whatever his true feelings were, Asaka liked its cash potential more.

They shook on it. Rudolph returned to his hotel the following morning, painting in hand, deal in bag. The best part? While the painting had been marketed to him for a cool eight million, he'd told Asaka that it was being sold for ten by an American corporation on the verge of bankruptcy, thus allowing him to pocket an extra two mil. Fuck it, who'd be the wiser? There was no law against buying low and selling high.

"Rudolph? They're here."

Madison stood in the doorway, blinking her tremulous blond smile at him.

"Already?"

Rudolph sprang to his feet. Catlike, he slid the laminated folder out of her hands. Provenance, condition reports, fact sheets, all emblazoned with his own initials—*RJS*—in crisp black serif font. God, would he ever get tired of seeing that logo?

"All there," she assured him. They exchanged a quick grin. Whatever else anyone says about me, he thought, I'm a damn good boss.

"Should I say you'll be there in a minute?"

"Be right down."

He waited until she left. Another flash in the mirror: he looked good. Pale, but good, his eyes still roaming restlessly around the room for missed imperfections. No trace, but no trace at all of that shy, gawkish boy, desperately trying to shoot a single hoop in gym class. Oh God, that milk-faced kid with a thick South Boston accent! Physically cursed with a crown of flame-red curls, ugly freckles, lips like a Hapsburg. Even his gait was effeminate as hell, a human bull's-eye for those malicious little bruisers now working blue-collar jobs. It was a time when kids could still call you a faggot, laughing while they kicked you in the stomach, and get away with it. Where were they now? Probably plodding police officers, male nurses, or firefighters popping pill after pill in Southie or Dorchester, he thought with a vicious little thrill of schadenfreude. Just a few more casualties of the opioid epidemic, and thank Christ for that!

"Rudolph?" Madison called.

He locked eyes with the Bélizaire one last time, crossed himself twice for luck. How beautifully it shimmered across the white concrete walls! So neatly contained, which was it should be. Because disorder—ugliness, poverty, unruly emotions—could not exist in this shrine of ice. The modern gallery was an organ refrigerator, devised to confine all messiness in the world to the red, dripping, beating heart of art, but outside? Every speck of dirt had to be scrubbed out, bleached out, frozen out. Collectors preferred this to the reality of life, and Rudolph—that shy, sensitive boy who'd grown up in a vat of dust and alcoholic failure and indifference—preferred it too.

He had a horror of mess.

3

RUDOLPH SAW THE THREE MEN WAITING DOWNSTAIRS THROUGH THE glass box of the elevator, before he heard the harsh foreign burr of their voices. Jonas, his contact, had one of those tanned, glossy Northern European faces that seem to have been smoothed out with butter. His corpulent frame strained against a navy pinstripe suit, cut just a smidgen too tight. Rudolph's lip curled to see his brand-new Lanvin sneakers, so tacky they might've come straight out of a Silicon Valley start-up. Then Jonas flew at him, yelling out, "Rudy! What's good, bro?" and wrapped him in a back-slapping hug that left Rudolph gasping for breath.

"So good to see you," Rudolph said, resisting the urge to punch Jonas in the face: Don't *FUCKING* call me Rudy, asshole. (It always reminded him of Rudy Giuliani, so baby boomer, so *lower middle-class*.) He turned to the older men standing behind Jonas and offered his firm, practiced politician's handshake.

"Rudolph Sullivan. Great to finally meet you," he said, broadcasting a warm smile at the two men. "I've heard a lot of good things, great things."

"Stefan Rathenau."

"Christian Rathenau."

Two rich uncles, one drunken nephew: Jonas. Excitement bubbled in Rudolph's stomach. Stefan, the taller man, closed his grip over Rudolph's. He was in his mid-fifties, with pale hair and one flat unmoving hyphen of a mouth. His probing eyes were instantly unnerving, chips of gray ice set in a gaunt, skull-like face. The other guy was a shorter, balder, chubbier version of his brother, his eyes softer and kinder. The second guy was the mark, Rudolph decided instantly.

"We have also heard many good things about you," Stefan Rathenau said in an impermeable tone. "You're a great friend of Jonas's, isn't that right?"

Was it? In truth, Rudolph had never seen Jonas in daylight. He was the kind of guy you met at the smoking section of the club, a part-time DJ who floated around the international party circuit talking about his big ideas for apps—all of which had thus far remained mysteriously unrealized. Jonas didn't even know how to code, but like many men who dislike work he dreamed of tech as a magic unicorn, if only he could think of one good idea—but Rudolph knew that he wouldn't. Jonas was a creature made for joy and festivities, with the flashing smile belonging to the sons of parvenus: huge, white teeth good only for crunching up ready-made fortunes.

"Rudy's a genius," Jonas boasted. "We met back when he was still working at Harry Olbrich's gallery in London, and I was trying to buy this painting by a really hot Belgian artist at the time. But Rudolph convinced me the guy was a one-hit wonder. Steered me in the direction of a '97 Gunter instead. And you know what? I made half a mil on that Gunter last year, half a mil!"

Stefan nodded, visibly unimpressed. And why shouldn't he be? Slick, well-fed Jonas was a guppy compared to him, a massive shark.

"The guy's a star, honestly," Jonas rambled. "Absolute fucking star."

Though he considered Jonas almost terminally stupid, desperately trying to live up to the accomplishments of his cleverer ancestors, Rudolph had always known that this spoiled grifter held the keys to the castle. His uncles were two sketchy German billionaires, the exact type of person whom Rudolph loved best. Stefan had been a computer whiz who'd started selling contraband IBM computers out of his East Berlin garage in the early eighties. After perestroika he had used the money to start his own bank, bringing on his brother, Christian, to help manage it. Slowly Stefan had climbed the ranks, investing first in Soviet commodities, then Western finance, and expanding the bank to cover the whole of Eastern Europe, kicking to the curb anyone who got in his way.

Rathenau was a golden eagle of the meritocracy, a genius of the markets, though some mud-raking journalists might call it a kleptocracy. But what, Rudolph wondered, was the difference between begging, borrowing, and stealing, when you put just as much sweat and blood into one as the other?

As he showed them around the gallery, Rudolph made sure to linger next to the Bélizaire. He was gratified to see their faces change: Christian Rathenau reached forward, brushing a shining glob of violet paint like menstrual blood on its surface. Stefan leaned back on his heels, pensive. Unreadable.

"It's for sale?" Christian asked. "Beautiful piece."

"Amazing, isn't it?" Rudolph said casually. "Very high demand, actually. It's going to a major exhibition in Tokyo next year, so . . ."

A look of disappointment crossed Christian's face. "What's the purchase price, just out of curiosity?"

"Twelve million," Rudolph said smoothly, adding a few digits here and there. "A real museum quality piece, which is the only thing I deal in—things that are incredibly rare to the market. This piece, I chased it for about five years to get the owner, very private man, to sell it to me."

"I see. So it's not available?"

Asaka hadn't asked him to sell it yet. But the opportunity to establish a relationship with the Rathenaus was too good to miss.

"For the right price, right home . . ." He trailed off. "Though I have to admit, I wasn't planning on selling it any time soon. It's too special."

The merest flicker of acknowledgment from Stefan Rathenau; Rudolph decided to let his case rest there.

He led them upstairs, to his cool bright shard of an office. It was calm and hard and pure like the inside of a chapel, or the nests of certain high-flying birds, though only the most magnificent of birds could inhale such thinness of air. An eagle might rest here. The Rathenaus went quiet, intimidated by its foreign mystique. Their eyes roamed anxiously around the room: past the Picassos, looking in confusion at the artfully arranged collections of stones. They were standing at the apex of culture and beauty, as the Italian princes once had. It brought home their own frailties to themselves, as it was meant to. Did they deserve it? Belong here?

Once you reached the top, the very top, what could the next level be?

Rudolph folded his hands. His eyes, in the celestial light, were cold and green. He was monastic, powerful, every inch the solid and trusted consigliere. Yet this world could not be bought. He was merely a priest, readying himself to listen to their confession, to their humble little desires, because it was up to him to open the gates of heaven. God himself—Rudolph might be able to put a word in.

"So. Jonas tells me you are thinking of formalizing your investments in art."

A silent nod. Madison came and went with tiny pots of espresso in an earthenware set by Edmund de Waal, the uncles' four eyes moving briefly across her tight skirt.

"You've started collecting more seriously in the past few years. I thought I saw your agent at the Christie's auction last week. The Richter, wasn't it?"

Stefan inclined his head.

"Smart choice. A dealer will always tell you to buy what you love."

Blank. He did not give a single fuck. This individualistic, you-deserve-to-buy-things-because-you're-worth-it language of late capitalism was never going to work on Stefan Rathenau, Rudolph could already tell. He was not some gullible American tech bro like Jonas, with a simpering matcha cookie girlfriend guiding him through galleries by the tip of his dick. He was frugal and ruthlessly pragmatic, of the post-Soviet milieu. It was lazy advice anyway, finely strained through airplane magazines and jewelry advertising before leaking into every art advisor's toothy spiel: *Buy what you love!* Time to switch gears.

"But I'm not most dealers."

That got their attention. Rudolph leaned toward them, spreading his hands out on the table, drawing them in.

"It's a dark and nasty world out there for those who want to buy art. Waiting lists, ranking systems, people pushing you bullshit that isn't half as historically significant as you think it is. Who to buy, and when, and how? No one will tell you the truth. Because ultimately, they don't care if you lose money as long as they sell the thing. Try and flip it six months later? You'll get blacklisted in seconds. But not with me."

Rudolph paused.

Stefan lifted his eyebrows. His ice-chip eyes looked only moderately more awake. "Go on then. What's so different about you?"

In for a penny, Rudolph thought.

He smiled. "Well, first of all, I've got all the connections you don't have but need. The real business is information, and I've got the best in the game—a Klimt that hasn't seen the light of day in ten years? Sold it. Convincing the Whitney to part with a perfect 'Piss Painting' Warhol? Obviously. I'm like a mole, burrowing under every hole for you, looking in places you'll never see. But that's not all."

This time they were both interested. "What else?"

"I put my clients first. I'm not interested in nurturing an artist's career by giving you bad advice. I'm not interested in picking a few bad apples to get a single really great one. I'm interested in picking all good apples, all the time. No—fuck that—great apples! And I want you to get great apples too."

Christian smiled and opened his mouth; Stefan cut him off abruptly: "How do you propose to get us these, as you say, great apples? Because right now, this is all sounding a lot like some millennial hedge funder riding someone else's wave. We've heard the pitch before."

Unruffled, Rudolph said calmly, "My strategy is slow. It's measured, curated. People say less than two percent of artists are really a good investment; well, I know exactly who those two percent are. I've located ten people, artists who got big in the eighties and nineties but never got their due. Until now. Bill Bowes, Gunter, Louise Lawler— just getting you the work you desperately want, that's baseline," he assured them. "I'll buy shares in paintings, hedge your bets, spread your portfolio. No one else is doing what I'm doing."

Stefan nodded.

"My first year out of college, I doubled secondary market profits for Harry Olbrich's gallery. That was 2009." He paused to let the year sink in. "Nobody bought art in 2009."

"That's certainly an astonishing turnover," Christian said, his long white chins rippling with excitement. His brother gave the tiniest of eye rolls.

"What would you say to those who think these high prices indicate a bubble?" Stefan pointed out. "Markets have crashed before. Personally, I don't see how a few licks on a canvas makes fifteen million dollars sustainable."

Stefan's face had gone blank; he wasn't at all certain about this venture, Rudolph realized with a jolt of alarm.

"My brother is worried," Christian said cautiously. "We hear the art market is volatile."

The ghost of fear, crossing Jonas's doughy face: Rudolph had secretly promised him a cut if the deal went ahead.

"There's a measure of risk involved," Rudolph acknowledged. "As with any investment, I might add. But when the artist's career genuinely merits the price, it's like gold. You can't fake it."

He looked each brother carefully in the eye, spreading his arms out wider: *I've got nothing to hide.*

"These artists adhere closely to a process I've developed to spy worth and reward. With me, your portfolio will remain in safe and stable hands. Always me. Never an associate. Never an advisor. We've entered an era of art as pure asset, and I consider myself a trader dealing in the most valuable jewels of our time. The possibilities," he added, smiling with the certainty of a convert, "are truly endless."

"There does seem to be something in the air. Some—madness, almost," Stefan conceded.

Rudolph nodded. That was what he loved about the art market: when you got it right, it was just like printing money.

"It's the future of finance," Jonas said excitedly.

"Exactly," Rudolph said, thinking, *Shut up before you jam my deal, you dolt.* "I can guide you, buy in bulk for you, guarantee you a continual line of profit. But there has to be a measure of trust in my skills, in my decision-making."

He leaned back in his chair.

"Let me tell you a story. Three years ago, I bought a Bowes for $362,000. A personal risk, mind—my own capital. This year I sold it. Can you guess what it went for?"

"Eight hundred."

"One point seven million," he said, enunciating the word *million*. "That's a four hundred percent increase. Could you find an investment fund with that kind of return?"

"I own a few Bowes myself," Stefan Rathenau said, his blue cabochon eyes glittering faintly.

They would sign the deal. He just knew it.

On their way out, Christian Rathenau stopped to stare at the Bélizaire again. This was Rudolph's cue to develop a fascination with the window. A pack of straggly haired teenagers had set up camp on the fire escape, and when they saw Rudolph frowning at them, in his stiff gray suit, they erupted into cackles of wild laughter over a large purple bong. Must remind Madison to get power sprinklers fitted on all entry points, he thought sternly.

"We will need a few days to think about all this," he heard Stefan say in his steely East German accent.

Rudolph made himself turn around slowly. "Of course. Take your time, it's a big step. We've sent you all the available information, I think?"

He kept the conversation light as he showed them to the door, inquiring whether they'd be in Miami or Palm Beach that winter, recommending a nearby restaurant, making a quick call to the owner to secure them the best table. How good life could be with Rudolph as your friend!

Outside, he lifted his hand in a slow wave as the men's chauffeur ushered them into a varnish-black Range Rover. Suddenly Christian Rathenau's head popped up like one of those plastic targets in a Whac-A-Mole.

"Don't sell it to anybody else!" he called over the howl of a passing ambulance. "The Bélizaire—put it on reserve for me!"

"I won't, Christian," Rudolph yelled. "A twenty-four-hour hold, that's the most I can promise, unfortunately."

He wondered if he was going too far with this last, but too late: Rathenau's head was already disappearing back into the car.

Greed was a lot like desire, he had found; like carnal lust, there were many ways to inflame it. One of the most effective was to pretend scarcity, basic economics, competing demands. *This one has quite the waiting list,* he'd say, or *Look, the demand is so high I can't promise anything—though I may, just may be able to get you this one, if you buy this one first* . . . This technique required balls, but then he had those in spades.

Their mouths watered with need, these powerful men reduced to quivering lumps, and yes there was something sexual about it, something mildly masochistic. They were so used to getting whatever they wanted that they couldn't bear to think that some fraction of the earth might not be theirs. So this, this *refusal*, notched their interest up by 100 percent. *I need that goddamn painting! Whatever it takes, just get it for me!* When that happened, rare as it was, Rudolph felt like the hottest girl at the party, surrounded by a dozen sweaty, panting teenage football players all begging for a blow job.

Putting on his headphones, Rudolph began to whistle, calling out, "Madison, I'm going for a walk!" over his shoulder. He threw a wink at the kids on the fire escape as he slammed the front door shut.

Haggard leaves fluttered down in sheets from the trees. Rudolph heard the bones of an old twig bend, then snap, under the firm step of his polished shoe. As he walked toward Meatpacking, he breathed in deeply, stertorously, as if he could breathe in with the cold air the intensity of his happiness, his zest for life. How fast and hard had he hurtled upward! In the bone-deep hierarchies of an industry that fed on nepotism and generational wealth, it was unusual enough to spark a flurry of whispers. Who was Rudolph Sullivan? How had a new-brained intern gained the ear—and, later, the financing—of one of the most powerful art dealers in the world?

People knew about his connection to the Sullivan real estate dynasty, and assumptions were made about the source of his connections, and of his wealth. All wrong. Rudolph allowed these rumors, and so much the better—clients trusted their own—but he had come up alone. Since birth, his uncle Lyndon had examined him with the contemplative displeasure he reserved for unwanted problems: gray, sad boy, doomed to sink into the bathos of his mother's mistakes.

Ella Fitzgerald came on. All those old fifties songs reminded him of so many Christmases at the Big House. Like tiny war chieftains, he and his cousins had dashed around Lyndon's sprawling Cape Cod estate, howling and swinging their tiny toy swords at each other. All year he looked forward to the holidays. It was a respite from the reality of his own life, which was tangled feelings, oppressive darkness. How long had it taken to see the faint disdain in his cousins' eyes?

Decisively Rudolph shook his head. He changed the music. Time for something a little more modern now, because you could not get lost in memories. Because it was he who had turned every deficit to an advantage, always scraping, mimicking, imitating, until he became somebody who could no longer be ignored. He smiled to himself, feeling joy now, as he walked by the cars, coated in a fresh white dusting of new snow. Because he was everywhere, his charismatic playboy smile lit up under the flashbulbs' bright glare. And when deepest winter came, only a concrete and metal exoskeleton could survive, only the strongest and richest and most ambitious of men could survive, and Rudolph Sullivan swore he'd be one of them.

4

MORNINGS, INGRID LIKED TO SMOKE A SINGLE PERFECT CIGARETTE ON the roof of Paul Bernot, watching the streets for action below. The little people scurrying about like ants on the corroded pavement, which gave up the smell of petrichor after last night's rain. It was a moment of calm, of peace, always shattered the second she saw Paul two hundred feet beneath her swinging legs, striding into the office from his classic Upper East Side six.

Today she was thinking about Claudia. Claudia, Claudia. Paul's top sales director and Ingrid's second boss, the more dangerous one. It had become almost a game to ponder Claudia and who she was. What she might do.

Ingrid loved to drift off at work. She had a big imagination, and, in truth, it didn't take much. Her duties were of a humdrum nature, though she did them diligently enough—which was all, she told herself, a boss could ask for. But every so often she would stare into space, the computers would disappear, and in these moments the wildest and most fantastical images would appear in her mind.

Paul Bernot Gallery on West 20th was painted in a swath of jet-black. Its exterior evoked the nineties—classic and formal in a way Paul himself was—and sometimes Ingrid would imagine the whole gallery as a boudoir on water, like some Japanese brothel from the Edo period, a floating world. She amused herself by picturing her colleagues as geishas, each distinct in their beauty, waving their beautifully filigreed fans at the collectors to usher them inside.

Ingrid knew she should count herself lucky to work there. She remembered her first interview. It had been two years ago now, an eon practically, but still she remembered how she'd sat on a bench in the lobby. Her knees had been shaking. She'd gripped her hands together as she waited to be called inside. She had looked around the lobby, thinking about how big it was, and how she wouldn't be getting a job here, even though she really, really needed one. It was then that she'd heard the faint rasp of feet in leather ballerinas. Ingrid had glanced up; frozen, transfixed by the sight, she saw a group of girls waft down the stairs. Look at this parade of swans, each wearing drapey, monochrome outfits in shades of black and white and gray, carrying bags that resembled ugly buildings but were, somehow, impossibly cool because of it: her jaw had literally dropped in awe. She had felt their eyes skim dismissively over her—it made her want to be their friend.

Paul had a reputation as a trustworthy man. He could be an asshole, but Ingrid respected him for giving her a chance. Even from the interview, though, she had been under no illusions that she was there for her zilch résumé. No, it was because she was pretty. Paul had gazed at her, hard, with his penetrating eyes. There was something of Anna Karenina about her, her ex-boyfriend Brian had once said—a dazed look, like a Russian émigré getting off a train.

So she'd been hired, to her surprise and pleasure. When she'd gotten the call, she'd thought: *Why me?* There had been other, more qualified girls in the interview room, as she was all too aware. But there was another reason, too, which Ingrid hadn't known about.

Paul only hired women. He disliked all men and felt competitive with, jealous of, and annoyed by them, including his own son—but nor did he like all women. It was Paul's policy to only hire women from two different categories of personality: sweet and malleable, or manic to the point of breakdown. Why? Because his life frequently bored him, and in these moments, he longed for a bit of pizazz, unpredictability, instability. Claudia fell into this camp. But on the day of Ingrid's interview, Paul had been swinging in the other direction. Claudia was driving him nuts. He'd started longing for some kind little person to help him out, a little sweetness, goddamn it, which would eventually take shape in the affair he conducted with the twenty-two-year-old German receptionist, Eva, downstairs, culminating in his ruinous divorce at present.

By nine the gallery had begun to fill.

"There you are, Ingrid," Paul sighed, placing his monogrammed pigskin briefcase on the desk. At sixty, he was still an attractive man, with longish salt-and-pepper hair that he kept as the one nostalgic remnant of his participation in some long-dead youth movement. Now it merely served to remind his clients that he was still cooler and more bohemian than they. "How was Dermott's thing last night?"

Lately it seemed that Paul was always beginning or ending his conversations with a sigh. Ingrid suspected that he secretly regretted leaving the security of his ex, a Belgian heiress to a tea towel company, for Eva—because, reader, he married her. As his new wife swelled with green juice, Paul started going around with a blank, hunted look in his eyes. Ingrid couldn't understand why he had done it so quickly after the divorce went through, except to say he must be very much in love. Or else it was a question of sunk costs: Paul hated to admit that he was wrong, was nothing if not an all-or-nothing guy.

She described the Critchley opening, watching Paul's nostrils flare with irony at the mention of the cow.

"God. How very early 2000s."

"Didn't you say that Duma Gallery's a front for the Dutch mob?"

"Exactly." He nodded. "They're money launderers, like half the people in the industry. But the mob, for Christ's sake!" He shuddered. "I'm sure Dermott is looking to jump ship as soon as possible."

"Should I schedule a studio visit?" she offered hopefully. "We could look at his work together, maybe?"

"No, no." He waved a hand. "Not yet. Claudia and I will take him to Cipriani, pour some wine down his throat. Give him a taste of things to come."

Ingrid spent the morning dividing a list of clients into a complex series of codes, which the gallery used to define how fast they could get a painting from the best artists. A curator smiling tolerantly at a diversity conference received a five for Influence, one for Wealth; a Fortune 500 CEO's wife received fives across the board, ensuring her spot at the top of the waitlist for their most in-demand artists. *Sanctions? Let's revisit,* Ingrid wrote under the art advisor to the Belarussian president. Artists could get a little touchy about their work going to dictators sometimes.

Claudia finally sauntered in around one. She flung her bag on Ingrid's desk and fluttered her glossy scarlet nails in Ingrid's face.

"Do you love them or do you love them? Honestly, I searched for years before I found the perfect shade. And would you believe, it's the same one Chloë Sevigny uses. I saw her walking out right when I walked in!"

"Oh my God, they look incredible."

Ingrid was seized by a desperate wish that she had called in sick. The familiar duet of Claudia's banalities and her own responses had instantly awakened her dormant hangover.

Claudia stood behind Ingrid, switching her head back and forth, as she slowly read Ingrid's emails. Claudia loved to stand over people's shoulders. She loved to read their emails. She was a little spy like that.

The blond hair, the tightly toned body. Claudia Harris was a beautiful woman.

Ingrid had heard rumors. Was she a terrorist? The Mata Hari?

Had there been a restraining order, a Swiss psychiatric intervention disguised as a spa break? Nothing would have surprised her. Sometimes Claudia would put her head on her desk and just sleep, the wheat gold of her curls spilling over one cheekbone, like a silky little kitten for the rest of them to coo over. Other times she would call you, screaming unintelligible verbiage, and fire you, minutes after sending you a cake for your birthday.

Claudia stood over Ingrid's computer, breathing on her. She had a glazed, beady look in her eyes.

Claudia was very good at sales. Yet her acts of minor insanity continued to pile up. She had fired many people. Everyone suspected that she had something on Paul, something bad, for him to let her behave like that. But Ingrid disagreed. Beneath the bluster, Paul was a kindhearted man. She felt a strange fondness for him, this tired sorcerer, whose graying head was always bent down over a sale—but always ready to snap back, to flirt with a client or charm an artist.

Paul's face changed when he looked at Claudia. It was a moment of rare humanity, an empathy so little seen in the art world, that Ingrid just knew something awful had happened to her. Rumors floated about the source of Claudia's madness, the source of her pain, put together by the minions who discussed her endlessly.

For example: Claudia kept a laundry list of the billionaires she was fucking, with pros and cons beside their names. Her own husband was a dud whom she was waiting to exchange. Everyone knew this because she left out her therapy notes, to which Ingrid and Rita—Ingrid's best work friend and a gallery sales associate—had once played a drinking game (a shot for the word *mindfulness*, another for *daddy*). Claudia was careless, but more than that, Ingrid suspected she actually liked to be feared and analyzed by her underlings. She had an exhibitionist streak, roaming restlessly around the galleries in spike-encrusted heels and a copy of her favorite book, *The Convert*.

It was Ingrid who'd recommended that book to her, though she privately doubted whether Claudia had ever read it. Since then, though, it had become a regular talking point. To clients, Claudia claimed to have bought the movie rights; last month, she had started putting on a show of actually reading it. In full view, she would sit at her desk and gaze down at the page laid open on the table, and sigh in contemplation as she twined a strand of hair around her finger. Five minutes later, she would glance around with a demure, secret smile to see if anyone was watching; once, as if to test her audience, Claudia had even been spotted brushing away a silent tear. It was part of her mystery for the minions to imagine the tears were real; but they would never know. Then, restlessly, she would close the book and sweep out of the room.

Ingrid choked out a few more compliments before Claudia, with a magnanimous nod, permitted a change of subject.

"Anyway. You know who I ran into last night, super randomly?"

"Who?"

"Simone Machado. That's your friend, right?"

Ingrid's stomach dropped. An old, familiar shame began to wind its way around her ribs.

"I was with—" She named a male tech billionaire whom Ingrid was sure Claudia had never met. "We've become *best* best friends lately."

"Oh?" Ingrid managed. "Where'd you see Simone?"

"At the Beatrice Inn. She's doing super well these days. Did you see her reviewed in the *Times* the other day? And so young!"

Obviously Ingrid had seen the *Times*.

"Yeah, it's kind of making me think about whether we could take her on. She doesn't have a gallery in New York yet." Claudia drummed her fingers on the table. "You know, especially since you have that relationship with her. Could be useful."

Ingrid tried to keep the muscles still in her face.

*   *   *

There was a time when Ingrid would have fought for Simone to be represented as an artist by Paul Bernot. Freshman year: she and Simone had been roommates. The sleepless ecstasy of realizing that here was someone who really *got* you: had the same sharp-edged sense of humor, thought Cecily Brown was the greatest painter alive, got emotional over the same sad indie music. It was obsessive. Sometimes they'd skip parties to lie side by side in their bony, dorm-issue twin beds, smoking a makeshift bowl of weed out of an apple core until three in the morning while The Cranberries wailed on.

After graduation, they'd finally done it. Moved to Brooklyn, begun their lives together. Simone had offered to let Ingrid share the studio her father had bought her, and they would split the bills in their Bushwick apartment. For nearly three years, they'd worked together—coffee and cigarettes till noon, deli sandwiches at two with their daily powwow and critical analysis of each other's work. At night, Ingrid would leave for her waitressing job, while Simone continued painting.

Ingrid had always known that Simone was well-off. Even in college, her father—a flashy Miami property developer who wore white linen suits and carried a crocodile-handled bamboo cane—had attracted notice. But at the small Rhode Island arts college they'd attended, trust fund kids were a dime a dozen. Everyone was always trying to look poorer and more bohemian than they really were, complaining about being strapped for cash, stuffed together with teenage hormones in the pressure-cooker of the dorm. Her college guidance counselor had assured her it was the best art school around, the glossy pamphlets sold themselves, and it was easy to forget about the constant deferral of her debt in that pampered prism designed like a playground.

Back then, Ingrid was considered the better painter. Simone claimed she couldn't live without Ingrid's advice: whether a painting needed a single drop of cadmium yellow or if she should just trash it and start again. Simone was so anxious, so desperate for approval, and when they first arrived in New York Ingrid had thought it was fun and glamorous to be broke and sleepless and working two jobs. She hadn't really noticed that Simone was *not* saving up, *not* going through the messy trial period of her early twenties, because Simone was already resting, waiting, planning for the fiery years ahead.

No trial of fire. Just fire.

Ingrid dreamed about fame. No, she dreamed about one day, just one wide-open day of painting, without the constant struggle to survive.

Simone rose in the clear hours of daylight to paint, calm and happy. Months passed, then a year. Her work was getting better. She'd been picked up by a small independent gallery. Ingrid's paintings began to look exhausted, drained, whittled down to the bone. She worried over them. Her future. What was an excuse and what was fate?

Two years had passed in this way.

Sometimes Ingrid dreamed about killing her. And yet. She wasn't so bad a friend that she could not feel excitement, too, for Simone. It coexisted, in a sense, with the corrosive jealousy. Was inseparable from it. In many ways they had lived in a cocoon together, a friendship as passionate as a love affair. But none of this explained why Simone had cut her off so cruelly, so suddenly, for reasons that were never clear. Friends drifted apart all the time, but she and Simone had been more like soul mates; and their separation still hurt Ingrid. Still wounded her to the core.

Ingrid stood up, almost knocking her cup of coffee to the floor and startling Claudia, who had been speaking at length without noticing Ingrid's expression.

"Everything okay?"

"I just worry that her work's a little too . . . trendy."

"Trendy" was a choice insult for any artist worth their salt, suggesting the antithesis of real, historical *significance*. Used correctly, it was like pouring antifreeze into a perfectly good wine. But a single glance at Paul's pensive expression, and she knew she'd chosen the wrong approach.

"Didn't you say she was a friend of yours?"

"Um—sort of." Ingrid went red. "Anyway, I just worry that it won't last past this, er, cultural moment. It feels a little too . . . zeitgeisty, don't you think? She capitalizes on the victimization of women. It's such a gimmick."

A short silence as Paul and Claudia absorbed this. Rita had slipped into the room too. Suddenly they all found themselves amid another impromptu Thursday-morning sales meeting, querying Paul's new favorite question: How to make money? He asked the heavens, as if they might hold the answer he sought, "Simone is Cuban, isn't she?"

"What? I mean, not really. She's from Miami."

"Right," Claudia said patiently. "So she's a Black Hispanic woman whose parents may have fled persecution in Cuba."

"Actually it was her grandparents—"

"I worry about getting canceled," Paul said ominously, "if we don't start working with more people like Simone."

"Can you imagine what would happen if someone does a profile on us?" Rita added, perching on Ingrid's desk with her legs folded up like an egret. "Staid, Establishment with a capital *E*, no inclusion? Saggy male artists? All-white staff?"

Behind Paul's back, she gave Ingrid a vaudeville wink.

"We need to change the narrative," Paul continued. "Show we care about human rights, diversity, social change, progress—all that stuff. I want ideas. Fast."

"What about a charity thing for victims of the Syrian war? Like, medicine and basic items for people seeking asylum in the US?" Ingrid suggested.

Claudia looked at Paul, whose eyebrows went up in disbelief. *Is this girl an amateur or what?*

"Sweetie, people just don't have the emotional bandwidth for that sort of thing right now," Claudia said gently. "It's all so depressing. People are already feeling really traumatized post-election. They need self-care. Not more negativity."

"We could try and diversify the intern pool, you know, structural change?"

"We need American stories, *profitable* American stories," Paul cut in. "Not interns. Not random shit happening in the third world. And it's not like we can put them on Instagram. We need *optics*—heroic artists, with happy endings."

Paul gave her a significant look, and Ingrid swallowed. What he wanted was Simone, and he wanted Ingrid to get her for him.

By the last six months of their friendship, most of Ingrid and Simone's old classmates had given up trying to be artists. It was too hard, too punishing. Ingrid had tried to lose herself in painting again, but spiky new anxieties tore at her concentration: the spiraling interest on her credit cards, the unpaid rent, her piling-up student loans. General instability and insecurity and fear. Ingrid had been living off her tips, which weren't even that great considering what a shitty fucking waitress she was, and she stank of smoke and grease and the ribeye some guy had wanted medium rare but she had delivered bloody.

Two years ago, Ingrid had returned home from work in tears. It was time to confront the obvious, to drop her pride. She had been hoping for some wine and advice. But Simone's face was rigid at the door—stiff, as if Ingrid had dealt her a terrible blow.

"I've been doing a lot of thinking," she said coldly.

Out of the blue, Simone said she had decided to break their lease. When Ingrid stammered that she couldn't afford to find another place right now, let alone another studio, she was shocked to see Simone drop her head in her hands. "Don't you think other people have problems apart from you?" she'd snapped.

Always Simone's cool smile glittered in her head, elusive. She'd wanted her out. No, there was nothing to explain, she just wanted to be alone now. Had Simone succeeded because of the money, or had she always possessed some inner intensity that Ingrid lacked? Ingrid could no longer ask; they had not spoken since that night.

Work finished at six. Ingrid wandered glumly through a grove of pillars in the station at 14th Street, trying not to go home. She could go out, but it was the end of the month. Her bank accounts were empty; and Rudolph hadn't texted, she realized with a melancholy little ache of disappointment. Nothing to do but get on the train.

For the past year Ingrid had been living in a second-floor Bushwick walk-up with Yuri, a Korean girl she had met online. Their apartment was small. Ingrid's bedroom faced the back of an alleyway where birds nested. She often woke up to a fresh curtain of pigeon shit, delicately shading what little morning light leaked in through the window.

Nearing Myrtle Avenue, Ingrid half-hoped to see the pale moon of her roommate's face at the window, framed by the glow of her computer, but Yuri was out, probably still working late at the bank in FiDi. Ugly brown furniture loomed over the living room-cum-kitchenette. Ingrid rummaged through the cabinets: they were empty. Finally she found a bag of old chocolates in the back of a drawer and began eating them whole, but just as quickly they turned to dust in her mouth. Spitting out a lump, she went out onto the fire escape and sat there, smoking. Listening to the dogs bark in a distant house. They were throwing themselves against a chain-link fence, over and over, in a rhythm so repetitive you could almost fall asleep to it. What an opera! It was not quite the life she had imagined for herself, as a teenager in the suburbs. Those starless black velvet nights in winter had seemed to swallow the sky. In her attic bedroom she would open a notebook, with Florence & the Machine playing from her computer. She'd start to draw, at first slowly, without knowing why. The drums thumped louder; cymbals crashed, Florence wailed, and Ingrid's fingers would fly across the canvas as though lightning had struck her hands.

Ingrid drew and drew and drew. Each morning she would wake up and count down the almanac of leaves on the willow tree outside her window, waiting, just waiting, for the day she could go to college. Each night she would slip into bed, hoping that time would magically speed forward to launch her into the glittering life in New York that she desired. But somehow even the waiting had been tinged with excitement. The future was ahead, after the never-ending dentist's appointment of childhood, and back then she had believed it would be solely under her command.

She was still smoking when her phone began to vibrate with a string of texts.

Hey it's Rudolph, the first one read. *I am actually having that party I mentioned earlier if you still want to come.*

He'd added a laughing emoji and the address.

She threw the cigarette into an empty planter, possessed by a sudden urgency she hadn't known existed until now. It was too late to invite Richard; she would go on her own. Rummaging through her closet, Ingrid found a dress. It was silk, yellow, she had bought it with her first paycheck at a Sies Marjan sample sale, with bits of gold lace and green tie-dye. Ridiculous to wear yellow in winter. Ridiculous but she didn't care, she loved yellow, she loved to make herself feel beautiful, and this was the most expensive and beautiful thing she had ever owned. Minutes later she was spritzing perfume on her wrists, willing a cool nonchalance she did not feel, and that's how she looked as she ran toward the cab that she couldn't afford: a twisting ribbon in yellow, fleeing from the cramped little apartment and out onto the street.

5

AN OILY BLACK SHOWER PELTED THE FROZEN STREETS AS THE TAXI skidded around potholes, passing the red lights of Little Italy. It pulled to a stop on a quiet street in the West Village, blocked from view by heavy rain.

A tall and elegant ivory building rose up between its neighbors. Arched, floor-to-ceiling windows lined each of its five stories. Ingrid got out of the cab. There were three or four kids in expensive streetwear on the stoop, peering doubtfully inside a paper bag.

"Did you get the ketamine?" a boy on the stoop asked her.

"What?" Ingrid said. "No. I'm looking for, uh, Rudolph's apartment?"

"Is that whose house this is?"

The boy took a swig from his flask and offered it to her. But the door was already opening, the boy shooting down the stairs, nearly tripping over the hem of his long green anorak.

In his absence stood Rudolph, towering over the bright crack of doorway. A tall blond in a silver Lurex jumpsuit was leaning against the wall behind him, eyeing Ingrid with evident suspicion. Ingrid's heart lurched. He wore a dark gray T-shirt and jeans, the T-shirt showing off muscles she hadn't quite been able to appreciate at the gallery. "Come in, come in!" his laughing smile seemed to say, promising to wrap up the strays and warm them in its blazing golden glow, assuring refuge from the elements.

Ingrid approached. Her arms were shaking slightly as she hugged Rudolph hello. Then, not knowing what to do, she moved awkwardly over to the girl and tried to hug her. But Silver Jumpsuit retreated, muttering, "Oh, we're doing this now?" before looking down at her phone with a smile. Shame glowed in Ingrid's chest—it was a mistake to come, glaring evidence of her aloneness.

"Let me show you around."

Rudolph led her inside. Even in the dark, Ingrid could tell it was an exquisite building, all jewel-colored stained-glass windows and soaring Art Deco beams. Loud house music pulsed from a distant upstairs floor. The blond girl had disappeared.

"Where'd your friend go?"

"Who?" he asked, then shrugged with disinterest. "Oh, her. Think she went out to the ATM."

"Oh," Ingrid said, relieved.

Rudolph opened a door. Music spilled out. Looking over his shoulder at her as he pushed through a mass of cackling girls, he shouted: "Sorry, it's a little loud. Can I get you a drink?"

"Just wine if you have it."

Her confidence from the gallery opening had dissolved. Now she was awkward, gauche, disjointed as a marionette as she moved spiderlike along the black-and-white tiles, trying to avoid being noticed. The apartment was bigger than anything she'd ever seen in Manhattan, not that that was saying much.

"Hey, let's go into the living room. I never get invited to parties," the boy in the anorak said to her, and she jumped. He was clutching a bottle of Fireball in one hand, his face creased and sloppy. Where had Rudolph gone?

"Oh, I see what you want," he said, gazing at her, and winked. "Come on, let's just sit in the corner and get away from all these people. I hate strangers, don't you?"

Reluctantly she allowed him to draw her by the hand. The living room was full of beautiful people with hair that was long and glossy or short and spiky; a pale-faced anorexic girl lay on a white couch with her eyes closed and bare arms covered in blue Sanskrit tattoos. People were draping their coats all over her motionless body, a living coat rack.

"Yo, I don't read the newspaper very often, but when I do I try to analyze the lies," the guy in the anorak slurred. "Know what I mean? See what's real, like, read between the lines."

"Filter it," Ingrid said, watching the girl's azure eyelids roll open.

"Exactly." The boy dropped his head on her shoulder, jerked upright.

"See, my girlfriend kicked me out, she couldn't wait for the VC funding," he told her. "This may surprise you, me being a hairdresser, but I'm actually on the verge of creating the first people-led quantum cryptocurrency. Technology will set you free," he whispered. "But sometimes my brain is firing on all cylinders. Sometimes my brain is firing so much that I can't complete a project."

He started to snore. She realized with a start that his anorak was old and coated in a thin layer of dirt. He must have wandered in off the street. Sleeping on the couch, he looked young and very tired. She put a nearby blanket on him and went out of the room.

Rudolph's apartment was strangely bare and featureless, all white marble and surfaces except for the multimillion-dollar art collection jumping off the walls, impossible to miss. Row after row of icy vitrines gleamed in the uncertain dark. One marmalade-colored Catherine wheel of metal sliced into the hallway, threatening to stab unsuspecting guests. It was scary and tarantula-like, twisting steel claws locked in perpetual spin like a child's plastic windmill grown to gargantuan size.

"That's his uncle's Stella. Only one edition ever produced," a girl's voice said coolly, and Ingrid knew without turning around that it was the girl in the jumpsuit.

"It looks like it should be in a museum."

The girl snorted.

"How do you know Rudolph?" Ingrid tried again, attempting a jovial note, but the girl's mouth turned down with instinctive dislike.

"We went to uni together. Goldsmiths." She had a rich, weighty British accent, as though she were gnawing on a mouthful of stones.

"That's in London, isn't it?"

"It is. Plus I've been friends with his cousin Hunter a long time." She paused. "Do you know Hunter?"

Ingrid didn't.

"Where'd *you* go to school?"

It was time to leave. She was moving toward the door, filled with regret at having come, when she heard the sound of her own name, cool as marble. It was Rudolph, stepping neatly down the hall with two drinks. He moved with grace for such a tall man, built like a baseball player, all long legs and sculpted shoulders. Now, she was sure, she'd be dismissed into the crowd. Clearly there was a reason the blond girl knew so much about him; she was his girlfriend, and he had simply invited Ingrid out of kindness. Pity, probably. But to her surprise he handed her one of the drinks and nudged the girl firmly on the hip.

"Catch you later, Corny?"

Ingrid released a breath. Corny didn't actually look ready to leave, but she knew she had been dismissed. Shooting another hard glance at Ingrid, she disappeared into the crowded living room.

They stood in the hallway together, alone.

"What are your thoughts, my little critic?"

"It's very striking."

"You hate it." He laughed. "It's fine, you can admit it."

Ingrid said nothing. He put a hand on her elbow, which was bare.

"I can show you the rest," he offered, in a low voice. "If you're interested."

* * *

They threaded their way past the people in the hallway, snatches of conversation floating by. Ingrid's heart thudded in her chest like a war drum. Rudolph opened a pair of doors, and suddenly they were in a glass-walled solarium, its noise-proof windows holding back the murky night. Ingrid was quiet. The silence of this room, after the music, was almost shocking. Then her eyes focused. In the center of the room was a pedestal. An enormous silver rabbit stood on it, staring out at them with the blank benign indifference of some ungodly totem of the future. It was a Koons.

"This is where you keep the pièce de résistance, huh?" she said, totting up the numbers inside her head. They almost took your breath away. "I can't believe you have this."

"So you like the rabbit?" his voice spoke up. She couldn't see him. He was leaning against the armoire, in the shadows. "I always think it looks like a sex toy."

Her pulse skipped a beat.

"That's exactly what I was thinking," she said. "I have the identical vibrator, it only costs about fifty million dollars less."

"Oh you do, do you?" he laughed, and she sensed rather than saw him ease off the armoire. "You're a real philistine, comparing a Koons to your vibrator."

"And you're a real capitalist, thinking price equals value."

He moved closer. "I thought you were less predictable than that."

"Well, I'm not. Sorry."

They smiled at each other.

"This is the greatest art of our time, because it *is* our time," Rudolph continued with new vigor. "It taps into the innocence of childhood— that natural immunity to the constant pressure of other people. You bought a toy, you saw a musical, you bought a fucking funnel cake at the fair and took it home with you. And you didn't give a shit about what it looked like. That bunny is the American dream."

"I see you drank the Kool-Aid." Ingrid gestured to the big silver carrot clutched in the rabbit's paw. "But I feel like he's sneering at us. How corny we are, how saccharine. The crystal-clear pool, the porno-hot wife, the house filled with tchotchkes. The eternal flame of *things*, you know? The dumb part is that people think that buying this rabbit makes them superior to all that, above it, even though they're the ones spending ninety million dollars on a fucking rabbit. But he doesn't see the hopes and dreams behind everything we long for."

She stopped. For some reason the words felt caught in her throat.

"Only the hollowness," she finished. "And it's just not fair."

A cloud drifted over the moon, plunging the room in chinchilla clouds of shadow. Only the rabbit stood out, its inhuman steel head emerging from a pool of liquid moonlight, frightening for reasons she couldn't understand. It had an air of permanence in the dark, of prophecy.

"You don't think it's enough for something to be beautiful?"

"No. Not to me."

But the instant she said it, she knew it wasn't true. When he spoke next, his voice was inside her ear, her body, a sharp point of fear needling her spine.

"You can touch it if you want."

Obediently she moved closer. The sculpture bore a perfect resemblance to the helium balloon that floated above the Macy's Thanksgiving Day Parade. When she frowned, the rabbit's sloping curves reflected it back to her in mercury. It had no face, no identifying features. Still, it seemed to grin at her, this sly metal god with the big carrot clutched in its fist like a child's toy, built for nothing but pleasure.

Suddenly Rudolph's shadow loomed in the reflection from behind her. Ingrid jerked back. Some primal fear of strangers reared in her throat—it was a moment of gut dislike, of instinctive revulsion. But when she turned around, his expression was light and laughing.

"You want to join the party or what?"

*　*　*

By midnight, Ingrid was talking to another guy, wondering what Rudolph was going to do. Were they playing a game? He was talking to another girl too. But the whole time he was staring over the other girl's shoulder at Ingrid, so hard and unblinking that she felt a little scared. Instinctively she crossed her arms over her chest. His green eyes were so pale they resembled celadon, so pale they were almost frighteningly blank.

Rudolph couldn't stop looking at her. She was Jewish, he guessed, or maybe Italian. But, at the gallery, he hadn't really seen. Now he was seeing. Red earrings jingled in her ears. The sound was hypnotic, like a windchime, a dog whistle. Sensing his eyes, she glanced up. Hers were as dark and glossy as a startled animal in a glade.

They started talking again. An unmemorable conversation, even pointless. She couldn't remember anything from that point on except talking, laughing and talking, without ever breaking each other's gaze. The whole room vanished, was a blur.

Afterward, just one thing from the whole night would stick in her mind.

"Your lips are so soft," he murmured as he leaned down to kiss her.

And she had replied:

"Elizabeth Arden."

It was all so ridiculous; she planned on telling her friends. But suddenly they were in his bedroom. What time is it? Ingrid wondered vaguely. Two, three in the morning? An old rap song still thumped through the halls of his white apartment. French Montana, or was it Kendrick? They were finally alone now, even though people were still outside. Rudolph's expression was tense, even despondent. Why did he look so serious? She wanted to tell him to relax.

He closed the door, locked it.

Their eyes caught. Ingrid's throat was so dry it was sandpaper. She couldn't talk if she wanted to. He walked over to where she was sitting on the bed and kissed her again. Outside, at the party, the music was still going. But here in this room it was their own private cell, self-contained.

She was good at sex. Talented at the disconnect. During the act, at least, there was a coldness inside her body that boys wanted to know how to crack. Her pale skin, her long brown hair, she was like a little china doll and they liked that. As a child she'd danced ballet and felt a sense of wonder and relief at seeing her body whirl, for a second, as she gave her personality up to the perfection of choreographed movements. The frenetic brain—it would disappear. Only with study and practice can true artistic freedom occur, Nietzsche had said something like that, and of course she was thinking about Nietzsche during sex—wasn't that part of the problem? Because she had always been practicing, acting, not free, it was the secret to her success, and when she looked down at a boy's face in the act and saw them groan it was with a sort of disappointed envy.

This, though. This.

The room receded a little. Her legs felt warm. It was a helpless, collapsing feeling, as though she had lost the ability to want anything else.

She touched his chest. His skin was so soft, but the muscles were hard, in fact she had never seen such a body before, and his sweat tasted like soap and alcohol. Lust had awakened something inside of her, something of a different breed. This desire was like the sea.

She had fallen in love before. Opened herself up to the possibility.

But not like this. *He leans over to kiss me.* It's like she's been thirsting for water and his body has suddenly emerged from the desert.

Quite frankly she was in love with him from that moment and already having to fight, to beat it back. She stares at him, his fingers wind over her neck. Harder, she says, I want you to do it harder. He tightens his fingers, still staring at her. Okay, he says, and does.

6

RUDOLPH WAS ON HIS LAPTOP, GLUED TO A DAY SALE AT PHILLIPS WHEN his phone rang. He was trying to sell a Sigmar Polke and buy a Bowes for his exhibition in London next October. Prices for both were soaring to new records, but hopefully he could swing a slim profit between the two.

"Ten million for *Untitled* by Bill Bowes!" the miniature auctioneer shouted from the blue glow of the laptop. "Ten million one, do I have ten million one?"

Rudolph watched, biting his nails, as paddles shot up from the crowd. He let out an exultant sigh. "Are you watching this, Madison?" he yelled out from his office, craning his neck. "You recording this? The market's going nuts! Absolutely nuts!"

He could see the pale blond blob of Madison's head bobbing up and down from beyond the fogged glass, a piece of floating beige debris on water.

"Crazy!" he heard her say.

But now his phone was wailing *JOHN JOHN JOHN CORTEZ*, and Rudolph groaned aloud. The fucking accountant again. He picked it up.

"Yeah?"

"Rudolph." Cortez sounded relieved. "Good to finally get ahold of you."

"Been busy. Auctions, you know. Sorry."

Rudolph picked at a hangnail, waiting for John to declare whatever bad news he was about to come out with. Cortez was always trying to undermine the enormous galumphing sales Rudolph slammed

61

down for the gallery with tremulous whining *hmm ah well I just think* reminders about risk and spending and checks and balances. A fragile, hysterical, useless man, not a big cat, not a great big prowling predator like Rudolph.

"No problem," Cortez said. "No problem at all." He laughed awkwardly. "Listen, Rudolph, I just wanted to go over the numbers for a minute. Have you got time?"

No I fucking don't, Rudolph wanted to scream. Instead he replied, "Sure," in the most bored tone he could possibly summon.

"Oh. Well, oh, of course. Well, ah, as we enter the new quarter, I just want to review the books, see where we can tighten things up around the edges a little. And, uh, things could be looking better."

Rudolph could tell John didn't enjoy telling him this; his voice was shaking with nerves. He tried to sound more patient.

"Okay, hit me. How are the numbers?"

"Well, as you know, turnover this year has been very high. Almost ninety million."

"But that's fantastic!" Rudolph exclaimed.

"Well—er, yes. Problem is, we also have a lot of outstanding debts on our plate now from old loans due to be paid. The Citi one, for example—Harry Olbrich's six million—"

"I'm aware of that, of course," Rudolph said coldly. "But we're a young business. It's normal to operate with debt, isn't it? Worse comes to worst, we'll extend our loans a bit longer."

"Er—thing is, we've already done that. Cash flow is tight, I will say. Like, are-we-going-to-make-payroll tight. I haven't calculated everything yet, but I'm estimating losses of around eight hundred K in 2016."

Rudolph gripped the phone. "How is that possible?"

"Well, there's a lot of spending." John sighed; Rudolph heard him leaf through files. "The New York gallery is costing us half a million a year—"

"Every gallery needs a space! We have to compete with the big dogs. Real estate's expensive—"

"To say nothing of the lease you have coming up for the London gallery. And, Rudolph, there's the personal spending. Client entertaining, first-class hotels, private jets—exhibitions and art fairs a hundred thousand a pop—"

"Necessary expenses—"

"But mostly, it's the purchase of art itself. Almost as quickly as we sell, you're buying new stuff. Do you realize there are half a dozen Bowes paintings just sitting in the warehouse?"

Rudolph could feel the rage rising up in his throat, acid and yellow. The man was a complete fucking dunce. Why had he ever hired him?

"John, they are a long-term investment," he said, very slowly. "The Bowes market is about to—is already exploding! I sell faster than any other dealer I know. I sell *more* than any other dealer I know." His voice broke; the stress was crawling up his spine like a trail of stinging ants. "Do you know how hard that is? Do you?"

"No one is saying you aren't working as hard as you can," Cortez said, nervously. "But can we afford to keep tapping into our capital like this?"

"John," Rudolph inhaled, "I hear what you're saying. I do. But these are solid assets, all right? Just need to hold on to them a little longer before I flip them on to the next guy. Eight, ten months—September, the Beaux-Arts is going to open a huge Bowes show in Paris. We've just got to bide our time to reap the biggest profits, okay?"

Rudolph remembered something.

"You said it doesn't make sense to keep the costs on our books. Is there a way to move them . . . off-books?" he asked delicately.

"What?" A long pause. "You mean, commit tax fraud?"

"More like creative accounting."

"That's illegal," John said flatly. "And I could be liable in the eyes of the IRS. So, no, I wouldn't recommend it . . . Anyway, we should really try and make some cuts."

Rudolph eyed Madison through the frosted glass doors, reaching up to the top shelf of the bookcase. She was wearing a pair of very tight pants today. "There are some people here who are extremely important to the general morale."

John sighed. "Let's just see what happens, all right?"

Rudolph collapsed into his burgundy leather 1972 Mario Bellini armchair. He felt nauseated; his jaw ached from teeth-grinding. The familiar black shutters of a migraine had already started to edge down over the perimeters of his vision. Fucking expenses!

The pressure of money was suffocating sometimes, like lying down in an open grave. Buried alive. In his dreams, he found himself merging with the dry earth, disintegrating in its rotten texture, and he was falling, falling, jerking forward as he tried to get up, the troubles of his childhood becoming one with the terrifying heights of his present. Merely the idea. Merely the idea of nothing made him go crazy inside.

And yet. His rage, his envy, they'd given him an edge. Most art dealers were dinosaurs, speaking in hushed tones about artists like they were some endangered species that needed protecting from the evil forces of capital. These patrician graybeards, talking on the phone with their arms crossed, looking down their long, thin noses at him. People didn't talk enough about negative energy, how it could fuel you, provide the jet flames to power you through every decision in your entire life.

He loved art. Loved it as purely and as truly as it could be loved.

But it was necessary to create a strategy that hewed to the clients' precise view of the world. His niche—the tech bros, the nouveau riche, the billionaires—they no longer cared about proving their cultural gravitas to an older elite. Why bother? They were so much richer than those snuffling old fogeys anyway, they lifted up their eyebrows at the Uncle Lyndons of the world in disdain: *You won't let me into the club? Fine. Fuck you.* They no longer cared about proving something to someone by displaying their most precious trophies to a salon full of guests—what thankless work! Let the wives do that.

They liked to speculate. They liked to chop art into shares and sell them as paper. They liked to shift art from cold storage container to cold storage container to avoid ever paying import-export tax—and Rudolph was the magician whisking their paintings into cosmic space.

A sharp ringtone interrupted his thoughts.

"Hey, dude, it's me."

Rudolph could hear the angry blare of cars behind Jonas's nasal out-of-breath voice, which always sounded as if he had a clothespin on his nose.

"Oh, hey."

Rudolph straightened in his chair, tense. He hadn't heard from Jonas, and after a few days he'd resigned himself to the idea that the Rathenaus weren't interested. Maybe he had played his hand too obviously. He was dying to ask *What's the fucking score?* But he didn't want to blow his cool.

"I just got back from a lunch with my uncle, okay. Christian, not Stefan. He wanted me to call you, actually, about the painting. You got it?" His voice jumped with excitement, gleeful as a child with the information he had in his hands.

"Did he like it?"

"He *fucking* loved it, man. *Loved it!* He said—he said it was the best Bélizaire he ever saw, bar none. Not even the MoMA has anything to compare, he said." Jonas made a happy little farting noise with his mouth. "You believe that?"

"And?" Rudolph demanded. "Does he want to invest in it? Buy a share?"

"Dude. Let me finish. He wants to buy it, okay? Not a share—he wants it for himself. Wants that shit on his wall! He just bought a new complex at Hudson Yards for some hooker Victoria's Secret model he's dating—but catalogue, man, not even runway, it's so jokes—he wants to keep it there so his wife won't see it . . . Listen, he's offering fifteen point five. I know you said nothing lower than sixteen, but what do you think?"

"I'll take it," Rudolph said immediately.

"All right, then. It's done. He'll make the first transfer tomorrow."

"That's amazing, Jonas." Rudolph exhaled.

"And—and—this is the best part. They want to sign the investing deal, too, starting in April. You buy low, sell high. Flip the art, they'll front the cash. Okay?"

"I can't believe it," he said, half to himself.

"Believe it," Jonas said. "You really are a great salesman; I mean that as a compliment," he continued, as if it could have been anything else. "And look—I get my five percent, right? For putting it together."

"Just like we said."

"Thanks, man. I'll try and get him to settle ASAP. I could use it, too. Things have been pretty weird in my family lately."

"I'm sorry to hear that, man," Rudolph said, and Jonas let out an edgy discomfited laugh. His father was an investor living off the dregs of his big brothers' fortunes. Something sketchy about him—Rudolph couldn't remember what, but he recalled seeing a *Page Six* about his assets being frozen. Now that the deal was done, though, Rudolph was itching to end the conversation. Jonas wasn't the sort of person he wanted to speak to during daylight hours. He made himself repeat earnestly, "Real sorry to hear that. Let me know if there's anything I can do to help."

"Yeah. Yeah, thank you. Speak soon, bro."

"Speak soon."

Rudolph tossed the phone on his desk. He felt like he'd just done a line of high-quality Colombian cocaine, the deliciously pure kind you could no longer get because everything was spiked with fentanyl these days. Fifteen point five million dollars! He imagined the money streaming in crisp green bills right into his bank account. Rudolph allowed himself a triumphant little jig, right there in his office. He was a genius, a prodigy, a wunderkind! Who said the American dream was dead? Who said? He was living proof that it was alive and well!

And if he used it to pay off Asaka?

He stopped dancing.

The problem was that the money was Asaka's. The painting was Asaka's, and all profits would be his as well. After Jonas took his 5 percent, what would be left for poor Rudolph? Nothing, basically.

Absently he stroked the antique leather of his armchair. It was impossible not to have money right now. Gallery rent, salaries, expenses—he needed a steady influx of cash. He needed to pay the PR lady who only wore Armani. Spelling out Rudolph's grand return to London as the director of the hottest new gallery. The rave reviews! The chatter! The parties and the money!

He was so close to becoming a god. But if he couldn't afford to put on the exhibition in the first place . . .

Unless—unless—he simply kept the money, held on to it for a few months, strictly for safekeeping, didn't tell Asaka about the sale—

After all, didn't all businesses move money around in this way? Rudolph asked himself. As soon as I get the investment seed money from the Rathenaus, I'll be able to pay Asaka right back. He'll never know it was gone in the first place.

He needed to walk. He needed to let the idea ripen inside his head, come to fruition. Harvest it.

Decide whether he was ready.

Outside, a cool light frost stiffened the air. As he walked, Rudolph was conscious of an old, obscure loneliness, a loneliness so part of his being that he might as well have called it by his name. He wanted to tell someone about his success, but he couldn't think of a person in the world who would care.

Know me. Need me. Love me.

He popped an Ativan. Rudolph had been addicted to sleeping pills and Adderall since his sophomore year at Deerfield. That was the year they all started partying in the city. Also the year he lost his virginity. He used to have a girlfriend in high school, a girl he really loved.

The girls. The icy, old-money, New York blondes he was always chasing after, treating badly, rejecting, being rejected by, so much confusion, so much pain. That was the year he had his first major crisis. He couldn't stop crying. He missed his mom, even though he hated his mom.

His anxiety was such that the Ativan was necessary, a soft pink blanket, like putting on a pair of earplugs to muffle a scream.

Here was the problem with the crème de la crème, the delicate blondes. Sotheby's girls, with eighteen-carat bangles that swiveled up and down their thin, tanned wrists as they walked. Under their gaze he felt like a flamboyant imposter, unable to compete with their fathers and brothers, certain they could see that gin-stained tenement in his past. The girls were obsessed with recreating their parents' status. Who gave you that bracelet? Daddy, Daddy. Though at first it had only added to their intrigue. He'd loved a challenge. Loved the wash of self-forgiveness that came over him when he looked into their eyes and realized that they had finally decided to trust him, despite their best intentions. Then Cornelia, who had scarred him in a different way. After fifteen years of this, he got tired of breaching all the boundaries. Beauty was commoner than toothpaste. Once you got inside, there was still that hollow feeling, so why the Fort Knox?

But this girl he'd slept with, this Ingrid. Quick as a diamond dealer, he'd measured her up. The edgy black clothes of a gallerina. Not his usual type. She had a wide-eyed, credulous, nodding way of listening, as if she really believed what you were saying to her. It was nothing special: he had seen the quality many times before in nice, polite twenty-five-year-old girls. Though it did have a certain freshness, especially when you yourself were no longer twenty-five.

He thought of her naked, in his bed.

But he had fucked a million girls before. His Lacanian therapist told him that he had a mortal fear of death and that he needed to bury it, often. Rudolph always enjoyed getting her take on his sex life, though sometimes she said other, more unpleasant things. Still there was something bad about an exposed body lying beside him in the morning. The dirty eye makeup, the condom on the floor: it all spoke of some disgusting vulnerability that drove him insane, and he would cringe away.

But.

Ingrid had one of those curiously expressive faces in which the emotions seem constantly to be brimming to the surface, a raw honesty, sketched into the ivory features. It was a childlike quality, almost like one of those sculptures of medieval saints. Yes.

Children, he thought suddenly, have the ultimate capacity to adore; they are the opposite of shame.

So many major, life-changing decisions could be put down to just this: an irritation with the old habits, a vague and lustful desire to replace them with something different, something new. In the morning her hands, on the back of his neck, had been cool. For a moment he had felt soothed, as though the hot crackle of a migraine pounding beneath his skull had finally gone away.

Where had she said she worked? Chelsea someplace.

He decided to take her to lunch.

7

INGRID WANDERED ABOUT THE HALLS OF PAUL BERNOT, STUDYING THE tourists. It was her job to check on the safety of the displays. People came into galleries for all sorts of reasons—to steal, to make fun of the art, to rest their tired heads in bad weather. She watched a stocky German tourist in Birkenstocks peer into the anus of a dead dog before flinching away in shock.

Smiling wryly, she turned on her heel.

Yohji Fujita had worked in obscurity for twenty years. Last year, though, things had changed for the shy and little-known Japanese artist. A famous actor had invited *Architectural Digest* to tour his house in Calabasas, where, on camera, he showed them his prize possession: a rare 1997 edition of Fujita's famous goat genitals, wrapped in his signature pink and red yarn.

"He's an artist's artist," the actor explained, disdainfully, just as his PR consultant had recommended. "Extremely niche."

Overnight, Fujita's fame had exploded. Someone made keychains, followed by a whole cottage industry of T-shirts and miniature plastic animals all shaped like pet orifices. Now that Fujita was finally getting the longed-for retrospective at the Tate, Paul had decided to put on a celebratory exhibition of the Pet Orifices here in New York.

She was about to go back upstairs when a flicker of movement caught her eye. There was a tall man with auburn hair peering at the biggest sculpture in the show—no, he was actually *poking* at the sculpture with his fingertip. What the hell was he doing? Ingrid started toward him, ready to tell him off in no uncertain terms. Then he straightened; the dim light caught the architectural jut of one cheekbone. Her mouth fell open.

"Rudolph?"

"Hi." His eyes crinkled into a smile. "I was just looking for you." Gesturing to the vacant space around them: "This place is kind of a maze."

"What are you . . ."

She trailed off, feeling more and more confused. Was he insane? A stalker? You didn't just walk into people's places of work after sleeping with them once.

He made a move to hug her hello. Ingrid stepped back so quickly she almost toppled a life-sized beheaded cat.

"Thought I'd drop by," Rudolph was saying casually. "Yeah, I was sort of in the area. Some of my clients are pretty interested in Fujita's work."

"Oh really?" Ingrid looked doubtfully at the sculpture.

"So talk to me. What's it all mean?"

She waved the press release at him. Read a line aloud in a droning monotone: "'Fujita elegantly bridges a gap between discourses reflecting on climate change and commercial consumerism, inviting viewers to experience the perception of spatial orientation and other forms of engagement with sites of reality—'"

"No, no, no." He rolled his eyes and smiled at her. "Cut the shit. I want to hear the behind-the-scenes digest. I want to know what you know."

Ingrid paused.

"Well, I guess he—Fujita—read a lot of Julia Kristeva and started searching for whatever looked as wounded and appalling as possible. Abjection, blood, holes . . . sacrifice pets to shock the bourgeoisie, all that fun stuff. It's like so Gen X, so eighties, but, you know, it's a continuation of his previous performance."

"Which was what, exactly?"

His interest surprised her; the way his pale eyes kept probing her face. The fact that they'd slept together felt like a conspiracy between them, paralyzing and arousing at once.

"He'd interrupt Broadway musicals to take a shit onstage. Critics loved it. They said it was a ritualized attempt to expel the forces of consumerism from his body. But it couldn't go on for long, obviously, because parents got too terrified to take their kid to see *Wicked* or whatever, like, it became bad for business. So he was forced to shit—to shift focus."

Rudolph motioned to the dog sculpture beside them. "What's that one?"

"That one is called *Dominus Rectum (Cobalt Blue)*. It's modeled on Yves Saint Laurent's dog's . . . Well. One of them. I guess his servants secretly replaced the dog with a new one every time it died so the guy wouldn't freak and blow a new season of designs. We got it from Sotheby's. Highest record for a dog corpse ever sold."

What are you doing here? she wanted to say.

"Very on the nose." He glanced at her out of the corner of his eye. "I'm not sure you're convincing me to buy anything. Still. I'm liking all these animal corpses, Ingrid. They're starting to become our thing."

She blushed at the sound of her own name. Was longing to cut the small talk, but immediately second-guessed herself.

"Anyway. Um, do you have a meeting with Paul?"

She motioned awkwardly to the ceiling, horrified to hear her old teenage stutter coming back.

"What?" He looked surprised. "I'm not here to see Paul. I came to take you to lunch."

"Lunch," she repeated, blankly.

"Lunch," he said. "You are in sales, aren't you? Just say I'm an important client."

He winked at her.

The answer to his question was no, and not likely to become yes. The people who succeeded in sales were glitzy and ruthless and well-connected, and if you weren't well-connected, then you had to have that killer instinct. Like Rita, who had texted Ingrid this very morning about a Fujita she'd sold, sight unseen, to a guy she'd met at the hot tub at Le Bain. The kind of person who could make a sale at a baptism or a funeral. Ingrid just knew she wasn't. She considered herself a drifting, floating, transparent sort of person, whom others valued most as a reflection of themselves.

"Um," she said. "I'm not really in sales. I'm more . . . sales-adjacent."

He ran a hand through his hair. His arms were golden, she noticed, freckled and covered in a sparse blond pelt.

"Hey, but I can be your first client." He grinned at her. "Come to lunch with me and I'll even buy one of those shitty dog sculptures. What do you say?"

"*Molto bene*, Geronimo." Rudolph smiled at the chef as they settled into a tiny red leather booth. Geronimo slid a bottle of Cabernet toward them, wiped his floury hands on a tomato-stained apron, and left. They were alone again.

"You speak Italian?" she asked.

"Oh no, no." He laughed. "Just a meaningless pretension."

She watched him pour half the bottle into two wineglasses.

"Though my father was Swiss, allegedly."

"Allegedly?" Ingrid asked. "You don't know who your dad is?"

She was joking, but his face immediately went tight.

"I mean," he colored slightly, "Sullivan's not his last name, it's my mother's. He sort of skived off when I was younger. There were certain . . . issues in my family, and he just—" He spread his palm out and blew on it. "Poof."

"Seriously?"

"Never seen him again." He laughed shortly. "That surprise you?"

No, she wanted to say, but it did. She had imagined some rich and cold-blooded childhood at the heart of a nuclear family of Connecticut WASPs. Big white house, cookies on the table, father the CEO of a major financial institution. But she had been wrong, or so he claimed.

What he did have was a perfect confidence. The expensively tailored clothes, the eyebrow-arching smirk, the way he lounged across the booth, his arms spread like wings. His eyes continued to stare at her. They were round, pale, with an almost angelic clarity that said *I have nothing to hide.* She had a sudden premonition: the man was a complete moral innocent. Untroubled by guilt, by second thoughts, by all the little hesitations and foundering that slowed other people down. Where others stuttered—stiff, awkward, sounding like liars though telling the truth—he just barreled forward into the future, the kind of guy who made history sag under his weight. How seductive; how curiously appealing. What must it be like to wake up with a colonizer's brain, not just believing the world was yours, but intent on possessing it fully?

"My parents were divorced, too," she volunteered. "My dad remarried this woman who barely believes in Western medicine. Lina. She bores you to death ad nauseum talking about potential toxins in food ingredients. Like, I can't even take a Tylenol in her house without almost getting sent to rehab."

He laughed, though she caught a wistful expression cross his face. So she tried again, seeking the brief flash of emotion he'd shown before:

"What's your mom like?"

"Um." Folding his hands together. "She's got a lot of problems. Consummate alcoholic. Pathological liar, too." His smile was wry and bitter. "No room for anyone or anything but herself."

Ingrid let out a nervous laugh. Was he the kind of guy who secretly hated women?

"I never would have guessed."

"Yeah, well. I'll take that as a compliment. Being someone else's full-time caretaker means growing up fast." He glanced up at the ceiling. "God, that sounded super self-pitying, didn't it?"

Rudolph had learned to drive at twelve, so he could take his mother to the liquor store. He had needed to teach himself, after she picked him up from a bus station drunk and totaled her car on a guardrail. From then on, he would always be driving through Boston, searching for her. Worrying about where she was and who she was with.

He recited it all, the dark liturgy: She would disappear frequently, sometimes for days at a time. Some of her boyfriends had been truly vile. As a child, he had often felt that he was living just for her. Just to keep her alive.

Ingrid stared at him. The story was so beyond her relatively sheltered childhood that she almost didn't believe it—the power being shut off, the horrible uncle . . . She listened, almost afraid to eat her pizza lest she seem to break focus in the middle of this Dickensian tale. Rudolph was talking rapidly at her, as if he suddenly needed to confess everything at once. Briefly she was conscious of embodying a blank, a Madonna figure haloed in gold, on whose anonymous lap he needed to sob out his tears. It was nice to be wanted in this way, she who had never been needed by anyone. But there was also something manipulative about it, a little too smooth. She got the feeling that she was not the first woman to hear this story, nor would she be the last.

Then he reached the climax. He straightened in his chair, looking visibly happier now. It was as though the entire story had been told for him to reach this point: a transformation, a rebirth, which would justify all the misery and pain. Rudolph had turned eighteen, gone to

London. Acquired a powerful mentor or two. The black sheep, finally shedding his coat on foreign shores. Where nobody knew who he was—and so he could finally become the man he hungered to be.

"God, I'm so sorry. I just went off on a real tangent, didn't I?"

"No problem. I like to listen." *Try not to sound like a doormat.* "Are you still in touch with your family these days?"

"Oh sure. My mom's doing great. Now the family doesn't have to look at me anymore, they've wiped their memories clean. Tabula rasa." He let out a bright, false laugh. "Have you ever noticed that people are always running away from their old lives and trying to walk into new ones?"

"I don't know," she said uncertainly. "But you grew up with your cousins, right? In Boston?"

"I mean." Shrug. "I suppose I was included in the family gatherings in the most marginal of ways. I hope my uncle sees a little more value in me now." He laughed again, that bright, relaxed laugh, as he poured the dregs of the wine in her glass. "But enough about me. It's so boring when people try and blame the void in their own lives on some random thing in the past, like they weren't just as fucked-up before. Tell me about you."

"Oh, there's nothing to tell."

The big jade pools of his eyes were warm and caressing. He played with the inside of her palm, tracing her lifeline with his long fingers.

"That's not what I see. I see . . . hmm, a long and fascinating life. You seem like the secretive type."

Ingrid blushed. The details of her past felt so small and pastel-hued against his grand verdure tapestry. She wasn't the type to weave such mythic scenes around the bare threads of her own life. Nor did she want to tell him about the death of her mother. It would derail the conversation into pity, and this—eyes glancing at each other, knees touching under the table—had nothing to do with pity and everything to do with being young and alive.

And yet. For some reason she found herself leaning into the red leather booth, telling him all about her whole abortive attempt at being an artist. It would have been better, she confessed suddenly, to have squandered her talent in some glamorous dissipated way, exploded out of history at twenty-five, rather than fading into the dull flowered wallpaper of some forgotten outer borough where washed-up New York hopefuls went to die.

To her surprise, Rudolph seemed to understand her conundrum perfectly.

"But it doesn't reflect on your ability at all," he told her. "Sometimes the world just isn't ready for a radical new talent. And I know that sounds cheesy, but it's true."

Ingrid almost gasped. He understood her. He understood—the shame, the regret, the questioning—of that whole lost future.

"That's nice of you to say, but you don't even know me." She cleared her throat, trying to regain control, tamp down the tremor in her voice. "I sort of shoved it all in a dark corner, literally and metaphorically."

He tilted his head appraisingly. A short silence fell. One hand darted across the table; a dry spark of electricity shot up her spine.

"Yeah, well," he said. "I'd love to see your paintings sometime."

8

DESCENDING INTO HER USUAL TUNNEL AT EIGHTH AVENUE, INGRID was so immersed in a bitchy email from Claudia that she hardly noticed the other occupants backing away from her side of the car. Thoughtlessly she sat down, scrolling until the oily, pungent smell of burning feces pierced her nostrils. A large curled-up man was sleeping next to her. He had a lit spliff in one hand and a broken bottle in the other, an explosive manure bomb just waiting to happen. Ingrid stayed, frozen, in her seat until the next stop, where she fled into the crowd to switch trains.

Outside a trendy Greek restaurant, the ruby and green lights of Chinatown shone over the waiting line of girls and boys in carefully distressed sneakers. Julia and Daisy stood near the front, talking in low voices.

"How's it going?" Daisy swept greasy bangs from her eyes. "We were just speaking about what hell on earth it is, trying to find love these days."

"I thought you were going analog with that." Daisy had recently deleted all her dating apps, a development they'd celebrated with great fanfare.

"Yeah, but it's so much more difficult to find people you actually like in the real world." She let out an elaborate sigh. "I just can't date someone with a nine-to-five job, you know?"

It was a trap, but Ingrid had to ask. "Why not?"

"I just feel like people with a really regulated working life mold their thoughts into something inherently smaller, you know what I mean? They adhere to structures of corporate capitalism. It's so not me."

Ingrid was never sure whether Daisy was joking. She doubted whether Daisy herself knew, either. A reedlike, chain-smoking English girl, Daisy was the scion of a long line of aristocrats who had alternately been linked to the Nazis and to the British royal family. Irony was the smug intellectual—"So there!"—the final polish of the shoe, conceived as an oblique rejection of capitalism. Destined to drift forever between uncompleted projects on the dregs of her diminishing trust fund, Daisy had created her persona—the hoarse reality TV–influenced vocal fry, the lime-green Y2K wardrobe—as a cultural parody and stuck to it as a kind of jaded homage, a critique. The towers had fallen. Reality was shaky. Personalities were nothing but marketing, and everyone knew authenticity was dead.

Julia, who had gone into journalism after art school, now held a coveted job on the culture desk of a national newspaper. She murmured, not looking up from her phone, "Sorry, my boss keeps chasing me. We're doing a story on the new Leonardo da Vinci, you know, the one that's just been rediscovered."

Ingrid shivered in her thin coat. She'd waited all day to hear the friendly familiar natter of their conversation, but the little group never felt whole without Simone.

On Halloween, two weeks before their final fight, Ingrid and Simone had gone to dinner at Daisy's. Simone had just sold her first painting to a gallery, and a joyous smile was tugging at her lips. Recounting the story of how the gallery curator had come to her studio—"A surprise, yeah. Total surprise. But actually, he's close to Roberta Smith—so I'm hopeful—and he said, how crazy is this, 'echoes of Judy Chicago'—"

After dinner, they went to a bodega for cigarettes and energy drinks. Ingrid's hands were shaking—she knew without a shadow of doubt that her card would be declined. When Simone dug in her own wallet for cash, Ingrid said, "I'll get the next one," but she found herself squeezing the energy drink so hard it exploded all over the sidewalk, fluorescent blue with rage.

When they went back to Daisy's, Simone had tried to change the playlist.

"You have the worst taste in music," Ingrid snapped. "Why don't you let someone else have a chance for a change?"

Simone's eyes went flat—her half-abashed, half-defensive happiness replaced by irritation.

"You're being really self-involved," she said coldly.

Ingrid's heart quickened. Daisy was Lolita that year, slowly painting on purple lipstick in the mirror, her face blurred under heart-shaped glasses as she and Julia got ready to go to a party. "Think I'm actually going to head out too," Ingrid said nonchalantly to Simone, who looked startled. It was against the rules to ditch each other for lesser friends, against the rules, especially tonight. Ingrid loved their traditions. They had planned to spend Halloween watching shitty horror movies together, Simone's favorite.

"Well, okay," Simone said. "I guess I'll just go home then."

She seemed to shrink in her colorful new dress, which now seemed a little dated, a little prudish and uncool beside Ingrid's black leather pants. Ingrid swept a placid uncaring glance over Simone, reminding her that after all it was she and not Ingrid who'd remained a Catholic school virgin until the advanced age of twenty-one, and who wanted to spend a night indoors watching B-movies anyway?

Wandering around St. Mark's Place by herself later that night, Ingrid had felt bad about the way she'd acted. In the morning, she had apologized. But some mutual trust in their ability to feel happy for each other's successes had been broken. Without realizing it, the ulcer in Ingrid's soul had eroded the friendship to the point where she could only think, *That was* almost *me. Your curator saw my work, too; he said it wasn't half bad.* She could be the most maternal person in the world, if only she was winning.

While they waited in line, Daisy told Ingrid about the progress she was making on her thesis project for the New School, an experimental film about shopping malls. Daisy, who had traveled all the way to New Jersey in search of the heartland, had been distressed to find her prize subjects in varying stages of demolition.

"It's just annoying, because the malls keep getting demolished," she groused. "It's like they want to steal my subject away from me or something. I wanted to do *Americana*, Middle America. But I'm still confident about getting to it eventually. I have a therapist—she's very unconventional—and she brought us together in a therapy circle where we underwent hypnosis. And we all discovered that we had been part of an underground witch cult in medieval Europe. We couldn't figure out the exact city, but I think it was probably Paris. Or Prague."

"Malls are so dead, they're basically an archeological artifact of the twentieth century," Julia said. "I kind of feel like it's been done before. Why don't you study the effects on their old employees, like, what are they doing now? Are they perhaps dying of the opioid crisis in some trap house in Newark or something? Because if they are, you could go there and film them shooting up and stuff."

"Wow, Julia. What a super idea," Daisy deadpanned. "So when it goes to Venice Film I can get pigeonholed as yet another exploitative political artist in search of cheap thrills."

They were nearing the front of the line now, but the host's eyes slid right over them. "You can go in," he said instead to another group of three: a perma-tanned girl swinging a monogrammed designer purse shining with newness, and two freshly scrubbed men in finance-bro vests. The girl was obviously excited about her new purchase; she was talking about it with pride, touching her boyfriend's arm.

"When the waiter lets a bunch of bougie fucking yuppies in first," Daisy said, eyeing the group with a basilisk stare.

At last the waiter waved them over to a cramped table lit with tea candles. They ordered orange wine for the table, calamari doused in salt and olive oil, a mess of tzatziki. Daisy's eyes hadn't left the group of three.

"It's a good anthropological exercise," she explained to Julia and Ingrid. "I love how they cover themselves in symbols."

"They're literally paying to be an advertisement to someone else," Julia said with a tiny smile. Unthinkingly she caressed her own bag, stamped with the word SCULPTURE? in bright red letters.

"Is your bag on the approved list of material self-expression?" Ingrid asked.

Daisy laughed. Julia eyed her.

"You're feisty today."

Ingrid said nothing.

Ingrid's friends. They were gaunt, unknowable. They wore thin gold chains around their necks and amphibious, professionally ugly sneakers. Construction worker hats demonstrated their allegiance to the working class. Julia herself was a master of this kind of rapid sussing-out, a bird of social manners, alternately moving close and winging away, depending on how cool a person smelled to her.

Ingrid had been so hungry to belong that it took her a while to understand why she felt so nervous and off-balance in their presence. They had mastered the art of giving *just enough* of a fuck, and this made them mysterious, paradoxical, desirable, as did their confusing and sometimes straight-up fascist politics. Initially she had seen it all as an aesthetic. But all aesthetic poses are also moral: a rejection of their parents, a rejection of what they saw as the dried-up shell of American politics, a rejection of what they saw as an increasing pressure on free speech, a rejection of the idea that any of this reflected America at all.

Ingrid could see it now, in the dark flush creeping over Julia's cheeks. "Whinnying white cavalry . . . blinders on," she was saying, somehow speaking of both her mother and the DNC.

Sometimes they scared her. They wanted a revolution. They wanted the empire to fall. At bottom there was always this cry, almost a howl, with which Ingrid could fully identify: *What is going to happen? Isn't anybody listening to us?*

But they loved to gossip. They loved to drink wine. Swap conspiracy theories. So information was being withheld and changed to suit the purpose of shadowy entities all around? How funny. All of this added to the unnerving sense that nothing was real and everything a posture.

Leaning forward, Ingrid whispered over the flickering candles:

"You guys, I've fallen in love."

Instantly they were all ears.

"Who? What? When?"

"Oh, Ingrid, you're always falling in love," Daisy said, pouring the rest of the wine into her glass. Ingrid disliked her intensely right then.

Ignoring Daisy, she recounted the whole story out loud.

"He even bought this sculpture by a horrible new artist we're showing," she finished. "It can't be serious. But I like him. I really like him."

"Sullivan?" Julia repeated, narrowing her eyes in concentration. "I know him. Or—well, I know of him."

"Really?" Ingrid's heart raced. "What do you know?"

Julia held up her hand for another bottle of wine. Then she started to shred up her napkin, rolling it into pieces with a deliberate slowness. Ingrid watched her do it, feeling increasingly disturbed.

"One of our columnists wrote a story on him a while ago, actually," Julia said eventually. "Just a little fluff piece—you know how people love a *Vanity Fair* series about these entrepreneur types giving out self-help advice on how to make it big—"

"So what did your colleague say?" Ingrid prompted impatiently.

"Well, his uncle is Lyndon Sullivan. You know that Boston real estate guy who got big in the eighties? One of those tycoons who sent thugs to projects to beat up tenants and remake the buildings into luxury apartments."

"Sounds like a wonderful person," Daisy said.

"Yeah. So my colleague thought Junior's whole business was funded by the family, but it isn't. Apparently the uncle hates him, cut him off."

"So who funds it?"

"Nobody knows." Julia snorted. "Although people say he works for all kinds of people. The Russians. The Saudis. Who can say? See, he runs that place like an investment fund. Bidding up prices, selling shares, providing third-party guarantees. People let him do whatever he wants because he's some sort of money-making prodigy. None of it's illegal, technically, but it's a risky game. It works, though. I mean look at the kid—what is he, thirty, thirty-three?"

Something about this explanation discomfited Ingrid.

"I think he used to get around, too," Julia was saying vaguely. "He's got a reputation as kind of a shark. Some English girl ... used to be on reality TV ... and the daughter of—" Julia named a famous Italian artist whose prices had recently gone off a cliff.

Ingrid nodded. The rest of the dinner ticked on into nothingness; her thoughts marched on alone. She was imagining Rudolph striding around a spotlit gallery as he screamed into a phone, a horde of assistants skittering after him like ants, and in this dream she herself was no longer one of them.

At home, Ingrid removed her socks. It had been raining, and her feet were still coated in a thin layer of grime. They were wet, smelly. For a few minutes she eyed them in amused silence. They were dirty like the man with the bottle of shit on the train. Some people fell through the bottom of a hole in society, and there was no one to help them get back up again. That sort of thing happened when you were alone, totally alone in the world.

She took a shower. The stall in her apartment was the color of a Band-Aid, one of those old fleshy boxes with grab bars. Ingrid rinsed off the day in graying streams, expertly executing a strategic nuclear strike with the showerhead on an errant cockroach attempting to dart past her feet. Only once she slipped into bed, rolling around for a minute to feel her skin on clean sheets, did she finally allow herself to do what she had been wanting to do since leaving the restaurant.

Ingrid had thus far resisted Googling Rudolph for some reason. Some masochistic desire to prove to herself that she was fine, not in love, would still be okay if everything dissolved tomorrow. Which made her next move even more satisfying. Ingrid opened her laptop. She inhaled, setting her fingers cautiously on the keyboard. There was a moment of silence as she typed his name into the search engine. The old computer made a little humming sound as it thought about it. Then the screen changed, and Ingrid began furiously clicking on every link that had ever pertained to Rudolph Sullivan.

The first one that came up was a lifestyle magazine article.

Socialite's Ex-Boyfriend Opens Chelsea Gallery— Prodigal Son Returns to New York

Fresh from running Harry Olbrich Gallery in London's pricey Mayfair district, contemporary art dealer Rudolph Sullivan has skipped over the Atlantic to hang his own name over the door on West 25th Street. I meet Sullivan at the grand opening for his first exhibition of sculptures by Tanya Singh.

Stepping out in a debonair Zegna suit, Sullivan is tall,

russet-haired, and aristocratically handsome, the epitome of the new millennial class of refined creative cool. Once known as the boyfriend of British canned soup heiress and reality TV star Cornelia Davies, Sullivan is nephew to real estate tycoon Lyndon Sullivan.

Those in the know flock to hot new artist Tanya Singh, who finds hunting trophies at junk sales and poses them in the act of mating. . . . "Her work really makes you think," enthuses one guest. "It's one of those things that's so surprising, you just think it's gotta be good."

Sullivan has developed a formidable reputation for aggressively pursuing works by Lucio Fontana, Bill Bowes, Ed Ruscha, and others. "He's the Bowes whisperer," art columnist Charlie Errol confides. "If there's a deal in the world involving a Bowes painting, you can be sure Rudolph Sullivan has his finger in the pie. He's a wunderkind that will be moving and shaking the art world for decades to come . . ."

Ingrid forced herself to stop reading. She strained her eyes to the laptop—closer, closer, closer—as if Rudolph's pixelated white grin might reveal the beating heart inside.

It was all so gross. The article's cloying tone, the rich and sticky daisy chain of acquaintances, how everyone was a Somebody or Somebody's son or daughter, the whole sugary-sweet abscess of incest and folly. She lay back on the bed and laughed. Then she stopped laughing. Her heart ached.

Please, please, she prayed. Please let me get what I want.

Just this once.

The way his ice-colored eyes had focused on hers, like a long-camera lens swiveling to attention . . . yes that was real. So real she could almost taste the adrenaline rise to the back of her throat.

Both come from fractured families, she imagined a couples therapist saying, ten years from now. *Death and divorce, respectively.*

She'd grown up in a town like others. Green lawns. Rough maples, shaggy at the edges, like friendly monsters, nothing too cultivated. Lived alone with her mother. The father had remarried when Ingrid was two. That was how she thought about him in her head, *the father*, because his image was so unimportant, so shadowy, a cardboard cutout of a man. He lived in Chicago with his new family. Her mother was the one she adored, the one she loved.

Lynn with her dyed blond hair and warm, rapid way of talking. She wore pedal pushers and had bright blue eyes that glittered when she was disappointed, so Ingrid had tried to never make her sad.

They talked constantly. Lynn was a rare perfect listener—patient, unstinting, offering advice. You could tell her a thousand times about a problem and she would still seem just as interested, just as passionate about finding a solution as the very first time.

The limits of that town were narrow and tightly proscribed. A sort of self-fulfilling prophecy about it. A single expensive French restaurant, to which Ingrid's mother always brought her on her birthday. Raspberries on a chocolate cake. Nothing seemed so chic as the white sparkle of fairy lights on a gate, the glimmer of water in the distance, even though she understood that these things would seem too simple, too DIY if she ever saw them again. It was for this reason that she never went back.

There had also been a mall, like the one Daisy wanted to film, and when Daisy had spoken about it, Ingrid had felt herself drift off mentally. She remembered the joys of the mall, its pleasures. Wandering through that big gray temple with aluminum heat pipes, looking in all the windows. The mall was a monolith of dreams, inviting you to envision a new life with each new pair of jeans.

A town like others. Green lawns. Ice cream. Making out with some stoner on the bleachers when you turned fifteen.

The death.

Ingrid had nothing to say about her mother's death. Nothing but, after six months of sleepwalking, she had woken up one day to find herself a completely different person. Alone in her father's house. Her throat ached and her heart was numb. Nothing was raw, nothing was bleeding. It was just that no one would ever love you again like your mother did.

Julia had made a number of rude comments about Rudolph tonight. She'd looked at Ingrid, significantly, as though the implication of something sketchy would immediately trigger Ingrid's removal from the situation.

Ingrid lay on her bed and stared at the ceiling.

Julia was the type of girl who thought the world owed you something good.

When she thought of her mother, one image came to mind. It was a persistent, unpleasant image, of Lynn, waiting in the high school parking lot. For some reason she had been stuck, with an irritable and vaguely hurt expression on her face. Forgetful. She was lost, and Ingrid was supposed to find her. Where had she been? Smoking weed in some guy's car, probably. A mistake.

Sometimes she still woke up, gasping for breath. The universe before her mother's death felt hazy in retrospect, like shaking the glitter out of the bottom of a kaleidoscope to see what was real, but everything was blurred. Talking as they walked through a park in springtime, magnolia blossoms on the trees, the silhouette of her own hand. She was a baby again, reaching for her mother's hair, so soft and golden and fluffy. The happiness of it. But these memories had become polluted with other, darker images. The parking lot. People were roaming there. She was afraid of God, afraid of the empty room. This grim little apartment with pigeon shit on the windows. It seemed to contain no color, no safety, no facets but the unquiet dark.

For once, she thought, I want to be happy.

Let something go right.

When she pushed this image away, another one came. Rudolph was walking up the stairs, she saw him going to a place where her mother lived. He was shaking her mother's hand, they were both alive, and he was saying . . . saying . . . *I'm so pleased to meet you*, with a big white smile on his face.

Ingrid froze the image, rewound it in her head. Played it again.

Last night, before Rudolph left for London, they'd stayed in bed together for hours. With his head in her lap Rudolph had looked like a little boy. He'd told her about the three turtles he used to keep as a child, all painted white. She'd told him about the sad mental decline and eventual suicide of her stepmother's cat. The narration had taken on a movie-like aspect; they'd listened to each other with wide eyes, half-parted lips, the kind of ruthless abandon that had no room for anyone else.

Happiness had overwhelmed her.

She closed her eyes. The pain of infatuation was starting. But after years of fighting a negative current, Ingrid wanted to be swallowed up. In the dream, Rudolph had on a white linen suit, the sun was warm on his skin, and he was laughing on repeat. A little silly, this dream, but . . . His voice had a reality, an authority, a control people actually listened to. Her hair would shine. Skin would glow. She would be privy to his secrets, his innermost heart, and everywhere she went, she would be greeted by the smiles that recognized his importance.

But what will it cost me? Ingrid's eyelids froze. Her lashes were palpitating lightly. Was there a shadow of boredom, of disgust? She had a confused sense of his hands tapping impatiently on a table. A dry sucking sensation at the top of her skull. Maybe she was in the background, becoming the woman he aspired for her to be, swallowing tranquilizers, her soul numb, dead, with only a taste of the real hopes and feelings—

He was so—obsessed with money—

Fiercely she pulled the fog back over the dream. There was no boredom. She was going to be happy, so amazingly happy. He was going to whisk her away from this life, this abyss of invisibility and non-meaning, and install her into real, perfect adulthood. The color of a pale blue sky, with not a speck of dirt in it. He was laughing, in her dream, and she smiled at herself a little as she fell asleep because the vision was so corny, so ridiculously untrue. But that was the thing about dreams. They existed just for you.

9

"WOULD YOU LIKE ANOTHER GLASS OF CHAMPAGNE, SIR?"

The emerald hills of England slanted into view as the plane dipped, revealing bubbling brooks and dark forests. Rudolph traced the clouds with his finger on the porthole window, listening to the beating rhythm of rain.

A pretty, blond flight attendant was smiling down at him from behind a cart of plastic cups and Scotch bottles. He couldn't help but notice her breasts. He tried not to look, but the plane was heaving slightly. Was she flirting with him?

"Maybe a mimosa," he said. "And some raspberries. Thanks."

"And just to let you to know, we'll be making our descent to London City in about twenty minutes."

He winked. "I'll chug it."

She flashed a piano-key smile at him. One incisor was stained with cherry-colored lipstick; his mental hard-on immediately deflated.

Rudolph gazed out at the fine gray drizzle, fastidiously tucking the complimentary cashmere blanket around his knees. The sticker price of flying private between London and New York was $65,000, and it was worth every penny. He didn't want to endure seven hours beside some blowsy Midwestern mother nursing her wailing baby. He didn't want to wake up to some dozing old hippie's beard tickling the tip of his nose. He wanted peace, peace and privacy, far and away from the great unwashed masses. Was that too much to ask for?

His friend Charlie, whom Rudolph had invited to fly with him, was snoring softly across the aisle. Charlie always wore the same uniform—a pair of safety-pinned red Adidas trackpants and cool sneakers—because he believed himself to be famous, an Andy Warhol–like person, whose outfits were worthy of being recorded and studied. Presently he was cuddling an empty bottle of wine, which earlier, the flight attendants had tried to pry out of his hands with little to no success.

Charlie Erroll was a glorified gossip columnist whose specialty was the art world. He had a rich wife, the daughter of a financier who'd been imprisoned for security fraud in the eighties and pardoned by Clinton; she was the reason Charlie could afford to follow his friends around with such ease. St. Moritz and Miami, Hong Kong and Paris, Berlin and London and Venice, party after party after exhibition opening after art fair, their world was exploding at a pace much too fast and expensive for your average critic to keep up.

Rudolph liked journalists—the idea of them, at least. Could you chase down the truth, pin it to a board like a butterfly? The bookish boy he'd once been was sure that you could. In college he'd even had some vague idea of going into the industry, but his gray-faced professors were always making morose about how hard it was to earn a living, how more and more papers were folding every day. So instead, he had chosen to make money.

That was fifteen years ago. Today it was almost impossible to distinguish a real review from an advertisement. Magazines were forced to solicit fake reviews from powerful galleries, laying false trails of glory for lucrative twenty-five-year-old artists, thus allowing the galleries to yank up the prices for their Hot Young Things. The nostalgic allure of Truth belonged to a pre-digital childhood now, a more innocent time, in which you'd actually believed it was possible to reach the heart of things.

Well, but ain't that the way it goes, Rudolph thought, stretching out his arms behind his head. Words existed to be molded and shaped, twisted around one's own agenda. Everything is spin, everything is for sale, and nobody knows it better than me.

Recently the editor of the most renowned art historical journal in the country had come to him, hat in hand, practically begging him to shell out a thousand dollars for a puff piece on Dermott Dermott Critchley, a painter he'd invested in. But the editor had made a mistake. Rudolph did not represent Critchley; more importantly, the journal would sink into bankruptcy in eight to ten months regardless. Strangely, though, and against his best interests, he had agreed.

Something about the old man had seemed so pitiful, dignified but pitiful. He had worn the puzzled expression of someone who didn't quite understand what was happening to him. Perhaps this was what had triggered Rudolph's desire to help: the memory, like a lost song, of someone he had once wanted to be.

Charlie stirred as they landed heavily at City Airport, Rudolph knocking back the last of his mimosa. Twenty minutes later, they were speeding through London in the backseat of a black cab.

"What's the plan tonight?" Charlie yawned. "I haven't even seen your new place yet."

Charlie's haggard face showed only traces of the wild youth he'd once lived in the early 2000s coke-and-supermodels scene. He was a tiny forty-something man with cropped brown hair and the sharp, clever eyes of an owl, earning his keep through a constant stream of cynical snark. Rudolph delighted in seeing his own words appear like clockwork in Erroll's columns, attributed to an "insider" or "a VIP guest" or a "highly placed source." What would his geeky teenage self have thought of *that*?

"You'll love it," Rudolph said. "I gut-renovated a Georgian town-house. Two doors down from Bianca Jagger's. And the gallery, the gallery's kind of like the one in New York—you know. Brutalist."

Charlie raised his eyebrows. "Can't wait."

"Anyway," Rudolph said, "the auction's at seven. We should be there by"—he glanced at his watch—"six-thirty. That gives you enough time for a nap. Then we can get a snack at Nobu with Fergus and Marina and whoever else." He wiggled his eyebrows. "And go out."

"Fantastic," Charlie said. "I'm just happy to get away from my beast of a wife for a minute. Tried to flush my antidepressants down the toilet the other day, you believe that?"

"Why'd she do that?"

"Some bullshit about how the label tells you not to drink on them. Told me my shrink was in cahoots with Big Pharma." He passed a hand over his face. "Whose shrink isn't, I ask you? Was it my idea to have a third child at forty-five?"

"If you weren't supposed to drink on them, every single person we know would be dead."

"Right? They were invented to drink on. Like a cocktail olive. It's utter," Charlie repeated, sounding more and more enraged, "fucking fantasy."

Charlie's favorite activity was complaining about his wife, whom he bitterly resented for her tight control of the family trust. That said, he did drink too much—they both did. As with many friendships, alcohol was the glue in theirs. But Charlie was twelve years older than Rudolph, and he actually had a wife and children, which seemed to rein him in somewhat. At least he didn't dabble in hookers and usually managed to get home at the end of the night, which was more than Rudolph could say for himself.

"Elaine's a good egg," Rudolph said amiably, thinking of this.

"I know, I know. I'm a horrible person. But right now I'm just exhausted, and my editor's expecting auction gossip bright and early." Charlie rubbed at his eyes. "I'm going to nap the rest of the way, if you don't mind."

"Be my guest."

While Charlie slept, Rudolph checked his phone. Emails came flooding in: a confirmation from the French curators at Beaux-Arts for his meeting tomorrow, Christian Rathenau's thanks for shipping the Bélizaire. Then a string of messages from Ingrid, bright and girlish and brimming with teenage love:

> Safe travels!
> Let me know when u land.
> Is it weird that I already miss u? ☺

He studied the texts with a scientific eye. Obviously she thought they were operating on a higher plane of intimacy, one that warranted daily texts about his safety and well-being. He wasn't sure how he felt about it, but for some reason he found himself composing an ardent reply.

In the four months since they'd met, Ingrid had seemed surprised and pleased by Rudolph's attentions, which had, at first, confused him. It wasn't that serious; she wasn't his type. So why did he keep appearing at her office every Tuesday and Thursday night, whisking her away for long, fuzzy happy hours that lasted until the early hours of the morning?

At first, he was careful not to give her the weekend slot, a subtle but firm move intended to show Ingrid her relative insignificance in his life. But at some point, this became yet another rule he'd forgotten to enforce. In the eternal gold twilight of a low-lit bar, they'd coil around each other's bodies, embarking upon a conversation that was long and meandering, which seemed to have no beginning and no end. They debated the merits of their respective ambitions—well, his ambitions mostly, Ingrid was just an assistant at a gallery no one had ever heard of. *He* was the one to show her things, teach her things, and when he spoke, her pale and luminous face rose toward him, the way a sunflower rises to meet the sky.

One wet February morning, they had been looking at mummies in the Egyptian section at the Met. A cold sleet beat at the roof. Warm inside the museum, they held hands in front of a turquoise statue of the goddess Isis, whose almond-shaped eyes and inscrutable grimace had reminded Rudolph of the antiques that his uncle used to collect.

"This one's just like you," Rudolph said, eyeing the statuette's tiny breasts. "Impervious to the desires of mere mortals like me."

"You little perv." And she had laughed, taken his hand. "Are you my Osiris, is that it?" But her clear olive cheeks had gone red.

It had become a nervous tic to see how much he could flatter and charm before people became suspicious. Spoiler alert: they rarely did. He was in the service industry to the megarich, and they were not like other people. Without the editorial limitations of affordability, their desires rambled on like unstoppable bores, both relentless and whimsical. To them, he was, at best, a trusted cultural attaché, providing a slick veneer to their shopping activities; at worst, he was little more than a used car dealer.

It didn't bother him most of the time. To cut out your feelings until every minute of the day became a separate and valuable transaction: that was the business. Sometimes, though, it did. Sometimes, when he heard his eager voice on the phone, he felt a well of shame and doubt so powerful it twisted his heart.

It felt curiously sexless to sell your soul. People joked that the art world was like high school. But who felt nostalgic about high school?

Those who had failed, he thought, socially as teenagers, and then spent their whole lives trying to re-create it, to prove they were worth it all along. When he looked around the upper echelons, he saw people who cultivated themselves, day in, day out, to become someone else's dream. Anodyne, bleach. Little Barbie dolls covered in cellophane. A long time ago he had realized that the appearance of effortlessness was the most effortful of all.

So you stopped caring. But it was your job, your work. You couldn't afford not to care. Still, you needed an escape. One night he met Ingrid's eyes across the table and sensed new possibilities coming awake. The thing was not serious. But. After twenty hours' separation, his whole body would itch to touch her, be with her, get out of work so he could visit her. At first there seemed something animal and almost awful about it: he was no longer in control of himself. He wanted to fuck her in the bathroom and then leave. But then, he realized, with a cool surprised feeling, he was grateful. Affection was a luxury he had never been able to afford until now.

Later, at the Carlyle, they drank martinis as clear as tears in front of the painted gold mural. They were talking, talking, talking, until their voices went hoarse, and suddenly he heard himself laugh out loud, with zero calculation. Emotion. She was everything he had ever wanted in a piece of art: beauty and emotion. Some kind of jazz was playing, and Rudolph let her talk. He was feeling loose in his body, and deeply relaxed.

The car rolled to a stop on a quiet street lined with trees. Charlie lifted his head, pressing his nose to the glass to catch a glimpse of the rosebushes. They had been precisely pruned, around the little gates, to protect each house from the prying eyes of observers like him. A beam of sunlight pierced the window.

Rudolph looked up.

As a student at Goldsmiths, he had often spent free afternoons taking walks around London. Meandering along the long, cool River Thames, he would fantasize about those jewel-box houses on Cheyne Walk, the most beautiful street in all of England. About tucking himself away. So when a house had come up on the block, six months ago, Rudolph had bought it in a flash. He had never felt so proud. Now the red bricks of his Georgian house glowed invitingly under a thin beard of ivy; a polished green door beckoned you in. The ceilings were sixteen feet high. The long glass extension led to a sprawling garden filled with lush plants and flowers, where visitors might lounge in a miniature Greek temple on warm summer nights, enjoying the koi pond spangled with fish the color of milk and rubies.

But its interior still felt like an empty stage. Discarded paintings were haphazardly propped up against the blank walls. The oiled parquet floors lay bare.

"It's gorgeous," Charlie said. "Really."

But his expression remained flat. Rudolph felt a dull pain in his teeth. He'd been grinding them again on the plane.

"I've ordered a bunch of furniture," he lied. "It's been delayed in French customs. You know how petty the douanes can be."

"Maybe it just needs a woman's touch."

"I touch women in here all the time," Rudolph joked lamely.

He watched Charlie, who kept looking around the room, as if he half-expected more furniture to suddenly appear. Charlie picked up a malachite Art Deco ashtray, running his hands over its smooth oblong weight.

"Who was that girl I saw you with at Carbone the other night? The dark-haired one."

"Oh, that was Ingrid." He cleared his throat. "We're sort of, uh, seeing each other right now."

"Oh."

Rudolph willed himself not to say anything, but the words came spilling out.

"What'd you think?"

"What?" Charlie laughed. "Oh, cute. Just that little—that little provincial look. Like she'd never been to a restaurant before."

"Well, I like her."

Charlie set down the ashtray. Glancing at Rudolph, he saw how the winds had shifted. He hadn't gotten this far in life without knowing when to quickly change track.

"Hey, I think that's great. She seemed—sweet. Like, wholesome. Anyway, it's not like things were ever going to get serious with Cornelia."

Rudolph didn't want to talk about that. Even years later, he still felt oddly defensive of Cornelia. More to the point, people thinking she was trashy or tacky reflected badly on him.

"Though I do have to say, that girl was a lot of fun." Charlie laughed richly. "Do you remember the three of us wrecking that hotel room in Hong Kong—?"

"I feel like I'm entering a new life phase, actually," Rudolph interrupted, frowning.

Charlie gave an amused look. "Whatever happened to Cornelia?"

"I see her around. We ball sometimes." Rudolph shrugged. "Listen, do you want to order some food?"

They ate burgers and fries on the only piece of furniture in the room, a low white sofa by Milo Baughman. Charlie, chewing with relish, didn't seem to notice the viscous yellow grease dripping off his fingers and staining the couch.

"God, I miss shitty food. Elaine's got me living on green juice—she's doing a summer detox before we visit her parents in the Hamptons. Now I think I need to sleep off these carbs, do you mind?"

Rudolph didn't mind, although Charlie hadn't even asked. He'd expected him to stay in a hotel or something. But when the situation demanded it, Rudolph was always the soul of politesse. He showed Charlie to a guest room with a flourish.

Upstairs, Charlie complimented a painting that Rudolph had just bought. Rudolph had liked it immediately: it showed a woman swinging madly in a park. One slender foot was encased in a blue slipper; the other shoe was flying off into a distant bush. Shades of the rococo, shades of the ancien régime, it spoke of fun times and pleasure and beauty. But now Charlie examined it, with a more critical eye. A marvel of illusion, he admired, pointing out its subtleties. Rudolph felt his stomach curdle. Somehow he'd failed to notice how ghostly the woman's face was, how her flesh seemed to be dropping off, and her pleasure park was submerged in an underwater grave.

10

Claudia had requested that Ingrid come in early to help with a client brunch, meaning her train was packed even tighter than usual with the sweating, silent, gray-faced masses. In charcoal, Ingrid sketched her fellow commuters, blowing the smudges off the page. No room for mistakes. The man in the black cashmere coat, barking into his cell phone about the next million. The Hispanic housekeeper in pink Reeboks. The Upper West Side mothers, towing their well-dressed toddlers up the stairs. Never once did they hesitate to push you out of the way. The city was rushing by, this cannibalistic place—always a step ahead, but there was a sense you could keep up if you just walked a little faster. Today, however, Ingrid was behind.

Ingrid called the caterer, Jessica. "I'm so sorry I'm late!" she apologized, hurrying through the grinds and shouts of construction work on Tenth. Jessica was waiting with a cart in front of the locked gallery, awkwardly shifting from foot to foot. Ingrid fumbled to help with the pyramid of food-filled freezer bags.

They spent an hour setting up in the dining room. Delicacies were carefully removed from each last scrap of tissue. Arranged on the gilt-edged Hermès dishes Paul kept for clients. At last, an elaborately constructed tower of cheeses stood at the center of the table, glistening with rinds and honey and plump violet grapes.

"Claudia will be so happy," Ingrid said, admiring the finished product.

Jessica thanked her. "With something this, you know"—gingerly she waved at the thirty-foot ceilings, the paintings—"there's extra pressure to get it right. You think she'll like it?"

"How could she not?"

"Good." She sounded relieved. "I've been up since three baking out of my apartment. I can't really afford to hire anyone else right now to help out."

Ingrid assured her that Claudia would be impressed.

But when Claudia came in at one, it immediately became clear that she was not impressed. The muscles in her forehead began to pulse. The blue vein. The blue vein in forehead was not a good sign. Rita, coming in swiftly behind her, took one look at Claudia and disappeared into the elevator. Claudia counted everything once. Twice.

"Something is missing," she said, ominously.

"I'm sure I double-checked everything."

"You've forgotten the sweet potato salad," Claudia said softly.

Ingrid could hear the little-girl artifice in her voice begin to ebb dangerously away. She watched Claudia slowly flex one fist.

The caterer paled. "I, uh, I didn't forget it. I mean, here's the list."

Limply she held out a piece of paper. Claudia snatched it out of her hand, eyes moving rapidly over each line of text. Finally she swung around to face Ingrid and said softly, her tone breathy:

"Who made this mistake?"

Please please please, let it not be me, Ingrid begged internally. Let it be anyone but me. "I should have the confirmation," she said quietly. "In my email, let me get it."

"I'm waiting." Claudia crossed her arms. "Un-fucking believable. Truly unbelievable."

A flood of relief ran through her as she pulled up the email—she had indeed ordered the sweet potato salad. In the same instant, she saw Jessica's face crumple as she realized what was about to happen. Looming over the smaller woman, Claudia puffed out her chest. A smile flickered across her lips before she started to scream.

"I cannot believe you have the nerve to blow such a simple request. I took a chance on you because I wanted to patronize a small, woman-owned business, because I'm a fucking *feminist*! But now I realize why you aren't working for someone bigger. It's because you have no clue how to run a fucking company!"

"I'm sorry, I really am," Jessica said in a frightened rush. "But sweet potato salad wasn't even on our menu—"

"This spread looks like dog shit," Claudia spat. "I am never going to hire you again. I am never going to recommend you to anyone. I want my money back. Now."

"Excuse me?"

Claudia pointed to the plastic change bag around the caterer's waist. Her eyes skittered disdainfully over the caterer's lunch-lady hairnet, torn cuticles, and Chanel-by-Chinatown purse.

"You've got money in your bag, don't you?"

Tears welled in the caterer's eyes. She fumbled with the change bag. Dollar bills fluttered out. They had a curiously beautiful appearance, Ingrid thought in a daze—like falling butterflies.

"Pick it up!" Claudia shouted.

A switch seemed to have been flicked; her eyes were bright and crazed. Ingrid and the caterer both fell to the ground, startled into a bizarre debasement by the violence in Claudia's voice. They scrabbled up the money. Beneath Ingrid's turtleneck, a clammy sweat was pooling. Without noticing it, they appeared to have exited a normal Tuesday afternoon and entered some darker, more lawless place. The red heel of Claudia's shoe, as she tapped it, was exactly parallel to Ingrid's face; and it seemed to rap faster and faster on the ground, until Ingrid feared she might crush her skull in with it. Finally Ingrid straightened up. She was still holding the dollar bills loosely in one hand. Claudia seemed strangely on edge. She stood looking into the distance but was different from before, lips parted, a dead spot in one eye. For a minute they simply stared at each other; Ingrid tried to keep her face blank. She would, she felt, be punished for seeing this.

Finally Claudia's lips twisted; she seemed to have realized that she'd gone too far.

Flapping her hands in the air, she swung toward the elevator, muttering:

"Just let yourselves out, I don't have time for this."

Jessica's eyes were red.

"Look," Ingrid said weakly, "I don't know what to say—like, I do know she's going through some stuff in therapy, though of course it doesn't excuse her behavior—"

"How is that my problem?"

Ingrid had to admit that it wasn't. But Jessica had already collapsed in tears on the twelve-thousand-dollar bench designed by Jean Prouvé, its sleek architectural lines resisting all forms of comfort.

After she walked the caterer out, Ingrid sat at her desk with her head in her hands until the drumming of blood in her ears drowned out the drone of the office machines. When she'd acquired this job, Ingrid had vaguely assumed that she, like every other adult, would find happiness in that distant faceless monolith called Work. Every teacher and parent and LinkedIn post she'd ever encountered had exhorted her to *Love what you do, and you'll never work a day in your life!* They had said *Follow your dream.* They had said *Productivity is the key to success.* From this safe distance, the temple of Work had shone silver in the sun.

Up close, though, it was more like an underground basement with fluorescent lighting. The jargon, the Olympic-level crawling performances required by power-drunk bosses in their own Lilliputian dictatorships . . . why hadn't anyone warned her? She considered the caterer. It hadn't even occurred to Ingrid to yell back at Claudia, to defend the caterer's work: that was the worst part, that oily, slimy feeling. Maybe she was just useless, as defunct as a cheaply made toy. Or else the place that everyone told her was a utopia was fundamentally hollow and empty—a much more terrifying thought.

Her phone buzzed in her pocket. Rudolph had just bought her a gift in London, a box of sable-tipped paintbrushes. Screw the workplace! Ingrid's heart swelled with joy. Was he thinking about her? She could picture him, peering into a window of a shop. Wondering—

"That your boyfriend?"

Rita had crept up on her without Ingrid noticing, so lost was she in Rudolph's texts. Ingrid dropped the phone.

"He's not my boyfriend. We're—I don't know." She stopped. Had no desire to psychoanalyze the budding relationship with Rita. "How was your date last night?"

Rita was clutching a cup of coffee, looking bilious and green under her sunglasses. She let out a low moan.

"Oh, awful. The guy was sweating through his shirt collar the entire time. I practically had to drink an entire pitcher of espresso martinis to get through it."

"Sleep with him?"

Rita slid her sunglasses down her nose. "No, thank God."

"Who was it again?"

"The usual. Aimless exec with a midlife crisis straight out of Cheever. Said his wife treats him like an old shoe." She exhaled. "Sat on the bed and ate a cheese plate while he talked about how he should have written the Great American Novel instead of joining the Fortune 500. His teacher at Iowa thought he had a lot of potential back in 1972." She pretended to play a tiny violin. "Cry me a river, you know? You're sending your fucking daughter to Nightingale-Bamford while I'm still paying off loans in blow jobs."

Ingrid watched her sort through the cash in her wallet.

Rita was two years older than Ingrid. She had bounced from college to a PhD in comparative literature with the frictionless ease of the intellectually gifted before even considering the realities of the academic world for a hopeful graduate, an arid desert with not a drop to drink. Result: she was in even more student debt than Ingrid.

It was standard practice for girls in art to have sex with older male collectors, hoping to bag a massive commission on a sale or—possibly—shove an elderly wife out of the frame. Rita was more honest. She disliked the blurred lines of dating collectors for free, preferring a clean and simple pay-for-play.

The older men who comprised her core demographic were mostly gray flannel suit types, who lived in Darien or Larchmont with their two bratty kids and hyper-disciplined, supposedly sexually indifferent wives. Ingrid admired her enterprising spirit, though she herself was far too fearful to follow in her footsteps. Once Rita had tried to get them to go on a double date, but Ingrid had gone home early. The old guys gave her the creeps. The desperation in their eyes, the way people looked at them together. She had never thought men were so pathetic. Plus a thousand salacious television movies were burned into her skull: women getting gang-raped, thrown into car trunks, and then chopped into pieces and thrown into a Texas oil field. But Rita would reproach her for her fears and prejudices. She was so bourgeois, said Rita. My clients are just middle-aged guys, regular and sad and wishing for a shoulder to cry on.

"What about Rudolph, huh?" She pushed Ingrid's shoulder. "He's been visiting the gallery a lot lately."

"I guess."

Rita was studying her with a practiced eye.

"You've never even had a real boyfriend, have you?"

"Of course I have," Ingrid said with indignation, her cheeks flaming red. She'd always been the worst liar. She pretended to flick a piece of dirt off her shoe. "Though not like a . . . super long-lasting one," she admitted.

"Define long-lasting?"

Ingrid thought of Brian. Shortly after moving to Bushwick, she'd posted online about needing a carpenter to help build furniture. Brian was a friend of a friend, who apparently had some skills with a tool belt. Two hours later, he'd showed up to build her IKEA bed. That it had broken shortly afterward was either a testament to his ability as a lover or his lack thereof as a carpenter, she still wasn't sure.

When not practicing carpentry, Brian had played in a band and helped manage a superfluous record store in the East Village. Ingrid had fantasized all day about how she and Brian would move into a dilapidated loft in Chinatown, where she would paint and Brian would write music. They'd live on sex and creative genius alone, like Patti Smith and Robert Mapplethorpe. Later people would make documentaries about their fiery, poverty-stricken youth, after they became famous of course—but the dream had never transpired. Ingrid had accidentally texted a long stream of frenzied armchair analysis *about* Brian to Brian himself instead of to Julia, the intended recipient. A rookie mistake, and Brian knew it. They had broken up soon after.

"It's hard to date in this city," she said finally. "People are just so scared to settle for anything less than the best that they think they can get."

Rita shrugged. "Well, don't worry. There's no need to freak out about it. What are you—twenty-five, twenty-six? Goddamnit, that's so young. You're so young, Ingrid. But maybe you should think about becoming a lesbian. We live in a culture obsessed with pleasure, haven't you heard? Heterosexual love is a site of oppression."

Ingrid felt helpless to disagree with someone as opinionated and self-assured as Rita. She said timidly, "I feel like people are looking for connection."

Rita laughed.

"Well, I think that's great. You might be the last romantic in this whole city. It's always the transplants, isn't it?"

Ingrid was just working up the nerve to point out that Rita was from New Jersey when the menacing *click-clack* of Claudia's heels resounded up the stairs.

"Are you ready to go, Ingrid?"

"Absolutely."

She glanced at Rita, who had stood up expectantly and slung her purse over her arm. Claudia's eyes moved vaguely in her direction, her shellacked lips forming a thin smile.

"I think it's best if only Ingrid comes with me, as my assistant," Claudia sang in dulcet tones. "You know, just so that we don't overwhelm Chastity and all. So we'll see you when we get back, Rita?"

A ripple of quiet fury crossed Rita's face. Ingrid grimaced at her apologetically. Rita had scouted out Chastity Peters herself; in fact *she* had been the one to suggest that Paul bring Chastity over to the gallery, but Claudia had obviously decided to cut her out of the equation.

"Should we take the subway?" Ingrid asked.

Claudia laughed merrily; she hadn't taken the subway in years. Seeing that Ingrid was serious, she replied in a somber voice, "I totally would, but my heels are just not up to wading through a whole throng of people right now."

So Ingrid hailed a cab, which screeched up to the curb in a cloud of filthy black exhaust.

II

THE AUCTION ROOM WAS PACKED WITH THE USUAL SHARKS AND minnows. Silvery lights bleached color from everything but the somber navy backdrop. Against this darkness, you saw nothing but cold glitter: enormous jewels on mottled hands, jaundiced teeth bared in mirthless smiles, high studded shoes straining across blue-veined feet.

Deeply bronzed art dealers schmoozed with dignified-looking older women. There was a lot of Chanel, a lot of '80s tweeds. A younger class of auction specialists swam restlessly about the room, trying to corner and cannibalize unwitting collectors, while frightened-looking assistants ran after them with manila folders and ringing cell phones. A Cecily Brown painting in fleshy tones of pink and brown stood alone on the stage, looking as if it just had been ripped wet off the easel.

An invisible caterer offered Rudolph a glass of prosecco. He accepted it, though Charlie waved the drinks away, saying balefully, "My ulcers are acting up again."

"Plus I don't drink cheap prosecco," he hissed in Rudolph's ear as they took their seats. Beside them, a woman who had had so much surgery that she resembled a third-degree burn victim was cradling a hairless dachshund in a tiny yellow cashmere onesie.

"Shut up, it's starting."

As the auctioneer strode across the stage, the audience fell silent. It was a silence dense with anticipation, with heat. The pressure of millions revolved abstractly in the air. Inside the pocket of his pants, Rudolph squeezed the lemon-shaped stress ball that Ingrid had knitted for him after he'd confessed to her about having panic attacks sometimes. He wasn't having a panic attack now, though—far from it. There was nothing so erotic as the thrill of an auction: the nail-biting tension of every minute, the fierce aggression of the pursuit, the jubilant climax of the winning bid.

"What're your lot numbers again?" Charlie murmured as the auctioneer extolled the qualities of the first lot.

"Fifteen, ten, thirty, and thirty-one," he whispered to Charlie. "They put the Bill Bowes paintings together. My Gunter is lot ten."

Charlie peered at the catalogue. "Beautiful—Wait. Isn't that the one that got wrecked in the flood? What'd you do to it? It looks brand-new."

"What we have here is a matchless painting by the Japanese artist Hashimoto Hara," the auctioneer bellowed in his cut-glass accent. "Ladies and gentlemen, I am going to start the bidding high . . . Nineteen million, ladies and gentlemen, can I get a nineteen million?"

Charlie craned his neck at the lot. It was a painting of a little girl in a catsuit. The man behind Rudolph raised his paddle.

"Did you see who that was?"

"Heir to the Al-Fahds," Rudolph muttered out of the corner of his mouth.

"Fuck me, that'll be a record," Charlie said, tapping the name into his phone just as the auctioneer slammed the gavel down and shouted, "There you have it, ladies and gentlemen! A new record for Hashimoto Hara, at twenty-five million!"

Rudolph shrugged. "Listen, you've got a paddle, right?"

Charlie indicated the paddle in his lap. "I'm buying for Elaine. A little Giacometti."

"Do me a favor. Bid on the Gunter."

"What, the one with water damage? I don't want that shit."

Rudolph had bought the Rudolf Gunter painting about six months ago from an insurance company that had written it off as beyond repair. A classic gold-colored Gunter, meaning that it resembled nothing more than the shiny metallic wallpaper you might find in some nouveau riche Miami mansion. But people would buy dog shit if you put million-dollar auction prices to it. The Gunter had been tucked away in some Geneva warehouse that had been flooded, damaging the painting beyond even the most creative restoration attempts. No one would touch it, but Rudolph had bought it for next to nothing and concocted a plan to make a quick buck. Harry Olbrich's Manchester accent jabbering in his ears:

"Rudy, let me show you something. See all that gunk?"

2008. Twenty-two-year-old Rudolph, a shy intern in Olbrich's Mayfair gallery, creeps into the boss's office to deliver coffee. Olbrich is crouching on the floor, shining a blacklight on a painting. Rudolph glances down in surprise.

"Is that—drool?"

Olbrich bursts out laughing, his hammy face jiggling with amusement.

"You believe that? Used to go to an auction, see a Picasso or whatever, and realize it was completely filthy with spit! Fix a bit of dirt or whatever . . . doesn't show up in the forensics . . ."

He hands Rudolph a tub of clear goop.

"Here, help me with this. Fake spit. People invented it to stop using their own."

"I found the special copper paint that Gunter uses on those paintings," Rudolph whispered to Charlie.

"No." Charlie's eyes popped. "You crazy bastard."

"Took me six months to find it. Only seasonally available in Germany. Madison and I repainted the damaged parts ourselves, bit by bit."

"That soggy piece of cardboard?" Charlie said in wonder. "You must've created an entirely new painting from scratch."

"Just call me Gunterangelo." Rudolph laughed and put his arms behind his head.

He loved to fuck with the auction houses like this. It appealed to his sense of the artificially composed scenery of the world, its randomness, its cosmic flukes and cruelties. Wasn't every price, in the end, no more than a collective belief in an arbitrary fiction? He considered his fakery a type of high-end performance art, known only to himself. Like Warhol, doing his Campbell Soup ads, Rudolph was making a commentary about the death of human originality. Only he was so cerebral, so fucking noble—he giggled to himself—that he was content to remain anonymous.

He surveyed the auction room in silence. Everyone else here took it all so seriously. They believed there was a direct relationship between object and value. He knew it all to be imaginary. He saw himself as an actor on a stage, with gold bloomers on, his shouts merging to be heard with the loudest voices of his day.

He kneaded Ingrid's stress ball. "Bid when it gets to two million."

"I don't have two million to spare, bronco."

"You won't win," Rudolph whispered. "Just trust me, okay? There's a lot of interest. I want to drive the price up a little." He waited.

Reluctantly Charlie nodded. "If I win, you're paying."

"Of course."

Rudolph had no intention of paying for his own painting. Clasping his hands behind his head, he waited for the Gunter to come up.

"The next lot is a wonderful 2015 work by Rudolf Gunter," the auctioneer boomed. "A frankly stunning copper Gunter, in marvelous condition. I'm going to start the bidding at one million seven hundred thousand, can I have one million seven hundred thousand?"

Hands flashed in the audience. Next to Rudolph, the woman with the dachshund lifted her paddle high.

"One million eight hundred thousand pounds. Any more? It's at one million eight hundred thousand pounds. Any more? One million nine hundred. Thank you. Thank you to the man in the green hat. Any more? Do I have two million?"

Charlie's paddle darted into the air, just long enough for the auctioneer to catch his eye, before it retreated between his quivering knees.

"We have it at two million," chanted the auctioneer. "Any more?"

"Fuck me, fuck me," Charlie moaned.

The white lights were hot, seconds stretched into hours. Rudolph sat rigidly upright, eyes glued to the auctioneer. He was pirouetting across the stage like a Shakespearean actor performing a soliloquy.

"Two million one hundred thousand pounds, do I have more?"

The other bidder's paddle flashed. With a decisive tap of the gavel, the painting sold for two million two hundred thousand pounds. Charlie was saved. He collapsed on Rudolph's shoulder.

"Oh my God, I thought I was a goner."

Rudolph patted his arm reassuringly. "See," he said. "I told you."

"Honestly, I need a stiff drink after this."

Rudolph wished Charlie would shut up already; the Christopher Wool was up, a white painting with the word FOOL printed across it in smug block letters. Behind him, a row of thick-jowled collectors perked up in their seats.

"An iconic Christopher Wool FOOL painting we have here, from an important, private, *aristocratic* European collection," the auctioneer boomed. "Let's open the bidding at two million, do I have any takers?"

Rudolph raised his paddle, but he was distracted by a bizarre tugging at the bottom of his trouser leg—a crisp midnight-blue Brioni suit he'd *just* had tailored. A sharp yipping noise ensued, but Rudolph was loathe to look away from the auctioneer.

"Two million one, with the gentleman at the front of the room!" the auctioneer shouted at another bidder.

"Get this fucking dog off my suit," he hissed at Charlie through gritted teeth, trying to shake off the tiny dog attached to his foot. "I'm about to lose the bid!"

As Charlie struggled with the dachshund on the floor, the woman with the botched face raised her paddle in triumph. The FOOL was hers to keep. She scooped up the dog, who'd managed to piss on Rudolph's suede shoes in addition to tearing his trouser cuff. "Beautiful Coco," she cooed in a thick Austrian accent. Rudolph snarled at her.

"Don't mess with that woman," Charlie whispered in his ear. "She threw a bag of hot wax all over her last boyfriend in an elevator. Ruined his face."

"She owes me a goddamn suit!"

"Relax. You'll get a new one."

Despite the loss of the Wool, Rudolph won two smaller Bill Bowes paintings he'd had his eye on for a cool nine hundred thou. When the auctioneer declared his winning bid he sank deep into the chair, pent-up adrenaline and jet-lagged exhaustion coursing through his body. He felt completely spent, like he'd just had sex for hours. He needed to isolate himself from the hangers-on and pour himself an ice-cold drink.

"Let's get out of here," he murmured to Charlie.

Stepping out into the cool night air felt like removing a suffocating pillow from his face. Charlie offered him a Gauloise with trembling hands; Rudolph didn't smoke, but he accepted it as a personal reward for making it through the Trouser Incident, as he was already calling it in his head.

"Come on. What's it to you?" Charlie said, sounding bored. "You make that much every hour."

"It's the principle of the thing," Rudolph responded. But of course Charlie was right, though it sent a wiggle of discomfort through his stomach—like such feckless spending deserved an equal punishment. He'd spent more on far less.

Speeding along the dark streets of Mayfair in a cab, Charlie took out a pocketknife and made a neat slit to the inside of his blazer. He removed a small vacuum-sealed bag of white dust and offered it to Rudolph.

"You brought that from New York?" Rudolph asked. "I've got a dealer right here."

"What's the point of flying private then?" Charlie tapped his nostril. "By the way, I invited Cornelia."

"You didn't."

Charlie grinned. "Hope you don't mind."

"Are you fucking kidding me?"

But Rudolph was pretending to be more annoyed than he was. Privately he felt that old thrill of lust, insecurity, and irritation that had accompanied all his rendezvous with Cornelia Davies. He considered himself basically a feminist—hell, he was all for shattering the glass ceiling! As long as it didn't affect his own salary, that is—but.

They had been twenty-five, twenty-six, twenty-seven. They'd been chattering all night to the pulsing rhythm of R&B and the yellow champagne of jazz. On Thursdays they spun drowsily from gallery to gallery, and he gulped down the cheap white wine because they were young and he still couldn't believe that it was all free. "I love it when people light my cigarettes," he remembered her saying to someone, in the gold threads of the dying sun by the window, while he watched. "Especially when it's a man."

They'd hurt each other sometimes.

Cornelia had been rotated around the friend group—and by God, so had he!—but you had to admit it was different for men. You were not *passed around*—you were the active prowler, buzzing from flower to buzzing flower like a happy little bee. There was no shame in it, no whisper of bronzer-stained pillowcases and used goods. It was simply vigorous and healthy, exactly what a man should be doing in his spare time. In the imaginary camera frame of public opinion, you got up from those sinful sheets—somehow you always left the camera frame first, even if it was your own damn house—and strolled casually, unhurriedly, down the city streets, leaving the woman sprawled naked, immobile, *encrusted with bodily fluids* on the sordid unmade bed.

Sometimes he still wanted to scream at her. *Conform, you tacky slut! Conform!* Didn't she understand that everyone else wanted to break the mold, too, only they didn't, only they chose to do exactly what everyone expected them to do?

He caught his breath. Why did he take it so personally? He didn't blame her for any of it, was aware that in many ways he had been just as culpable, just as guilty. It was the darkness in her eyes that he hated, like they were some sort of doomed toxic fate couple, Romeo and Juliet for the twenty-first century, the presumed knowledge of what he was and what he was like. He hated that. Hated her. There had been something dirty and shallow and predictable about the relationship that made his stomach turn.

No. He forced his eyes open. He didn't hate her, he assured himself. It wasn't that deep. Still had a lot of fondness for that girl in certain ways, although it was no longer romantic. Merely the distant affection of a brother toward a messed-up sister.

Nobu was Nobu, all glittering black marble and sensual gold lighting. The usual people staffed its long bar. Beautiful women, sparse on conversation, curled up cozily next to balding businessmen with platinum watches. Hands rested on smooth tanned thighs. Russian escorts. Wannabe influencers in bodycon dresses, photographing themselves placing juicy clumps of pussy-red sashimi between inflated lips.

Rudolph loved and hated it in equal measure.

They ordered the Chassagne-Montrachet and a plate of ceviche. Rudolph was buzzed and not at all hungry, but Charlie wolfed everything down like a starving man emerging from the desert. His voice became louder as he drank, divulging increasingly salacious gossip about mutual friends. Rudolph listened in silence, taking mental notes for anything he could use.

"Fucking bitch!"

They heard a loud clattering noise. A furious-looking man strode past shaking wine off his hands, his small entourage scurrying after him with napkins.

"What do we have here?" Charlie said. His voice was laced with delight. "Stage left. I think your hapless bride has entered the scene."

Rudolph didn't bother correcting him. His eyes were too fixated on Cornelia. She was moving doggedly toward their table in a tiny red kimono dress, which somehow managed to escape the spilled wine, and from beneath a veil of sooty eyelashes her big lemur eyes peered out at him in surprise. No pink streaks. She used to have pink streaks in her blond hair. Clumping along in those six-inch heel platforms, that baby giraffe walk he knew so well. The messy ingenue. He examined her for signs of aging, signs that life had finally begun to take its corrective toll, and found none. But why be surprised? When you were Cornelia Davies, hard living could be swept away, as with a cool cloth dipped in cucumber. On the soul—well, he didn't know.

"Corny, my princess!" Charlie kissed her on both cheeks. "How goes it? Haven't seen you in years."

"We were in Hong Kong together last May," Cornelia corrected him, sliding into the booth. Her eyes rested on Rudolph's face. "You must remember."

Rudolph nodded but didn't say a word, letting Charlie waffle on.

"Oh yes. I was so busy running around all the parties, strictly for business of course, but that was a fun night, wasn't it, Rudy?" He punched him on the shoulder.

"So fun," Rudolph said mirthlessly.

"Ah, my wife woulda killed me if she'd found out," Charlie said, putting on the hammy Queens accent he brought out when he wanted to seem down-to-earth. "Are you still doing the show?"

This was pure cruelty on Charlie's part. He must know that *Horses & Hermès*, the reality show in which Cornelia had briefly played a supporting role, had sadly been canceled months ago. When she was still on the hard stuff, Cornelia had nearly been forced off the show for hitting another cast member in the face and screaming at her, mouth full of spittle, "You fat fucking turkey!" Though, if Rudolph recalled correctly, it had been ratings gold.

Rudolph watched Cornelia waft around the question. "Oh, no, I couldn't do it anymore," she said. "I was advised not to. Certain people at our family's PR firm . . . Anyhow. I've been working a bit for Daddy at his new club in Soho."

"Of course," Charlie said. "How wonderful that must be."

Cornelia appeared not to have heard. She reached across the table and seized Rudolph's hand, breathing, "I've missed you, how are you?" in a low, throaty tone.

Steered by Charlie, conversation shifted to the surprising successes of the night.

"I just couldn't believe the Cattelan sculpture of Hitler," he was saying. "Twelve million pounds . . . You know, my mom was adopted from Polish Jews murdered in the war. The price itself is a spit in the eye."

Cornelia was Googling the sculpture. "This one?"

She pushed her phone toward Charlie, who winced. A pint-sized wax Hitler knelt on the floor. He was frighteningly lifelike, in a gray wool suit that Rudolph recognized from old German newsreels. The hands clasped together. He wore an unreadable expression—guilt? Agonized shame?

"It's hard to look at," Rudolph acknowledged.

"It's pure perversion, in my mind," Charlie said. "Why would you even try to joke about something so bleakly awful? It's sick."

"I don't know," Rudolph said. "It's an element of history that we have to confront. No image has greater power to embody it than Adolf Hitler. I mean, we watch movies about the Holocaust, Hollywood actors play Goebbels and Goering. So why can't we stand to look at a permanent sculpture? What's this instinctive desire to look away?"

Rudolph was leaning forward in his seat now, immune to the warm florals of Cornelia's perfume.

"We've lost our religion. Why do you think the price of art has skyrocketed lately? Way beyond any other luxury good. It's because people have a spiritual abyss inside of them. They want to believe in something." He caught his breath. "And the terror of this work is that it refuses to reassure. You look at something awful like the Holocaust and this art, you want it to provide meaning; it does nothing of the kind. All we see is the short little guy."

Charlie was nodding. "I see. You're thinking of Arendt."

Who? No, he'd just been spitballing, but Rudolph nodded anyway. The spiel was running ahead of him again, weaving and twisting and knotting itself together with a salesman's instinct.

"You realize the weight of all that death and destruction rested in the hands of men like you or me, who went home to their wives and played with their dogs. It's the realism of this work that scares us, plain and simple. We ask questions—and there no answers," he finished.

Charlie was nodding. "I see your point. But still"—he shuddered—"who could live with it?"

"I think it's a cop-out," Cornelia said, surprising them.

Charlie regarded her with frank astonishment.

"Why?"

Cornelia shrugged. "Look, he's tied Hitler up as if he's praying for forgiveness. But that's not what happened, is it?"

Rudolph frowned. He was displeased that Cornelia had seen something he hadn't, yet vaguely impressed too.

Charlie peered at the photo. "You're right. See, this just proves my point! It's so cheap. Hitler never regretted a fucking thing, he was too thoughtless to even see his own evil, too married to his own worldview." He banged a fist on the table, causing an eel roll to leap off his plate in surprise. "Nothing is fucking sacred anymore."

For a minute they sat in a morose silence. Cornelia stared into her empty glass.

"Things are so miserable, aren't they. Out there."

"Oh God," Charlie said. "Cheer up! Here we are, friends all. Feasting on spicy tuna rolls that'd probably cost the Uighurs a years' hard labor at the Zara factory."

"Yeah, and it all just feels so meaningless sometimes," she said despondently. "Like what right do we have to be here. People are dying, and stuff."

"You want a pick-me-up?" Rudolph was enjoying the charming looseness that came with that second glass of wine, without which it would be impossible to get through dinner. "I've got licorice sticks in my bag," he said absurdly.

Cornelia giggled. Her hand moved to Rudolph's leg under the table.

Charlie groaned. "I'm looking away, I'm looking away now. Oh good, look, it's Fergus."

Through a haze of white wine, Rudolph saw Fergus's pudgy face looming above the table in a pair of red trousers. His wife, Marina, was picking her way behind him in a lacy blue dress. She was a pretty brunette with a square, sticky face and curly brown hair.

"Cupcake," Charlie murmured, and Rudolph nodded in agreement. For a certain type of British man, the ideal girl was like a prize horse. Good bloodlines; a docile attitude. A taste for long walks in bad weather. The frumpy rusticity was part of it, like the homemade jam—proof positive of centuries of aristocratic inbreeding.

"Rudolph!" Fergus brayed, slapping him on the back. "Good to see you, my man."

But Rudolph had ceased paying attention entirely. *You're so beautiful,* he was whispering to Cornelia, burying his nose in the musky scent of her long blond hair. He didn't know why, other than when she'd mentioned the plight of the Uighurs he had shivered, as if he'd caught a faint chill in the air.

As students, Rudolph remembered how they would lie on their floor drunk out of their minds, blearily shouting about the transformation of Labour while the girls nodded wisely in a corner. Candles melting into empty wine bottles. Cigarette ends. Always this sense of excitement, though, about the night. With each dusty blue twilight, a new world might open: you could meet a girl tonight, find a whole new reason to live.

Now Fergus's nose was red with wine. He was talking about a charity dinner he'd been to.

"They served a disgusting little summer trout. No one interesting. Everyone just talks because they like to talk, and it was the dullest thing you could imagine. I was sat next to the granddaughter of the Nazi ambassador, von Ribbentrop. I asked her why she'd never thought to change her name. Can you believe what she told me?" He raised his eyebrows. "*Oh, oh, it's an old, old German name,*" he mimicked her. "I thought, dear God! Just change it!"

"We went to the South of France last week," Marina said. "We're thinking of buying a place in the Dordogne."

"Problem is," Fergus sighed, "the French are so fucking awful. I absolutely despise them, as a people."

Peals of surprised laughter. He glanced at all of them beseechingly; Charlie was watching him with a gimlet eye.

"They're such socialists," Marina chimed in. "They're so entitled. They think they can just wake up, and like, *receive* the government's money. It really doesn't set a good example to people in this country."

"Is it because you don't speak French?" Rudolph teased.

Fergus puffed up. "I certainly do speak French, bear in mind it's a bit rusty now, but at Harrow I did learn it—"

"But it's not like," Marina said, "the French have an incredible cultural empire stretching back more than five hundred years." She looked around with a slight smile. "Like *we* do. I mean, what do they have?"

"How about," Charlie said, "Zola, Flaubert, Proust, de Beauvoir . . . And that's just for writers, I could go on and on."

"Well—that was like a hundred years ago." She threw her hands up. "What right do they have to be such snobs? *Nothing,*" she uttered decisively.

Charlie shook his head sadly.

Fergus leaned over the table, his shirt now dappled with spilled Bordeaux to match the red trousers and bloated jowls. "My thoughts have changed on Brexit," he was saying, "if you look at the farmers, for example—"

Charlie, cutting in: "The farmers don't understand that they're being manipulated by the elites in a cynical bid for power."

"If you listen to the farmers," Fergus said loudly, "you'll see very well that we're supporting absolute hordes of migrants—"

"Brexit had no public backing until Murdoch's newspapers got behind it!"

Stop, Rudolph wanted to say to Charlie. I'm planning on selling Fergus a Bowes later, for God's sake shut the fuck up—but he was prevented from signaling by Cornelia, who was kneading his pants—

Fergus sighed and looked into his glass with an expression of infinite patience.

"Look, at the end of the day I think this is quite an instinctive, national, *British* feeling," he said, gaze swiveling accusingly toward Charlie. "And I mean no offense, but I don't think you can really comprehend how *real* Brits feel, salt-of-the-earth types—"

"And you can?" Charlie asked, flipping out a hand at the five-hundred-pound-a-bottle wine locked in Fergus's grip.

"I'm a country boy at heart," Fergus blustered. "I grew up in North-umberland." He mopped the eel off his lips with a napkin. "Say what you will, but I believe the greatness of the British spirit to be absolutely vital. There is something that—unites—*us* from Stonehenge to the Battle of Waterloo to Brexit, quite apart from European concerns. They have their own agenda, see—"

He was speaking into the distance, with the intent, noble look of a sea captain on his face.

"Bloody hell," Cornelia said, when they were safely tucked away in the bathroom. "The farmers, the farmers. I can't bear Fergus. He used to be so sweet. Now he does nothing but practice his boring little Parliament speeches on us, have you noticed?"

Head swimming, Rudolph was unable to answer; he sat down on the toilet and snorted, regaining his faculties.

"But he's a collector," he explained, kindly. "Charlie's got nothing to lose, but I do. I have to keep listening to him because I'm trying to sell a painting."

"What painting?"

"A very expensive painting by an artist called Bill Bowes."

"Bowes?" she said, with deep suspicion.

"Everything that looks like play is work for me," he said. "It always has to feel like the best time of their lives."

He didn't know why he bothered; Cornelia would never understand. She was like all the other girls he knew who did nothing at all. Hothouse flowers, clustered in a stifling glass bubble, waiting to be married so they could fuss over the toxins in tap water. As if clicking *buy* on pink crystals could ever fill the gaping void in your soul.

He sat on the toilet, watching her cut lines. "Child-sized, child-sized," he kept saying under his breath. Cornelia seemed different now in a way he didn't quite like. She used to rattle around rooms with a hysterical energy he'd found almost calming. But now her face looked pale, slightly wasted. He worried about her, about her insobriety. Only her perfume was recognizable—Portrait of a Lady, by Frederic Malle. Scent of patchouli, sandalwood, and rose. It made him happy to know this one part of her remained the same.

But now she was looking at him like she loved him.

"I wanted to tell you, Rudolph," she said. "I really—I mean, I can't get over some things—"

As if by instinct, his hand floated up her waist.

"Look, Cornelia—I'm not . . . I mean."

He tucked a strand of golden hair behind her ear.

"I need to tell you . . . Something's wrong with me. I'm not, I mean, I'm emotionally—fucked up."

"What are you trying to say?"

"Huh? Uh . . . I mean, I don't know . . ." The last sober part of himself was still trying to warn her off. *I'm immature!* he wanted to scream, *I'm not good for you and you're not good for me.* But he didn't really want to stop. Jesus Christ! Was he speaking to an infant? She should know. By God, after everything they'd been through, she should really fucking know.

They were so close, in this toilet, almost touching.

"I think you're amazing," he said drunkenly, sniffing a grainy ball of coke up one sweaty nostril. "But I—"

"I just want to know we're . . ."

Awkwardly she touched the lapel of his blazer.

"Not like it was before. You hurt me, you know? But I seem to find everyone else so—God that sounds pathetic. There's just no one in London who really—do you know what I mean?"

"I know," he soothed. "Hey, let's not talk about it right now, okay?"

She laughed. Her eyes were so sad. She was trying and failing to say what she wanted to say, and if he were a better man he would've told her to just stop. But tonight, at least, he could not be that man. He was not a good person and had never claimed to be.

He closed his eyes. London, Paris, Berlin. Every apartment they'd ever stayed in together had felt haunted. Cornelia was always wanting to move around, trying to eke some earth-shattering transformation out of her life. Sage burnings. Incense. He thought perhaps she had wanted to wake up a new person one day.

The skin hot. Her thigh sliding toward it.

Like magic his hands were in her hair, he was inhaling the scent of roses. No. Don't do this. The feelings of sickness had started, of guilt. But sometimes his body felt like it didn't belong to him. Was merely a vessel for the powers of night, infecting him, possessing him, they'd already made up their mind, and this sick, twisting feeling? Was part of it. Yeah, it was part of it.

12

SUDDENLY THEY WERE AT A CLUB IN SLOANE SQUARE, IN CHELSEA, with a carnival of images dancing before his eyes. There was apparently some kind of a Mexican theme, like Día de los Muertos, and Rudolph felt alert. Drugs were running through his bloodstream in silty, quickening jabs, piercing his heart; he was on autopilot, a mixture of blankness and paranoia, losing time. Boggling death masks swam out of the crowd; they had painted black lips, eerie black holes in the place of eyes. He stumbled away. Omens, bad juju, he wanted to get out. Someone had brought LSD. Cornelia was giggling, dancing on the table, the bitter taste of her lipstick was smeared all over his teeth along with the gritty dust of cocaine. Fergus was dancing with some girl who wasn't Marina, mouthing the words to a Latin club song while he pulled hard on a silver vape. *Until the break of day, until the break of day*, he remembered someone screaming. People were coming and going, getting lost, getting found, reappearing with trays of green shots that glowed in the dark.

They had been standing in line, like ordinary people, until Rudolph, disturbed by his lack of special treatment, had decided to go up to the bouncer and buy a VIP table. He'd even invited some nice girls in the line. But it turned out the girls had not been so nice; Cornelia's wallet had disappeared. They'd spent some time looking for the wallet before losing interest and returning to the bathroom. Rudolph was listening to himself talk, with the faint surprise that always came when your body had floated up to a secondary plane of heaven, disassociated from your mind.

"This coke is shit. It's fucking cow dewormer," he was saying, in slurry, toneless accents, Cornelia hanging off his neck. Her laughter was animalistic, smelling of mint strips and the sour-sharp tang of gin. "Get your guy to come," he heard himself say. "Get your mother-fucking guy."

He and Cornelia were bouncing along in a cab, quarreling about whose fault it was and why. The rosy tendrils of dawn crept over the London skyline. A knot of churning desperation formed: the bald world was refitting itself together. Realized he needed to drink it away—

Rudolph opened his eyes. There was a vape on the bedside table. Bright sunlight pooled on the bed. Something had happened last night, but he couldn't remember. Except a horrible, prickling feeling had attached itself, like an alien body, to the back of his head.

For a while he simply stared at the ceiling. Then—misery—the whole crazed montage of the last twelve hours downloaded in one neon whoosh to his brain. He squeezed his eyes tight at a final, searing image: a faceless woman, naked, her tiny breasts poking him in the eye as he tried and failed to fuck her with his limp, coked-up dick—

Fuck. Was she here? A quick glance revealed the bed to be empty. Pain sharpened its needles—this room, with its stale smell of smoke, was a hairline too close to a nauseating regression. In this moment Ingrid was not so much a specific personality as an alternative to Cornelia and everything she represented. Ingrid with her clear face. He kept his eyes shut, focusing on milk, puppies, green grass. Scrambled eggs. Yes, that was what he needed, scrambled eggs.

He stumbled downstairs in his boxers.

"Ah, the man himself. Looking unusually sober, I see."

Charlie was calmly leafing through a newspaper. He peered at Rudolph over his tortoiseshell-rimmed glasses. The sobriety of others, when you were this hungover, always felt like a shocking insult.

"Guess so," Rudolph managed hoarsely. "Not so good right now, though."

"Have some coffee." Charlie pushed a cup over the marble island. "I got bagels, too."

Rudolph tore the bread into pieces. He caught a glimpse of himself in the mirror: his face was as sallow and pale as used candle wax. Each swallow was painful, his liver struggling to digest the poison congealing his organs into a gelatinous bile.

"Uh, did you come out with us? Did I—"

Did I embarrass myself in front of everyone? he wanted to say. Did I say something I shouldn't have? He had a horrible memory of himself: *Well, I really shouldn't be saying this but* . . . with a big shit-eating grin on his face.

"I left after we got to the club," Charlie said. "A major cultural appropriation faux pas, all that Mexican shit." A disapproving sniff. "I hope you didn't miss any meetings."

"Oh, no." Rudolph chewed his bagel. "I don't do that."

This much was true. He was always early, always smiling and polished and ready to sell a painting, regardless of whatever he had done the night before.

"Um," he said. "Did I . . ."

He stopped. Cleared his throat.

"Who—?"

Charlie laughed. His eyes sparkled; his cheeks glowed with health.

"Who, who?" he mimicked. "You an owl? Cornelia's upstairs. If that's what your question is."

"Fuck." Rudolph massaged his head. "Why did you let her in?"

"You let her in," Charlie said. "So—good luck with that."

He found Cornelia curled upstairs in the TV room, watching cartoons. When he came in she gave him a quick covert glance, and he noticed that she had found an old prep school T-shirt of his. With it on, a bowl of cereal in her lap, she looked like a little girl. Forever young. An image of his mother floated into his head, the way she'd flip through daytime television with the curtains drawn on weekends, never once venturing outside.

"Hey." She raised her spoon in a laconic half-wave. "Hope you don't mind. Froot Loops was all I could find in your kitchen."

"Yeah, well," Rudolph managed, his skull pounding. "I'm barely here these days."

She laughed. "Right."

He stared at her until she said, very formally, "Do you want to sit down?" and he shook his head no, wondering how on earth he was going to get rid of her.

The electric sizzle between them had vanished in the face of cold reality. When Cornelia was around he became immature, teenage, the cruelest version of himself already written in her disappointed gaze.

Avoiding her eyes, he steeled himself to check his bank balance. The card transactions, last night—his heart dropped.

He clapped his hands authoritatively and said, "Listen, it was really fun last night, but I've got a lot of stuff to do."

"What?"

"Mm," he said, guilty and irritated at her shock. "Don't get me wrong, Cornelia, it's been fun. Real fun. But I just have a couple of very important meetings I need to attend to."

"With who?"

"Some people from a museum in Paris. I can't really talk about it."

Cornelia eyed him.

"You used to tell me everything," she said.

"Can we please not have any weirdness right now?"

Out of habit, he reached down to massage a triangle of skin on her skeletal bicep. She really was more anorexic than ever, he noted with concern.

She stood up. Some torturous battle seemed to be taking place behind her eyes.

"Okay?" he pressed, but her blond eyebrows drew together in anger, and instantly he knew he'd pushed it too far.

"I'm *sorry*," she sang in a high sarcastic voice. "I'm *sorry* for imagining that we could have a real conversation about things. I'm sorry for imagining—Do you remember anything of what you said to me?"

"Look, can we just not get into this right now?" he snapped. "I have shit to do, honestly, and I thought you understood—"

When she looked up her eyes were shiny and round as buttons.

"It felt like the start of something. Again."

"The start of what?" Rudolph asked, genuinely confused.

Cornelia had been smiling; now her lips curled into a wounded grimace. She began an elaborate pantomime of getting ready—fussing around with her gold bag, with the hollow crucifix that contained her supply—as Rudolph hovered. A strange feeling lashed about his entrails. He half-wanted to kick her out, half-wanted to beg her to exonerate his mistakes.

"Oh, no, believe me," Cornelia said, in a high, mincing voice. "I understand perfectly. It's Jekyll and Hyde again, isn't it? Peter Pan who never grows up."

"Hey, hey—"

"Blaming all the women in his life . . . Poor little me! I'm miserable, I'm a fucking little orphan boy who needs to be loved . . . But once you've used people up, you toss them aside. I've been nothing to you but a used Kleenex. Don't you think I know that? Genuinely, Rudolph, you're a fucking sociopath."

He laughed, almost relieved she had decided to be vicious, because now he could be mean, too.

"We were never," he said slowly, enjoying the lie on his lips, "even together. Why do you think I never introduced you to my family?"

Cornelia's face went a dark red. Wordlessly she flung herself at him, intending to—what? Scratch him?—but Rudolph grabbed her arms and she opened her mouth and suddenly they were kissing, her lips hard and furiously angry. Half of him just wanted to fall into it, like he had so many times before, this savage push-pull stirring his numb stomach—No.

"Please just go, like I asked you to," he sighed, pushing her away.

"You're a piece of shit," Cornelia said, but without conviction, as if she'd already admitted defeat.

She made her way downstairs, Rudolph watching to make sure she actually left.

Rudolph writhed around in his big bed, feeling like one of those tortured saints you saw in medieval iconography. He was St. Sebastian penetrated by a thousand arrows, head thrown back in ecstasy. Or the martyr to Chinese lingchi he'd seen reprinted in Georges Bataille: disemboweled piece by piece by the mob, then shredded to the bone like a juicy piece of chicken. There was an almost sensual pain to this hangover, a self-flagellating weakness, like he was earning back the night before.

Somewhere in the distant tangle of sheets, his phone was ringing. When Rudolph croaked out a dry hello, he was displeased to hear the tremulous tones of his least favorite person in the world.

"Rudolph. It's good to get ahold of you. I've been trying to get in touch for a couple of days now."

Rudolph said nothing.

Cortez rushed to fill the silence: "So, ah, great. I just wanted to give you some updates on our recent numbers. Sales are better than ever, as you know—our main problem is we're cash-poor because of the debts coming due this year, but we should be in the clear soon."

"Did you see we made two hundred thousand on that Bowes at auction? Price is up, just like I said it would be."

"Rudolph," Cortez said patiently. "I'm not denying for a minute that your earnings are very high. You're carrying this whole gallery. But we still need to cut down on things, just to fill our coffers until we get to a better place. Like the house, for one."

The house in Chelsea had cost six million pounds. Rudolph had justified it to himself as basically an exhibition space, which was pretty much true since he was constantly hosting clients. Three thousand sprawling feet in the heart of London! The stained-glass windows and fuck-you fireplaces! . . . I *earned* this house!

"It is my company," he replied coldly. "What's the point of doing all the hard work if you can't pay yourself the salary you deserve?"

"No, no, absolutely," Cortez agreed. "In theory. Look, I just want to address a couple of other issues, well, expenses that seem, uh, unnecessary to me." Papers shuffled in the background. "The charters from New York to Martha's Vineyard and back—"

"A necessary expense. I had to meet a client there, extremely reclusive guy. Didn't have time to get a ferry."

"Right. I see you got a villa and plane in Ibiza—"

"Business development—"

"—then there was also another expenditure of—er—eight thousand dollars in St. Moritz, which I don't fully understand. Just a bank transfer." Cortez waited. "Obviously I have to declare it."

"Client-related expenses," Rudolph repeated. So sue him! One weekend he'd been feeling a little bit lonely and gotten a girl off OnlyFans to go skiing with him.

He sighed, tried to sound penitent.

"Look, John. I get it. We're going to be getting a lot more conscientious around here. You hear about the sale of the Bélizaire?"

"I did," Cortez said. "And that's great, but we still have stuff to work on. I'll know more when I go through this month's invoices."

Miserably Rudolph tossed the phone aside. It was so hard to keep up with the Joneses, to pal around with the superrich when you were a self-made man. Other gallerists inherited money, or married heiresses, or were simply ruthless and rapacious and clever, and he was supposed to be the same. And if he wasn't, who was he? Just a loser. Just the same fat schmuck no one had wanted on the lacrosse team at Deerfield—

"You okay, Rudy?" Charlie called, knocking on the door.

Fuck off, Rudolph willed. Instead he called politely, "Just taking a little nap before my meeting!"

Mercifully he heard Charlie say something about heading off to Whitechapel, followed by the slam of the front door.

Rudolph sat up and threw the covers off. He needed to be smarter about things. More capital. Less partying. His current strategy was a good one; with the cash from the Bill Bowes exhibition later this year, the gallery would be swimming in profits. Just need to get through this fallow period without making a bad misstep. But he was confident, after all these years, that he wouldn't.

Sometimes he longed to confide his financial anxieties to someone, but there was no one, really, to turn to. The illusion of money reassured people, engendering more success by telling people you were doing well. It was a lonely way to live.

He padded into the bathroom. It was capacious and silent, swirling Verde Alpi marble, with flecks of emerald winking up at him from the sink. He'd commissioned the stonework after seeing the Villa Necchi in Milan. The daughters of prosperous industrialists, the Necchis had been one step closer to the chilly heights of Milanese society than their parents—and one fraction was all you needed. So they had built the

Villa Necchi in the 1930s as a temple to their good taste, designed by a famous Italian modernist. It was a strategy that had worked a little too well, enticing even Mussolini to turn the villa into his government's headquarters during the war years. Shadowy daughters, inviting the fascists to tea. Gold-rimmed teacups and big black boots, crushing mud into the carpets.

This imagery pleased Rudolph's private sense of the secret parallels between things. There was a brutality to money, he had always believed. The people who acquired it most naturally were a little harsher, more productive, more demanding than regular folk. People who had no problem crushing the soft, the kind, and the meek under the big black soles of their boots. You saw them do it. Then you decided which kind of person you wanted to be. And maybe once you got a little more money, it became a little easier, or at least you never had to face the sight of the blood and guts under the tread of your shoe. Any obstruction was something to be leapt over, as you ran into an ever-more glorious future at a fast pace.

Rudolph turned the shower on. Pushing his face up to the steam-fogged mirror, he examined the shadow of a pimple emerging from his jaw. Experimentally he sucked in his stomach, turning this way and that.

His dick was hard. His fingers twitched.

He had always been an anxious, obsessive kid. Now he stepped inside the shower. Excitement pulsed beneath his skin, almost shuddering, crawling under the weight of it. Early on in his childhood, he had developed small rituals to quell the feeling of worthlessness, of something dark and amorphous lurking behind the corner. He balled up his fist and began to beat at his chest, first slowly, rhythmically, then harder, back and forth and back and forth and back and forth.

"Rudolph, Rudolph, Rudolph," he chanted, beating his chest, reminding himself of his own name in case it somehow slipped away from him, in case he became nothing and no one and of no conse-quence to anyone . . .

Once, Cornelia had caught him doing it and balked. She'd backed wide-eyed out of the bathroom, and neither of them had ever mentioned it again. In a way he had never forgiven her for that. In a way he had never forgiven her for being his mother. Sometimes you chose people not for who they were, but for what they brought out of you, and sometimes that thing was a terrifying meaninglessness that you needed to drown. Sometimes he had to beat himself more viciously to be soothed, and today was one of those times.

He beat and beat until the water ran cold.

13

ON THEIR WAY TO LONG ISLAND CITY, CLAUDIA GAZED OUT OF THE CAR window with a dreamy unfocused look. Ingrid watched her twirl a bright gold strand of hair around her finger, wondering what limited thoughts passed beneath that taut and beautiful skull of hers. Claudia was always most mysterious in these moments of silence, with a little smile playing at the corner of her lips, as though she were brooding on some future assignation. An air of secrecy. Was she planning a dinner party? Solving a complex math problem? Or did the beauty of her smile lie in its actual nothingness, in the complete absence of stimuli to the brain? *When I think not of myself, I think not at all.*

Suddenly Claudia reached over and pressed her hand to Ingrid's knee.

"I'm so glad we could do this." She smiled generously. "It's not every day that you and I get to spend a bit of alone time together. Just, like—getting to know each other. Outside of the office. You know?"

"Oh, definitely."

"Isn't it nice, being just us girls?"

"It's wonderful. It's really, really fun." Ingrid hoped the terror suffusing her body wasn't visible. She didn't think so.

Claudia blinked at her lazily, lizard-like.

"Let's just chat, huh? Tell me more about what you're doing outside work these days. How is your boyfriend?"

Ingrid was flustered. Claudia had said hello to Rudolph several times when he'd dropped by the gallery to pick Ingrid up after work.

She had no trouble imagining them running into each other at some museum event or cocktail party, either. Claudia's eyes flickered. Had they—?

"He's really great," she stalled. "Really, really great. Uh—we're just hanging out, really. He's in London, actually, for the auctions."

Claudia's eyes glowed with interest. "Really? What's he bidding on, do you know?"

Ingrid told her.

"Oh." Losing interest, she resumed her steady blink. "Nothing Paul's buying, that's good. He's pretty interested in Bowes, huh?"

Bill Bowes was one of the most famous artists in America, although Ingrid had always found his work a little soulless. Though maybe that was the point. He painted faces, over and over, blowing microscopic pores up to a colossal size, before translating them into prints and Polaroids and collages and daguerreotypes. Bowes, who was lauded for his investigations into the heart of American narcissism, had done the same thing for half a century. He painted everyone from the homeless to the First Lady and his friends and families in this way. There was a certain type of artist whose style never deviated. Inadvertently, Ingrid felt, Bowes's own narcissism had become the real subject of his paintings.

"Big, ugly pictures of noses," Claudia commented. Then her eyes brightened. "I heard something funny about Bowes the other day. Apparently he gets his hottest students to help him at the studio, you know, because he's a professor a few days a week at Parsons. And he, like . . ." She dropped her voice delightedly, pretending to be scandalized. "Screws them. While his wife is in the next room! She was his student too, you know. He did that famous erotic series of her in the seventies, the one that got banned from all the museums."

"I thought he had Parkinson's?"

Claudia shrugged. "He's unstoppable, clearly."

Ingrid had no idea what to respond. Silence ticked past as she searched her brain for more small talk.

"How's Victor, by the way?"

"Ugh, you know. Same old," Claudia said dismissively.

"Is he still looking for a job?"

Ingrid had heard Claudia's husband alternately described as an investor, an entrepreneur, and the son of a Bank of America chairman. He had been in between jobs for as long as Ingrid had known him, though he always seemed busy enough, moving fluidly between the Racquet Club and the Yale Club and various high-powered steakhouses with an empty squash bag and an air of louche self-importance. But Claudia herself seemed to vaguely despise him, and when he came to the gallery they brushed each other's cheeks with the cold formality of business partners.

It was said that Claudia's top choice had been a married collector from her previous job, but there had been some sort of scandal, an abortion, and that man had gotten her fired instead. Watching Claudia stiffen, Ingrid felt an unexpected flash of pity. Someone had once seen Victor screaming at her in public, down the hallway. Was that why she was the way she was? The unhappiness of the relationship seemed etched into her face. But sometimes she would laugh at a joke—there were moments of friendliness, sweetness even—and her jaw muscles would relax. A younger and happier person seemed to be locked inside of her, unable to get out.

"He's working on a couple different projects," Claudia said now. "A few big lunches, taking phone calls, investing here and there. Networking, mostly."

Ingrid nodded. It was typical coded gibberish used by the ultrarich to disguise the fact that they didn't really work.

"It's difficult for him, though," Claudia continued. "Because he does go to interviews sometimes. And this is really un-PC to say, but it's just like so hard to get hired as a white, upper-class, privileged man these days."

Ingrid kept nodding, like one of those bobblehead toys you find in gas stations.

"That's why I don't really believe in the concept of white privilege. Because even though I'm like, really, really lucky, I worked my ass off to get to where I am."

"Mm," Ingrid said in a neutral tone. "Why doesn't Victor just work at his father's company?"

"He could," Claudia said. "But he doesn't want to take a job away from a person who really needs it." She stared listlessly out the window. "He tries to think about the less fortunate, you know."

Ingrid mulled this over. Then Claudia said breathlessly:

"I want you to record the conversation with Chastity today, all right? He's being called the next Kerry James Marshall. He's like friends with all these cool celebrities, went to RISD. Didn't you go there? You're not friends with him, too, are you?" she demanded, peering at Ingrid with a sudden new interest.

"He was older than me," Ingrid confessed. "But I've read about him. *Vogue* did a profile, didn't they?"

"Oh," Claudia said absently, leafing through the artist's résumé. "I don't know."

"Is there anything I should be looking out for?"

Claudia appeared to consider her words carefully. The diamonds on her steepled fingers glinted white against her black silk shirt.

"Keep the conversation light," she emphasized, "for now. Catching an artist is like hunting a deer—softly, softly."

"What a dump. This is why I don't like leaving Manhattan," Claudia whispered as the car drove away behind them. "Look at all this shit on the ground."

Thick clouds milled about the overcast sky. Claudia kicked ineffectually at an old Coke can, sending waterlogged cigarettes tumbling over the ground. The Doll Factory loomed above them like the rusted-over skeleton of some long-lost dinosaur.

Ingrid gazed up at the building. Ghosts seemed to prowl the deserted parking lot. This building had been a sewing machine factory in the nineteenth century; in the twenties and thirties, it had been children's toys. And for a moment the phantoms of a crowd of women in sturdy dun-colored dresses seemed to hurry by her, under a dawn lit to a blood-red glow. Polish and Italian and Irish girls, who'd signed their names inside the book at Ellis Island. This rotting structure had been destroyed by fire. Even the oldest of the last factory workers must be dead, or at least rotting away in some forgotten nursing home on Staten Island. In their place, Ingrid saw a silent group of teenagers pass around a soggy joint as they loaded up their camera equipment. She could see why they wanted to film here. The air seemed saturated with a leftover fog of hope, of exhaustion, of urban toil, baked into the disappeared reality of the city's sweaty industrial past.

"Can you call Chastity and tell him we're here? I don't feel completely safe out here." Claudia shuddered.

Ingrid bent to examine the ceramic shards scattered among the overgrown weeds. Something small and hard crunched under her foot: a china baby doll face with shattered holes for eyes, lips eternally locked in a coy raspberry pout.

"Don't touch that!" Claudia yelped. "Seriously, that's so fucking creepy. You don't know where it's been." Begrudgingly, she handed Ingrid a tube of hand sanitizer.

"I see you've found a doll's head."

The voice was low and powerful, rasped over with smoke. Ingrid looked up. A tall man with long dreadlocks was striding across the gravel toward them. Instantly Rita's interest became clear to her: with his broken nose and ripped jeans, he had that indefinable charisma of a rock star, a sort of twitchy sexuality oozing off him. Silver crosses jangled in his ears; onyx rings gulped light on his paint-stained hands as he waved hello.

"I'm Chastity."

"Ingrid. Nice to meet you."

"We are so excited to be here!"

Claudia's voice was at its most musical. She flung her hands at Chastity like startled doves, and they performed a series of delicate hugs and air kisses while simultaneously managing not to touch each other at all.

"We absolutely cannot wait to see the paintings. I don't think I've seen you since—can it possibly have been the Armory party, last year?"

"Did I see you there?" Chastity said. Claudia's face flickered with displeasure. "Things have been so crazy busy. You know how it is."

Claudia nodded energetically.

"I haven't had a single minute to spare," she confided. "The gallery is wildly busy, you know. But what a fantastic location!"

"Oh, thank you, thank you. I'm so blessed to be here. There's been a lot of interest, I do have to say. A lot of interest."

"Oh? Who? Who's interested?"

"I mean, like—" He named one of the top galleries in Los Angeles. "I'm doing an exhibition there this summer. In the Hamptons. A bunch of great people are involved."

"Really," Claudia said, her eyes glittering.

"Yeah, well, people are really starting to notice my stuff. It's been busy, so busy. But enough talking!" He let out a loud, throaty laugh. "Let me show you around the space."

Chastity grasped the door handle. Even his knuckles were cool, Ingrid couldn't help noticing. Tattooed with blue dots, with Roman numerals. He was the sort of person whom you would see in a coffee shop and instantly think of as famous—which, for an artist, was already half the battle won. Ingrid could sense Claudia becoming more and more nervous as she contemplated the possibility of some other gallery poaching him first.

"That's so impressive," she said, jangling her gold bracelets. "Obviously it makes so much sense. You're a once-in-a-lifetime talent. Let our social media manager know about the details for that show, and we'll promote it to our followers. We have a vast audience, you know. Absolutely vast."

Chasity's studio was cold as an icebox. It had double-height ceilings and smelled strongly of turpentine from the wet canvases that littered the floor. Like a wind-up toy, Claudia readied herself to unleash a stream of praise; then she let loose, bending and touching and putting her nose up to the paintings.

"Oh my God, Chastity, they're soooo gorgeous. They're fantastic. They're captivating. I've never seen anything like this, actually."

Chastity had hung a framed print of his *Town & Country* cover on a wall. It depicted a polo player in Gucci Spring/Summer riding toward a white mansion with a golden ball in one hand. Conversely, *Aristocracy in Flower* showed two boys in eveningwear, lounging on a yacht. Ingrid's initial reaction was confusion. The figures' faces were so gray and sadly malformed that they resembled victims of fetal alcohol syndrome. They were just so . . . empty.

Then something clicked. No wonder the collectors loved him, Ingrid realized. Shadowed by the liberal guilt of their generation, making money just didn't seem good enough anymore—even though it was what they'd built their lives around!—but the press and critics were saying no, you had to support marginalized peoples, blah blah

blah . . . It was too tacky nowadays just to nail that blithe Slim Aarons portrait of perma-tanned supermodels lounging around a pool at Cap Ferrat, way too tacky—not unless you wanted to look like a tone-deaf philistine. And yet they did not really want to be challenged, they did not really want to be made to think. They secretly *liked* the Slim Aarons portraits! Luckily with Chastity, they got both. He venerated their billions back at them, glorified their superiority as the rightful rulers of this earth, but eradicated the guilt because he was Black. Good God, he was Black! It was perfect. Now when they put up Chastity's resort wear advertisements, a warm glow of well-being lit up their insides. *We absolutely adore Black people,* Ingrid imagined some whippet-thin white person boasting at a dinner party. *Equality and progress are so important to us. Here, look at this fellow I just found—*

The more Ingrid stared at the paintings, the more she had to ask herself if Chastity was not actually a genius. Was this some kind of meta joke? The figures were so horribly deformed, the scenes so transparently obsessed with yachts and mansions, that she wondered whether Chastity was making fun of his clients.

"They're absolutely revolutionary!" Claudia was crying out in awe.

"Nostalgia for a different era, you know?"

"I couldn't agree more. The world is just too complicated these days!"

Claudia swanned on in this vein a little while longer. Then she said, "I've got to step out for a minute to take this—private museum in China—really interested in your work. But please, talk to Ingrid. She's going to write about you to a major donor at the Broad. We have the best contacts in the art world, you know. The absolute best."

She nodded encouragingly and slipped away. Ingrid got out her pen and paper and waited for Chastity to speak. His catlike eyes were fixed on some spot beyond her.

"I'm very particular about the way I'm described," he began slowly. "Very particular. I identify as kind of like a melancholy fallen aristocrat who's been ripped out of the past. Like F. Scott Fitzgerald, or—or Picasso. A time of simpler pleasures, more romance, more poetry."

He repeated the phrase "very particular" several times, apparently hypnotized by the cadence of his own voice.

"What are some of the ideas behind your paintings?"

"Ideas?" He laughed, cast her a skeptical look. "I don't know about ideas. But I enjoy looking at spaces of glamour from times past. Debutantes, the Newport mansions, Eton ... Claridge's ... society balls. My favorite thing in the world is just to go to Paris and play chess at the cafés—I stay in Saint-Germain, you know, the Hôtel de Crillon— with whatever strangers I meet. Writing poetry till dawn. Getting up to ... oh, you know." He let his heavy-lidded eyes rest briefly on her face. "I think of myself as sort of a flaneur, creating little scenes of depravity and debauchery all around the world."

Ingrid imagined him pacing the streets of Paris in a beret, demanding stressed-out French office workers play chess with him at his five-star American hotel.

Chastity lit a cigarette.

"I'd love to see some profiles comparing me to poets and artists in fin de siècle Paris," he added coolly, pronouncing it *Pah-ree*. "Like ... Jean Genet, Sartre. Hype up the sort of rebellious, melancholy elements in my persona. And when it comes to wardrobe, it'd be great if we could score some Brunello."

"I'm sure we can do that," Ingrid said agreeably. She consulted her notes. "You're living in a hotel now, aren't you?"

"The Plaza." He laughed a little. "Yes. It's kinda old-school, but I'm subversive like that," he said, rolling the s's around his tongue. "In the past it was seen as not cool for an artist to make a lot of money. But I'm proof that money can be cool too, money can be rebellious and fun and limitless. You know?"

"I see. You're breaking the rules."

He flashed Ingrid his diamond-studded Rolex. The studio fluorescents—colorless, bleach-white, drained of all warmth by design—shuddered off his grin.

"I think making money is the most punk rock thing you can do. Write that down, will you?"

By the time they left Chastity's studio at three o'clock, even Claudia looked exhausted behind her impeccable Botox.

"Wasn't he so demanding? Artists these days," she said in the car to Ingrid. She rifled through her bag again, studio photographs spilling over her black silk shirt. "He's so cool, though. Like the fact that he's African American, he has that whole cool like . . . jazz, basketball thing going on," Claudia mused, furrowing her brow.

Ingrid winced. Then Claudia stabbed at a photograph with one red nail. "See that painting with the clocks, hanging? I *love* that one! There's, like, this hidden meaning."

"What's that?"

"It's like he's, like, thinking about time. You know? It's so relevant right now, because, also, so many of my clients are trying to diversify their portfolios. With minority artists, I mean. Trying to give back and all." Her eyes darted rapidly around the vehicle. "There's a lot of PR potential. It gave me a great idea for our exhibition, actually."

"Tell me?"

"I was thinking . . ." A pause for effect. "*Race Through Time.*"

"What?" Ingrid asked, wincing.

"Get it? It's like a pun on the phrase 'race through time.' Because it'll be about a bunch of artists looking at, like, race. And then also time, and then just, like . . . whatever else." She sighed, exhausted now by her mental efforts.

Suddenly Ingrid's phone buzzed inside her pocket. Looking at the screen, she felt her heart drop. She blurted out: "Weird. Simone just texted me."

Claudia's eyes narrowed. "Simone Machado? I thought you were friends, no?"

"We used to be super close, yeah. But we, er, kind of fell out."

Silence. Claudia stared out the window. They were driving through the dark tunnel that connected Long Island City to Lower Manhattan, the wheels revolving slowly through traffic.

"Personally, I'm going," Claudia purred, "to get a manicure and go to the gym. I really need to get fit before Victor and I go to Sag this year. So many collectors' wives will be there who've literally just been to Pilates and that's it for the entire year, because they don't work."

"Lucky bitches," Ingrid said without thinking.

Claudia gasped, laughing as if Ingrid had said something blasphemous.

"Of course," she said loftily, "no one could convince me to quit my job. Not even because I, personally, need to *work*"—Claudia allowed a discreet pause to elapse—"but because it's so important to my, like, sense of inner self, you know?"

"Of course," Ingrid said. "Me too."

"Simone's studio is around here, isn't it?"

"Close," Ingrid said. "She works near Chinatown."

"Hmm."

Shadowed by the darkness of the tunnel, Claudia continued to stare out the window. Ingrid marveled at her self-control. What private thoughts, what calculations, must be rotating behind that smooth forehead? Yet her face remained glazed, reptilian. Dissociated.

The car emerged into sunlight.

"I think," Claudia said casually, "that you should take the rest of the day off. Go and hang out with her. Remind Simone," she said, with a sidelong glance, "that we absolutely adore her work and think she is just incredible."

"Oh, really?"

"Uh-huh." Claudia rapped her knuckles on the glass panel separating the driver. "Can you let one of us out here, please?"

As Ingrid climbed out onto the street, Claudia put her head out the window and looked her appraisingly up and down. Suddenly Claudia's beautiful violet eyes, staring at her, filled with a deep warmth and interest in Ingrid's life. It was a trick she had only seen Claudia direct toward people with wealth, or power, or both, in the past. Never at her.

"Ingrid," she said. "If you did manage to sign Simone, that would be a huge coup for the gallery. And we might revise your position accordingly—like, to artist liaison. With a pathway to other promotions after that. Do you see what I'm saying?"

Ingrid sucked in her breath. Then her smile became real. Becoming Simone's artist liaison would make her a gatekeeper to the gallery, and more importantly, spirit her away from Claudia's sticky hands. It was an unhoped-for win.

"I'll do my best," she promised, and watched the cab roll toward Chelsea Piers.

14

BY THE TIME HE ARRIVED AT THE ITALIAN RESTAURANT IN ST. JAMES, Rudolph had just about managed to shake off the sweatiest dregs of his hangover. He'd gulped down half an Adderall with his green juice, slapped color into his pallid cheeks, and shaken off the tremor in his hands. The room chimed delicately with the hushed tones of gray-suited businessmen and ladies who lunch, picking at their wilted spinach and eggs Florentine. At the zinc bar, a man in a white tuxedo tossed cocktails in a sleek silver shaker. The restaurant was pretending to be a simple Milanese barbershop from the 1930s, though their truffle risotto cost over a hundred pounds apiece.

The four of them—Rudolph, Frederick Asaka, and the two French curators—had gathered here, at Asaka's bequest, to negotiate a transaction of sorts. Asaka was a major supporter of the Palais des Beaux-Arts, and Rudolph knew he longed to sit on its board. To this end, he'd asked Rudolph to lend the museum his two best Bill Bowes paintings for the Beaux-Arts' major retrospective this fall. Rudolph was happy to cultivate a new relationship with the curators, happier still to have Asaka in his debt. A two-year loan would represent a temporary loss of income, but it'd be worth it once he saw their prices surge.

Frederick Asaka waved at him across the room, black eyes large and opaque in his jaundiced face. As usual, he was the best-dressed man in the room, and Rudolph felt that curious blend of warmth and unease— almost fear—that always accompanied his rendezvous with Asaka.

He could be so soft. So gentle, so discreet and sophisticated until he *wasn't*; he reminded Rudolph of a tiger shark, silently swimming a hundred feet below the surface.

Beside him sat a tweedy type whose smudged spectacles and balding head shone like a feather-strewn egg under the lamps. Presumably the curator, Leclerc. He sat beside another, taller man in a dark velvet waistcoat, who was smiling at Rudolph from under his long Roman nose. So this must be the aristocrat—and the chairman of the board—Olivier d'Erlanger. He launched into his prepared speech with the silky élan of a man accustomed to taking control of situations.

"We're grateful for the introduction. It came at the best possible time, because in addition to the exhibition, we're very much looking to expand our permanent collection of Bowes paintings. And your version—the early nineties nude from the Streetwalkers series, very large but still extremely precise, before his brushstrokes became rather loose with old age—it's really almost perfect among his oeuvre."

Leclerc nodded in agreement. Asaka smiled his velvety smile. Rudolph was only vaguely listening, but he snapped to as the chairman finished his sentence.

"Thank you for those kind words. It's heartening," Rudolph said, looking around the table with big, tender eyes, "to see his work finally appreciated by institutions in the way that it deserves. I mean, for so long Bowes was totally under-recognized because he was so ahead of his time. He's almost like a Robert Rauschenberg figure in that way— so radical it took people a while to catch up to his genius."

Leclerc's egg-like head bobbed enthusiastically. "Exactly. Exactly. We couldn't agree more."

"Which is why," d'Erlanger continued, "it is so essential that any donation comes in the right way, you understand."

"Rather than a commercial institution," Leclerc added.

"In order to truly canonize Bowes in the eyes of a European audience, the donation would look well coming from Frederick, who is so respected in Paris."

Rudolph glanced at Asaka, trying to conceal his shock. Donation? What was this about a donation? Could I have been so out of it? No, he was absolutely sure no one in the email chain had said anything about a donation. It was a loan, that's all. A loan. He couldn't be expected to give up five million dollars of work!

And the way Asaka just sat there, smooth and blank as an ivory idol—something was off. Why would he assume that Rudolph would donate a painting? A clammy trail of sweat began to work its way down his neck. He put his napkin down, signaled to the waiter for another glass of ice water.

"This is somewhat unexpected."

Leclerc glanced nervously at Asaka, who remained silent.

"I'm sorry, we were under the impression that this had already been agreed upon?"

"We know it's an enormous request," d'Erlanger said. "And yet I certainly feel that this retrospective will be absolutely transformative for Bowes in France."

Rudolph sipped his water. His stomach was beginning to churn again.

"I'd be delighted to make the loan. As you know," he added with a burst of inspiration, "I myself am opening a Bowes exhibition this autumn in London. I'd like to publish a catalogue, and of course it'd be an honor if you might write something for it."

He peered keenly at Leclerc, who coughed.

"Generally we're not really supposed to write essays for commercial galleries—"

"Though we do make exceptions," d'Erlanger interrupted in silky tones, "for patrons of importance."

"Can I consider the prospect a little longer?" Rudolph asked.

"Absolutely."

"Though we do need to know by May."

"That's fine. I'll call you."

"Wonderful. We're most grateful. Now we have a meeting with the curators at the Tate—same purpose"—d'Erlanger showed off his dimples—"so, *malheureusement*, we do need to leave you."

The polite chorus of goodbyes; then they were gone. In the watery green halo of the stained-glass window, Asaka remained seated, his face silent and unmoving. Rudolph motioned to the waiter. His hands were beginning to shake.

"Drink?"

"None for me, thanks. Oh, well—perhaps just a coffee."

Rudolph watched him out of the corner of one eye. Asaka rearranged his belongings on the empty seat, neatly fitting a Chinese museum catalogue into a leather bowling bag. He reminded Rudolph of a vulture, languidly surveying a corpse who didn't know he was dead yet.

Finally the coffee arrived. Rudolph, stirring sugar into the hot liquid, allowed a moment of silence to elapse.

"I didn't realize that you wanted the donation to come from me. Without compensation."

"Yes, I think that would be best."

"That would represent a rather significant loss of income for my gallery. Around five and a half million pounds, maybe more. You know how Bowes's prices have skyrocketed lately."

Asaka laughed. "I'd be an idiot to have missed that."

"Is there something I'm missing here?"

"You know, I think there might be." He recrossed his long legs in their elegant wool trousers, picking loose an imaginary thread. "Rudolph, where is my Bélizaire?"

Rudolph's heart dropped in his chest.

"What do you mean? It's right where we left it, in the Geneva freeport."

"Is it?" Asaka said with a tiny smile. "That's not what I've heard."

There was a whirring sound in Rudolph's ears, a strange muteness. He considered what, exactly, Asaka might have seen or heard, but the possibilities were too awful to linger upon. Suffice to say that he, Asaka, was in the same room with Rudolph, arranging an exhibition six months hence, so he must not be planning to terminate their relationship anytime soon. And yet. A quick glance at Asaka's cold smile, and something slipped into place. He *knew something*, Rudolph realized with a bolt of terror. Knew it with absolute certainty.

"What have you heard?"

"I was at my club the other night," Asaka said calmly. "And what do you know. I happen to hear a German guy talking about a big, beautiful Bélizaire he'd purchased. Just astounding, apparently. 1981 Bélizaire. Got Cyndi Lauper's face in it—funny, that, because I thought there was only one left in the whole world with Cyndi Lauper's face in it. So I hear all this. And my fingers start to tingle—see?—like that."

He waggled his fingers at Rudolph to illustrate the point.

"Your painting is safe in the storage container in Geneva," Rudolph repeated. He raised an eyebrow. "I think you must have misheard the man. But, after all, we agreed that you were only keeping it there to allow the price to appreciate. I *have* shown it to other people, to see if I could get a better price for you. Obviously."

"No. The guy had bought the painting."

"Frederick. With all due respect, I think you may have misunderstood."

Asaka stroked the edge of his crystal glass.

"Bet you're hoping I didn't compare notes?"

He smiled slightly.

"Anyway. I'll get to the point. I want my fucking painting back."

A drum beat in Rudolph's ears. He had the feeling that Asaka was circling him slowly, scenting for weakness, for blood, and he knew it was imperative to maintain eye contact, even though Rudolph's eyes felt bone dry, even though his entire body felt parched and eviscerated by Asaka's black gunpowder stare. Because of course the Bélizaire was long gone. It was probably already hanging proudly over Christian Rathenau's girlfriend's artificial fireplace in his skyscraper penthouse at Hudson Yards—those strange, silvery towers that Charlie had once called a "demonic anti-neighborhood for demon billionaires."

"Your painting is safe," Rudolph said. "Frankly I'm astonished that anyone would say that to you, absolutely stunned. There must have been some mistake. An easy one to make, though. So many of them look very similar."

"I thought you might say that. I'm guessing the painting is already gone. So, in lieu of the Bélizaire, I'd like," Asaka said softly, "the Bill Bowes donation made to the Beaux-Arts, in my name. For starters."

"There's no need—"

"And I want my money back on the Bélizaire. I think it was fifteen million, wasn't it? That's the price the guy paid." He smiled at Rudolph. "I had a chat with him, actually. Your name came up. Germans are so friendly, don't you think?"

Rudolph resisted the urge to mop the sweat from his brow. It was a tic, a tell, though possibly they were past that point now.

"The painting's in the freeport," he insisted for a third time. "This is all just an unfortunate mistake. I think the potential client in question might have gotten a little carried away, bragging about a piece he doesn't own—"

"There's another option, of course. I might like your help, if you'd lend it, to facilitate various transactions, house certain works in your galleries—I do have friends and acquaintances abroad, all eager art collectors, and they'd like to ensure their purchases with no . . . *legal* delays. To do with moving currencies around, and"—he waved his arms in a leisurely fashion—"all that boring stuff."

Oh fuck.

Rudolph stared at him. He rattled the ice in his glass, aware that his hands were shaking now.

"And where do your friends base themselves?"

"All over the world. It really doesn't concern you, but in the interest of transparency, many of them are based in Dubai. The Virgin Islands. Brazil."

"I see," Rudolph repeated, and he did. Asaka wanted him to launder money. The last thing he needed was to get involved with terrorists or mercenaries and have the Feds breathing down his neck!

"I just, I really need to think about this. What you're asking me—"

It's crazy, he wanted to say. *I can't do it. I won't.*

"Frankly, there's nothing to think about."

"Look, Frederick. I just . . ." Sweat beaded the back of Rudolph's neck, staining his crisp white shirt with the sour smell of fear. "You're overreacting."

The smile dropped off Asaka's face. Underneath it his eyes were terrifyingly blank, as stony and pitiless as an abandoned cave.

"You can't see an opportunity when it presents itself to you, huh? All right. No friends. Make the donation, then. Give me my motherfucking money."

"I find this all highly suspicious," Rudolph said, trying to regain control. He felt as though he were on a high-speed train that had veered off the tracks and was suddenly heading for a cliff. "If you were really that concerned, you'd take legal action. I want nothing to do with your friends, and I don't know what you've heard, but you're sorely mistaken about the painting."

"Listen, Sullivan, I'm getting pretty tired of your bullshit right about now," Asaka said in a silky voice. "But I *will* ruin you if you don't get me my money back. In ways you can't possibly imagine." He stood up and dusted off his trousers. "And now, if you'll excuse me, I've got custody of my son today. We're playing football in Regent's Park. Perhaps I'll introduce you to one of my friends soon," he added, smiling.

Rudolph stared at him.

"Cat got your tongue?" Asaka grinned.

"Frederick, don't push me." Rudolph stopped him with a raised hand. His hand seemed to be floating in the air, staving Asaka off, protesting the inevitable. "I'll make the donation, but as to the rest—"

Asaka waved a hand. "Don't worry about that. These people are the soul of discretion. You'll never catch them on any list. Under their names."

Asaka's black eyes were now sparkling with mirth. In fact, Rudolph realized with growing unease, he had never seen the man look so damn spirited.

After he paid the bill, Rudolph began the long walk home. It had begun to drizzle again. This time he kept his eyes to the pavement, hardly noticing the redbrick luster of Sloane Square under the thin sheet of gray rain. He felt sticky and gross and unwell, his stomach roiling with fear and nausea from his hangover.

Things were not going well. Things were not going well at all. If only he had a tiny bit of financing help. If only—

But how? he wondered, despair growing thick and heavy as a block of phlegm stuck in his throat. How could he possibly plan for the worst thing imaginable?

15

TO REACH SIMONE'S NEW STUDIO, YOU HAD TO NAVIGATE THE chattering dining room of a Chinese restaurant, perfumed with the eye-watering scents of Szechuan beef and peppers. A clanging chorus floated up the dark stairwell as Ingrid made her way: hostesses yelling out phone orders in Mandarin, clattering dishes, the sharp cry of a busboy burning his hand.

"God, I don't know how you resist eating Chinese food every single day," Ingrid said, as she and Simone exchanged a stiff hug.

"Oh, I don't. It's part of my daily regimen as an artist. You know how MSG gets the brain juices flowing."

Ingrid laughed politely, and Simone shut the door. They remained standing about three feet apart, seconds of silence ticking away. Finally Simone asked her if she wanted a cup of tea.

"Sure."

Ingrid coughed. Unwilling to look Simone in the eye, she pretended to explore the new studio. It was larger than the one they'd occupied two years ago, brighter too, with a choice deployment of Moroccan rugs and poufs. Street furniture. A cacophony of plants spilled from the windows, lemony-green in the sunlight.

"Is turmeric okay? Or I have green if you want?" Simone was saying.

"Turmeric is fine, thanks."

Simone's paintings glistened on the walls. Stark fragments of letters dripped in the blue-black colors of blackberry juice down the pale canvases. Each scene seemed to narrate the path of a woman, shown in cell-like boxes that resembled a comic book strip. Ingrid could feel Simone's presence, intimately, and a nameless sadness washed over her; it was like seeing an old lover move on without you.

Simone handed her a mug Ingrid recognized from their old apartment. Her lips were pursed, thin and awkward.

"What are these paintings for?" Ingrid said finally.

"Oh, gosh." Simone seemed relieved. "Those are for a group exhibition in Milan I'm doing this fall. The theme is the female body, so not very groundbreaking, but anyway. What do you—" Simone hesitated. "What do you, um, think of them?"

"Me?"

"Yeah. I mean—is that weird? I've kind of, like . . . I don't know." She twisted her gold rings. "I miss hearing your opinion on new stuff I'm working on."

Surprised, Ingrid glanced up. Simone's eyes were liquid with unspoken apologies.

"I like them very much," Ingrid said, choosing her words carefully.

She mentioned a few technical changes Simone might make to improve them, a shade of sienna to enliven the curve of a back in one painting. And suddenly they were talking over each other, Simone explaining that she'd been looking at old Marvel comics and thinking about abortion rights in America in the new paintings, Ingrid asking about the charcoal passage here in the corner . . . It was the perfect moment to mention Paul Bernot, but Ingrid chose to let it go.

Watching Simone laugh felt almost like old times, when they were still close enough in age and ideas and circumstances to joke about being twins separated at birth. By the final months of their friendship, Ingrid had become Simone's shadow, her confidante, fading into the smudgy darkness as Simone stepped forward with a bright smile. Her life and art would be endlessly chronicled and argued about and recorded by critics and curators and historians, while she, Ingrid, disappeared without a trace. A cold wet chill sank over her whenever she remembered it, got into the marrow of her bones, but today Ingrid forced out a new thought: I do matter. I matter to Rudolph, and he loves me. If I died today, at least I would have made a mark on one life.

"I'm really happy that you're getting all this attention," Ingrid said. But the words rang hollow. Simone looked briefly embarrassed.

"Thank you." Simone cleared her throat. "That means so much to me, honestly."

A moment of silence.

"Look, do you want a drink? I know it's only four, but . . . we could go up to the roof terrace—or at least, a roof which is now my terrace. I got a letter from the city saying it was declared derelict, but when did that ever stop us?"

"Remember when we used to jump over the rooftops at parties?"

"God, that was stupid of us."

They giggled, remembering the summer they'd turned nineteen. Equipped with a handful of broken plastic lawn chairs and six handles of Tito's vodka, they'd held a birthday party on the rooftop of their old apartment on Irving Avenue. Dared each other to jump from one building to another. In those days it had seemed impossible to die, impossible not to be young, not to look forward to every next birthday with a sort of itching and breathless anticipation.

"I always read those horror stories in the *Post* about kids dying when they did that," Simone said, shaking her head. She squatted over the miniature fridge. "Should I make mojitos? I know it's only April but I'm feeling kind of festive. Or do you want a beer?"

The light above their heads was just beginning to fade, darkening to thin stripes that painted the sky with infinitely subtle variations, violet and ruby and amber and pink. Simone tipped back her head to soak up the sun's last rays. They'd been sitting on the roof for over an hour now, sipping mojitos, watching the limes float to the top of the glass pitcher.

Ingrid was rambling, talking about her job, about how lost and adrift she'd felt these past months. Without Simone—but that remained unspoken. All that need coiled up inside her seemed to have come undone in the soft red gleam of this late-spring afternoon.

"It's been good in certain ways, I guess," she concluded. "I mean, it feels great to earn money—even if it's nothing in the grand scheme of things. But at least I can make rent." She thought of how Simone had allowed her to use her studio, gratis, for almost three years. "It's just . . . not what I thought I'd be doing. I thought I'd be making a name for myself, doing whatever it took, and now, well, I barely paint anymore. Maybe—maybe failure robbed the joy from it, I don't know."

Simone made some soothing noises about how Ingrid was definitely not a failure, there are many different paths in life, etcetera. Ingrid let her talk. She was feeling good, on this spring afternoon, with the mojitos inside her. Then Simone asked:

"What are they like?"

"Who?"

"The collectors," Simone said. "I should know, but I sort of avoid the socializing part. I don't—" She hesitated. "I don't like to waste my time."

Ingrid grimaced. "I understand."

She thought about the collectors.

"I don't give much thought to them," she finally said. "They've become something else in my mind, like a symbol. Of everything that's bad. But there's nothing wrong with them individually, I suppose. In fact, when I really think about it, they're probably the better kind of rich out there. They're giving us—the artists," she corrected herself, "money. But you see things you don't want to know, sometimes. For example, they're all mostly men. Finance guys, tech. The women— their job is to look good. The art is part of it, like the clothes. It makes you wonder sometimes."

"Wonder what?"

Ingrid drank her mojito.

"Why should they have so much when others have so little?"

Simone laughed.

"Cruel twists of fate," she said, studying her nails with an empty gaze. "There's probably someone halfway across the world thinking the exact same thing about you."

Ingrid let out a reluctant laugh, too.

"Yeah, but this is America." She focused her eyes on Simone. "But I know there are things I can't change," she told her.

Simone was silent.

"I wish I could, though," Ingrid continued. "Like, go back. Go—"

"Revisit it?"

Simone took Ingrid's hand and put it in her lap. Gently she petted the inside crease of Ingrid's palm. As if she were asking a question— or asking permission, Ingrid thought confusedly. She remembered other nights—talking till dawn until their voices grew hoarse; falling asleep in each other's beds. Moments of such intimacy, such extreme closeness, that this thing between them had seemed to occupy Ingrid's whole spirit, her entire soul.

"Why did you kick me out?" Ingrid blurted, then bit her tongue sharply. It was the one question she'd told herself she would not ask.

"Hmm?"

Simone looked up. Her eyes were still drowsy, but the spring temperatures seemed to have evaporated slightly. She drew her legs up to her chest and covered them.

"You know what I mean," Ingrid persisted, knowing she was being annoying but unable to stop. "Why did you—you know? Not call me, not see me, after I left. Ghost me, practically. Why now? After two years? I've thought about it—oh, incessantly."

"Have you?" Simone said softly. "Have you really?"

"Yes."

Simone shifted toward the edge. Ingrid had a sudden fear that she would slip, fall off the roof, that her delicately molded skull would crack like a swollen egg, brains and blood splattering on the concrete below in a gelatinous red ectoplasm. And what would Ingrid do with that? She wanted to grab Simone's hand, to tell her—tell her—

Simone jumped up toward the stairs leading to her apartment, almost jogging.

"I'll tell you why, but first I need another drink."

Ingrid waited on the couch while Simone cracked open a couple of tiny Mexican beers, dumping a bag of potato chips on the upturned basket that served as a coffee table. Simone stuffed chips in her mouth, drank half a beer, squeezed lime into another, and still Ingrid waited in silence for her to speak.

"Do you remember," Simone said at last, "that old studio art professor we had in senior year? The one who taught figurative painting?"

"Ellis? Sure."

"Yeah. Well. Do you remember how he'd get his old painter friends from the eighties—remember he used to talk about going to the Mudd Club with Patti Smith and all those people—he'd get them to visit and do lectures sometimes?"

"I'd forgotten about that. He got Katherine Bradford, Chris Martin . . . Who was the other?"

Simone was staring at the brick wall beyond Ingrid's head. She wore a strange expression, so blank and impassive that Ingrid felt momentarily chilled.

"The other artist," Simone said slowly, "was more famous than any of them. He painted portraits, stitched together lots and lots of pictures of people."

"Commentary on the digital age, and all that?"

"Yes. And later, after we moved to the city, I—well—I saw a poster of him at the Whitney, and I remembered." Simone took a breath. "So I called him up. Asked if I could help out in his studio."

"I didn't know that." Ingrid was startled. "When was that?"

"Must have been around 2013, 2014," Simone murmured. "And he said yes. He said I could do some summer work as a studio assistant, or more like his assistants' assistant. I didn't say anything to you at the time, because—I don't know—" She gave an artless shrug.

Ingrid nodded. *I didn't want to.* She understood perfectly—they'd all jealously conserved their contacts in the art world, not wanting their peers to succeed without them, not wanting to ruin their own credibility by promoting lesser friends. *Pick me, pick me!* Swearing up and down that they despised the Establishment, when each and every one would've sold their souls a hundred times for a single Uptown gallerist or journalist or curator or *whatever* to give their work a second look.

"Anyway, so I started helping out at the studio on Wednesdays and Thursdays. Not far from here, just off Bleecker Street. He was so busy, going to museum openings and parties and stuff, that I didn't even see him for a while. It was summertime, you know? He'd come down from the beach every so often, bring us sandwiches and lemonade from the deli nearby, and I thought—nice guy. Real down-to-earth."

"He didn't want to supervise what you were doing?"

"Not at first, no. I mean, he'd gotten it all fine-tuned to a tee, he didn't need to be there much. He'd been doing the same thing for fifty years, you know? Most of the summer I was there, he'd take a bunch of Polaroids, choose one. If he was in the city, he'd go in at night, when no one was around," Simone said. "Then he would leave detailed instructions for the studio assistants, before signing them himself. It was very Warholian—almost like a factory."

"Okay." Ingrid wondered if this was an intellectual property story. Had the famous artist stolen Simone's ideas?

"But he was very, very specific about how he wanted it to be. Intensely creative. And, you know, he was getting old, had some physical difficulties. The assistants said he was working on his marriage—this has-been supermodel, stashed away in East Hampton. Too expensive to split up. You know that kind of marriage?"

Ingrid nodded, though she had no idea.

"Anyway. Finally, in September or something, he came back to the city. He was in the studio every day that fall, even sleeping there sometimes. God, I really did love his drive! The guy was a workaholic, obsessive, eccentric, shredded every canvas that didn't meet his standard." Her voice echoed with admiration. "Things he'd worked on for months. And he was very protective of his portrait models. Had cordoned off an entirely separate floor, see. Would lock the blue door, so we knew they weren't to be disturbed."

Ingrid's scalp prickled. She looked at Simone. Simone was tapping her nails absently against a glass bottle, making a hollow ping.

"And I mean, the way he created his paintings—unbelievable. When I was there he was working with tar. He'd paint these beautiful portraits, like Old Masters, in colors that could never add up to the tones of flesh. But somehow by the time he was done, it became this hyper-realistic likeness. Then I saw him pour the tar. This enormous bucket of hot, boiling tar, so toxic you had to wear a respirator around it, just bubbling right out in a huge industrial cauldron. And he was pouring it all over the paintings! I was shocked—I got so angry the first time. This hot poison, boiling and bubbling all over such a precise likeness—it was like watching him commit a murder. Then it solidified into the cracks and crevices, almost instant, leaving a black sheen like a map, a geological formation, and afterward you were left with this picture of—of devastation. It was a face, but a face of apocalypse."

Simone made a quiet humming noise. "That's when I knew he was a genius. Because he was willing to let it all go.

"He started to trust me in the studio. I mean, I—I would've done anything he asked, you know? At first I was just some dumb kid—they had me priming and stretching canvases, making phone calls, buying paint at the store. But then he sort of . . . I don't know . . . took me under his wing. Showed me how to choose the best photographs, how to pick out the gradient of colors in a complexion, how light reflects off the sweat in your nose. How to capture fleeting micro-expressions, passion or boredom . . . He knew about things we always recognize in social situations, but never how or why we do . . . I was fascinated. He was a master at work."

Ingrid watched her in silence.

"After a few months, he started to trust me enough . . ." Simone hesitated. "He asked me to sit for a portrait. And I felt so flattered, of course. Actually, I leapt at the chance. So I started coming in on Fridays, too, and I'd spend the whole day in his modeling room. What a privilege, I thought, to spend time alone with this iconic artist, talking about his life. His advice. No one else was allowed in. I felt like—this is our little secret."

"A secret," Ingrid repeated. "And was it one?"

"Not exactly." Simone exhaled. "He never said anything, but they knew. The other assistants—they were jealous, actually. They started acting a little cold, standoffish. Maybe they thought he was showing favoritism to this dumb intern, I don't know. Token Black girl. Hey, they wouldn't be the first." Simone laughed grimly, and Ingrid was conscious that she was talking about *her*. "But I didn't care, because he—the artist—was top of the food chain. His was the only opinion that mattered, right?"

"So what—"

Simone spoke rapidly, as if she wanted to get this part over with:

"He started asking me to model nude. I mean, whatever, it was a little uncomfortable, but that's the price of art, you know?" Tipping the bottle to her lips, Simone drained the beer. "I wasn't going to be a prude about it. His work's in every museum in America, for God's sake! But he knew I was uncomfortable, so he'd pour me a glass of scotch so that I could relax a little. Get into the mood."

An icky feeling was crawling through Ingrid's stomach. She imagined Simone disappearing behind a heavy blue door. Long silences in the cold white walls of a loft. Simone naked, breathing quietly, the nameless artist's eyes fixated on her body.

"Then he started making comments about my, um, hair . . . not the hair on my head. And in our conversations, he started to talk about his sex life, his affairs. He asked me what I preferred to do with my boyfriend. I told him I wasn't going to answer that, and he got kind of mad and said he didn't like to work with people with bourgeois sexual hang-ups. So I, uh, I apologized."

"I see," Ingrid said quietly, and she did see.

"One day when I was sitting for a portrait I sort of . . . fell asleep. I remember waking up when he came to me. He, um, asked if he could touch me. I kind of laughed and said no. But then . . . I tried to push him away, but it was like I had no strength in my arms. It was hard to stay awake. I felt paralyzed, so paralyzed I could hardly speak. His heavy, wrinkly body touching my skin . . ."

The rush of words stemmed its flow, stopped. Simone's gaze remained fixed on the wall.

"When it was over he said he felt nauseous. Asked me to leave. It was like he didn't even know who I was anymore. I wonder, did he feel guilty? Or was he just finished, finished with me?" Simone fiddled with a fraying thread on her sweater. "Probably the latter. So I went home. I took a scalding hot shower, and I passed out for like twelve hours."

Ingrid's whole body tensed.

"Were you drugged?"

"Who knows?" Simone shrugged. "I think so. But there's no way to know for sure. When I woke up, I picked up my clothes—so soiled, I just wanted to burn them—and the most disgusting thing was, his semen was all over my jeans. He'd wiped it there, as if my clothes were nothing but rags to him."

Ingrid shuddered.

"As if I," Simone repeated, "were nothing but a rag to him."

A cloud raced over the ebbing sun. Ingrid shivered, as if Simone had summoned some dark presence to the threshold. She tried to wrap an afghan around Simone's shoulders, but Simone shook her off. She got up and opened the refrigerator, the white door hiding her face again. The beer fizzed loudly in the silence between them.

"Anyway." Simone sounded resigned. "I didn't burn those jeans after all. I kept them, like some sick little badge of honor or something."

"You kept them?"

"Yeah."

Ingrid stood up.

"So that's, like, evidence or something. We could go to the police."

"What?" Simone laughed dryly. "Come on. It doesn't matter anymore."

"Of course it fucking matters!"

For reasons beyond her own understanding, Ingrid found herself shouting. Simone was watching. There was a coldness in her eyes—she seemed almost on the verge of laughter, like she had already sifted through the whole event and come to whatever conclusion she could about it. Like she'd never needed Ingrid's help in the first place.

"Sit down," Simone said. "Yes, I know it was harassment—"

"More than harassment—"

"Let me speak!"

A bright furious flame had lit up in Simone's eyes.

"Don't you dare make me out to be something I'm not." She crumpled the beer cap and tossed it behind her. "I decide what I want to do with this information, not you, okay?"

Ingrid went quiet. Simone was drinking so fast she'd almost gone through a six-pack, plus the mojitos, yet she didn't seem drunk but in the grip of a cold, set fury.

"It took me a while to grasp the facts," Simone said distantly. "I just wanted to—get away from the trash, the dirt of it all. The sickness. The city, I mean."

"And that was—what, six weeks before you—"

"Before I asked you to move out. Yes. Don't worry"—Simone fished at a fallen moth in her drink—"you weren't the only one. I didn't want to talk to anyone. It wasn't that bad." She looked Ingrid in the eye. "Anyway, nobody really compared to you."

Ingrid felt nauseated.

"I never realized. I should've—God, I could just kick myself! I should have known that something was wrong."

"You couldn't have known," Simone said, but her voice was hard.

They sat in a heavy silence, considering the lost years.

"Did you ever go back? To the studio?"

"Yes," Simone said. "See, that's the worst part. I actually did go back. Because I thought, I thought . . ."

She bent over her stomach, as if she were in pain. Ingrid reached for her—she was ready to help, to comfort. A feeling of relief washed over her. Then she saw Simone's face. Simone was *laughing*, she realized in shock—wheezing, in harsh and breathless gasps.

"I thought he owed me. Isn't that fucking hilarious? I still went to that studio when I couldn't even hold a *brush* because my hands were seizing up with fear. Because I thought he owed me, that he would feel guilty or—or fear me, you know? Fear being exposed. But he didn't look at me the next day. See, he obviously thought he'd imparted his wisdom, done me a favor by letting me work there, and beyond this, he didn't give a fuck. I was nothing to him, and he owed me nothing in return."

"But that's exactly how he wanted you to react!"

"It was, though. I was. I wish—I mean, I wish—"

She lapsed into silence.

Ingrid aimed her arms around Simone's shoulders. This time Simone let herself be embraced, though every muscle in her back remained hard, every muscle in her entire body remained as hard and unyielding as a tightly curled fist. Ingrid had the queer feeling that they were play-acting still—rehearsing the roles they felt they ought to because neither knew how else to behave. At least, Ingrid was. Simone herself was not reacting the way Ingrid felt she should be, though she knew this was a despicable, heartless thought, a thought she tried immediately to wipe from her mind. It was just that Simone's body felt so heavy against hers. It felt so heavy that some frightened animal part of Ingrid wanted to push her aside. She restrained herself, continued petting Simone's hair, but the thought remained. This obscure fear, however outlandish, that some dark and viscous contagion inside of the other woman had managed to crawl its way beneath the surface of Ingrid's own exposed skin.

16

"Sir, the line for US citizens is over here."

A grim-faced Swiss border guard in a security uniform stopped Rudolph mid-stride as he marched toward the Geneva Airport arrivals hall. For a fraction of a second he couldn't breathe. They're not mind readers, he reminded himself, and quickly marshalled his thoughts.

"*Mais je suis Suisse,*" he explained with a smile, flashing his Swiss passport. The border guard held up both hands in surrender, lips twitching with amusement.

"*Allez, monsieur.*"

Rudolph sailed past the long line of doughy-faced Americans. There was a single man waiting for Swiss citizens at customs. Thank you, Father, for giving me this, he thought. If Father is what you were.

Going to Geneva had been a split-second decision, more of an impulse to flee than anything else.

After he'd left Asaka on Jermyn Street, Rudolph had ambled back at a slow, unhurried pace that belied the panic jumping in his throat. Home at last, he'd collapsed into his big Vladimir Kagan armchair, cold drink in hand, the sumptuous velvet stained wine-red like the inside of a Medici cardinal's sweeping, ermine-lined cloak. He'd bought it at auction for ten thousand dollars, hoping to bring some warmth into the pale, dry room, but instead it resembled an open heart that had somehow been flung into a void: bleeding, too red, foolish.

Somehow he'd forgotten how alone he would be. Charlie had left to visit a friend in the countryside; Cornelia had vanished hours ago, and by his own request. And this is a family house, he thought, glancing nervously about the big empty rooms with their double-height ceilings, the haughty parquet floors begging for adornment. A house built for parties and dashing children, not a peripatetic bachelor in his mid-thirties.

He uncorked a bottle of his prized vintage *baijiu*, a rare 1974 Kweichow Moutai he'd picked up years ago at auction in Hong Kong, and took a long pull. Two bottles had set him back 150,000 HKD, or just over nineteen thousand dollars, and it tasted slightly sweet, like soy sauce, on his lips. Tonight. Tonight was the time to drink one of the bottles, while his thoughts still lurched unsteadily from side to side like sailors on a storm-tossed ship.

He imagined Asaka. That sleek little pilot fish, alert in attendance, with his pale sawpit of a mouth. Smiling at him.

His stomach turned. But Christian Rathenau owned the Bélizaire now, which left Rudolph only one option: get Asaka the money fast enough to shut him up. And if he didn't? A public lawsuit, facing a small battering army of highly paid lawyers, the loss of his business and reputation and credibility . . . Christ, it would mean the end of everything. But Rathenau had paid for the Bélizaire three months ago. A quarter of the cash was already gone, spent on salaries and office rent and who knew what else?

I need a way out of this, he thought. Absurdly he wished he had family to turn to, confess the gravity of his mistakes, and for a minute he tried to imagine calling his mother and telling her everything. But the fantasy—himself crying on the phone, his mother soothing him, offering him advice—dissolved almost as quickly as it came. Eloise wasn't that kind of parent. She resembled a child, with the kind of pale, delicate Ophelia complexion that had been marred by alcohol and misuse, withering like a white rose at thirty. She would blink slowly and say in her breathy voice: "But I'm sure this'll all sort itself out, though, won't it?"

The idea of asking his uncle for help was even more unthinkable. Rudolph's skin crawled with humiliation at the thought. The man despised him—would see in his ask some fatal confirmation of a tragic flaw he seemed to have seen in Rudolph since birth. Why give him the satisfaction?

Alcohol seemed to focus his thoughts. You can't lose all this . . . shit, man, he thought as he gazed around the room. This house, these objects, they *were* his success: not just its trappings or rewards but the winning itself lit up in rich and luminous color. They were his crown and scepter, manifesting his social worth, his taste, his right to stand on this earth. People trusted him to sell the best, to *be* the best, because they looked around at his life and concluded he must be worth it. Without this stuff—the cars, the girls, the houses and restaurants and clothes and vacations—how would anyone know he was making it? How would anyone know that he was fucking alive?

Panicky now, the misery writhing in his gut, Rudolph thought of the man with the oily comb-over. Jorgen Gris, the least of father figures. An embarrassed half-smile in the corridor; the warm perfume of whiskey and oranges nestled into a tan suit as someone carried Rudolph back to bed. Life had been brighter, back then, his parents' voices murmuring then clashing together, even if he had never understood the source of their strain. He only remembered the feeling of watching them. The sense of some great mutual effort, straining at the seams.

Then—nothing. No one spoke of Jorgen, ever. When Rudolph had questioned his mother, she'd compressed her lips into a grimace and turned away.

Something compelled him not to ask. A cloud of darkness shrouded his memories of Jorgen, radiating poison like a chemical burn.

The only thing *he'd* gotten out of the situation was the Swiss passport in his hand. Ensconced in the armchair, Rudolph traced the outline of the white cross on grainy scarlet leather with his pinkie. More attractive than other passports, more ruthless somehow, a sleek homage to the efficiency of Swiss design. Or was he confusing the document with the seductive appeal of its conferred advantages?

Almost of its own volition, his other hand kept pouring more drinks into the crystal glass, beginning to slosh the *baijiu* a little more with every pour. Forgetting to add ice. The exhaustion of the day had seeped into the very marrow of his bones, and at some late hour he must have drowsed off, hardly noticing the door between waking and sleep slip open on its hinges.

He was back in New York, on that bitterly cold February night when Ingrid had introduced him to her friends for the first time. They'd gone to an East Village dive bar where you could still smoke inside. The night had been strange, but in Rudolph's sleeping brain it became even stranger, polluted by the alcohol that swirled through his memories, tinging them violet and neon pink and magenta in an electric haze, giving everything a hallucinatory cast.

"Everything's on me," Rudolph announced, raising a pitcher of margaritas bright with salt and lime. "To Ingrid!"

He was rewarded with artificial smiles.

From the moment they'd locked eyes, Rudolph could tell they disliked him. It was a question of lifestyle, of jealousy, of total incomprehension. Daisy was smoking Camel Reds, an untouched volume of Camille Paglia at her side. Julia was a spiky journalist from New Jersey who obsessively refreshed her Twitter feed with a running verbal update, dominating the conversation with long speeches about truth and justice and Our Fractured Political Landscape. She resembled a scowling little sausage dog in her skintight brown jumpsuit, slamming her fists on the table or waving them in the air to demonstrate a point. He could almost cry it was so goddamn boring, and he had heard it all so many times before.

Seeing his lips twitch, Julia turned on him, quizzing his strategy of buying art. Didn't he care that struggling artists weren't benefiting from all this money he tossed around? It could savage their careers, flipping hard-earned masterpieces for a million a pop. They're people, she told him loftily, not stocks. As if he gave a fuck.

"When you sell a used car, do you pay the car company twice?" he answered in measured tones. "It's trickle-down economics. I pay the big bucks, and eventually those profits drip down to younger artists. Whose careers are skyrocketing like never before, by the way."

"The American dream," Daisy murmured. "Yuppies selling to old white guys."

She lit a cigarette with a soft smile.

He laughed easily. Lightly, flexing his fists under the table. "Well, yeah. But unfortunately, it's the old white guys who rule the market. Money is money, and at the end of the day, that's what I'm about."

Something in Ingrid's face moved fractionally toward disappointment; too late, he realized that he'd made an error, slipped out of character.

"But this is all just a means for Rudolph to finance his next project," Ingrid interjected. "He wants to open a gallery for new artists from underprivileged communities."

Rudolph attempted a grin.

Oh, shit. He'd forgotten about this story, which he'd invented in a moment of drunken vanity. You could get addicted to the speed of infatuation, that need to see a constant flash of adoration in the other person's eyes. But sometimes he said so many different things it frightened him, like he'd lost the plot of who he was supposed to be.

"Everyone in the system is shady," Ingrid continued, sounding defensive. "Claudia's the perfect example. She makes me wire money all the time to our clients' Swiss bank accounts without even checking with finance. Literally, these people are unlisted, we have no idea who they are, I mean it's like the Wild West out there—"

Snapping to attention, he came gallantly to her rescue:

"My long-term strategy is all about giving back a little. This is simply about using the inequities of the banking system against itself to benefit the careers of underprivileged people I truly believe in."

Take that, you sad bohemian layabouts. Rudolph leaned back in his chair; he'd explained it so convincingly, he almost believed it himself. Ingrid tilted her head at her friends: *See what a good guy he is?*

"How charitable of you," Julia said dryly, her brows lifting in disbelieving little half-circles.

By the second round of margaritas, Daisy had moved on to her favorite topic of conversation: the wicked habits of the bourgeoisie. *Another,* Rudolph mouthed at the bartender.

"It's just so depressing to get these people who are saying 'Yeah, I'm a vegan,' with a tube of coke up their bloody nose. I mean cocaine is run on South American slave labor for fuck's sake, it's the most unethically produced thing—it's just these fucking yuppies, man. It's like my friends who do it who are yuppies."

"And how do you define a yuppie?" Ingrid inquired.

"It's not how *I'd* define it," Daisy said. "There's a strict anthropological definition. A young, corporate-seeming urban professional." She let her eyes drift dismissively over Rudolph. "Like him, for example."

Smothering his laughter, Rudolph glanced at Ingrid's face. She was squeezing a quartered lime with such force he thought it might fly at the wall.

"And what's wrong with that?" Ingrid asked. "You don't fall into that category, because you don't need to get a high-paying job. You're allowed to be the perpetually unemployed free spirit, because you're being financed by other means."

"Hey." Daisy gazed at Ingrid with an expression of real surprise. "I am just trying to live a life that feels authentic to me." Helplessly she shrugged. "Isn't that all we can do?"

Though Rudolph's expression remained diplomatically bright and cheerful, it was all he could do not to roll his eyes. At least his friends wore their snobbery openly; Daisy cloaked hers under a thin layer of bohemian languor, your classic champagne socialist. It was only the hereditary rich, he thought, who didn't care about money, who refused to see how it oiled the wheels of their own lives. He wanted to push her down in the mud and see if she could get back up.

Instead, he said easily, "That's a really good point. Actually, I agree." He laughed, waited a minute. "Hey. Do you guys want to go out? I need a real drink."

It was at China Chalet that the dream started to change—and later, when he woke up, Rudolph would think that this was when the hidden cogs of his own subconscious began to reveal their inner machinery to him, to reveal the project of fate. Conversation and memory blurred. He'd promised to brave the bar for another round of drinks. But, in the tranquil logic of dreams, he remained trapped in Ingrid's body, riding the luminous purple roller coaster of her mind. Both spectator and protagonist, he watched himself disappear into the crowd.

Julia was peering intently at Ingrid. Daisy flung herself over the torn leather banquette and began taking pictures of the fake rose petals.

"Remember when you were a Marxist in college?" Julia asked, unwrapping a piece of gum from its silver jacket and beginning to mash it forcefully between her teeth.

"Huh?"

"Do you mean the empty classroom where we all ate Entenmann's donuts and tried to figure out how to unionize the student body?" Daisy asked.

"I just don't get it, that's all. It's like a little bit hilarious to me that yesterday you're a Marxist in college, dating Brian the carpenter-slash-guitarist, and now you're dating an apex predator flying private jets to Mustique."

"What's to get?" Ingrid said lightly, sensing her aggression. "Things happen."

She lit a cigarette with a Zippo she'd found on the floor. Selling out—wasn't that what Julia was accusing her of? But how to explain the magnetism, the intense physical longing, his voice playing like a skipped disk in her head? The leap from nothing to everything was lurching and senseless, as animal and inexcusable as sex or death.

"I just feel like we're meant to be together," Ingrid said finally.

Julia looked at her awhile.

"That's it, though. You seem so different around him. Like—spellbound."

"I'm exactly the same."

"Chill out, you guys." Daisy laughed. "Some people are just better at falling in love. I choose guys with no job, Ingrid chooses titans of industry. Or whatever."

The music was getting louder and louder, strobe lights staining their faces like slabs of broken cathedral glass. Julia took another big swallow of vodka, her voice rising:

"This is the kind of guy who only sees dollar signs, a massive social climber who pals around with billionaires. Doesn't that bother you? I just feel like you used to be so much better than that." Her face was growing pink. She seemed impassioned, grabbing Ingrid's arm with an energy that surprised her. "I know you love him, but I just wonder if you'd be happier with somebody else. Who understands you. Who would never ask you to compromise yourself."

Ingrid blinked at her in surprise. She felt suddenly shredded, as though Julia had torn a slit through her vision of the world. In its absence lay doubt, and all those emotions she had never allowed herself until tonight.

"This is my life now," she said.

Julia seemed almost on the verge of tears. She was very drunk.

"What about being an artist? You never even tried that hard."

Ingrid's face flushed an ugly red.

Real artists did suffer, didn't they, she thought. A flood of misery washed over her. They subsisted on bread and water and painted on cardboard until they made it. And I didn't do that. I couldn't. I—

She opened her mouth, incandescent with rage. A mad urge to ask Julia what she meant by that. Then she made the mistake of looking into Julia's face.

Julia looked ill. She was covered in sweat, rambling, sipping her drink, and at the same time blinking back tears. The more Ingrid observed her, the more pity replaced the urge to scream. Then she saw this final, damning sight; and more than anything, it convinced her to dismiss the whole thing. Julia was scanning the dance floor, searching for romantic prospects, with a bare desperation born of loneliness in her eyes.

From his occupancy in Ingrid's body, Dream-Rudolph watched Rudolph approach with vague disquiet. He was holding a tray of drinks, his wolfish teeth lit up violet by the strobe lights. Quick as an athlete, he spun her out on the dance floor. Ingrid was awkward, stilted, allowing herself to be twisted into the mass of bodies, swarming with heat. She felt aroused and slightly sick, dizzy with the music, a seventies Eurotrash song they'd put on to rile up the crowd.

"You look so happy," she said to him.

He lowered his head to speak into her ear. Lips touching the razor's edge of her cheekbone. He could taste the salt in her sweat, the sugary shimmer of sticky purple glitter on her eyelids.

"You make me feel so—so great, Ingrid."

"That's so cheesy," she shouted. But he only smiled and spread his arms out uncaringly, like, *So what?*

A plague of uncertainty overtook her body, flailing inexpertly on the dance floor. Julia's words gnawed at her brain. What would happen if she said no. Then she'd be alone again, alone in her apartment with her piling-up bills and no one to talk to and no one to—

"I'm so in love with you," she heard herself say.

"What's that?" he shouted, pretending not to hear.

"I said love me!"

She took a step forward. The music was rising to a crescendo. It was rising, rising, into some kind of pagan religious chant. The floor exploded into a rainbow of pink and acid violet and Prussian blue, so startling they had to shut their eyes. The crowd was shoving them together, the margins of their bodies becoming one, and even as he started to lie, he realized with a sudden frightening clarity that he really did love her, and a heaviness came over his body like a claustrophobic gas. She was crying. Then he leaned down to kiss her, and the chorus hit another dark peak and wave.

Rudolph opened his eyes, fragments of speech still caught inside his throat.

"It's like the Wild West out there," he said aloud.

He ran his tongue over his dried-out lips, remembering the sugary taste of Ingrid's cheap purple glitter. His poisonous hangover was mysteriously gone. For the first time in days, his mind felt as cool and clear as a new dawn.

Straightaway, he'd bought a plane ticket to Geneva. He knew what he had to do.

17

INGRID HAD RARELY DRIVEN HERSELF HARDER FOR THE GALLERY'S ENDS.

It was a cool April morning. Making her way across the steely floor of a corporate café in Chelsea, Ingrid saw Simone. She was sitting in the blank light of a window seat, her long brown curls shining in the sun. Streaked with caramel now. A feeling of awe and irritation swelled up against Ingrid's will. Not only was Simone a genius, not only did she have to come out with a terrible story that made Ingrid experience guilt and regret rather than the bitterness that had become so natural to her, but Simone had to be beautiful, too. In college sometimes they'd pretended to be half-sisters—jokes at a party, laughing at guys, but it was believable because they shared a vague resemblance. Only Simone's features were more striking, more intense. Ingrid was the weaker version of her in every way.

For two weeks now, they'd been tiptoeing around each other, like two people deciding whether they wanted to date. Yet the ease of their dorm-era friendship seemed to have tightened into something more muscular now. Frozen in space. Ingrid was all too conscious of what she needed from Simone. She could feel Simone sitting back and watching her, letting the gallery seduce her with promises, while at the office, Claudia and Paul's eyes were a gun to her head, a constant pressure. Even now they waited upstairs. It was both exhilarating and strange.

"So," Simone said, picking at her prosciutto sandwich.

"So," Ingrid repeated, studying Simone's face.

Seal the deal. She forced a smile. "So, I feel like I'm ready."

Simone glanced at Ingrid, waiting for her to fulfill her role in the courtship ritual they both knew lay ahead. But perversely, now the moment had come, Ingrid wanted nothing more than to delay its realization. *Let me have this one thing of my own!* she begged the universe.

"I don't want to beat around the bush forever. I feel like, with you there, it just makes sense for me to be represented by Paul Bernot Gallery."

"That's great," Ingrid said. "So you think you'd want to do the exhibition next month?"

Simone shrugged. "It depends."

"Paul's really keen," Ingrid pressed.

"I'm willing to talk, for sure."

"Pick your date, he said."

Simone leaned back in her seat. Her cat eyes glowed with an otherworldly focus.

"Look. Put my cards on the table. I've brought my portfolio, not that that's particularly needed, but . . ." She hesitated.

"But?"

"But . . ." Simone's eyes were opaque in the half-light of the café. "I've been thinking about what we, ah, talked about before," she said. "I would like to make some kind of statement. Not right now, it's not quite clear yet, but it will be. Just need to let the idea . . . germinate a bit."

Ingrid eyed her in confusion. She'd thought they were talking about the exhibition, but Simone seemed to be focused on the rape.

"What kind of statement? Like a press release?"

"Mm. Maybe. I don't know what, exactly."

Simone tapped her fingers on the table, distant now.

"People approach you. They want to take something from you, right? Because everyone wants to take. So you give, you give and you

take, and you're hoping life comes out roughly even in the end. Right?"
She took a breath. "Then *you* report your rape. Because, whatever,
you want to take something too. You want to take back your pride, you
want to confess, you want him to pay. But what kind of justice is served
in foul play?"

Mechanically she laughed, leaned forward to look Ingrid in the eye.

"The girl who cries wolf becomes a piece of used toilet paper.
People stop taking you seriously. And don't bother to protest, because
we both know it's true. People want to hear it, of course, they're
ravenous for it. Pain's exciting. But soon that's all they can see. You
become a site of invasion to them—a raw and wounded living vagina
who can never heal. So you get up on your soapbox," Simone continued.
"And everyone pities you. Everyone pities you until you age and fade
away, like all the other soiled, screwed-up girls."

"But it's not just about you and him," Ingrid said, squirming in her
chair. "You might suffer, yes, I'll admit. But he will suffer more. He'll be
penalized for it. And other women won't experience the same."

"Other women? Why should I give a fuck about other women?"
Simone repeated, growing angry. "The imaginary sisterhood compris-
ing half the planet? All we've got in common being fucking tits and a
vagina? That is just some pathetic PR department trying to force me to
buy a . . . a pink razor or whatever. It is not my fucking responsibility."

Ingrid watched her in silence.

Simone sighed.

"All the same, I'm not completely heartless. I don't want this to
happen to anyone else. I just think, if the world is going to mine *my*
quote, unquote 'trauma' for their own entertainment and leave me with
the shreds, why shouldn't I do it first? In a way that serves me? Like a
Tracey Emin, *Everyone I Have Ever Slept With* type thing. She really
made a name for herself with that, didn't she?"

"Straight to the Tate," Ingrid affirmed.

The piece in question had been a shock to the staid London art world of the late 1990s. Emin had sewn the name of everyone she'd ever slept with into the nylon surface of a cheap camping tent. She had torn herself open and sold her pain to a museum and it had worked.

"But doesn't it feel passé these days?" Ingrid wondered. "I mean, everyone commodifies their trauma."

"It's not passé, it's precedent." Simone leaned forward. "You don't understand. I'll give them a single person to focus on, a single scapegoat. Tracey Emin didn't do that, but I will. Not just an isolated work, I want—I want a movement. I have to get it right."

"Wait, you're serious?"

For a moment Simone looked narrowly at Ingrid, as if she were searching for something. When she shook her head and looked away, Ingrid had the wounded sensation of having been found lacking.

"Look, Ingrid. I'm so used to being reduced to a symbol. Do you think I don't know why this gallery is so interested in me right now?"

"You're a great artist," Ingrid said awkwardly, and she meant it.

"Thanks, I guess." Simone sighed. "But you know as well as I do that there are a ton of great artists out there. I have to do something twice as original, twice as good, if I want to transcend the—the genre, right? Plenty of artists fade away after one exhibition, one real hit, and then still end up being like—a banker or a farmer or whatever. But I want to last."

"Look, I understand that. I totally understand it," Ingrid said, stumbling. "It's your vision, not ours, and you have to follow your heart."

Paul is relying on you. Help her.

"I guess one thing you could do," she said finally, "is create a work that comments on the ravenous appetites of the public itself. You know? Expose him, yeah. But also point out how desperate people are to cannibalize your suffering. They want to hear the dirty details, don't they? So give it to them, and laugh."

Simone was nodding fiercely now. A smile broke across her face. Ingrid's relief was instant: her best friend was back.

"God, I knew you would get it! There may be a couple of legal disputes, but I'm sure we can deal with them piece by piece. I just need freedom to create, that's the main thing." She squeezed Ingrid's hand across the table. "I've really missed you, you know. And now we get to work together, every day—it all feels so perfect, doesn't it?"

Legal disputes . . . ? But the thought faded away in the wind of Ingrid's happiness. For a moment they held hands, each locked in her own unknowing thoughts.

It was time to put things in motion. When Ingrid suggested they go see Paul and Claudia, Simone nodded. Ingrid guided her out of the café and up the stairs of the gallery. Into Paul's office. Seeing the minute incline of his head—*you've done well today*—she closed the door and stood outside it for a minute, listening.

Then a sort of languor went through her. Even this appetite to listen felt somehow faked. She had the recurring sensation of faking her own actions, because there was something about this new, knifelike edge to Simone that she honestly disliked. Revenge. These violent appetites, these violent delights, seemed finally to match Paul's and Claudia's ambitions for Simone, but that did not mean Ingrid shared them.

A small frown creased her face. She'd forgotten to ask his name. The rapist. Or maybe she had been afraid to ask—afraid to ruin the uneasy trust springing up between them again. Part of her wished she could whisk Simone away, into the past, to recapture the happiness they'd lost when this mysterious abuser had poisoned their lives. The sunlit studio. He'd ruined it. She didn't even want to know his name. In her mind he had already become a black hole, a void, a symbol of everything that had conspired to break up their friendship. If it wasn't for him, Ingrid might still be working in the studio today. With Simone, not for her. *Anyone can be a banker or a farmer because they didn't make a mark . . .* Ingrid flinched, Simone's voice ran contemptuously through her mind.

Still. She pressed her lips together. The promotion, the tangibility of success—within breathing distance.

She walked away from Paul's office, smothering the low polite buzz of their voices beneath the closed door. Later would be time to listen, because soon enough, Paul and Claudia would invite her in. It was her hope, her future, her only choice at this point. Nor, she thought with grim amusement, did the rapist's name matter. Whoever he was, Simone was going to tear him apart.

18

THE PALE BLUE RIBBON OF LAKE GENEVA GLITTERED UNDER THE SUN as the taxi drove by the circling swans in all their heartless beauty. It was fifteen minutes from the airport to the hotel. Rudolph watched the neat streets of Geneva unfold row by row before him, armies of gray-suited toy soldiers rising to the march.

His destination was the Hotel des Bergues, a giant creamy wedding cake towering over the shore with stony grandeur. The driver parked in front of the entrance. Nabokov, he remembered, had lived at the nearby Montreux Palace for twenty years in exile, in those heady days when the best European hotels were still cheap enough to live in on a near-permanent basis.

"Forty francs, please."

Rudolph paid the stratospheric fee in silence. The anonymity of hotels made him feel like an actor, maybe, or a ghost: a bottomless pool of nothingness waiting to be filled up. He could be anyone or anything; he could be a figment of his own imagination, or even someone else's. He passed through the vast marble lobby, imagining himself unseen.

A smiling receptionist ushered him up to his suite, and he briefly checked out his digs: rich and spacious in pale pastels like the frothy inside of a lavender macaron. Some invisible person had nestled a cold bottle of white wine in an ice bucket beside a box of Rohr chocolates. All very nice, he told himself. But in truth, his heart no longer beat harder to see all that luxury spread-eagled before him. It was simply de rigueur.

I need more to get excited these days, he realized with a dull ache. But he couldn't explain why his eyes prickled sharply at the thought of having to push himself further and further with each passing year, endlessly seeking some fresher or more beautiful or more exciting thrill.

He flopped on the bed and opened the box of chocolates, unwrapping each candy from its jewel-colored foil and dropping it in his mouth. As a child, he'd practiced doing this with the baskets of candied fruit and truffles people gave his uncle at Christmas, playing a silly game with himself: How much can I eat before I puke? Even now the chubby specter of his boyish self lingered at the doorway, patiently waiting its turn to invade his body once again.

The room felt oddly cold. Suddenly struck by paranoia, he got up and closed the yellow drapes. There's nothing to be afraid of, he told himself.

It was the blue hour, that strange empty time between afternoon and evening. With its dusky gilt mirrors and cracked leather wing chairs, the empty hotel bar resembled an interior decorator's fantasy of a prewar gentleman's club crossed with Marie Antoinette's boudoir.

Sitting in the silent hush of the deserted bar, he ordered a strange purple cocktail that tasted like perfume, sipping it while he watched people drift in and out of the lobby. Harried-looking business executives. Saudi princesses in blinding pastel bling. A girl who looked like Cornelia floated by—same gaunt elbows and injured expression— and, like the repetitive strains of a monkey's accordion, their old song struck up in his head. "Please Please Please Let Me Get What I Want." It had been a mournful chart-topper by the Smiths they'd once danced to at a wedding . . .

"Another drink, sir?" the grizzled bartender interrupted kindly, and Rudolph realized he'd finished the purple drink a long time ago.

"Whiskey. On the rocks."

All of a sudden he missed Cornelia. With all her faults, she'd understood him better than anyone. Knew he was weak, fallible, prone to mistakes. He wanted to call her suddenly, if only to see that mirror in her eyes.

"Would you like our list?" the bartender prompted.

But no—he couldn't. Shouldn't.

Remember what's good for you, he told himself, and fixed his icy gaze on the bartender's expectant face.

"I don't need to," he said. "*Le meilleur,* please."

He woke at eight in a cloud of tangled linen, heart juddering in his throat. Vague memories of tumbling into bed with the contents of the minibar, a bag of peanut M&M's, and a bottle of vodka . . . Shut up, he told himself fiercely, you aren't breaking any laws yet. Sweat it out and you'll be fine.

Rudolph pulled on his running clothes: a pair of sneakers, a sweat-wicking terry cloth headband to protect his delicate waves from harmful oils. Outside, the sun glinted off the platinum lake. The swans spread out their snowy wings in a gesture of indifferent welcome as they waddled along the shore. As he ran along the bridges, a lightness, almost painful, entered his heart, and he was briefly able to imagine himself with no material ties to anyone or anything. Free.

If I stop now, I could still afford to buy a quiet house in France. I could go and live there by myself, doing—what?—small-scale organic farming, running a cookery class, giving hiking tours to visiting tourists . . . hearty, useful, back-to-the-land stuff.

But then he imagined having to serve *pain de campagne* to some arrogant city person like himself. He could already picture the patronizing small talk. *You get many tourists down here in the winter?— You know, these grapes aren't half bad! . . .* The indignity! The silent, servile background creature, unnoticed as a lump of furniture or an ugly child. No, no, everything depended on his ability to convince the Swiss bankers to open his account. He needed to find a way to make money disappear.

His appointment was at eleven. For thirty minutes he killed time looking in the shops of central Geneva, which wasn't hard. You could tour the whole city by foot in less than two hours.

Objects gleamed from their pedestals. Shiny watches, python bags, jewels of all colors lit up from above and below in silver and gold settings, much the way saintly icons must have been illuminated by candlelight in Byzantine churches. These modern relics attracted a similar religious fervor from the tourists lingering before the icy vitrines: burning eyes, a naked need that bordered on the fanatic.

Smiling and chatting to the saleswomen, Rudolph practiced his French; he had already decided not to reveal his American citizenship unless absolutely necessary. Nonresident Americans were strictly prohibited from opening Swiss bank accounts due to issues of tax evasion and other sketchy attempts to move assets offshore; and Rudolph had no desire for anyone to ever link Rudolph Sullivan with this identity or account. His French wasn't perfect, but then plenty of kids here, stationed in Swiss boarding schools by watchful parents operating out of undisclosed locations, spoke bad French with perfect LA accents. It was a country of people with no country, united by only one thing.

When the big clock struck ten forty-five, Rudolph hurried toward the bank.

There was nothing like spearing a real Moby Dick of a masterpiece to make a guy open up, Rudolph knew this from experience. Once they'd shaken hands over a deal and settled down into plush armchairs, legs spread wide and pudgy fingers gripping an ice-cold drink, many powerful men became generous in their secrecy. Buzzing and pink-cheeked with alcohol and the thrill of the hunt, they let their minds drift to other, equally reassuring examples of their wizardry. Fantastic alchemies could be performed over seemingly rigid legal strictures; laws were merely guidelines after all, not meant for people who contributed so very much to the national GDP.

Names were traded in the fireside hush of hotel bars: this loyal fixer to spirit away an aggressive lawsuit or crazed memoir by some long-forgotten ex-girlfriend. Another to conjure up a friendly foreign citizenship to some far-flung Caribbean locale. To forge your children an unbreakable trust, mighty as a fortress against any attempted attacks, no matter how legally troubling ... Rudolph was a good listener—you never knew when things might come in handy—and with this in mind, he always, always listened to talk about banks.

Most banks took an irritatingly hard line about pesky things like background checks and income reporting. But some, he learned, did not. And the kindest, most forgiving minority of banks actively sought out their clientele among the shadiest political and financial personages that could be found.

Inside the cool blue headquarters of Allard Group Bank, he was gratified to find himself whisked upstairs to a significant-looking corner office smelling of lemon wood polish. The banker stood by the long windows, the chilly Northern European sun illuminating his silhouette in hard gray lines.

"Yves Müller. A pleasure."

"Rudolph Gris. Good to meet you."

Rudolph shook his hand, projecting confidence. Jorgen's odd surname fit like a lie in his mouth, though it was not.

"How can we be of help?" the banker inquired once they had exchanged pleasantries.

"I'm interested in opening a new account. I believe my father banked previously with your agency."

"Ah?" The man showed no trace of recognition. "That may be so. May I see your passport, please?"

"Certainly."

Rudolph slid the passport over. Why had he mentioned his father? Jorgen had never banked here. He was chewing his tongue—off and running—imitating some dumb trust fund kid with nothing to hide. Müller's blazer rode up as he reached for the passport, revealing stiffly laundered shirt cuffs embroidered with his monogram, *YM*, in swirling purple cursive. A baroque detail. Twisting his sweating palms together, Rudolph watched the banker type something into his computer.

"Everything seems to be in order," he said eventually. "So you'd like to open a numbered account. For what purpose?"

"Well, I own galleries, see, in New York and London. And I've decided to expand to Geneva, especially since much of the art I deal in transits through the Swiss freeport. It just makes financial sense."

"I see." Müller wrote something down on a pad of paper. "And may I ask, will this be followed by a physical site for the business?"

"Absolutely," Rudolph said calmly, improvising as he went along. "I'm looking at sites for a third gallery close to where the Pace offices are, at the Quai des Bergues."

Müller looked at him inquiringly. *Tell the truth, just not the whole truth.*

"Many of my clients are Geneva-based—at least in terms of their fiscal assets—yet the auction and gallery scene is relatively thinly spread. Mostly jewels and Old Masters. There's lots of opportunity for growth, for starting new conversations and generating energy based on the high number of Swiss proto-Impressionist landscape artists coming out of the regional provinces of St. Moritz and Lugano, given the algorithmic data on collectors who are interested in a certain breed of late-nineteenth-century post-Freudian pointillism . . ."

He spouted on and on, making up a grand imaginary history for Swiss art, trying to fill every sentence with words as dense and impregnable as possible. Artspeak. He could see Müller's eyes glazing over with boredom, though he kept up his thin-lipped greyhound smile. Good. Let him think I'm just passionate about the job, some excitable youngster ready to start up another short-lived business with Daddy's money.

Finally Müller interrupted him with an icy glance, full of Swiss froideur: "Makes sense."

He couldn't give less of a fuck, Rudolph realized with a flood of relief.

"Sorry if I'm running on a bit," he apologized with a broad smile. "I just love this beautiful city so much, you know? I think there's such potential here—maybe to open another art fair, like a Basel competitor . . . I have a lot of great contacts . . ."

Shut me up, he willed. *Give me the goddamn account and get me out of your office.* But he had to make the effort. The millions he could offer the bank were not enough to warrant a complete flouting of rules; it took *billions* to make people stick their asses out for you, billions like his clients possessed, and the idea of it dredged up another wet surge of rage—

"That sounds very, very amusing indeed," Müller said, while examining his computer. "But it's not required for us to know every-thing about your company's strategy. Everything looks quite standard, and I don't anticipate any problems with opening this account. The only thing we will need to see is proof of address. And business statements, to verify the transactions going through the accounts." Müller looked at him curiously. "Only the initial ones, I should say."

"Of course."

"There is a higher fee associated with these accounts," Müller concluded. "As well as a relatively high opening deposit."

"That's no problem at all," Rudolph said crisply.

"Right." Müller paused. "Well, once you've sent everything over, we'll get Compliance to go through your credit history and business records, and we should have an answer for you in the following week or so."

Rudolph hesitated, not wanting to sound sketchy but needing to know the answer. *Can anyone trace me to this account?* Instead, he asked in a casual tone:

"How strict are your confidentiality laws surrounding these accounts?"

Müller gave him a long, appraising look, a you-haven't-fooled-me-for-a-minute look.

"Discretion is everything to our clients, as you must know. US citizens and residents are subject to a separate set of foreign account reporting rules, meaning they are required to report assets abroad to the US government." Pause. "But I don't suppose that would apply to you."

Müller righted a purple Post-it, slipped from its golden pad.

"I wouldn't worry. We're very loyal to our customers at Allard, you know; we think of them as part of our little family."

They exchanged a coded glance. Inside, Rudolph cringed a little: Did Müller know? Could the bank's credit history database have access to information about where Rudolph lived and where he kept his real financial holdings? No, it was impossible—but it was time to end the conversation, all the same. He offered his politician's parting handshake.

"Thank you very much for your time, Mr. Müller. It's been very informative."

*   *   *

It was eight on the East Coast and 2:00 a.m. in Geneva. Rudolph lay in bed, cradling a glass of whiskey as he listened to the dial tone. Ingrid would be home, just come back from drinks. They'd texted earlier.

"I want to ask you something," he said before she could speak. "Just don't say no until you hear it, okay?" Then he cursed himself. Bad start.

"What is it?"

Ingrid sounded different, more drained. His heart beat faster. "Are you okay?"

"Julia said some things about you tonight," she said after a pause.

"What things?"

"That you are a bloodhound." Ingrid giggled, an uncomfortable tinkling noise like bells on a dog collar. "That—oh, you know how she is, but she thought it was unethical. Says you've got a bad reputation for selling shares in art and stuff."

Rudolph listened to the gaps and crevices between each word, interpreting the meaning behind them. She sounded tipsy.

"Julia's a fucking idiot," he said coldly. "And I don't need to explain to you why."

"But if you did?"

Rudolph exhaled. "I don't have time for this right now, I've got meetings all over town tomorrow. Why is Julia an idiot?" he repeated. "She's an idiot to think there ever was a line between the pursuit of beauty and the accumulation of assets. I hate fucking intellectual snobs who cling to these stupid passé notions."

He heard her sigh, as if this wasn't the response she'd wanted.

"This is what I hate about journalists," he continued. "They feel personally offended when the world doesn't live up to their ideals. They genuinely believe they're standing alone in a mire of corruption and decline, trumpeting their moral shock—"

He broke off. Even he could hear the anger in his voice—the bitterness, which seemed somehow ugly, misdirected. The yellow drapes fluttered in the wind. Who had opened them?

"What's wrong with that?" Ingrid asked. "What's wrong with having ideals?"

"Nothing. Nothing."

He stopped pacing. His voice sounded calmer now.

"Let me explain something to you. Everything, arguably, is about money, but everything that concerns material things *really* is about money. I know this must be quite a shock for you."

"That's not—I really feel like the best art shows us the truth of our time, reflects something we can't see in ourselves."

"Hey, I'm not denying that at all. I'm just saying art isn't born in a vacuum. In a way, I think all those ideas are just a shield. Money and power are the only real motivations in this whole world, but people don't want to know."

"Ideas, passions, that's what makes people tick," Ingrid countered.

"Are you really so naive? Money stirs us more than anything else on earth." He laughed. "Look, Ingrid. Didn't the Medici dukes hire the most talented artists in Italy as status symbols, to spread word of their political might through Europe? *That's* how the Renaissance got started—it wasn't some chill guys sitting around having a beer. The ways of the world don't change. People are just more honest about it nowadays, that's all."

Romantic ideals are also for sale, he almost added, *and they're the most expensive of all*. But he was too tired to corral the confusing fragments flitting around his mind.

Ingrid was silent for nearly a minute. Then she said quietly, "You may be right. It's humiliating. It's degrading. But maybe I don't want to think like that all the time. Otherwise, what's the point? For most people, there's nothing waiting on the other side. So maybe I don't want to be a realist. I want to see the—the beauty, the fire to create."

What a contrast, what a prize, to have this beautiful girl talking about loving art for art's sake! It was fresh and hopeful and sincere, great dinner-party chatter, proof positive of his own sophistication and imperviousness to material greed. He had the sensation of being a child again, purified, able to see the world from a new set of eyes. But tonight, as he sank into his plush pile of gold-rimmed pillows, Ingrid's featherweight dreams weighed heavy on his shoulders. She had a peppercorn salary; she was hundreds of thousands of dollars in student debt. She did not understand the sinking pressure of a business, he told himself as he lay facedown on the bed, or the need to support people who relied on you.

"Everything's for sale, Ingrid," he said in a small voice.

"Not everything. Not love."

His heart leapt. His voice was full of need.

"Do you really believe that?" he wondered aloud. "Would you love me if I were a cashier at Walmart? A starving poet?"

"Of course," she said. "I would always love you."

How strange that a mere string of words could feel like the most intoxicating thing in the English language! Her words were a cool hand pressed to a hot forehead when you hadn't even known you had a fever. Guilt overwhelmed him.

"Hello? Are you there?" she was saying, after thirty seconds of silence. "Rudolph?"

"I wish I were there," he whispered.

"Me too," she said, sounding happier now. "Now what did you want to ask?"

He licked his lips. Cognitive therapy breaths, in out. Calm. Relaxed. Then, before he could lose his nerve, he said, "Look, I have this thing in Paris on, on June 3. Would you want to come with me?"

A short silence. "Paris?"

"Yes, Paris."

He shifted across the bed, unbuttoned his piped blue pajama shirt. She sounded so reluctant. He felt hot, sweaty. Why was she not jumping at the chance?

"Don't you want to?" he asked.

"I do," she said. "It's just . . . Simone's show opens that day, and—"

"So what? You can come straight after, on the red-eye from JFK to Charles de Gaulle. I do it all the time." He waited, suddenly nervous. "Don't you want to come?"

"Well, yes—but it's out of my price range. You know I can't afford big trips."

"Is that all?" He laughed more freely, enjoying himself now. Everything's going to be all right, he thought with a sudden wash of relief, you are going to make her life better, not worse. You'll be the hero, the knight in shining armor.

"I'll pay, obviously, Ingrid. Don't be silly. I'm going there next month, anyway; I've got this boring gala at the Palais des Beaux-Arts and I really want you to come. Okay?" he pressed.

"I've never been there before," she said slowly. "People here seem to go all the time, but to me it's always had this, I don't know, unattainable allure."

"Everything's attainable." He smiled into the phone, hiding a gulp of irrepressible laughter. "So it's settled. Pack a nice dress, okay?"

They hung up. The whiskey in the Baccarat glass lay still on the gilded Boulle table. He started laughing, laughing so hard and maniacally that he could no longer control the shrill jubilant peals of his own voice. There was something so awful about his manic baboon squeal, in this strange gold room: it revolted him to the core. Picking up the glass, so drunk his head was spinning, he hurled it at the wall where it smashed and shattered into the soft-pile Persian carpet.

19

INGRID WAS PROMOTED A FEW DAYS BEFORE SIMONE'S EXHIBITION OPENED.

It was one of those blooming, burgeoning, green-gold spring mornings in New York that set your teeth on edge with pleasure. She walked to work for the first time in months, under the trees swirling in the wind like falling umbrellas. A new season in the air, as if you too could become a new person along with the budding cherry blossoms.

Downstairs in the gallery, a crew of technicians had been working since dawn to take down the Japanese pet orifices. The show had sold out. Now, whenever she walked downtown, Ingrid saw people wearing bright purple hoodies emblazoned with an image of Fujita's signature naked dog parts. Graphic T-shirts riffed on Magritte's *The Treachery of Images*, showing Fujita's now-familiar sculpture of a dog anus with the legend *Ceci n'est pas un cul de chien*.

"Ingrid," Paul shouted. "Get in here."

He was waiting in his office, a discarded plate of sushi lying beside him. "Bad tuna," he commented, seeing her glance, and gestured to a chair. "Sit down, all right?"

After thirty, forty years in power, Paul strode into rooms like a powerful prize bull. He was nothing like Rudolph, that whirling quick-tongued animal; not even Paul's recent melancholy could shake the overriding sense of a man in absolute control of his kingdom.

Ingrid sat, wondering if she'd done anything wrong. For the first time she noticed Claudia, coiled up in the chair behind Paul's desk, her watchful eyes flat and silent. Ingrid had an icy premonition that she was about to be fired.

"So, we just wanted to have a little chat with you about a couple of things."

Paul cleared his throat, pushed his square-rimmed glasses up his nose.

"You are very well liked in the office," Paul said consideringly. "Respected, even."

"Oh—thank you."

"I'm aware that we haven't had much of a chance to thank you for what you've done for us, with Simone. Bringing her on, I mean."

"I couldn't have done it without Claudia's help," Ingrid said, trying to smile.

"But of course." Paul waved a hand, as if he'd expected this. "Claudia's let me know how much she helped you. But it is still impressive. In fact, it's about the biggest opportunity someone in your position has ever offered us. And, well, we like your gumption."

Ingrid thanked him again.

"I'll get to the point," he enunciated slowly. "We've decided to make you Simone's artist liaison."

Ingrid stared at him. Paul was still speaking, rattling off benefits and a salary raise and a title change and needing to interview a replacement assistant, but his voice became a low inchoate buzz.

"With more money comes more responsibility," he warned her. "There will be no one to blame for your mistakes now. But you could become—you have the opportunity to become the most valuable, the most irreplaceable person here." He leaned forward. "There's an opportunity here, but you need to grab hold of it with both hands."

He peered hard at Ingrid. Paul had a way of looking at you, with his icy, penetrating stare, his pale blue eyes probing your face like the long pools of a lighthouse casting its search lamps out to sea. Her heart turned over. For a minute she felt paralyzed: Could he read her mind? She wanted to cry out, *No! I want to be an artist!*

But that path was closed to her. She gathered her wits and said, as fiercely as she could, "I do want this. I really want to work here."

"Good."

He settled back in his chair, his eyes shining with faith now. He wants me to succeed, she realized with a start. I *can* succeed here. If I want to.

"Really, Paul, I—I won't let you down. Thank you. Thank you both."

Paul gave a stiff nod, awkward at the praise, and waved her away.

"All right. Well. That's all, Ingrid."

She thanked him again and went back to her desk.

This morning, she had been doing her lipstick. She had chosen a new color—raspberry, much darker than she would normally have chosen—but strangely enough, it suited her. In the mirror, looking at herself, she had stopped, momentarily taken aback by what she saw. One of Them. Her blinking reflection in the mirror seemed to inhabit the body of someone older, sharper, glossier. Someone more like . . . Claudia.

In the meeting, she had vaguely noticed how Claudia's face, while Paul was speaking, had remained very still. She had said nothing during the entire meeting, Ingrid realized. Not a single word.

Be careful, a voice inside her whispered.

The day of Simone's exhibition opening flashed by as quickly as money changes hands. All morning Ingrid fielded alternately desperate, pleading, enraged calls from clients, everyone begging for a shot at Simone's work. The answer was always the same.

"I'm so sorry, but all of the works have been previously sold. But if you want to buy a work from another part of our program, we might be able to move you up the list."

"Realistically," one tech prodigy shouted down the phone, "realistically, I can buy you and your shitty little gallery ten times over if I wanted to. I'm a third-generation collector and my family's got a lot of assets, so you don't get to ask me about the rest of your program. The only thing worth a dime anyway is Simone Machado. I want the best and I want it now, and realistically you should beg for my patronage—"

But Ingrid had already hung up.

Then she was dashing up and down the stairs, arranging wine-glasses, soothing an anxious Simone, talking to yet another inquisitive journalist on the phone. What was Simone like? they wanted to know. Why did she use those colors? What was the meaning behind the shadowy figures in her paintings, the half-eaten apple on the bed? Was it true that she had specifically re-created the exact Canada balsam glaze Titian had once used to paint *Venus of Urbino*? Even Paul was shocked by the chaos, the sheer all-devouring appetite threatening to consume Simone's show before it had even opened.

"I've never seen anything like this," he said, shaking his head. "Not in thirty years."

Having no way of comparing, Ingrid restricted herself to a simple nod of agreement.

"And do her paintings even really merit it?" he wondered aloud.

He eyed Ingrid with a dubious look. It was not, she thought, a stupid question. In this upside-down world, sometimes you could not tell the difference between good and bad.

So he and Ingrid looked up. Simone's paintings hung on the walls. Nude women roamed darkened cells; their lips dripped blue-black juice, and their unblinking eyes, scrubbed of pupils, stared out at the viewer with a sharp ferocity, as if they might slip out of the paintings and into the gallery like violent ghosts. They confused Ingrid. Still, she sensed their power. Simone seemed to have captured something beyond her own knowledge, beyond her own environment. Like a message for the future to decode: They burned with life.

*   *   *

Ingrid had been running around for so many hours that she hardly noticed the absence of Claudia at first. The whole gallery was in such a celebratory mood, talking and smiling and opening a bottle of wine at four to toast the party tonight, that Ingrid was just happy that Claudia hadn't appeared yet to ruin it. Minutes before the reception began, though, Ingrid received a curt email. It contained orders to pay a client for a painting they'd apparently bought months ago.

Paul will be livid with you if it isn't paid by tomorrow, Claudia concluded tersely.

Gripping her phone in one hand, Ingrid made her way up the office. It was empty, isolated, but for a few forgotten Pet Orifices in the corner.

How typical of Claudia to try and flex her muscles one last time! She was always forgetting to pay clients on time. She loved for Ingrid to dodge the proper approval processes, reminding her, constantly, of Ingrid's loyalty to her above anyone else. $2.85 million, though . . . Should she get the finance director's approval?

Ingrid reread the email. It was bitchy all right.

All week Claudia had seemed fragile, strange, wearing a big black pair of sunglasses indoors like she had an eye infection. She was always swishing into Paul's office before glancing around and then banging the door shut, as if she half-suspected a horde of spies to be in pursuit. Maybe best to make her happy. Other people's promotions often awakened a deep paranoia in Claudia, a hysteria that could quickly become fatal for the other person.

Two freeze-dried cat eyes stared bleakly out at her from their bubble wrap.

Ingrid decided to make the transfer. The recipient's address was a corporation. It was in the Virgin Islands or someplace like that— she watched the money drain out of the company's bank account, so frazzled and excited that she no longer cared. Paris. In two hours, she'd be on a plane to Paris.

"Ingrid? Ingrid?"

Simone's voice sounded tinny and childlike. She must be standing on the landing, in her new red dress, too nervous to go downstairs and talk to everyone. I have to go help her, Ingrid realized, and she switched off the lights.

Like symbiotic parasites, the right sense of buzz required a balanced ratio of young and cool versus old and rich. This exhibition had gotten it right. Ambiguously gendered students with pierced noses and dirty sneakers mingled with eccentric artists, then rich, aging collectors. Claudia towered smilingly over the crowd in skyscraper heels that, aesthetically, called to mind both the hooves of a deer and the female genitalia.

From her vantage point at the bar, Ingrid watched her bend over a small yellow-haired child and pop an enormous cupcake in the little girl's open mouth. The girl's mother was a spectrally thin blonde in a fox-fur vest, who kept one hand on her child's head and the other gripping three huge shopping bags from Bergdorf's, rather more tightly.

"I saved you this cake because you're going to be a rich and famous collector one day," Claudia cooed at the child with a beatific smile.

Ignoring her, the girl stuffed her face into a mound of glittery pink frosting while her mother looked softly on, blitzed on some unnamed prescription.

"I've been looking all over for you!"

Ingrid turned; it was Simone, fizzing with delight, clutching a bottle of Japanese beer in one hand.

"I can't thank you enough for doing all this for me."

"Oh, it's nothing!"

"I'm serious. It's unbelievable." Simone was trying to appear unfazed, but a look of disbelief kept creeping over her face. "I'm just—I couldn't have made it up, you know?"

Ingrid forced a smile back. "You're only getting the attention you deserve."

Simone searched Ingrid's face for the lie. People had only recently begun to fawn over and flatter her. The gallery types—thin and glamorous and sharp of tooth and claw—weren't her usual milieu.

"I never know when people are telling the truth," she told Ingrid, breath hot with alcohol. "But you wouldn't do that, would you? You're so honest. The most honest person I ever met," she said to herself faintly. "And I know that."

"Never," Ingrid assured her.

But that was another lie, and in a moment Ingrid realized how far she had already traveled from the world of raw ideas she'd once inhabited. Untruths came easily to her lips now: it was all about managing control, herding artists like animals in a zoo with such subtlety and diplomacy they hardly noticed the change.

I'm learning, she thought with horror.

"Simone—" she began, but Simone's eyes were flickering around the room, moving spasmodically from billionaire to editor to curator to artist and back again.

"Holy shit—that's the woman who curated that show at the Whitney. And Lary Schmaltz is here! Do you think I'll get written up in *New York*? Wouldn't that be incredible, Ingrid? Wouldn't that just be incredible?"

But they had both changed, Ingrid realized, with a dizzying sensation. And there was no going back.

She followed Simone's gaze. The biggest art critic in New York was scrutinizing her largest oil painting.

"This just feels absolutely trenchant," he explained importantly to a crowd of waiting women.

Nods all around.

"Machado is expressing something that feels particularly *urgent* about the unfolding space of unreality inherent in our broken political system, into the space of being a woman. Who. Is. Alive. Today! Ladies and gentlemen, this is what activism in art looks like!"

"It's absolutely wonderful," one of the women murmured.

"In the age of Trump, is there anything more powerful, more necessary for the modern artist and collector? Than to stand, to stand unflinching and pay witness?"

His gaze roved from face to face. He appeared to be waiting for a response. The women watched him in silence. Then, slowly, he removed his glasses.

"I, personally, think not."

There was a sudden wild rush toward the painting, a morbid horde of skeletal Issey Miyake–wearing women clawing and gnashing their bleached teeth. Ingrid saw a credit card fly into the air as someone tried to press it into Rita's hands. "I want that painting," the woman was saying. "I want everything available by Simone Machado, now."

"Unfortunately it's already been offered to a significant institution," Rita said smoothly. "So sorry to tell you."

Ingrid felt relaxed, even physically numb. It was true that the rich were like other people, as she had told Simone. But it was also true that they weren't. Everything about them seemed honed to a white marble, monochrome, bloodless by nature. She watched them scramble for the paintings. Some of the wives called Rita just to talk. Out of loneliness. Just then, she did not envy them. The frictions, all those everyday flare-ups over money and problems—a part of life for her and for everyone she knew—could also feel like a connection to the rest of the world. Like reality, and perhaps they felt its absence. It reminded you that you were human.

Someone nudged her shoulder.

"Everything's going great, isn't it?" Claudia said, her teeth gleaming brilliantly inside her mouth. She smelled like sex and roses. "I've already been asked for two different interviews. Simone is such a hit. She's already being called the voice of a generation. Can you believe it?" She gazed at Ingrid. "I'd be good in an interview, don't you think? Paul says I'd be perfect."

"Of course."

Ingrid coughed. It always disconcerted her when Claudia sought her approval.

"You know." She summoned her courage. "I actually think I've found someone. For Simone's last unsold painting."

"Who?" Claudia's eyes narrowed to slits.

"Charlie Erroll."

At Claudia's silence, Ingrid rushed in. "I just, I, ah, I thought it might be good press?" she squeaked. "She, I mean his wife, is on the board of the Brooklyn Museum—and he writes that art column. What do you think?"

"How do you know the Errolls?" Claudia asked, smiling. "They're huge collectors."

"Oh, he's an old friend of Rudolph's."

Claudia's glazed smile was becoming more and more dangerous. Ingrid tried to backtrack.

"Of course, only if it's okay with you, if you haven't already—"

Suddenly Claudia's doll-like eyes sharpened into focus. Her long red fingernails tightened around Ingrid's wrist, bruising it.

"Ingrid, let me offer you some advice," she whispered. "I've had a few people work for me who have sadly had to leave. They now work in shitty little suburban galleries in places like Orange County or Palm Beach or fucking Atlantic City, do you get me? And that's all because, unfortunately, they didn't know their roles, their *place*. The thing is, Simone is my artist. Mine. I found her. I'm saying all this because I really want to *help* you, all right? I just want you to understand your *place*. You do not try and get into sales, no matter who your fucking boyfriend is. Do you get that? Do you feel like you understand your *place* a little bit more now?"

Ingrid blinked. But Claudia had already swiveled around by the time Ingrid had time to digest what she was saying. She saw Claudia wrap her arms around a stiff, frail-looking collector, guiding the elderly woman to a chair with a daughterly smile.

It was time to go to the airport.

The opening reception was shifting now. It was dropping its stiffness, more young strangers were gatecrashing, drinking all the beer, and Paul was smiling tolerantly because he knew they were the sign of a good party. A tabloid had arrived. People were having fun, starting to get that hazy, bright-eyed look of free alcohol, as Ingrid made her way outside.

The spring air was cool at night. Ingrid huddled in her denim coat, waiting with her suitcase. People were smoking and discussing whether it was the right move to go to the Jane. But Paris was calling, Rudolph was calling.

She watched a girl in skintight jeans try to throw up behind a cab. She was making tiny choking sounds, like a strangled cat, while her laughing friends tried to film her.

"Body positivity!" she bellowed, briefly surging to her feet and throwing a peace sign into the air. Then a thin green stream of vomit came hurling out of her mouth, spattering on the gum-encrusted sidewalk in a bilious mess of acid and white wine.

"Immaculate," her friend said, clapping. He began zooming in on the video, setting the surge of vomit to a dubstep track, repeating quietly to himself, "Viral, viral, immaculate."

Ingrid got into her cab. She pressed her face to the cold window. Outside the little cars were going by. Moving fast, in the other direction, toward the deathless green-and-amber sparkle of the city. For a moment only, the whole chandelier hung bright in her mind: all the restaurants, the streetlamps, the millions of lives. In a second she imagined the whole flight of time. Where the river met hay, where the fresh blue-green breast of land had once existed, wild and untamed, before the roaring untrammeled ugliness of the highway rose up to seize it; memory swallowed it all, but Ingrid could imagine. Then the taxi raced forward, past the dark gleam of the horizon; until, like diamonds growing rapidly in reverse, one by one, to specks of carbon dust, she watched the tunnel snuff out the lights.

20

IT WAS 11:00 A.M. AND SUNNY BY THE TIME INGRID ROLLED HER
battered nylon carry-on into the crowded baggage hall at Charles de
Gaulle. The room seemed to breed relief: stiff Parisian parents greeted
returning university students; rows of businessmen marched out of the
tunnels, shaking off the stale airplane smell of fuel and carbonated farts.
Ingrid watched them turn on their phones, a look of renewed energy
tightening the faces she had seen become loose and exhausted in sleep.
Only Rudolph wasn't here, she realized, searching the crowd for his
angular figure.

Minutes passed. He wasn't here, he wasn't here, he wasn't here,
and the ensuing disappointment sliced through her like cold metal.
Ingrid waited at the carousel, watching the abandoned suitcases rotate
round and round. Should she call someone? But there was no one she
wanted to call but her mother.

Suddenly her spine began to prickle with an alien knowledge;
the chattering airport voices faded to a blue haze of nothingness.
He came up behind her and slowly unwound the thin cotton scarf
around her neck, cupping his hands gently against the back of her
head as if she were made of something thin and breakable. Ceramic,
maybe, or glass.

"Should we go?" he said, kneading her hip. "Forgive me for being
so late. I was stuck in this interminable meeting with the advisors for
the Pinaults."

It wasn't a question, she thought as she stared up at him—tall and
auburn and radiating the June sunlight in his cool white sweater—but

of course, she forgave him. Right then she would have forgiven him anything.

They would, Rudolph decided, drop off their bags and go straight to lunch. Ingrid, sleepless with exhaustion and dazzled by the bright mosaic of streets, allowed herself to be led to the wine bar on the Rue des Petits-Champs, though Rudolph seemed tense and edgy, double-checking the swerving roads with an eagle-eyed stare as they walked.

At the wine bar, a certain stilted strangeness seemed to freeze their attempts at conversation. They ordered Sancerre. Ingrid drank quickly.

Before Rudolph, Ingrid had tended toward guys who wore black T-shirts and frequented independent bookstores. They were, quite publicly, into film. Weekends, they went to the IFC and read Foucault, Adorno, n+1. If you weren't aware of these things, not to worry. They would remind you.

Rudolph was different. The way he walked and talked sometimes reminded her of a charming little sailboat, its billowing white sails propelled by sun and wind alone. Rarely delving beneath the surface—why should he? The world's mine, he seemed to say; I own it. Me. His arrogant good looks had already bewitched the bar, people half-turning in their seats to let their eyes linger. It made her want to lean on his shoulder in the middle of the street, exulting in the glance of passersby recognizing that she was his and he, hers, she alone bathed in his rosewater perfume of luck and confidence. But now his face looked almost shocked, like an awkward boy who'd frozen up and lost his power of speech. Could he be having second thoughts? Or just the natural anxiety of their first trip together?

The silence had gone from odd to suffocating when it was broken.

"You should try the duck pithiviers—" he said, just as she said in a rush, "Have you read the news today?" thinking to broaden their conversation with some casual talk about the State of Our Democracy or Sino-American relations. It was the wrong thing to say.

"I haven't gotten around to it yet."

Ingrid picked at the duck pithiviers, whatever that was. It was delicious—tender and flaky and encrusted with a thin layer of sea salt—but in her nervousness she could barely taste it.

"How do you speak such good French?" she tried again.

"Why do you ask so many questions?" he snapped. "Sorry. God, I'm sorry, that was super uncalled-for. It's just—it's been a stressful day at work."

"Anything you want to talk about?"

"Oh no no no, it's totally fine." He sighed. "I learned French at boarding school. Anyway, it's always useful, isn't it? I have a couple of business interests in Geneva."

Ingrid leaned forward. "Switzerland is so creepy to me. Paul says eighty percent of all art is just, like, hidden in storage containers there. Like a ghost town."

"Oh sure." He touched his mouth with a cloth napkin, smoothing away an errant blot of grease. "You can hide anything in Geneva. It's the craziest place—more like a display window than a real city. Cash, gold, jewels, guns, anything that can be liquidated. Kinda makes me wonder who my dad was, but, you know, I told you how weird my mom gets."

"Will I ever meet this famous mother?"

"Oh, obviously. I'll probably go up and see her this summer, actually. I'd love an ally."

He smiled shyly at her, and she began to relax. The ice between them was cracking, frozen pieces shifting into something more like the romantic trip she'd fantasized about.

"But you haven't thought this through at all. What if this trip's a complete disaster? You'll have to disinvite me."

"I guess I'll just have to cross that bridge once I come to it."
They both laughed, as if he were joking.

After lunch, Rudolph decided to buy Ingrid some new clothes. Ingrid protested; she wanted to go to Brancusi's studio, and anyway, she was uncomfortable with him buying her expensive things. But he insisted, his voice taking on a hostile edge:

"What's the point of going to Paris if you don't go shopping?"

She kept looking at him in a hurt way as they walked along the Avenue Montaigne, offended he didn't think her current wardrobe was up to scratch. Oh, well, he thought, keeping his eyes locked ahead. Get used to it.

Inside the sea-green walls of Prada, salespeople fluttered around Ingrid, crowing over her beauty. Rudolph sat on the velvet sofa designed for waiting spouses, imagining a better, more improved Ingrid in the new clothes: warmer and more malleable, more toothlessly tender Winona Ryder in *Autumn in New York* than judgy, diffident, critical Winona in *Girl, Interrupted*. Because disquietingly, a more ambiguous emotion had replaced the unmitigated awe she'd once showered him with. Sometimes he was frightened by her clever eyes, scrutinizing him.

But it was too late, he realized with mild shock; he'd gone much, much further than planned, too far past the critical threshold to press the escape button. He wanted to swell up like a bantam rooster even as he wanted to beg for her approval, he couldn't bear to think of her secretly mocking him behind his back—

Don't laugh at me, please!

"*Mais cela est incroyable,*" he heard a saleswoman say.

Ingrid's double stood reflected in the glass, her dark eyes fixed on his. The black dress made her look taller, thinner, its backless silk plunge decorated with a single silver chain to show off her long expanse of pallid spine under the colorless lights. Suddenly she seemed like all those other girls in high school who'd ignored him, who'd left his texts on READ, and he was overcome by a deep fear that she would leave him. For who? Why? Didn't matter. One day she would be there and gone, that was all. He hated her for it, absolutely despised her, and he had a brief hallucination of twisting the silly chain around her throat and strangling her right on the dressing room floor, how her eyes would fly open in surprise and the saleswomen would scatter madly like hens—

Let me be happy! he pleaded with the demon inside him.

"Do you like it?" she asked.

He rose to his feet. "I think it's great. Let's get it."

Curling his knuckles at the saleswoman:

"Can you wrap that up? And we'll take this, this, and this too."

At the cash register, he offered his gleaming Chase Sapphire card for the saleswoman to run through the machine. Each swipe of his credit card was like a religious ritual in miniature, a quick burst of celestial calm and happiness that only lasted fifteen minutes. Some vision of himself, zen and perfected, seemed to grow closer with every purchase, a joyful completed man bounding off into the sunset—one more thing, he always promised himself, one more thing and I'll have all the things I could ever need . . .

"I'm sorry, sir. This card doesn't seem to be working."

Reality was a cold snap. Ingrid looked at him strangely. *Let's just go,* he heard her say. *We don't have to get it.* The saleswoman's smile had cooled by one or two degrees.

"Try this one," he said, handing her another. *Fuck you.*

His feet felt bolted to the floor as they waited for the card to go through. What if the banks cut me off? No, that's crazy. They can't do that, I'm making money, I'm successful, but what if—

"Thank you, Mr. Sullivan. That's all set for you."

Everybody was smiling now.

They left the store carrying five thousand dollars' worth of clothes, crisp sea-green boxes wrapped in featherweight tissue and satin ribbons. It was funny what money could do to a room, he thought with a touch of sadness. Fix things, change things. Instill fresh love in an anxious girlfriend's heart. How bad would it be if all his cards had gotten declined? Though neither of them would've ever admitted it, he feared it would have ruined things for good. An odor of unalterable awkwardness would have seeped into their vacation, spoiling the taste of fresh love like milk gone sour in the fridge.

Money was who he was, what he had to offer to the world.

All the more reason to carry out his plan. Not that he could stop the cogs from turning now, not even if he desperately wanted to.

21

WHAT A PERFECT NIGHT! EVERYWHERE THEY WENT, YOUNG AND OLD Parisians lounged under striped awnings bejeweling the city like spots of amber, smoking and laughing and drinking wine, their serpentine language swirling beneath the dusty sky. As they trotted down the Place de la Concorde, Ingrid admired the white Haussmann buildings edged in soot, each embroidered with black strips of iron balcony curling upward.

"It doesn't go public for another week," Rudolph assured her, quickening his pace as they walked to the Palais des Beaux-Arts. "This is for patrons only. Very exclusive."

Small trash fires flickered where the homeless warmed their ragged hands. Immigrants bundled under threadbare tapestries of old coats and aluminum tents against the cool June night. Rudolph's eyes slid innocently by; you couldn't spend so much time in big cities without becoming used to the dizzying gap between opulence and rank poverty.

One man with wild, haunted eyes held out his hands, wordlessly asking for a cigarette. Ingrid gave him one but shook her head when he asked for change, though she had cash in her bag. There is nothing, she told herself firmly, that you can do.

"Paris can be so dirty" was Rudolph's only comment.

They rounded the corner toward the pale marble block of the museum. Rudolph halted in shadow, gazing up at the light. Velvety crimson curtains stood sentinel at the window, guarding a thousand precious trophies; the golden melody of voices and violins and the gentle clink of champagne glasses floated down.

Ingrid watched him in silence, vaguely unnerved.

"Should we go in?"

The sound of her voice startled him; he swiveled around with an odd blank look, as if she were a stranger. Then the spell was broken; they were climbing up the stone staircase, through Corinthian pillars the height of elephants, into the waiting flood of light.

Globalization ensured that the wealthiest of the West looked everywhere the same. Still, many of the guests looked vaguely European in that rich, scrawny, elderly way: high sophistication combined with distressing hints of bad postwar nutrition, or a life lived on leek soup. Brittle women glided past in black or beige cashmere and silk, their husbands tottering after them, gold cuff links flashing dead feudal names from brown-spotted hands.

"Champagne?"

Rudolph plucked a glass out of the waiter's hand. Like a celebrity, he had the trick of switching himself on; now he blazed with light and laughter under the crystal chandeliers. Pinching Ingrid's elbow, he steered her over to a French heiress he'd met at Art Basel and had been pursuing as a client ever since.

"Catherine? Catherine Langlois? How amazing to see you here! When was the last time I saw you—that conference at Basel?"

"Oh God! You were so bored you started eating a bratwurst. That conference really was disgustingly dull, wasn't it?"

A flurry of catching-up talk; Ingrid tuned out. Then she heard the woman say: "And this is . . . ?" glancing doubtfully at her own person as if unsure whether she was an escort or a maid.

"Oh, this is Ingrid. Ingrid, Catherine."

He wrapped an arm around Ingrid's stiff shoulders. All in all, Ingrid was a good plus-one; but sometimes, just sometimes, it'd be better if he could make moves alone.

"Bonsoir," Catherine replied, making no move to kiss Ingrid hello. Her accent was just heavy enough to be sexy, Ingrid noted, and though she looked around fifty she was beautifully well-preserved: thin as a blade of flint in her black Armani suit, with the ramrod posture of a former ballerina.

"I didn't know that you were a Bowes fan, Catherine," Rudolph was saying. "Doesn't seem your style, somehow."

"Mm. No. But Grégoire contributed to the museum's new wing, and . . ." An elegant shrug, making it clear she'd only deigned to come for everyone else's benefit. "You know how it is. I actually find Bowes a bit—how would you say it?—ugly. Klutzy. *Provincial*," she uttered finally. The kiss of death.

"Don't hold yourself back now," he joked.

"When I have a portrait painted, I want it to flatter. His sitters are so *disgracieux* and ugly, it's all a bit . . . *retardataire*." She sighed. "I suppose the realists, like the poor, will always be with us."

Ingrid, standing quietly, soon noticed that Rudolph was not-so-subtly flirting with the older woman, laughing at everything she said. Steady, flattering eye contact, the kind of unbroken gaze she might have thought meant he was utterly fascinated by Catherine Langlois, if she hadn't just seen him do the same with the person behind her.

"You have one of the best collections I've ever seen in my life," he said, gazing at her with pupils black and swollen like a hypnotist's.

"Rudolph. You always know how to flatter." Catherine poked him flirtatiously in the chest.

"No, it's true! I've never met anyone so well-versed as you are, Catherine—I mean, you should be writing monographs on this stuff. Honestly!" he exclaimed to her delighted crow of disbelief. "I was just poring over a monograph on Guyton last week thinking, how much better would this be if they'd asked Catherine Langlois to write the foreword? Who else has grappled with the work like you have?"

"It's true I've really worked hard on the family collection. Ugh, it's become positively cheerless these days to chase down new work!"

She let out a world-weary sigh. Women like Catherine Langlois loved to talk about how hard they worked, with a staff of six and no job save the charity circuit.

"But Rudolph," she added to Ingrid, "is absolutely everywhere at once. Every party, every art fair." Pause. "Flitting so quickly between cities! Like a little time traveler."

"Oh?"

"Though less so, these days. There are about a hundred women on the circuit from Hong Kong to Miami who must be missing you right now." Laughing. "What are you doing, shutting yourself up in Manhattan?"

"It does feel a little empty without you there!"

Ingrid's throat was seizing up with jealousy and disgust. The dogged pace of their mutual masturbation, all so fake and boring—fuck this! If he wanted to flirt with another woman right in front of her—

She muttered something about the bathroom and fled the room. Over her shoulder she heard Catherine Langlois say, "Oh yes. Then Verbier, of course. Will you be there for the Hauser charity thing?"

"Of course," Rudolph replied, and she could hear the relaxed smile in his voice.

Ingrid locked herself in the bathroom, retched up champagne. She sat on the toilet for a good twenty minutes, half-listening to some Russian woman natter on the phone, trying to convince herself to go back outside. Even the bathrooms in this place shimmered with gilt, golden basins; carved swan taps, lifting up their burnished throats to be twisted. And though she knew it was just tacky painted gilt, like anything you'd see in New York, under her eyes it glowed with the unimpeachable light of the real.

* * *

Rudolph was sweating inside his charcoal Anderson & Sheppard suit. Catherine Langlois was a sure thing—her husband had come over to ruin their conversation, but not before they'd fixed a date to talk about buying a couple of paintings. Oh, she was eager all right! he thought speculatively. Husband thirty years older, puffy old windbag with a bright red nose and a gimp leg. Clearly she's got a lot of needs going unmet, he thought.

He scanned the room, looking for someone else to talk to.

Spotting Olivier d'Erlanger across the room, he made his way toward the chairman, who smiled at him, whispering: "Just in time!" The glittering room swayed in his field of vision. Exhaustion—jet lag, another white-knuckled sleepless night, fear revolving round his heart—was becoming more and more difficult to cut with his ADHD pills. He felt panicky, uncouth even—but nothing showed, not from the outside.

D'Erlanger tapped his wineglass with a little gold fork. The crowd hushed.

"I'd like to thank you all for coming here tonight," he said in French, his fundraising voice rolling richly outward like melted chocolate. "To thank you all for endowing the exhibition with your patronage. Because, like Rauschenberg in Europe or Lucian Freud in America, we believe that Europe has not fully understood Bill Bowes's work. Until now. I myself have been painted by Bowes—yes, me!—and there was nothing, but nothing more shocking than seeing my own visage exposed like a piece of meat! Warts and all!"

Polite laughter, the sounds of toasting. The crowd didn't quite know what to make of this, though all congratulated themselves for supporting an artist as radical as d'Erlanger made him out to be.

"These portraits have always had the power to shock," d'Erlanger continued. "Critics accused Bowes of being a common hack, photographing the most average people off the street. But I think that resistance lay in fear. You see, Bowes carves up his subjects' angst, their humiliation, in sagging weak chins and base desires. It's frightening to confront the truth about ourselves, n'est-ce pas? Bowes celebrates the anti-ideal. He stares into the void of the self."

Smatters of real applause. Rudolph remembered seeing his first Bowes painting at the Institute of Contemporary Art in Boston at sixteen, the way it had made him feel so naked, so exposed. Looking at Bowes's work was like acknowledging something basically repulsive about yourself, something you tried hard not to think about. He found it strangely soothing to think that others, too, had secret shames, hidden in the night.

Where was Ingrid? He suddenly realized she was absent, missing his triumph. You're not paying your part of the bargain, he thought with a surge of rage. Why do you think I bought you all the clothes, the jewelry?

"I would like to thank all of the patrons who contributed to the exhibition," d'Erlanger announced, smiling. He ticked them off: rich industrialists, banking tycoons . . . the woman having an affair with the tech billionaire . . . third-generation grocery store scions . . . Rudolph was dizzy with greed to hear his own name.

Ingrid appeared behind an older woman, looking pale-faced. "Where the fuck were you?" he hissed, grabbing her arm. His voice sounded needy and raw, even to his own ears. "You're missing it! They're just about to announce my donation to the museum."

"I was in the bathroom."

"Frederick Asaka has donated one of the most significant works in the exhibition to our permanent collection, *Portrait of Elinor Ripley*, from 1979. Rudolph Sullivan, a tireless champion of Bowes on the commercial side of the art world, is here to present the painting. Mr. Sullivan, thank you! What an honor it is to have you here with us tonight!"

He swished one arm dramatically downward. Invisible hands whisked the navy curtain away, spotlights trained on a hidden portrait: a nude woman looking out at the viewer, arms hugging her knees. Ingrid felt cold. Something familiar in that weary expression, almost exhausted—

"Is there anything more important in the Western tradition," d'Erlanger suggested, coolly eyeing the woman's painted breasts, "than capturing the female form at its peak?"

Heart in throat, Rudolph watched d'Erlanger raise his wineglass.

"I know I speak for the whole of the museum in thanking you, Mr. Sullivan, for your support."

Everyone in the room was beaming at him now. He felt famous in exactly the way he wanted to be, known only by everyone in the know. Rudolph toasted the chairman back, smiling so broadly he half-expected his teeth to tear his cheeks open, split through the muscle-covered pads of grit and blood right down to the bone.

22

INGRID LAY IN BED A FEW MINUTES AFTER WAKING, LUXURIATING IN a shaft of sunlight streaming through the open window. The creamy sheets felt warm and forgiving under her airplane-knotted back; sprigged blue toile curtains floated in the cool continental breeze. Beside her, Rudolph snored in a plush pile of gold-edged pillows. The hotel was pure spectacle, the kind of place Saudi princes stashed their mistresses on shopping trips to Paris with their wives.

A knock on the door startled her; a uniformed bellhop in black, pushing a domed silver cart. "Your husband asked for breakfast to be delivered to the room at nine," he explained to Ingrid's questioning look, and even after last night's irritation the word thrilled her: *husband*.

"Would you like this set up on the balcony?"

"It's a little cloudy, isn't it?"

"Oh no," the bellhop assured her. "From this suite you have the best view in all of Paris."

With the grace of a matador he shook the tablecloth out into the air and fanned it over the balcony table, arranging plate after plate of golden croissants and raisin-studded sugar pastries, delicate smoked salmon curled up like pink babies. She watched with the faint shame and excitement she always felt around hotel staff, unnerved by their obsequiousness, secretly feeling closer to employee than guest. Finally he left. Ingrid poured herself a cup of coffee. For thirty minutes she sat on the balcony, admiring the Parisian skyline and thinking about the day to come. Then Rudolph moaned in his sleep.

"What is it?" she asked, getting up and shaking him awake.

"Work dream," he mumbled, rolling away.

"About what?"

"You left me. You didn't want me anymore."

He buried his face in the crook of her neck, her terry cloth bathrobe growing damp with his tears. "You do love me for real, don't you?" he added plaintively, his pool-green eyes growing red and watery. "You're not just faking it?"

Ingrid was puzzled; she felt guilty but didn't know why.

"Rudolph, you're not making sense. I'm here now." His head lay on her chest. Ingrid petted his hair, feeling moved and also a bit disgusted. It was like holding a big overgrown child who had cried himself to sleep.

"Did you like the breakfast?" he asked.

"Oh," she said in surprise. "It was great. I was just expecting us to get a croissant from a bakery or something." And seeing his eyes open wide with sadness, like a little boy who's gotten a bad grade, she assured him hastily: "No, no, but I loved it. Honestly."

"You sure?" he asked shyly, needy for approval. "You said you never saw the Eiffel Tower. I only want you to have the best, you know."

On impulse, she kissed his cheek. He wrapped his arms around her, and they had slow, forgiving sex under the pale azure sky of the canopy, last night's argument forgotten.

Ingrid watched the pearly motes of dust rise from the carpet, Rudolph's head settling into the soft curve of her thigh like a small furry animal seeking comfort.

Sometimes it was as if they were operating on two different planes of reality: brief moments of real, honest emotion undercut with a sort of enforced stage-acting that felt difficult to break away from. She'd always had trouble relating to men without some sort of script, a guideline of jokes and niceties cobbled together from books and movies and women's magazines telling her what to say and when. Now I want to throw out the script, she realized with a start, but some hard knot of coldness prevented her. What lived under the script was raw as meat, it had never seen the light. Gone was her ambivalence, passivity, indifference—now she experienced every pleasure as a future pain, the fear of separation.

"I'm not the sort of person who feels comfortable around people," she whispered to him, thinking he was sleeping.

But he was awake. "Neither am I," he said, seeming to register her surprise. Leaning over the piles of pillows he bit her lip, savagely, enough for her to flinch.

Then he was leaping up from the bed as if it had never happened, tearing pants and a polo shirt out of the wardrobe where they'd been pressed and hung by some nameless entity. "We're going to the countryside," he declared. "Get dressed."

She went off to shower. The bathroom filled with steam. As the mirror fogged up, she noticed a red smear in the reflection. It was hers, she realized with a vague unease: on the shoulder of her towel robe, where Rudolph had wiped his bloodied mouth.

Fontainebleau was one of Rudolph's favorite historic sites and Ingrid had never been; plus it was a good chance to test out his dormant driving skills. Hell, he'd even rented a jazzy little Alfa Romeo for the occasion, glossy wet red like the bright maraschino cherries in the Shirley Temples his mother used to order for him at the bar. He'd sit under the barstools, drinking them one after another, waiting and waiting for her to be ready to go home.

Away from the city heat, the summer wind blew a warm violent perfume of spruce trees and gasoline over their faces when Rudolph rolled down the windows. They pressed out of traffic down the long broad highway to Perthes, stopping for coffee and gas about thirty miles outside Paris. The high quality of French gas stations impressed Ingrid, a far cry from the shit-covered tributaries watering the average American highway.

The bulky weight of his phone pressed into the seat of his pants, hard and discomfiting. He felt strained and jerky; he kept glancing at Ingrid. When the phone rang Rudolph snatched it up like he'd been waiting all day for Asaka's shrill, sharp bleat.

"How are ya, Rudy?"

Rudolph exhaled in relief. "David." David Gibson was an art dealer who worked at one of the biggest galleries in New York. They often swapped difficult-to-sell paintings that the other might have a client for—pocketing a double commission along the way, natch.

"Watching the game today?"

"I wish."

Actually Rudolph didn't watch sports. But David was a big football fan, and around such men Rudolph felt a desperate desire to impress with his masculinity that went straight back to middle school. *I am normal, fuck you!* He made his voice sound deeper, laughing. "I'm with my girlfriend in Paris right now."

This was partly for Ingrid's benefit; after the museum gala last night she had stormed around the hotel room, too inexperienced to see his conversation with Catherine Langlois as the empty courtship ritual it was.

"How about you?"

Gibson laughed. "Oh, I'm in Sag."

"Yeah?"

"Uh-huh. Surprised not to see you at the Surf Shack last night." Rudolph could hear rap music and shouts of laughter in the background. "Leo's having a party right now. Lotta girls here, I have to say."

Rudolph experienced a deep twitch of resentment, that old restlessness telling him to move, go. *He* should be in fucking Sag

Harbor! *He* should be in Sag Harbor partying on Leo's boat, not running museum donation errands around Paris for goddamn Frederick Asaka.

"Huh," Rudolph said breezily. "Cool. Well, hope you're having fun. We're about to go for a private tour of Fontainebleau—I'm thinking of buying a similar place nearby—so let me know if the service cuts out."

But David wasn't in the mood for a dick-measuring contest, not today. Suddenly businesslike, he cut in:

"Rudy, I actually wanted to talk to you about the Twombly we mentioned last week. Remember? Big old late work, about sixty inches wide, from the *Coronation of Sesostris* cycle. Whaddaya think?"

Rudolph considered. He knew the series well—in fact, he'd written an essay on the ten-part work in college. They were iconic paintings, typical Twombly, an Italophile from Kentucky who had taken care to always be photographed in white linen suits. Rudolph appreciated a guy who could brand himself. Twombly had been obsessed with the classics, translating their epics to the canvas in wild scribbles of charcoal paint: warring gods and men, Bronze Age migrations from the smoldering ruins of Troy to the empty plains of Rome-before-Rome. *Coronation of Sesostris* was about a mythical Egyptian pharaoh who had died in battle, rowing his funeral barge into the land of the dead. According to legend, though, he'd later come back to life. Twombly modeled his journey on the sun god Ra, who rode his chariot to the heavens, day after day, in a cycle that ran from morning until night. Growth. Decline. And then—resurrection.

Yes, Rudolph had a few ideas for buyers, and he told David as much.

"I thought you might."

"It's yours?"

"Nah, but we've got a two-year contract to sell it. Texan couple owns it—guy owns some fast-fashion company. Wife only wears The Row, obviously."

"Not the Carlisles, is it? Big Trump donors, aren't they?"

"Yeah, well, they're from Dallas. It is what it is." Rudolph could almost hear his indifferent shrug on the other end of the line. "If you get beyond the man's vulgarity, of course, you've gotta admit that his tax policies are a real step up from Obama. I donated to the campaign myself, not ashamed to admit it. 'Cause at the end of the day, I'm just looking out for who's going to be best for my assets."

Rudolph made a noise of acknowledgment. He was afraid to openly agree in front of Ingrid, whose ears were already twitching with curiosity.

"Well, thanks for thinking of me, David. Appreciate it. What're we thinking, six-month agreement?"

"Yeah, yeah, we can extend it if needed. I will send a guy over tomorrow—you do want it in London, don't you?"

"Definitely. The buyer I'm thinking of is a Frenchwoman." He felt Ingrid's gaze rest on him briefly. "Money comes from vacuum cleaners, you believe that?"

"Oh, without a doubt. You'd never think of all the money that comes out of these humdrum fucking appliances—one of my best clients is the owner of a multinational toilet paper company."

"Everybody's gotta wipe their ass."

Gibson laughed appreciatively, and Rudolph laughed along with him. It was the kind of dumb low-caliber joke he'd grown up around in his seedy Boston suburb, one he'd never dare to make in his current circles. But David was different, slightly chippier, a short, hostile Atlantic City guy who reacted to the extreme wealth of his clients with a kind of subtle sustained macho vulgarity matched only by his aggressive pursuit of a sale. *Prove it, you slick fuck. You a man or what?*

"You're a good guy, Rudy. Thanks a lot for doing this."

"No problem at all. Hey, we bag the sale I'll take you out to a game."

"You got it. Talk soon."

Rudolph felt Ingrid staring at him as he put the phone down. "What?" he said irritably, glancing over.

"I thought we were on vacation. You've barely said a word to me."

"Oh God. Don't be so dramatic."

"I'm just an accessory to you! Your work dominates the room, wherever we go."

He looked over at her, all tensed up and fragile like an anxious pet. She's the only person in the world who really needs me, he thought, the only person who cares, and some tight balled-up knot inside of him loosened. He reached for her hand.

"Hey, I'm sorry. One more call and I'll be yours all day, okay?"

She shot him a grateful glance. Trying to be as quick as he could, he called Madison to ask for a sales essay on the Twombly, stat. Not too lyrical, he instructed; and by God make it sound expensive!

"The Egyptian pharaoh Sesostris—you got this?—conquered all of Asia Minor and made his way into Europe. The Greeks say he conquered the whole world. Even erected a pillar in one capital with a vulva on it to make fun of how the other side fought like women. 'Kay? Actually, no, take that out, I don't need to get skewered online by some fucking feminazis for using real historical details in a press release . . ."

He could hear Madison typing rapidly on the other end of the phone. "Okay, thanks. Do you want the draft by tomorrow?"

He looked over at Ingrid, her tense shoulders. Quickly he came to a decision.

"No need. I'm offline the rest of the week."

At Fontainebleau, they walked slowly arm-in-arm toward the sprawling château, stopping every few minutes to examine a shop window or exchange a kiss under the cool shade of an awning. It was a student city even in the summer months, filled with rangy young people eating gelato or sipping pints of beer as they leaned against the stone walls casting slow desultory glances at the passing tourists.

"Did I hear you talking about Trump donors on the phone?"

"Yes. David Gibson is one, apparently."

Ingrid shook her head. "What a sham. At least artists are rebelling against the administration. Trying to make a statement."

He eyed her. Wanting to puncture her little rose-tinted bubble.

"Lots of people in the art world support him," he said deliberately. "Lots of rich people, lots of people in general who just want a tax break, artists who aren't as heroic as you think behind closed doors. Because nobody is. Or maybe to shove it to the people who think you need to go to Harvard Business School to get the job done. There's a simmering rage out there, don't you get it? All these fake liberals in cultural institutions mouthing off about how vulgar Trump is, his terrible etiquette . . . it's totally empty, dinner-party chatter." He sneered into the breeze. "Because the entire system runs on exclusion and elitism. To the core."

Ingrid shuddered. "That makes me sick to hear."

"But look who was elected, Ingrid. Be realistic about what Americans really think. Trump sees a worm; he encourages it to squirm out of the apple. You, you're trying to pretend the worm doesn't exist. That will never work. The worm grows bigger and bigger until it develops teeth, a maw."

She sighed. "I hate it when you talk like that. It feels so nihilistic—like you don't ever believe things can really change."

"Nihilism just makes sense though, doesn't it? The Earth will probably heat up and explode before our kids reach adulthood, right?"

She looked at the sun. It shone on the green gardens all around them, the palace's pride, cultivated for centuries for such vivid blue and red flowers to grow.

"I try to vote for the earth," she said eventually. "There are artists whose work is worthy and good. They are struggling. What about supporting them?"

He laughed harshly. "First of all, I don't give a shit about anyone's career but my own. I'm only looking at value. And most of the rising artists you're talking about are a flash in the pan. I want the sure thing."

"But aren't you ever worried that a push toward diversity could damage all those old white guys you're so into?"

"No way," he assured her. "Not in any serious, long-term way. It's a wave, that's all. A mad rush to exploit the prices of Black, brown, women artists to cover up deeper structural problems, yadda yadda yadda. And I'm all for new artists succeeding—but when it comes to the past, history's already been written."

What if a new history is written? Ingrid wanted to ask. But she sensed Rudolph had reached his limit. He was rubbing his eyes, the sun white-hot, stifling against his strained facial muscles.

"Let's talk about something else, okay?"

"All right. I'm boring you."

"Nooo," he said soothingly. "I think it's great that you care so much. And I care too, all right? But I also want to enjoy our vacation. Trump will still be waiting by the time we get back. God knows we won't have missed anything."

They fell silent as they approached the castle. It was too beautiful to argue, too beautiful to do anything but gape.

Napoleon's gold eagles blazed from spear-topped gates. Fontaine-bleau was a sand-colored palace cut around a manicured green court-yard, built by a dozen different monarchs but somehow coalescing into a captivating whole. Friends again, they wandered from room to room, taking in the furniture encrusted with treasures. Honeycombed walls intricately carved with crescent moons of Diane de Poitiers and her lover, the king; Directoire chairs tightly embroidered with imperial flowers. Immense marble gods and goddesses leapt from the walls. Marie Antoinette's delicate Turkish boudoir shimmered like a mother-of-pearl oyster in silver silk.

Yesterday on Rue du Mont-Thabor he'd spied a sparkling diamond bracelet so extravagant he'd itched to buy it for Ingrid. It was like something Marie Antoinette would have worn on a casual Friday, dashing around the Petit Trianon in her fake peasant gowns with her little lambs dyed pink and purple like Easter eggs. *Let them eat cake!* Rolling around in the grass laughing while the real peasants outside munched on maggot-chewn black bread and got their sticks and torches ready. No wonder they'd cut off her head, the jealous cunts . . .

"Can you believe people actually lived here?" he heard Ingrid saying, her eyes wide with awe.

"I can."

He could imagine it all. Walking into the tiny yellow jewel box of a theater in buttery puffed satin: Empress Josephine, swishing into a midnight showing of *Orpheus*; stiff-necked Nazis clicking their polished heels in heavily medaled military jackets, the theater of Vichy collaborators electric with desire to please their false masters.

At least the aristocracy of the past had to be on show. They'd performed a ritual service, dutifully exposing their babies in gold carriages for the roaring pleasure of the mob. People needed a spectacle—they wanted to see the lives they could not live—but oh what a dangerous game! Because sometimes your eyes rejected so much shine. Then it was time to tear things apart, howling for death to purge yourself of this flurry of images that represented your own exile from the divine.

His clients hid in darkness to avoid this fate. They paid for their search results to be wiped off the internet, their money nestled tight as a matryoshka doll at the bottom of a dozen shell companies. Yet they exercised the wealth and power of ancient kings. Just substitute the fading tapestries for a tech titan's Zen waterfall or plaything of a private museum, the baroque grandeur for cold blocks of steel and glass. It was easy to decorate like Marie Antoinette when you had no fear of the guillotine.

Ingrid said it reminded her of paparazzi photos of Putin's palace, but Rudolph had a faraway look on his face. He was remembering the past. Nothing so dispiriting as the long bleak drive to dingy Roxbury as he watched the happy faces of his cousins fade out of sight. Crouched in his dark twin bed, he'd listen to the shrieking neighborhood kids play kick-the-can, neither knowing nor caring that he was Rudolph Sullivan. A thousand, a million times he preferred to lose himself inside the vivid, fantastical, baroque books on the Italian Renaissance that he had stolen from his uncle's house—pressing his face with delight to their yellowing pages under the blue glow of the nightlight. All the tension in the world seemed compressed into that one electrifying moment: God, rushing toward Adam from the roaring red cauldron of heaven, ready to animate his lifeless body with the spark of one arched-out hand. If only Rudolph had such power. If only he could escape into the vaulted blue sky of that painting, swallow up all the knowledge in the world in one long greedy gulp.

They decided to take a detour toward Blois on the way back, to a vineyard in the Loire Valley reachable only by rambling dirt road. A weather-beaten old vintner fed them pungent saucisson studded with peppercorns, tiny glasses of Anjou Rouge. Though Rudolph longed to drink every drop, he pushed the glasses over to Ingrid, saying he needed to drive.

Maybe I should camp out in France a while, he thought idly as he watched her bite into the charcuterie. Asaka, the gallery, all of New York would fade into nonexistence. Suddenly his heart ached for the phantom cottage at Fontainebleau, the perfect place to leave everything behind.

"I've been thinking of buying a little château," he said carelessly to Ingrid. "Maybe in Auvergne. What do you think? We could open up a bed-and-breakfast. You could paint."

She laughed. "I'm sure my boss would love that."

"Maybe that will change."

"How would it?"

He gave a nonchalant shrug. But she was right; it could never work. Where was the energy there, the verve? Who would see him? David Gibson would be sitting on Leonardo DiCaprio's boat while Rudolph gardened in the dirt like some perverted old man.

They left the vineyard with a bottle of olive oil and six cases of wine.

Only once they'd finally gotten back to the hotel room that night did Rudolph allow himself to do the thing he'd been itching and burning to do for several days now.

First he went to the minibar and slowly, ritualistically poured himself a stiff drink. Grey Goose martini. Three olives. Twist of lemon.

Sipping it, he perched awkwardly below the French windows to watch Ingrid sleep. He even got up, pacing restlessly around the room, to check her breathing, but she was out cold; he'd made sure of it, slipped an Ativan in her drink. He envied the type of rest she must be having right now.

Thus assured, he went to his suitcase and removed the second cell phone tucked into an interior pocket. Opened it. He scrolled past the other apps before finding the small, dated-looking bank icon he was looking for. At last the numbers flashed up on the screen before his eyes, and they were everything he'd hoped for, anticipated. Two point eight five million—he let out a sigh of relief. It was enough. Along with the spare cash in the gallery bank account and what was left from the Bélizaire sale, it would be enough. Quickly he executed the transfer, then stepped gingerly into the dark hallway.

"I've got your money, okay? Are we done here?"

He heard Asaka chuckle, low as the drawl of a saxophone, and once again he wondered uneasily: Who are you, Frederick Asaka? That terrible drop in his stomach when Asaka suggested, *I've got some friends—successful businessmen I thought you might like*—it was knee-jerk, the gut instinct of a cornered animal.

"You got lucky, huh?"

In the skewed reflection of a picture frame, his own face looked blurred. The toile wallpaper strained sickly green in his vision, acid chartreuse his old Freudian art history teachers might have said. The color of psychosis. But when he spoke, his voice was controlled.

"You could say that."

Tiptoeing back into the room, he undressed and slid into bed beside Ingrid. She was asleep. In the moonlight, a single curl sliced across her temple in a dark arabesque. He brushed it carefully out of her face, thinking she was very beautiful in the dark. Then he tried his best, his very very best, to go to sleep.

23

HALF OF INGRID STILL FELT FOUR THOUSAND MILES AWAY AS SHE maneuvered into the gallery brownstone on West 20th on Monday morning, a shelf of coffees from the deli balanced on her hip. The empty motions of another workday—greeting the receptionist, rearranging fresh flowers in the lobby—felt robotic, the whir of a machine on autopilot. Inside she was still sifting through scenes of recent memory, weighing them up like jewels under a loupe.

Paris had run on like a pastel-tinted dream: the hotel, the sunshine, wandering around the Jardin des Tuileries. "No more fuckups—we're going to the bakery every day this week," Rudolph had promised after the failed hotel breakfast. He'd brushed scattered crumbs off her jacket; almond cookies, they'd eaten almond cookies every day.

People walked out of one life and into another all the time without realizing it, but it was rare to recognize the precise moment of transition. Of irreparable crossing between paths. In Paris, Ingrid had sensed it. She had held her breath, hoping and hoping these tall medieval churches would usher her into a place where she would always be this happy.

Stepping out of the elevator, Ingrid noticed the air was strangely frigid in the office, a sharp twenty-degree drop from the June heat outside. Only the white noise of the air conditioner buzzed over the muffled din of honking cars.

"Hello?"

She peered into Claudia's cubicle, then Rita's. Both were vacant.

"Ingrid."

Rita materialized in the doorway, framed in her black clothes by the gray light leaking through the windows. Her face was pale and unreadable.

"Hey!" Ingrid perched on her desk, eager to catch up on everything she had missed. "How's it been here? Did Simone's exhibition sell out?"

At first Rita did not reply. She was watching Ingrid with a strange, withdrawn expression under her big dark sunglasses.

"Look, Paul wants to see you," she said finally.

"About Simone?"

Rita eyed her for a full second. She paused at the door. Usually, Ingrid thought with a queer sense of misgiving, she would've asked me about my trip by now.

"To be honest," she said slowly, "I don't really know."

Ingrid had once read a short story in which an American woman and her daughter go on holiday to a hotel in Paris. A few days into their trip, the woman comes down with a strange fever. Her daughter goes to buy medicine at the pharmacy, and when she comes back, the hotel is gone. Her mother gone with it.

A new hotel, with a different name, stands in its place. This hotel is blue, not yellow; the interior is completely different. Even the street numbers have changed. The doctor they'd seen doesn't recognize her; nor does he remember the mother. Their names and passports appear in neither the hotel log nor the French customs system. It's as if they never entered the country at all.

The event is inexplicable. The daughter looks and looks and looks for her mother, but there is no trace of her presence. She simply no longer exists. Defeated, exhausted by grief, the daughter returns to America, but she never finds her mother again.

After her own mother died, Ingrid had to move from St. Louis to Chicago to live in the home of the father she barely knew. She read the story over and over, hurting herself with it: the only person on earth who seemed to know or care that her beloved mother had died and was never coming back. Everyone else forgot things so quickly.

Later, she read the author had based the story on a tale he'd heard about a freak incidence of bubonic plague in 1920s Paris. The mother died after being bitten by a rabid rat while the girl was out at the pharmacy. Police were called; strict orders handed down from the French government. Together, all—doctors, lawyers, police, and hotel staff—rapidly conspired to stamp out a potential city-wide panic by erasing every trace of the infected guest's presence.

Now she remembered the story again. The dry shock of it: going on an ordinary errand in the morning and locked out of your own life by nightfall. Because for all practical intents and purposes—and life is made up of them—the truth only existed if other people believed in it too.

Ingrid followed Rita to the polished rosewood boardroom upstairs, where Paul held his most important meetings. The silence was deafening, brittle now, but Ingrid told herself everyone was probably in the Hamptons. The office always emptied out during the summer, didn't it? Didn't it?

"Ingrid. Sit down."

Paul was leaning back in a leather chair at the end of the long, long table, seeming very tall and far away. His back was to the sky. Unwillingly Ingrid's eyes drifted to the open window: the little cars moving jerkily through midmorning traffic like flying gravel. Paul's crisp navy suit was unusually rumpled, his eyes bloodshot as if he hadn't slept in days. Must be the new baby, Ingrid told herself, but that same strange choking feeling wrapped itself tight around her throat.

"Ingrid," she heard him say again.

She tried to smile at Paul, to catch his eye, but his eyes were roving around the room and he didn't reply. His fingers were curled viselike around a black mug of coffee emblazoned with the *New Yorker* logo.

"I'm sorry, Paul, I was just about to bring in your coffee—"

"Sit down."

She sat. A switch seemed to have been flicked; there was no sound in the frigid room. The hair on her arms prickled against the low constant hum of the air conditioner.

"What's going on?" she asked.

"Claudia," Paul called out. "Get in here."

The slow click of Claudia's heels, muffled in the soft carpet, moving nearer and nearer.

She heard Paul say something about an email. An error in judgment. No choice in the matter.

At this point Ingrid's vision darkened. A single pinprick of light illuminated Paul, speaking angrily at the end of the conference table, waving his arms about while Claudia sat silently behind him, eyes glued to her phone. Ingrid could see her fingers flying across the keyboard, texting, telling somebody about someone, something, and Ingrid suddenly understood that it was her own scandal causing some unknown recipient's eyes to fly open in titillated shock.

"—been linked to unauthorized activity."

"—have to explain that there's been a data breach to the clients. We've tried to get forensic accounting to track down the money, but it's very complicated—"

"—tracked as far as the Channel Islands. But we can't go any further."

Why is this room so cold, Ingrid caught herself thinking.

"Can anybody turn off the AC?" she managed, teeth chattering.

"Are you even listening to what I'm saying?" Paul shouted.

Claudia smoothed down her leopard-print suede skirt. Ingrid watched her lean toward Paul, whisper something in his ear, using her long white hands to smother the sound. The flash of her gleaming nails, sharp and poisonously red. When he turned back toward Ingrid, Paul's pale blue eyes were cold.

"So. Do you understand?"

"Understand?" she echoed stupidly.

"It's quite clear that you can no longer work here."

"But I swear to God I've done nothing wrong!" Ingrid cried. "Claudia asked me to wire the client transfer, I mean—I know we're supposed to check with Finance, but she's asked me to do it late several times—"

"That's a preposterous lie," Claudia cut in with an acid glare.

Shock gripped Ingrid's chest, then panic, terror. She was struggling across the table, trying to show him the emails—show the proof—

The phone flew across the conference table and skittered to a jerky stop in front of Paul. Paul made a move to reach for it, but Ingrid watched Claudia place a delicate hand on his arm to stop him.

Paul sighed.

"No, Ingrid, I'm sorry. It's hard for me to believe that a nice kid like you could get wrapped up in this, but here we are. Best-case scenario, you did something perilously stupid—worst case, you've stolen almost three million dollars." He shot Claudia a look. "Now, whatever anyone else may think, I can't believe you masterminded this scam, but . . ." Sighing, he looked almost regretful.

"But how are we going to explain this, I ask you? I won't even be able to pay my staff this month. That's how bad this is. We've had to report it to the FBI."

"Wait, Paul—let me explain—"

Claudia was smiling a glassy, false smile at her; even she, Ingrid noted foggily, seemed discomfited by this meeting.

"We'll need to take that, too," Paul said in a remote voice, indicating her cell phone with a jerk of his head. He was too dignified to reach for it, but that too was implied.

"Right now?"

"It may be relevant to the agency's investigation."

Paul was looking over her head. His face was blank. Tears were swimming behind her eyes; she had never felt so desperate, in so much disbelief that they were behaving like this, like they didn't even recognize her.

"Please," she heard herself say. "I really don't want to leave."

For a second Paul examined her as though there might be something to forgive. Then he sighed again. This time, it was the executioner's sigh.

"Don from Security will come with you to get your things."

They believe I've committed a crime, she realized with brief, stinging clarity.

She licked her lips. "Can I talk to—"

Paul looked at her. "Of course, you can understand why we'd prefer to keep things quieter. But Don will send anything of relevance forward. From your desk."

"What about Simone?" she asked helplessly. "Are you going to—"

Claudia barked with laughter. "Simone's a gallery artist now."

"I'm sorry," Paul said briefly. "This whole thing is just extremely unfortunate."

Slowly she got up from her chair and made her way back to her desk, somehow remaining upright while Claudia shadowed her down the stairs about three feet behind. Rita's wide-eyed face loomed up from a great distance, distorted like in a funhouse mirror, saying, "What happened?" But all the wires in Ingrid's head seemed to twist together and she couldn't respond. Carefully she placed into her purse the uneaten ham-and-cheese bodega croissant she'd brought for lunch.

The security officer watched her do it with his arms silently folded across his chest, in case she was tempted to make a scene. Everyone else was watching.

There wasn't much else to do than shoulder her bag and leave.

Twenty minutes late to dinner already, and not answering her phone, either. Rudolph had locked himself into a red leather booth at the back of the restaurant. He was holding a gin martini like it was the only thing tethering his muscles to Earth. Truth be told he'd expected this, just not so very soon.

It should've been easy to forget your troubles at Minetta Tavern. Pink and green neon signs glowed in the warm summer darkness; inside, the familiar atmosphere of lamps and crisp tablecloths transported guests to a clubbier and more manageable New York of old, where accents were regional and small-town dreams could still land big-time glamour. Now everyone sounded like they were from Calabasas. Now you had to pay thirty-six dollars for a burger to feel you were living in that imaginary past for an hour, only an hour—but people would pay that price, any price for nostalgia, as he knew so well.

He made a few quick calls: updating David Gibson on a couple of clients who seemed interested in the Twombly. New directions for Madison on an Anselm Kiefer. A typically effusive yet awkward email from his mother, inviting him to the Cape for a couple of weeks with Lyndon and the cousins. Fuck, no.

Eight-thirty now. Had something happened to Ingrid?

Trying to distract himself, he began composing a careful refusal to Eloise—*I'm so sorry, Mom*, the word stiff and unwieldy in his mouth, *I would've loved to come but work's crazy right now*—when he realized with a flicker of irritation that this time, no bullshit, he might actually have to go. Three years since he'd been home . . . and most important, though he hated to admit it—Lyndon would be trapped at the Big

House all of August like an insect pinned to a board. Surely he wouldn't say no to an investment opportunity now, with all of Rudolph's recent success . . .

Eight forty-five. Forty-five minutes late . . . what if something had happened to her? What if she'd been hit by a car, pushed in front of a train by some schizo, stabbed for her wallet in Times Square? He was really starting to worry now—Then suddenly Ingrid was in the doorway, drenched with rain.

She was crying.

"You're late," he said.

"Am I? I hardly noticed." Her face was covered in streaks of mascara; she scrubbed at it rapidly with one knuckle. She wore the frantic, out-of-it look of someone too focused on their own failures to notice what was really happening. "They took my—they took my phone. And then I was wandering all around Chelsea for hours, I didn't—I didn't know what to do."

"What happened? What are you talking about?" He tried to arrange his face into some semblance of casual shock; finding this ineffective, he reached out and gripped her arm. "You're scaring me!" he barked like a bad actor. "What the hell is going on?"

"It was the transfer," she babbled. In a muddled stream it all came out: "Remember that transfer I told you about—Claudia asking me to transfer almost three million dollars to her client, right before the opening . . . They said it wasn't her. It was someone else, Rudolph. Someone else sent that email, we—they don't know who. And now it's just lost, gone. Completely irreversible."

"And they fired you for this?"

Behind Ingrid, the waitress was approaching; he discreetly shook his head, and she wheeled around with a sympathetic look over her shoulder.

"Yes! As if I were nothing to them. As if I hadn't worked there for almost two years! In less than ten minutes they'd escorted me out of the building," she cried. "They took away my keys, my phone—"

She was shaking, in that state of humiliation so deep that you can only repeat yourself over and over like an automaton, hoping against hope that someone believes you.

"They thought I had something to do with it," she sobbed. "That I—I stole the money."

"How could they think that?" he said, drawing himself up in a righteous fury. "You know, I bet it was the Russians or Chinese. Just look how they got into Hillary's emails . . . think of Edward Snowden," he added darkly, as if the CIA might be involved.

"I just feel so blindsided."

"Look, Ingrid. It's devastating, but try not to take it personally. You did nothing wrong. These people are ex-KGB, professional hackers. They rip Grandma off for millions every day." He took another sip of his martini.

"I just, I thought everything was beginning to make sense. You know? A job I actually liked, Simone—you . . ."

"Come on," he said with a trace of irritation. "You hated that job."

"I didn't hate it!" Ingrid took a ragged breath of air. "It was complicated, sure. Like any job. But they were nice to me—they were people, just like anybody else."

No one is *just like* anybody else, Rudolph thought, his guilt leaching away; he really *had* saved her, swept her away from a toxic environment she was simply too naive to see. Claudia had wanted her dead; he'd seen it as soon as he took one look at her. It was only a matter of time. He reached for her hands and said soothingly:

"You're right. And I'm sorry—look, fuck these people, right? They're terrible people! This is going to be a new beginning. Because

Paul and Claudia, they seemed like awful, awful people. They didn't understand you, did they? They would've never let you rise, not in the way you deserve."

"I do feel like Claudia had something to do with this," she reflected, and he nodded urgently in agreement. *Yes, yes, yes!* "It just seems like her all over. So sketchy—like, how could this person have known how to frame the email in such a plausible way? But I don't think I could ever prove it. Ugh, how am I ever going to find another job again?"

He made some reassuring noises, but the industry was small. People would talk. It would be difficult indeed, and the roiling nausea of guilt was lurching around his stomach again. Suddenly his tongue detached unplanned from his brain.

"What if you stopped trying?"

She lifted her face and stared, black tears spilling like ink.

"Trying to what?"

He licked his lips; they were bone dry.

"Trying to get a job. Look." He seized her hand across the table. "I've been thinking. You could move to London with me."

"To London?"

She was still looking at him with that blank, stunned expression. He wanted to offer her a Kleenex, but he didn't have any. So he kept going, the words spilling out:

"I'm getting a little sick of the New York environment, you know what I mean? It's disgusting—so shrill. So dirty. And the people, so superior. They think they're so much better than you, you know? It's like the whole city's an enormous goddamn purity contest and you just can't get it right."

He broke out into a harsh, rasping laugh, and for a minute surprise flashed over her face. Quickly he went on:

"Rent's skyrocketing. Pollution's out of control. Subway's filthy, buildings are too tall to see the sun . . . People act like this is the best city in the whole world, and I'm sick of it. Besides, my whole Rolodex is mostly based in Europe. I'll need to put a lot more energy into the London gallery anyway, especially with the Bowes show opening in a few months."

"But what about the New York gallery?"

"Oh, I'm not worried. I'll fly back and forth, manage it from afar. And"—a sudden brain wave—"I'll make Madison my deputy."

"Madison. Your assistant Madison?"

"Don't act so shocked. She's pretty qualified. She went to Barnard for Christ's sake."

"That's not what I'm talking about." Ingrid stared at him. Her face was bloodless. "I just don't know what to say. Your idea is crazy."

"How so?"

"I don't have a job, I don't have a visa—" She started wringing her hands; he could tell that she was about to start crying again. "We'll have to split up—"

"I love you, Ingrid," he said recklessly, and suddenly it seemed imperative that he convince her, right here, right now. "I can't imagine my life without you. Not there, not anywhere."

"But what about my career? What about—"

"We'll create one for you. In London. I have so many connections there, I can get you a job in like two seconds." He snapped his fingers to demonstrate. "Or you could try your hand at being an artist again. Why not give it some oxygen? Really breathe some life into your paintings?"

She said nothing. Now, he thought, is the moment to play my trump card. Slowly, deliberately, he said:

"Listen, Ingrid. Your career here in New York is finished. At least for right now. It's a small industry, and word gets around. If they think you had anything to do with this . . ." He trailed off and shook his head, once, solemnly. "And I know you had nothing to do with it, but that's not what they'll think, unfortunately. It's best to just move on."

"I still don't have a work permit, though."

"So come as my fiancée."

She stared at him with wide-open eyes.

"What are you saying?"

The snippet of metal from the wine cork was still lying on the table between them: in a single smooth gesture, Rudolph picked it up and twisted it neatly around her finger.

"Let's get married. And before you ask, yes, I'm being serious."

"For a visa? That's not the most romantic proposal I've ever heard."

But a tremulous smile was emerging on her lips. She wanted to say yes, he could see it.

"Marry me."

He was getting hungry now. He wanted her to agree already, because the waitress was walking toward them, and he'd already waited an hour to order a bacon cheeseburger on bleu. Ingrid touched the makeshift ring, admiring its dull sheen under the yellow lights.

"Say yes," he said, looking her in the eye and squeezing her hands. "I love you, I can't live without you, and I need you to come to London with me, Ingrid. What do you say?"

As he held Ingrid's shaking body close, feeling her tears of happiness stain his shirt, he watched a group of pink-cheeked tourists trying to look sophisticated. They were probably the best and brightest of their class, from some crappy Podunk town in Florida or Ohio. The prettiest and most athletic too, even if they felt in their heart of hearts that they didn't quite fit in. They'd watched *Sex and the City*, they'd read *Bright Lights, Big City*, they'd saved up and packed the U-Haul thinking determinedly *I will make my mark*.

What they didn't realize was that they couldn't afford it, not now, not ever. What they didn't realize was that this city would chew them up and spit them out when they were emotionally bankrupt and no longer young. What they didn't realize was that this city was nothing but a scam, a dream of a place that never existed outside of some stupid writer's head.

Later that night, lying in bed with Ingrid asleep beside him, he tried to analyze what he had done. What he'd set into motion. After she'd said yes, after they'd ordered another bottle and he'd told the waitress they were getting married, after someone brought over cake and champagne and the sloppy jubilant kiss under the vivid neon glow on Carmine Street—his mind kept ticking.

Maybe it had seemed rushed and irrational—even if it had *felt* spontaneous enough—but something inside him had been percolating, gathering, taking shape for a while now. And it wasn't just guilt, he reasoned. No, he'd never let himself be led by an emotion as shallow as that. He'd promised himself, after the squirmy thing with Father Dean all those years ago—and he still wore the cross out of sheer superstition—but Rudolph had decided right there and then that religion had nothing to offer him. Christianity was for poors and sentimental women, people unable to confront the Void. The truth was that you died alone, and then there was nothing.

He had a different god now. But he still got lonely sometimes—nobody'd told him how cold and goddamn lonely this life could be.

The marriage made perfect sense the more he thought about it. Business was beginning to get a little uncomfortable for him in New York; the bank calling on his loan, suppliers at the gallery . . . Better to move, get out, leave.

And what better way to usher in a new year of stability, grace, and financial success than a beautiful new wife? Why not? Wasn't marriage a feudal arrangement, a deliberate decision to combine strengths, to build a thick stone fortress between yourself and all the world's fearsome attacks? He could use that right now.

How it would change the way people looked at him! They would see a man who was finally *established*: no longer a feckless playboy but a pillar of society and family life. Ingrid would be the antidote to all that messiness. Quiet, but smart enough to talk to people at dinner parties. Pretty but nothing tacky, nothing like Cornelia. Her artistic aspirations would be the bohemian feather in his luxurious velvet cap.

And he owed her one, didn't he—

How smoothly it had all gone! Really, he couldn't believe he hadn't thought of it before.

Any traces of guilt, he thought as he watched the red dawn rise, would be quickly expunged in the warm and pleasant glow of newlywed happiness.

24

WHEN PEOPLE ASKED INGRID HOW LONG SHE PLANNED TO STAY IN London, she said forever.

This at least was true: the whole idea of New York filled her with an indelible embarrassment now. She expected people to ask why she was leaving her job, and she had an answer ready: It just didn't feel enough like *me*, a classically vague millennial answer to which there could be no response. How could you argue against lack of passion? No one would ever waste time trying to breathe life into a dead heart.

"But then you'll be dependent on a man," Julia said, her nose wrinkling in disapproval. "Why don't you stay here? Find another job, keep trying to do art on the side?"

Daisy, for her part, was irked that Ingrid wanted to go to London instead of LA, where Daisy had decided to set up a skincare brand inspired by the zodiac with the last dregs of her trust fund.

What choice do I have? Ingrid wanted to ask. I have six hundred dollars left in my checking account, no healthcare, no way to pay my student loans. Office jobs were just like she'd read in Houellebecq: dull and draining, thankless in the end.

"It kind of just feels like you're giving up," Julia said. "Like the world's too big to confront, and you're too afraid of failure, so you're hiding away with your rich husband in your cute little cave. Nothing can be your decision, you're a victim of fate—"

"I plan on practicing Marxism in the domestic sphere, that's all."

Ingrid told everyone this in the same flat giggle, to show she knew very well her participation in the most ancient of dynamics, *she knew that*, and yet she would remain herself. Always.

"Yeah, whatever." Julia sighed. She chewed her gum with a hard, dissatisfied look. "But what do you actually want out of life?"

The only thing Ingrid had ever wanted to do was become an artist. What was so bad about being a kept woman if she could finally do what she'd longed to do? What was so bad about choosing love, adventure—even tragedy, as long as it was colorful? Leaving New York was not so much an acceptance as a refusal to be swept away by the banal currents of a predictable future. The drab beige life of her parents in their drab beige suburb, every day the same—no. It just wasn't for her.

A passionate love. The excitement of the unknown—that was what she wanted. And the world would reward her for her sacrifice, or at least she hoped so.

Still, Julia's questions prickled at her, rubbing away at some sugar crust of denial. She remembered her mother leaning over her as a child. Insisting, with the fierce shining eyes of a woman who'd had her own regrets after the divorce: *You need to make your own money. It's up to you to rise. Men will try to put you down, but think of all the women who'd die for your opportunities—*

She recalled old CNN frames of Iraq, Afghanistan, blown-up villages and gunfire, devastated people watching the alien khaki tanks roll by. The invading army erected schools, universities for girls to attend. Earn their own money, agency, power. The American way.

What do you want?

She remembered Lenin, Marx, Engels in the college rearview mirror. The books of struggle made sense to her imagination: the capitalists, the unhappy masses, she could see them all around her, in the stained and straw-haired men who slept on the train. How could adults just sit around watching? Why didn't they do something about the poverty, the unfairness all around them? How certain she'd been of busting out of art school, guns firing, catapulting into fame like Rothko or Kandinsky!

Doubts crippled her when she moved to New York. The distant dazzle of towers, it suggested a human addiction to inequality that she felt powerless to change. At some point, her beliefs had withered to empty aphorisms in the mouth. Maybe they'd never been strong. Now she and her friends donned watered-down New Left talking points like glittering dresses at a party, discarded when they got home.

Ingrid had always been conscious of these dualities. Hypocrisies, dissonances, ugly truths her friends refused to see. But her guilt was never strong enough to stop herself from doing the same, even though she wanted to. Now she saw her whole future unfolding, youthful brokenness scrabbling up against adult precarity, this endless sucking feeling at the end of the month. But when she thought about being with Rudolph forever, everything felt sunny.

There was just one fly in the ointment, and that fly looked a lot like Julia. It wriggled around in Ingrid's brain, smirking at her with Julia's patronizing face. Julia was a journalist, her think pieces fierce and argumentative, questioning the environment, urging specific change. Julia would only date writers, changemakers. Julia was standing on her own two feet, hard as it was. Julia had integrity, while Ingrid was a coward, afraid to face life on her own terms.

What do you want?

After Paris, the apartment on Myrtle Avenue had seemed especially cramped. Ingrid went to the florist. She had been hoping to re-create the Jardin du Luxembourg. Beds of peonies, sprawling roses, irises. But flowers were too expensive, so she compromised: green ficus and ferns, cacti and ivy.

You're too much of a purist, Ingrid argued with the Julia in her mind. Purists could never see where self-evident truths faltered so badly when subjected to rigorous examination. Painting perspective 101: life curves where the laws of physics have ruled straight lines.

But I thought you were a purist, too.

Ingrid looked at the plants now. They sat on her windowsill, wilting slightly. The room was dark. Framed by the pigeon shit, they seemed so small, small and bright and vaguely pathetic. The sight depressed her: they seemed so thirsty for water and air.

So did I.

Then it made her angry. Those plants couldn't grow here; those plants needed light.

June passed into July. Things had significantly slowed down since the initial flurry of packing. Her clothes were hastily unfolded into Rudolph's closet; she found someone to replace her on the Bushwick lease.

In August, a veil of sweat descended on the city. The sun beat down on the burning pavement, trash bags crawled with insects slurping up the rotting remains of milk shakes, shit-covered diapers, old crusts of pizza. The city had a garbage problem and people wrinkled their noses at the putrid stink, which hung rich as melted toffee in the shimmering air. *I hate this city*—you heard it all the time.

Alone, in the airy white halls of Rudolph's Christopher Street apartment, Ingrid looked down at the sweating people dragging themselves to work. A refreshing change. She went out and bought flowers, huge and pristine, with stems so crisp they arched into the air like something you could hold on to.

Jubilation won out among her family. Considering the gravity of her decision, their approval surprised her, but then they'd largely laid her aside long ago, resigned to losing her, like all ambitious daughters, to the grinding mechanical jaw of the city. Her father's new nuclear family was difficult to breach. They viewed the idea of her settling down with someone who *would take care of her* with the unexpected relief of one who finally finds an old sock they lost a while ago behind the washing machine.

Her stepmother, Lina—who had always viewed Ingrid with a vague if well-meaning sense of surprise—even offered to host an engagement party for them. "In New York or Chicago, wherever you want. Within reason, of course! We can make it really fun, really girlie!"

Then, surprisingly, her apparent joy had collapsed into sadness.

"Oh, Ingrid, I'm really going to miss you," she wept.

Ingrid, listening to her cry with real shock, decided that this was Lina's pent-up, confused guilt rushing out. Lina knew she hadn't quite done Ingrid right, hadn't given this motherless stepchild the love she needed all those years ago.

Only her father's voice went a little quiet on the phone. He'd never even met Rudolph, though she didn't know why her stomach lurched so uncomfortably at the thought. Nothing could change the fact that he had been a shadow, a timid and introverted corporate lawyer who'd left her mother when Ingrid was a baby. Their custody battle had been ugly, competitive, and her mother would stroke Ingrid's hair and talk affectionately about how boring and conservative John and Lina were, how she, *she* had always loved Ingrid best.

What's done is done, she reminded herself. It was clear that both she and her father were comfortable with the contractual terms of their polite, arm's-length relationship: an annual Passover visit to the ugly brown prerecession McMansion. Lunches at some anodyne museum café once or twice a year. He did write good birthday cards; she'd always appreciated that.

*   *   *

Rudolph was always jetting off somewhere, a fact she seemed to have missed before. The Hamptons, Ibiza, Mallorca and Milan and London. Private jet, business class. Other people's jets. Things were picking up for him—more sales, more clients. More money.

"Why are you leaving again?" She was lying on the bed she still considered *his* bed with her head propped in her hands. Watching him stuff boxers into a suitcase.

"Following a lead. Some guy owns a big nude Bowes, around 1970—his best period. It's expensive but the market's skyrocketing—if only I can wrestle it away from the family, in a couple of months it'll be worth double."

"That's great," she murmured.

Sometimes it was like they were speaking different languages. Rudolph was steel and metal, stretching into the sky, slaking his ambitions, going up and up and up while she sat in her head all day. *I thought you were going to stay home more*, she wanted to say. And: *Is this my life now?*

Glancing at her, he seemed to realize her discomfort.

"What are you going to do without me? I worry about you getting cooped up in this apartment all day."

He reached playfully over to mess up her hair, but his hands slowed to drag over the back of her neck. She stared up at him, her dark eyes large and luminous.

"I'll keep busy, don't worry. See some friends or whatever."

"Oh yeah?"

She pulled him down on the white linen sheets.

Then it was only the heat, the heat, the heat. The heat so hot and tight it seemed its flame would burn her up if they didn't have each other, right now. His arms tense and hard where she gripped them, pulling him down with her palms, his groan stifled into her sweat-soaked chest. An ambulance wailed outside, his face intent; when she closed her eyes she felt a sudden discomfort so sharp she gasped with the sensation of something firm and raw breaking apart.

"Are you okay?" he murmured, reaching down to coil a damp strand of her hair from her throat around his finger.

She nodded yes, yes, willing him to keep going.

"Do you want to stop?"

Already he was receding away, she felt the lost echo in her body like a tiny death. The nameless fear that preceded every strong emotion, sorrow or joy. She twisted her hips to keep him there; agony creased his face.

"No," she whispered. "No, I don't want to stop."

Seeing her friends was a lie; the truth was, she'd always had trouble caring about more than a few people at a time. *Let go of negative things that are taxing you mentally, emotionally, and spiritually,* the cool voice on her meditation podcast intoned. When Julia sent her a text in mid-August, Ingrid put her phone down and did not reply. Day after day she made the same slow migration from couch to kitchen to fire escape, occluding the smell of cigarettes in the rank warm air.

The thought of painting decoratively was unbearable, like some frivolous nineteenth-century housewife who gave out still lifes for fun. She would have capital *P* Purpose or nothing at all. Instead she concentrated on the flawless execution of a dozen mindless little tasks: ordering medication online, scrolling through comments on a newspaper article, taking Rudolph's suits to the cleaner's.

What do you want?

The city had eaten up her bones and merely enjoyed a light popcorn crunch. Luxuriating on the bony white couch, she felt fragile and erotically powerless, as if nothing could possibly be her responsibility or her fault.

* * *

"Let's go up to the Cape this weekend," Rudolph said one day over breakfast, his eyes fixed on a spot on the wall above Ingrid's head. His voice was vaguely accusatory, like he expected Ingrid to object. "It's too hot here. Everyone else is in the Hamptons. And," his voice became softer, "you're not feeling yourself, are you?"

She probed at a lump of blackberry jam in her oatmeal.

"Am I?"

"What do you think?"

Ingrid had no real desire to disturb her current lassitude. But, she thought despondently, there's no way to get out of this.

"I mean it's fucking ridiculous for you to have not met my family right before the wedding," he continued, growing anxious. "It's socially unacceptable, even if they are a bunch of shits."

"Do they know I'm Jewish?"

He snorted. "Come on. What does that matter?"

"I don't know. You said they were a bunch of chilly Republicans from New England, so I'm just picturing no Blacks, no Jews—"

"Don't be silly. They're not like *that*. Of course not."

Ingrid pursed her lips. She was sure that in her research on Rudolph, early on, she'd read some unflattering profile on Lyndon Sullivan—something about the racial policies he'd overseen at his golf club—but she let it drop. Silently she picked at her oatmeal while he watched her, carefully attuned to fractional changes in the atmosphere.

"You know, once we go to London, we could get a dog."

She looked up.

"A dog?"

"A dog," he repeated slowly, leaning back in his chair with a smile. "It's animal cruelty to keep a dog in a cesspool like this, you know that. They need space to run around in. But in London, I've got a yard the size of a house. It's perfect for a dog, just perfect."

"I didn't know you liked animals."

"I'll love them," he assured her. "I love them now. I just can't have them here."

"But there you can," she suggested, hopeful.

"Yes, there I can. There everything'll be perfect."

And he reached over to kiss her cheek.

25

THEY DROVE THROUGH CONNECTICUT AND RHODE ISLAND IN Rudolph's new car before reaching the Bourne Bridge at five. It was Friday afternoon, August 18.

"Cocktail hour," Rudolph said, removing a silver cocktail shaker and two glasses from the duffel bag tucked under his seat. Ingrid yelped, "Car!" and yanked the shaker out of his hands. The wheel spun.

In silent symbol of protest, she'd decided to wear head-to-toe black: big black Doc Martens, leather jeans, a black organza blouse. Rudolph had arched an eyebrow humorously at her outfit but hadn't said a word otherwise. Now he asked, "Aren't you going to put your hair up?"

"It is up," Ingrid snapped, prickly with nerves. "I'm a curly-haired Ashkenazi Jew, that okay with you?"

"Okay, okay."

He rested his palms lightly on the steering wheel, sweat coagulating on the buttery gray leather. Ingrid was becoming less manageable than intended, and it wasn't what he needed right now.

"Listen, just don't smoke around them. Okay?"

"O-kay. Don't worry," she said in a more docile tone. "I know how important this is to you."

"It's not—" Rudolph stopped. "I just don't see them very often." Weakly, he added: "Thanks, though. I appreciate it."

They reached Hyannis by six. Ingrid had watched a documentary about the Kennedys to prepare, but the grubby neon decals of Hyannis were not what she had envisioned. In faded color under the bright

Indian summer sun, letters missing here and there, they sputtered LIQUOR & BEER, PASSPORT PHOTOS IN ONE HOUR (OR LESS!) and DOLLAR STORE 50% OFF NOW! The ugly concrete sprawl of chain pharmacies and fast-food drive-ins and dying shopping malls had the same apocalyptic joylessness of any small town in America, and she noticed Rudolph's lips curl into a resentful sneer.

But then he drove further. Suddenly they were breaching the armor of a row of tall green hedges, the car slowing to a leisurely amble as they passed silent electric gates. The tall shadows of summer mansions burned against the sun's orange flames, an ancient necklace of ash-colored beaches clinging obstinately to the eroding coast.

"This is Hyannis Port." There was a note of pride in his voice. "What do you think?"

"It's like walking into *The Truman Show*," Ingrid said, watching an elderly couple in matching pastels walk a spaniel down the road. White, of course. Everybody was white.

"Well, yes."

He laughed, pleased, and put a hand on her knee.

Rudolph's uncle owned one of the largest homes, a rambling three-story colonial saltbox with a lawn like a baseball field. Neat rows of hydrangeas and rosebushes lined its ashen shingles; Ingrid glimpsed the aquamarine glimmer of a swimming pool, beyond a guesthouse the size of her childhood home.

Rudolph parked beside Lyndon's ostentatiously battered green Volvo and two five-year-old silver Audis that must belong to his cousins. Somehow his beautiful midnight blue Porsche 911 seemed out of place, trying too hard, he thought queasily, though he'd specifically chosen the least flashy color. He'd been away too long, forgotten the precise visual dialect of their pretensions.

"Let's go?" he asked.

Ingrid was brushing a stray crumb off her shirt. Looking up, she saw a copper weather vane of a roaring eagle spinning in the wind, its eyes big with fire.

"Rudolph!" a man's voice bellowed.

A symphony of family greetings filled the air. Two big blond men bounded out of the house like a pair of hyperactive golden retrievers, a blur of white teeth and thickly muscled legs pumping across the lawn in Nantucket reds to match their sunburned noses. An English mastiff galloped with them, licking Ingrid's knees with a joyful slobber. Either Hunter or Trey—she couldn't tell which—offered to carry their bags inside, and Ingrid said yes. Rudolph said he couldn't possibly allow it. They made their way through the ash-colored doorway, the dog nipping playfully at Ingrid's heels. In the neurotic seconds that followed, she made a quick map of exits, noting the vaulted ceilings and threadbare Persian carpets. A cold draft lifted the hairs at the back of her neck. Someone barked, "Close the window, the guests are here!"

Guests, Ingrid thought. So they don't consider him family.

She had a chance to wander the sunken living room while Rudolph and the cousins shouted upstairs. Bookcases lined the walls: yellowing 1970s coffee table books on the Impressionists, Giotto, Mantegna, and Perugino; heavy biographies with the names of Churchill and Roosevelt embroidered in gilt. Edward Gibbon's *Decline and Fall of the Roman Empire*. To her untutored eyes, the house reeked of old money. But Ingrid had done her research, and she remembered what she'd read about Lyndon Sullivan. It was all public information: Gatsby-like, he'd worked his way up from nothing, which meant that everything—the aging monogrammed silver, the dog hair on the needlework cushions, the banged-up Volvo in the drive—was fake. Careful clues to a four-hundred-year-old *Mayflower* history that had never existed, placed here for the benefit of people who would recognize them.

"Ingrid, I am so overjoyed to finally meet you," a woman cooed in her ear in a breathy, little-girl voice like a bad Marilyn Monroe imitation.

Spinning around, Ingrid came face-to-face with a tiny thin woman with graying blond hair, spreading her arms out in welcome from a vast muumuu of sea-green gauze. Ingrid was surprised to see her bright, desperate, hollow eyes—so different from the oppressive woman Rudolph had described. She weighed no more than a child, Ingrid realized as they embraced. But her face was strangely old as a Mesopotamian idol, puffy with alcohol, gouged out by some lifelong hurt.

"Thank you so much for inviting me, Mrs.—"

"Call me Eloise, honey. How was the drive?"

She plopped down in a leather club chair, rapping one polished pink nail smartly against a sweating Waterford crystal glass on a card table beside her. The cousins thumped downstairs, laughing and shouting behind.

"Get you a drinkie? There's gin, tonic, wine—oh, basically everything you could think of!"

Rudolph kissed his mother perfunctorily on either cheek, doing his filial duty. Ingrid had never seen him so stiff, so drained of color.

"Wine would be great, thanks."

Eloise rose to fetch it with alacrity, asking about the city, the drive, the weather.

"Long," Ingrid said, summoning her best daughter-in-law smile. "I'm so glad to be here. I've heard so much about you."

"All good things, I hope!" Eloise cawed, her eyes flicking over Rudolph's for the briefest half-second.

"We've all been dying to see who Rudolph's been hiding," said Trey.

"Finally, a woman in these parts," Hunter echoed. "Eloise does not count."

Everyone laughed. Eloise joined a second or two late, smiling from cousin to cousin, though her expression remained happy and relaxed.

Rudolph's mother shared his pale green eyes, but where his were piercing, hers were misty, somehow unfocused, as if there were things she preferred not to see.

"We're going to be great friends, I just know it," she declared, clinking her glass to Ingrid's with a smile.

"Show us the ring."

They'd arranged themselves in a circle around the living room, Hunter leaning forward with his eyebrows raised at Ingrid. Trey lounged beside him in a faded green leather chair, his muscular legs spread aggressively wide, his arm wrapped around the narrow hips of a tall woman of about thirty with honey-colored hair—Jordan, his wife. She stood tolerantly beside him, smiling at Ingrid, allowing Trey to fondle the circular thrust of her perky, spin-toned ass behind the chair.

"Stop it, you guys!" Jordan chimed. "You're scaring poor Ingrid."

"No ring, no bring."

"That's always how it was for me too," Jordan said cheerfully, shooting Ingrid a reassuring smile.

Ingrid extended her hand. Rudolph had given her the ring two weeks after the night at Minetta's, opening the velvet box with a small ironic smile and saying:

"Who can find a virtuous wife? For her worth is far above rubies."

The red stone shone on her finger, bright and oddly heavy in a dark antique setting. She wasn't used to its weight.

"Gorgeous," Jordan cooed, waving her white-nailed manicure at Ingrid to compare. "Trey and I got married on the Vineyard. Just a couple miles from here. Afterward everyone came back to my family's place—just this dinky little cottage my great-grandparents bought, like, a hundred years ago—super casual really, just oysters and champagne. But we got a good crowd. Are you guys planning something similar?"

"Nothing really—"

"As in, we haven't planned anything yet," Rudolph interposed with a quick glance. "It's been so sudden. A whirlwind romance, in the most classical sense of the word. We're definitely thinking destination wedding, though."

Were we? Ingrid echoed silently.

"Like Amalfi, something like that. Maybe a little bigger than yours," he mentioned offhandedly to Trey without looking at him.

"That would be gorgeous," Jordan bubbled. "Trey and I went to Lake Como for our honeymoon. It was amazing, though nobody even tried to speak English to us."

"I've been doing Duolingo in Italian for a couple of years," Trey added. "So I'm pretty fluent at this point."

"Whatever happened to just shouting in their ears and seeing what sticks?" a booming voice rang out. Instantly, every man in the room tensed to attention.

Lyndon Sullivan lumbered down the short flight of stairs to the living room, thumbs looped in his cowboy belt. He was a big, broad-shouldered man with the closely cropped hair and stiff upright bearing of a military commander, every square inch of him immoveable as stone. With a paternal smile affixed to his lips, he let his gaze roam around the room.

"Rudolph, my boy," he said jovially. "How are you?"

"I'm great, Lyndon. Really great."

"You mean *well*."

They embraced briefly. Watching them collide was like seeing a serpent squirm over a concrete wall: Lyndon barely moved, while Rudolph projected a reptilian discomfort.

"The prodigal nephew returns," Lyndon replied, his smile opaque. "And with a new fiancée, I see?"

New? Ingrid thought. Rudolph sat down again. He was gripping the sides of his chair like a support rail, avoiding Ingrid's gaze.

"What happened to the old one?"

"We were never really engaged, Uncle Lyndon. That was just a joke."

"Oh?" Lyndon laughed. "Sure seemed pretty serious to me. But what a pretty girl this time, Rudolph! He always had good taste," he stage-whispered to his sons, who started laughing too. "More than he could afford, even!"

Ingrid was afraid to look at Rudolph. She sensed but could not see the dark flush creeping down his cheeks.

"Remember how goofy-looking Rudy was at Deerfield?"

"The worst hand-eye!"

"I just remember Alexis Crawford saying no when he asked her to prom. Remember that?" Hunter sniggered. "He couldn't pull for shit."

"God, yeah. We all thought he was a fucking fag."

There was another little silence while Ingrid absorbed this.

"Oh, boys, don't embarrass your cousin," Lyndon said approvingly, glancing at Rudolph to gauge his reaction.

Rudolph had paled beneath his Ibiza tan. He sat with his loafers elegantly crossed at his slender ankles, offering his uncle a grim polite smile that read *I hate you.*

"Sorry, dude," Trey said with a lopsided smile, punching Rudolph lightly on the shoulder. His fat gym-enhanced pecs pulsed inside an old gray Trinity lacrosse T-shirt. "We're just busting your balls."

"Haha," Rudolph said. He cracked a forced grin, and Ingrid wanted to wrap him up and whisk him away from this malicious little family. "Very funny."

Ingrid didn't get a chance to ask Rudolph about his ex-fiancée, real or imagined. Hunter and Trey, who explained almost immediately that Trey was a nickname for Lyndon Washington Sullivan III, roped him into a game of touch football on the lawn, an activity as alien to her as she imagined a game of chess would be to them. Anyway, did she really want to know about this past fiancée, fictional or not? The jealousy might quickly become crippling.

Reassuringly, the women of the house were certainly treating Ingrid as the Chosen One. They crowded around to look at the ring in great detail, *oohing* and *aahing* when Ingrid told them about their plans to go to London. So romantic! They didn't bat an eyelid when she told them she'd quit her job and had no plans for another one: for them, she realized, it all sounded quite natural.

"Trey and I," Jordan said, arranging her white skirts over the couch with an air of significance, "agreed I'd stop working at Goldman after we got engaged. I always hated my job anyway, you know?"

"I do think the idea of loving your career is a totally late-capitalist notion."

"Totally, totally," Jordan agreed. "But first I needed security. I wanted to live like my parents lived, you know? Nothing less. And, so, like, it took a while. Basically, I was thirty-one when we got engaged—in agony, practically. But my psychiatrist always told me, Jordan, you've got to manifest the ring. And guess what? I manifested the exact four-carat, emerald-cut diamond I wanted. And I always say this to my friends!"

She raised one finger to the light, rotating each efficiently carved facet of the diamond for the other women to admire.

"Girls, you've got to *manifest* it."

Ingrid sipped her wine. She thought about Rita. At least Rita was able to walk away with her mind and integrity intact; at least Rita didn't have to swallow her tongue to get through the day. Was this her future too? No, it couldn't be. She loved Rudolph; he was so different from these people.

"Where'd you meet?" Ingrid asked.

"Trinity," Jordan smiled. "Trey was in love with me from afar, but my sorority didn't approve. He had, like, a little bit of a reputation."

She giggled, allowing her listeners time to consider her husband's remarkable sexual prowess.

"Junior year, I finally let him take me to his fraternity's spring formal. There was a little bit of back-and-forth after college—needing to sow his wild oats and stuff, but luckily . . . luckily . . . he knew I was the one. Sometimes you just have to wait it out, you know? Anyway, we were both in banking for a bit, but I quit before the wedding. Because, you know, I had to plan the entire thing for five hundred people."

"Right, right."

"It was so boring, so exhausting, and even though obviously I'm extremely privileged and was a hundred percent blessed to be in the position of being able to hire a wedding planner, it was still, like, super hard, you know? But *someone* had to do it, right?" she huffed, sharing a conspiratorial eye roll with Eloise and Ingrid. "Because it's certainly not going to be *them*."

Eloise squealed like a pig.

"Oh, Jordan. You're so naughty!"

"I'm just saying. It's true!"

Jordan let out a cackle. She raised her eyebrows at Ingrid, who smiled tentatively back.

"Trey's like a little baby. He's like, I can hang a painting! I mean, not that we need it, but . . . You know how men are. Always wanting to take action and do stuff. And then here I am, two hours later, having to call the handyman."

"I know the feeling," Ingrid lied.

"My ex-husband," Eloise cut in, "was completely useless around the house. Useless, useless! Couldn't fix a lightbulb, totally disinterested."

"Rudolph's father was Swiss, wasn't he?"

Uncertainly Eloise's eyes flicked toward Ingrid.

"Swiss? No, dear, no." Eloise giggled. "Good old American."

Ingrid leaned forward. "What happened to him?"

"Oh, who knows?" Eloise smiled, and Ingrid heard the topsy-turvy tinkle of alcohol in her laughter. "Rattling around some bar in Back Bay, probably."

"But Rudolph is part Swiss, isn't he?"

"Oh, no, that's just—"

Eloise stopped. There was a slight teetering moment: suddenly her drunkenness seemed to snap together like a button, from slipshod to tight control. Her voice became crisp.

"What was I saying? He's persona non grata in these parts anyway. And, Ingrid? I wouldn't bring him up again, not in front of Lyndon."

She mimed zipping her lips. Ingrid smiled and nodded, trying to look accommodating, but inside she felt destabilized, shaken even. Rudolph had told her his father was Swiss. Why would he lie?

"Anyway," Jordan continued. "I have so much time to do the things I want to do now, like ride my horses and garden and plan events for our homeowners' association committee in Rye, and attend to my, you know, philanthropic responsibilities." She beamed at Ingrid. "And so will you. Like, I used to just be on flipping Excel all day. How boring is that!"

Being on a homeowners' association committee sounded like the most boring thing in the world to Ingrid, possibly even more boring than Excel. She wanted to ask why Jordan didn't just lie on the couch and watch TV all day, really give in to the nothingness of pure lassitude.

"Oh, and I've gotten so into the planet since I left work. Trey just bought me this flower-arranging class, and it's totally revolutionized our dinner parties. I usually twine Madagascar roses around a thick central twig to keep them structured."

"That's fascinating," Eloise said, draining her drink.

"Also, you know," she continued, giving Ingrid a nervous glance, "we want to have a baby soon. That's the most important work you can do, right? Divorce is an epidemic these days. Looking good and, like, continuing to keep things fresh in the bedroom is so important to creating a happy home."

Nods all around.

"But, Ingrid, I need to give you the number for my facialist *before* you start organizing your wedding-planning calendar. Not that your skin isn't good, but everything could use a little work before the engagement photos, don't you think?" Jordan beamed at her. "I've got a guy who injects radioactive foreskin particles into the smile lines. It's like Chernobyl for wrinkles, trust me."

"Sounds pretty intense," Ingrid said. "Well, I've got a lot to learn, obviously. Though I'm not looking forward to planning a wedding."

"You're *not*?" Jordan exclaimed. Eloise's eyebrows darted upward in surprise.

"I mean, it's just like you said," Ingrid said, trying to regain control of herself. "It's just all so overwhelming. I kind of wish we could just elope or something."

"Oh, don't worry," Jordan said, relaxing at once. Eloise made a sympathetic humming noise. "We'll help you, of course we will! Literally reach out to me any time. Day or night. And I can give you the number for my wedding planner. Amanda found me the exact same cake that Kate Middleton used at *her* wedding and got the chefs to actually come out to the Vineyard and make it for us, using all-local gluten-free ingredients. It'll be even easier for you doing Amalfi. You might only have to fly them out from London to Bellagio."

Dinner was intended to be al fresco, laid out on the splintering pine table on the wraparound deck, but Eloise decided there were too many mosquitos. In the dining room, fat buttery lobsters sat alongside summer zucchini picked from the garden and bottle after bottle of Lyndon's favorite California zinfandel. Eloise swanned around the house, commanding the housekeeper, chivvying Lyndon's sons as if she were their mother. They seemed used to her, replying in the monosyllabic tones of teenagers, with the same brusque affection you would give an old stuffed chair. There was no sign of a Mrs. Lyndon Sullivan.

Ingrid couldn't shake the feeling that a lot had changed in the fifteen years since Rudolph left Roxbury, which he had described as a mire of dust and bottles and piled-up dishes, Eloise's unsavory boyfriends rotating in and out interchangeably. Now Eloise appeared to live in the big house, and she and Lyndon whispered into each other's ears like lovers. It was obvious to Ingrid that Rudolph's presence had somehow disturbed the fragile natural laws at work here, broken some tenuous understanding between the aging siblings.

"Are they full siblings, your mom and Lyndon?" she managed to whisper in Rudolph's ear as he carried a plate of raw hamburgers and Swiss cheese to the grill. Trey waved a smoking spatula at them cheerily.

"Huh? Half, actually. My mom's a lot younger, not that you'd really know it anymore."

"Oh."

Ingrid peered out at Lyndon and Eloise, talking alone at the edge of the deck. Blocks of ice clinked in Eloise's crystal glass, her slim white hands moving like wings while Lyndon nodded seriously in agreement.

"Why do you ask?"

"They seem very . . . in sync. I guess I just thought it was a difficult relationship. When you were a kid, I mean."

"Things have changed a lot since then." His mouth twisted. "My childhood was nothing like this. They were estranged a long time, but . . . even when they fought, they were always weirdly . . . uh . . . close."

"Yeah." Ingrid watched sister and brother hover flirtatiously around each other. "They seem very . . . attached."

"It's better now that I'm gone." He sighed. "I know it must look a little strange to outsiders."

There it was again. *Guests, outsiders.* Ingrid wondered if flower arranging classes might help her belong to this family after all.

After Rudolph went off to help grill burgers, Ingrid walked over to the edge of the deck, watching the slate-blue Atlantic splash against the silver beach below. It was quiet here. She leaned over the rotting wood railing, painting a picture in her mind: the aging sailboats, bobbing feebly over the waves. If she were to do a Turner . . .

Suddenly she became aware of a foreign presence behind her. Her discomfort grew.

"What a magical place this is," she said nervously.

"Isn't she lovely?"

Lyndon had crept up noiselessly behind her, despite his large size. His voice was low and gravelly. He was smoking a cigar, the tobacco wafting pungent trails of white smoke into the violet sky. She watched him. The shape of his head was blocky: it reminded her of the stone faces at Easter Island. In this light, the red threads in his gray hair became visible, traces of a younger man.

"I built this place in '82. But Eloise and I had been coming here, oh, every summer since we were kids. We used to race lobsters on a deck just like this one. Old fishing shack back then."

"Oh?"

"Yeah, that was fun. Most of them were thrown straight into the pot, but the fastest lobster escaped, got to live another day. We threw the winner back into the ocean, see." He laughed, a deep-bellied *harharhar.* "Survival of the fittest."

"Fun game," Ingrid commented, strangely disturbed.

"It was. Maybe a little sadistic, you could say. But the rules of the game always favor the fastest person in the room."

Guess I never got the memo, Ingrid wanted to joke, but she had a feeling he wouldn't find it amusing.

"Only Rudolph doesn't have that problem," he continued. "He's always been a little too ... quick. Needs to slow himself down. Or maybe speed up—can't quite figure out which."

"Well, he's just really ambitious. Maybe he takes after you in that way."

Ingrid saw his hands grip the railing, go white. Then he snorted with laughter.

"That kid's nothing at all like me, let me tell you."

Ingrid paused.

"He just wants you—I mean, his family to be proud of him."

Lyndon quirked an eyebrow.

"Come on. You can't really believe all that psychobabble bullshit, can you?"

"Rudolph wants artists to succeed," Ingrid said loftily, trying not to let her irritation show. "He's encouraging creativity in society, putting his money into beautiful and original things that help people find meaning in their lives. What he's doing is important. They're noble ideals—ideals I share, actually."

"Uh-huh. I sure can see why he likes you."

Delicately he pulled the cigar out of his mouth and leaned against the railing that prevented people from hurling themselves into the sea. The bush on the cliffs was dark and unyielding, prickly looking.

"I helped her, didn't I?"

Lyndon's voice was wistful, as though he were talking to himself alone.

"Nobody can say that I didn't. But she never wanted to try. Hell, my sister's problems have lasted her whole life. But she's my blood. I always—"

He cut himself off with a short, cruel laugh. His eyes were open and looking very far away.

"You'll forgive me if I'm a little stiff with all the platitudes and niceties. It's been a long time since I was an idealistic young person—I was one too, you know. Once. But there is one thing that Rudolph wants in this life, one thing anybody wants above all other things."

"No," Ingrid said quietly, wanting him to stop.

But it was too late. He continued to speak.

"Money. Filthy lucre."

He gestured out to the long white sands below, the boats and the dock and the extravagant pool house.

"He wants all that belongs to me, and more. But he will never, ever get what's mine," he sneered.

Ingrid was stunned into silence. Then the paternal mask fell like an iron curtain over his face.

"Anyway, my girl, I'm very glad to meet you. How old, did you say? Twenty-six. Ah, to be twenty-six again! Well, I'd better get cracking on that garlic butter sauce. Pleasure to chat."

He smiled, kind and fatherly. It was as if the earlier conversation had never taken place.

"Careful on that railing, now," he added, turning to leave. "The wood's rotting in places."

After dinner, everyone drifted off to their separate activities, but Eloise insisted on staying up with Ingrid. Ingrid watched her future mother-in-law get drunker and drunker as the night progressed, ten, eleven, midnight . . . Eloise, rambling about what shit luck she'd had with men. Life sure doesn't turn out the way you think it will, does it? Well, you know what they say—open your door to a good day and get ready for a bad one. Isn't it great Rudolph's found a girl like you! Of course he's got a tendency to butt heads, but men sure are stubborn creatures . . .

Ingrid wished Jordan would reappear, with her well-meaning bubble of narcissism, but she'd long since gone to bed. Eloise had that bright desperate glitter in her eyes of someone who refuses to let the night go without a fight. Finally Ingrid forced out some apology about being tired—Eloise said winkingly, "Now, I wonder why that might be?"—and excused herself.

The bed in the guest room looked cool and pristine, but Rudolph was nowhere to be found. Must be watching TV with the cousins. Ingrid slipped into the egg-yellow pajamas Richard had assured her were perfect for meeting the in-laws, brushed her teeth in the bathroom, and decided to pour herself some water. Then she realized she'd forgotten to get a glass from the kitchen. Well, everyone should be asleep now. She was tiptoeing down the stairs to the kitchen when the echo of a familiar voice froze her mid-step.

". . . ask about the possibility of investing . . ."

"If I've told you once, I've told you a thousand times!"

A silence fell, heavy with rage. She heard Rudolph murmur something in a voice too low to hear.

"What a goddamn waste to send you to that expensive school," Lyndon said audibly. "Against my better instincts. I should have let you duke it out in Roxbury. Like every other kid in your circumstances, I might add."

He said something about delusions of grandeur, but Ingrid was already fleeing up the stairs with her heart in her throat, trying to muffle her footsteps in the carpet.

Once safe in the guest room, she slipped under the faded navy quilt embroidered with stars. Her heartbeat slowed down a little. Stop creeping around, she told herself sternly as she hid under the covers. You've got to live with this fucked-up family forever now—only think how humiliated Rudolph would be if they caught you eavesdropping!

And it was true what they said, about living near the sea. Smell of salt in the sheets. The slow lapping of waves lulled her to sleep within minutes.

* * *

The next day Rudolph received an urgent work call over pancakes. They'd need to leave early: a Saturday client dinner. Apologies, flurried excuses. Very unexpected, yes. Then—hardly looking at each other for fear of acknowledging an illicit desire to flee—they packed up their bags and got in the car.

They sat in pensive silence until the dark blocks of pine trees were left behind. As the car eased its way through a bottleneck of traffic at Bourne Bridge, Rudolph slid his sunglasses on. He looked as if he were trying hard not to cry.

Ingrid thought of the family on the front porch waving goodbye, the yellow dog wagging its tail in the side-view mirror as they'd edged around the steep driveway. By chance, she'd glanced back a moment to see Lyndon, guiding Rudolph's mother into the salt-eaten house. He had one hand on the small of her back, a strange expression creasing the iron profile as he looked down at her. A devouring expression.

She considered again the red threads in his gray hair. The stiff, hawklike nose under watchful eyes. It was funny how neither of his sons had that hair.

Rudolph was looking straight ahead, his hands clamped on the steering wheel and the black sunglasses shielding his eyes. She couldn't see his face; but she could see everything around it, like a photograph with a dark stain of water blurring the center. She glanced at him, once, regarding him carefully. The cold northeastern sun glittered off his auburn hair once more.

DESCENT

26

EXCITEMENT POURED THROUGH THE AUTUMN MONTHS, COMMOTION, many shouting voices surging and gabbling together as if their lives depended on it. The crowds of art and fashion swirled endlessly from exquisite steel city to exquisite steel city, they were exhausted, they had *notaminutetospare*, but when another must-see art/climate change/conference/corporate-sponsorship event opened up, they always went. The prospect of missing out was too humiliating to even consider.

Rudolph was everywhere at once. Within weeks of arriving in London in late August, his PR team began their work. A couple of excitable puff pieces came out about a charismatic New York art dealer who was opening a big new gallery. He was invited to speak on a podcast, then an industry documentary. A sustainability conference was held by an art-fintech start-up in Düsseldorf.

He was becoming a public figure.

It made him laugh to think of how Uncle Lyndon had shaken him off. When Lyndon's own worthless cockroach sons were the most boring and vapid investment bankers imaginable, *no* talent, *no* insight or creativity, nothing to speak of for themselves. And still—!

I am doing it all, he said to himself in a fury of satisfaction. I have built an empire of millions from a steaming pile of shit alone.

His life had a sheen to it, a patina. It was going fast fast fast like the fast black cabs he hailed down the potholed tarmac of Piccadilly Road that screeched to a stop when he flung up his hand and yelled *Taxi!*, his monogrammed silver cuff links flashing in the low English sun. Then he'd clamber up into his flying chariot, disappearing inch by inch: the antique diamond pin winking in his lapel, the Italian loafers, his bronze head ducking under the roof of the car as it lurched off to his next appointment.

It was the whirl. The social whirl.

Buying, buying, buying. Selling, selling, selling.

The whirl looked like this:

Breakfast at the Wolseley. Pheasant shooting up at Fergus's estate. Lunches with the director of Frieze or the editor of *Harper's Bazaar*, dinner with clients and artists and journalists and curators and more clients descending into feverish booze-fueled benders at the three Cs: China Tang, Cecconi's, C London, table after table groaning with uneaten food. Rudolph always paid without a word, he was the soul of discretion and subtlety and charm, and his clients expected it— because the richer you got, the more things became free.

Distracted as he was by the frenetic pace of his growing business, he'd been nervous about bringing Ingrid in. She was shy and hesitant; she would require a measure of attention he did not currently possess. Their relationship so far had been a dance, laughing over drinks and dinner and vacationing in Paris and going home when they got bored. But now she would be his wife, in this lonely new city, with no friends or job or life beyond his. She wanted a simple civil ceremony, not the opulent wedding he'd imagined, and he worried about this. Worried about her. She was embarrassed about not having any friends in London, about the circumstances of her leaving New York—a faint pressure broke out above his eyelids whenever he thought about it.

What if she regretted her decision? Left him, fled home to New York? What if—God forbid—she found out that he was tiny and dull and boring, a tiny boring little man who could never be tall enough to make up for the life she'd left behind? What if he failed to excite?

What if he failed?

It was a possibility too terrible to acknowledge.

She would be happy, he decided, if only he showed her that he could support them both in the style to which he'd tacitly promised. Everything had to be pitch-perfect.

He spent days dashing around the empty house before her arrival, plumping pillows and frantically arranging violet hydrangeas in vintage Swedish vases. When Ingrid arrived in early September, he dogged her around the house, anxious for approval ("Do you like it? Do you like it?"). She roamed the vast marble bathrooms, the high corniced ceilings, the original Georgian fireplaces. Finally she sagged into the couch, looking defeated.

"It's just a lot," she said, and closed her eyes.

It was a lot, he knew this. It was a lot. In a matter of weeks, she had transformed from a downtrodden twenty-six-year-old assistant in debt, living in a roach-infested apartment in Bushwick—to broke and fired—to the pampered wife of a London multimillionaire. A city she hadn't even visited before.

Yesterday she was a caterpillar, he reminded himself. Today a butterfly, emerging dewy and confused from her chrysalis.

On the plane to the Düsseldorf climate change conference, Rudolph suddenly realized he didn't know a thing about sustainability. His entire business was premised on the shipping and flying of artwork and people across the world at insane cost to the global carbon emissions threshold. But would anyone at the conference care about such petty details?

At the conference, he spoke at great length about the importance of recycling. Of like-minded people coming together to create a better planet for the children. (Whose children?—Not the point.) He also spoke of a deep personal belief in an exciting new form of digital media.

An NFT was essentially a picture on a screen. Like a screenshot—indeed, to the naked eye there was no difference. Except for the all-important fact that NFTs could be sold for millions, whereas you could take a screenshot for free.

Actually, NFTs were even more harmful for the planet than other forms of art, because of the complex and carbon-wasteful blockchain on which they were built, but Rudolph did not waste time in mentioning this to people who had spent millions in fuel flying private to a two-day sustainability conference. People liked solutions, they liked shiny expensive new solutions.

When he finished speaking, the applause was astounding. Silver-haired businessmen came up to him, wanting to know more. "You've really *got* something," they said excitedly, pumping Rudolph's fist. The organizers had given everyone free recycled water bottles and T-shirts, and you saw people waving them virtuously about like religious totems, handing out freshly printed business cards to network the dying climate away.

Meanwhile the prices kept spinning higher and higher, the market was burning hot as a cauldron with a pure gemlike flame. The discourse was powered by an overriding sense that, somehow, five-million-dollar paintings and parties and sustainability conferences could wipe out the toxic political wasteland the Western world was generally agreed to have become. This was the real purpose of the pricing madness: an antidote, a cure. A more virtuous future.

Profit was the defining mark of merit—actually, there was no other.

Everyone congratulated themselves for being there.

27

RUDOLPH INVITED INGRID TO FRIEZE IN REGENT'S PARK, WHERE HE sat lounging in an Eames chair, leisurely sipping a green juice. In his nervousness about the upcoming Bowes exhibition, he hadn't been sleeping. People drifted quietly from booth to booth, the low tinkle of laughter interspersed with the flat patter of money negotiations. A certain anxiety had crept into people's voices—it was warm for October, too warm. Willowy women shopped for art, their faces tight and shiny as boiled sea bass, while their men flew high above the earthly world. They were planning an escape to Mars in case things down here didn't work out.

"You okay?" Rudolph asked her. "Happy?"

His eyes looked bruised under the sickly lights.

Happy? she asked herself. *Are you happy?*

"Of course," she said. "Of course I'm happy."

In truth, she felt rather tense. Unmoored. London shimmered before her, silver and green and coated in a thin layer of fog. The days stretched endlessly, like rows of blank dominoes.

At least she had Rudolph. After all those months of longing! He was hers now, all hers, and the rush of happiness felt like champagne bubbles in her throat. In bed she clung to him, but in the mornings he'd gently pry himself away. Outside he strode, tightening the buttons on his crisp new shirts, while Ingrid watched him go from the doorway, still dressed in an old terry cloth bathrobe.

The saving grace of her shell shock were her visits to Hyde Park. In the autumn sunlight, she would paint abstract watercolors, sketches really, of the swans that lingered on the lake. But it felt unnatural to start up again, and many hours in the day remained unconsumed. Work and commuting, after-work drinks with friends, the pressure of bills— she hadn't realized how much these banal routines had structured her time. She wandered blindly about the streets of London, searching for something to hang on to.

One morning she came across an article Julia had posted on Twitter profiling the upcoming sale of a newly discovered Leonardo da Vinci. Julia, she remembered, had first mentioned it about a year ago. "Such a ruin, it's literally untouchable," she'd said, laughing. "It's not even by da Vinci."

Except now people were calling it the eighth wonder of the world. Rumors swirled—it could go up to fifty, seventy, maybe even a hundred million. Chinese billionaires and Saudi princes were said to be locked in a savage battle of wills and bank accounts. The general tone was of gleeful disbelief.

Thank God for the internet. When the long, muffled afternoons rolled blankly by, the internet provided a cacophony of voices that felt almost like friends.

Lately the voices had taken on a shrill, helpless edge. A civil war was coming. Drought, fires, school shootings, threats of nuclear war. A long-awaited and painful awakening over racism. The horror, the pain, the rage out there shocked Ingrid, who resolved to put Rudolph's money to good use.

Along with the house, she decorated her social networks, donating a hundred dollars to Greenpeace, Planned Parenthood, pro bono lawyers volunteering for the ACLU, fanning out vintage red Moroccan carpets on the floors. Every dollar helped. Sometimes she couldn't resist posting her good deeds online, rallying quotes, heatedly debating the news with acquaintances as she burned her fingers on a new turquoise Le Creuset pot baking tiramisu. Perhaps *debating* was too strong a word—they mostly agreed. The algorithms had learned what she wanted to see and hear.

Occasionally, though, doubts needled. To whom was she speaking, in this wilderness of mirrors, crying out the same clarion call? Other voices, other echo chambers glinted darkly through the glass. Ingrid forgot what she had read or bought or posted less than five to ten minutes later; her outrages were easy, skin-deep, as were her excitements. The news renewed itself endlessly, a thousand times a day. It existed to be looked at.

But she was a person on the Right Side of History, with the Right Sort of Opinions, and there was a wan saintlike comfort in this knowledge despite the bleak malaise outside. In past years, Ingrid might have read news sites of different political affiliations to make up her own mind. Now, though, a new orthodoxy of purity clichés flooded the headlines—*being aware of your privilege, protecting your mental health, educating yourself*—in the finger-wagging tones of a sentimental parent. It was like everybody had suddenly convinced themselves that being comfortable was the solution to the problem. So if you read an offensive or alien tone, you should click out of it. Controversy became dangerous; it risked breaking ranks.

Many urbanites, rich, and upper-middle-class people breathed a sigh of relief when the white working class voted for Trump. It was confusing enough to a voter like Claudia to have been persuaded in the decades since Reagan to feel sorry for immigrants, minorities, and unmarried teenage mothers—but frankly their sympathies were finite, and resented being stretched too far. They'd long suspected that poor people were a bunch of badly dressed, lobotomized savages from Florida—and, finally, you could say so!

Where did those other barbarians go, whose words had become too controversial, racist, or rage-filled to live on Ingrid's internet? Plotting their plots, she assumed, as her side plotted theirs.

* * *

"Why don't you go and buy something for the living room?" Rudolph suggested, looking up from the press release the French curator had sent him for his Bill Bowes show. A gigantic, animated sculpture of colored lights loomed over the Frieze tent, the maze of white booths strangely cold beneath its fake pink glow: *YOU WILL OWN NOTHING AND YOU WILL BE HAPPY.*

The realization struck her like a tire iron. I am no longer free, she thought dizzily. He controls the money, therefore my life.

"I'm painting something, actually," she murmured, turning away to watch a pair of London art dealers.

"Look at the chum," the first art dealer complained. "D'you remember when Frieze was meant to be the antidote to all this? Damien Hirst's first install—kid without a shirt, straight out of Goldsmiths? And now he's gazing down at us from his thirty-four-million-dollar palace over Regent's Park."

"How quickly they learn," his companion deadpanned, and they laughed.

Rudolph was watching her alertly. In the past few weeks he'd noticed her aimless drifting, but work had tightened his attention to a single pinprick of importance.

"I worry about you sitting at home all day. What if we go out to dinner with some friends next week, huh? Fergus and Marina— wouldn't you like to meet them?"

Ingrid shrugged. But Rudolph, filled with a sudden burst of enthusiasm, spun her around until they fell into the Eames chair, breathless with laughter.

"Hear me out," he said, planting a kiss on her shoulder. "Just until you find your feet, why don't you plan us a honeymoon? Something over-the-top—since we're not doing a big wedding?" He spread his arms out expansively. "Sky's the limit. We could go in December, after the Bill Bowes exhibition ends."

"Like where?"

Hearing a faint note of interest in her voice, he brightened.

"Well—Italy, for example. We could charter a boat. You know I'm pretty good at sailing. Or we could do a tour of Antarctica? Have you seen those cool luxury igloos where the seals, like, paddle up to your feet . . . or . . ."

"Southeast Asia?"

"Anywhere you want."

He caught a strand of her hair and wound it around his finger, tight enough to cut the blood flow. They both watched his finger turn white. A thread seemed to be weaving itself between them, in these moments: closer and closer, as though nothing could break through.

Her dark eyes met his green ones. A smile lifted the corner of her lips.

"I'd like to introduce you to the love of my life. Guys, this is Ingrid."

Ingrid had never seen anything like them in her life. Marina was physically plain and milquetoast but carried herself with all the contemptuous pride of a queen; Fergus, with his shawl-necked cardigan and aging Barbour jacket, resembled a strange cross between a Brooklyn hipster and an Edwardian country squire. His cheeks were flushed with wine, his nose hard and swollen as crumbly old cheese, but still she found him obscurely handsome in that arrogant decadent way of men on a journey to decline.

"Ingrid," Fergus said, kissing her on both cheeks. "So pleased to finally meet you."

"So great to finally meet you guys," Ingrid said, looking back and forth between them. "Rudolph talks so much about you."

"We absolutely adore Rudolph," Marina said. Fergus nodded in agreement, echoed: "Adore."

"Since university—Rudolph and I both flirted with arts courses before realizing"—he laughed loudly—"that we might as well do something sensible with our lives! I did, at least."

"Rather than potter about with a load of paintbrushes the whole time!" Marina joined in.

Ingrid noticed the slight, but Rudolph seemed not to. He was laughing too, although he had dedicated his whole life to the arts.

"Ingrid is an artist, too," Rudolph interposed.

"Not really," Ingrid said quickly, her cheeks heating with embarrassment.

Fergus fiddled with a gold leaf ice cube in his negroni. He offered: "I always admired Churchill's watercolors at Chartwell. I'm in politics, see. Big history buff. Churchill, Chamberlain, Disraeli."

"What kind of politics are you in?"

Rudolph nudged Ingrid under the table. A sad-looking waiter took their drink orders, his drooping black moustache and red velvet waistcoat straight out of Soutine.

"Conservative," Fergus said easily. "Of course. Although it's nothing like your Republicans at home. We're much more civilized over here, I mean we actually do believe in climate change and so on, though it's been totally overstated by the liberal media."

"The Guardianistas!" Marina added darkly.

Ingrid asked how they'd met. They seemed bored by the question and by her. She saw Marina cast a swift cool glance at Rudolph, like she'd expected more from him.

"Family friends since we were—this big." Fergus put his fingers together to demonstrate.

"Destined!" Marina said. "Our families knew it. But I had to let him have his time messing about"—she turned to Ingrid and put on a maternal expression—"before we could be together. I'm sure you understand," she added slyly.

Ingrid nodded. Fergus had a high social status in their world, a large fortune no doubt; and careful Marina, good old family friend Marina, *she's like a sister to me!* Marina had waited and waited until he was too fat and tired and coked-out to bother chasing skirt. Around his thirtieth birthday she had sprung into action, scheduling his dinner parties and sending Christmas presents to his mother and generally organizing his life to the absolute max. Fergus—easily convinced, too lazy to run—fell rapidly into a state of dependence. Marina had wanted it so long, she'd failed to realize he was the one who really benefited. But men, Ingrid thought, were like that. They grew dependent extremely quickly. Then dropped into your lap like a stone.

Now Marina was smiling across the table with her rictus smile and frightening, doll-like blue eyes. Ingrid struggled to think of more to say.

"And you, what do you do?"

From the microscopic change in Marina's expression, she understood that it was the wrong question, gauche and American and overly businesslike. She could practically hear Rudolph shouting in her ear: *Whatever you do, do NOT ask them what they do!*

Marina had started a private social networking app. An address book of sorts.

"Like *Tatler*?" Ingrid asked, and Marina winced. Then she summoned herself.

"A bit," she said kindly. "Though more . . . exclusive."

"Fergus is training to take up the House of Lords, after his father," Rudolph said. "They have a wonderful estate up in Northumberland."

Boyishly Fergus flicked a lock of hair: "Family footsteps and all that. Bit annoying really, but what can you do?"

"Political power is passed down through male lineage in this country?" Ingrid couldn't help herself. "I didn't think that happened anywhere in Europe still."

Infinitesimally Rudolph's grip tightened around his sweating crystal glass, but Fergus offered a forgiving smile.

"We are not European, though," Marina said. "You do have to remember."

"You may think us English old-fashioned," Fergus said in an affable tone, "but politics is more of a duty than anything else. And at least we don't have the American system—I mean, you all are just so extreme in that country. Guns, race relations. We would have never elected such a buffoon." He shuddered. "I suppose it's just, uh, the lower classes," he added vaguely, and Marina offered a faintly pitying moue. "Sad, isn't it? To be so uneducated about one's own best interest?"

"Very sad," Marina agreed.

"Whereas Boris, Boris is an extremely qualified man all round, top-notch debater. I'll be voting for him next election, for sure. The only reason he's hated is that"—he wagged his finger instructively—"he's a boy's boy, went to Eton and Oxford. There is so much jealousy and hatred of our kind, even though everyone knows social inequality is so much worse in America."

"But is inequality such a *bad* thing?" Marina cried, laughing. "People just want everything handed to them these days!"

Ingrid choked on her wine; Rudolph hit her on the back, making soothing noises.

"Anyway, it's not like Washington. Fergus really cares about his constituents," Marina continued. "We've bred our dogs with the same people over sixteen generations, real ear-to-the-ground type stuff."

"They call it Londongrad, don't they?" There was an edge to Ingrid's voice. "The oligarchs, they buy up all the nice houses, make rococo palaces modeled off all those crumbling English estates—"

"Not the real ones," Marina said loftily.

"—the Tory politicos take their money and give them a wing at Oxford. I've read about it lately."

Rudolph seized the chance to change the subject. "Ingrid is very well-read."

"It's easy to get mixed up when your ideas come from books and not real life," Fergus suggested.

"Fergus's sister, Poppy, is a bit of a communist too." Marina cast Rudolph a sympathetic look. "It's a phase a lot of well-bred girls go through."

"Oh," Ingrid said. "But I'm not very well-bred."

Fergus laughed, amused. He exchanged the faintest of eye rolls with Marina, who emitted a long, honking laugh. *How many times did you practice that laugh?* Ingrid wondered.

"Then what are you doing here?"

Their food arrived: Ingrid had chosen the Dover sole, Rudolph a steak, and Marina and Fergus the guinea fowl for two.

"Not a vegan, are you," Fergus said to Ingrid with relief. "Poppy is. Every meal a living hell, believe you me. Thank God she still likes a good hunt."

Fergus was getting bored of Rudolph's new fiancée. Americans could never take a joke—but he perked up when a pretty, black-haired teenage waitress came to check on their table. Siobhan, she confessed, blushing when he asked her name. What did she like to do? he inquired, gently flicking her elbow in the most delicately flirtatious way.

"Trying to make a bit of cash before uni starts back," she said, refilling their wineglasses. She had a thick cockney accent Ingrid strained to understand, nothing like Fergus's crystalline BBC presenter tones.

"Where you off to then?"

"Liverpool," she said with pride.

"Smart girl, hey? What course?"

"Philosophy, politics, and English."

Fergus whistled, mock-impressed.

"That's the course all the politicians do here," Rudolph whispered in Ingrid's ear. Siobhan ducked her head, smiling with embarrassment.

"Good on you!" Fergus exclaimed, making his plummy voice sound self-consciously casual. He was, Ingrid noticed, blunting the crisp syllables as he spoke to Siobhan: *Ha, ha, I might be super posh but I'm on your side!*

Marina was good enough to wait until Siobhan moved two feet away before she said sourly, "PPE, with that bloody accent? What's the point?"

Fergus, smiling, said something louche and inaudible that made Marina squeal with laughter.

"They're saying she's too low class to take a course in politics? Like she's too low class to be a politician?" Ingrid whispered to Rudolph.

He gave a half-embarrassed nod-shrug: *It's not for us to judge.* It was then that she realized how Rudolph's voice had subtly reshaped itself in their presence. It, too, had become clipped, more English somehow, as if he had left some old, forgotten part of himself behind.

A planned ski trip to Verbier was discussed. "Oh, you must come, you absolutely must," Fergus said enthusiastically, his gaze roving restlessly around the room.

At one point Rudolph appeared to engage Fergus in a long conversation about a Twombly painting. Many things passed Ingrid by: what morning suit Fergus should wear to so-and-so's wedding, how drab their pile in Scotland was; Fergus waxing nostalgic about the country; a thick, complicated network of references to villas in Mallorca and Provence and "my father's little place at Cassis." When dessert arrived, Ingrid was so exhausted by attempting to parse the social dynamics that she could barely crack the glazed caramel topping of her crème brulée with the tip of her silver spoon.

Glancing at her, Rudolph saw it was time to go home. Ingrid, he explained to Marina and Fergus, was still jet-lagged from her travels. She wasn't used to flying much.

"Oh, gosh, neither am I anymore," Marina professed, politely ignoring the fact that Ingrid had arrived six weeks ago. Fergus made sympathetic noises from the back of his throat.

"Absolute delight to meet you, though."

"And we'll see you at the wedding!" Marina cried as they waved goodbye.

Chilled with drink, Ingrid leaned against the fogged-up window on the cab ride home. Rudolph stared out at the black oily streets.

"Well, so what'd you think of them?"

"Oh, well. I thought they were . . ." She searched for the right words. "Interesting. Well, unexpected."

"Unexpected?" His voice was edgy.

"I guess they seemed very . . . entitled. Well, the way they talked to the waitress."

"Waitress?" He frowned distractedly. "Well, they're English. I mean I know they're not perfect but—" He laughed, wounded by her dislike. "God, you're hard to impress."

The shrill bleat of her ringtone interrupted him; Rudolph subsided into the cocoon of his coat. Simone was calling, Simone who hadn't sent her a word of concern or acknowledgment since Ingrid had left the city, and briefly she longed to flee back to her old life. In a way, Simone had been her greatest love. She had understood her best. But the city had swallowed her up without a ripple, and she pushed away the phone with a sigh.

"Look, tell me what it is that you want me to do," Rudolph was saying. "To make you happy—what is it? Tell me and I'll do it, I swear."

A dizzying wave of spite filled her stomach; furious at her powerlessness, she spat out, "You've lived your whole life without me, I don't see what difference it makes."

It was a lie—they both knew it made all the difference. Rudolph clenched her hand in a tight grip. The streetlights burned amber in the dark night, but inside the taxi, nothing seemed to exist beyond the tense muscle of their two hands, fused. Her breath slowed down, she was calm now, and her black eyes shone up at him like two plums in cold water, hanging just out of reach. If he leaned closer, he could kiss her, taste the spray of bitter orange and vermouth on her lips.

For a second, he waited.

Something mortal floated on the air, something in this moment that he never wanted to lose, some ragged second of wanting and wishing and waiting that could never come true. But on a silent signal he kissed her anyway, as if that answer might lie between her lips, as if her perishable breath might make his absolution complete.

28

THEY MARRIED ON A COOL BLUE MORNING IN EARLY OCTOBER, WITH Marina and Fergus as their witnesses.

Such a beautiful day, Marina kept saying as they walked toward the stone steps of Chelsea Old Town Hall, rising tall through the trees. Rudolph's palm felt hot and sweaty in hers. He wore black sunglasses and a nervous grin—impromptu bachelor party with the boys last night, he'd said.

Of the ceremony itself, Ingrid remembered little. Inside a small and dated room, a man was waiting. A bowl of white roses lay on his desk. She examined the roses to calm herself, each cool white petal touched with a single diamond drop of dew. Flowers in a still life, someone had once told her, were always ironic. They symbolized life, but by the time you saw them they were already dead—cut for that purpose.

The man intoned words. Ingrid was conscious of only two things, a breeze blowing through the open window and her bare knees like ice under the ivory wool dress.

"Congratulations," the man said, smiling.

She looked up.

"That's it?"

"That's it."

A dizzy elation rose high in her chest. She watched Rudolph slip the gold band down her knuckle, sliding into place beside the ruby ring. Outside, they emerged into the harsh blue daylight like two startled rabbits. "Pictures!" someone shouted, and rice was thrown. Confetti. It's only 10:00 a.m., they kept saying to each other with a kind of exhilarated shock. It's only 10:00 a.m. In the picture where Rudolph throws up her hand, she is smiling so hard her face hurts, uncomfortable with the flashing camera. He is looking at her, his needy eyes searching for hers, but her gaze is fixed on the glowing sun.

If I had been looking, she thought vaguely—for a sign, an omen, a harbinger of our life together. I couldn't have asked for more than this, could I? I couldn't have asked for more than this bright, cloudless sky, blue without a flaw or trace of rain, blue like the heart of a jaybird.

29

THE MORNING OF THE BILL BOWES EXHIBITION, RUDOLPH WOKE EARLY
to run around the river. The streets of Chelsea were long and silent
and preternaturally clean, and the brown autumn leaves blew gold in
the pale dawn. Water stretched out calm and fathomless beneath his
flying feet, a vast silver ribbon of river with no end.

Afterward he was exhausted, sweat coming off him in animal
waves of heat as he strode around the kitchen, tossing bananas and
apples and kale into an industrial-grade blender. The machine came to
life with a whir of steely efficiency.

Choking down the murky liquid, he scrolled through his inbox.
Already two dozen people had accepted his invitation to the opening,
including the owner of a private museum in Shanghai, a curator at
the Tate, and the powerful heir to a powdered macaroni-and-cheese
dynasty who never touched the stuff himself. All signs pointed to a
sold-out show, in which case—he and Madison had worked the figures
out last night with rising and joyous disbelief—*in which case*, he stood
to make a profit of 30 to 40 percent. Millions upon millions just waiting
to hit his bank account.

After his shower he crept back into bed with Ingrid, who avoided
exercise at all costs. Burying his face in her hair, he let his eyes fall
shut, the warm solid feel of her body lulling him into a light doze . . .

He was alone. Or no—talking to someone. Someone was telling him
something important, a person he recognized or feared, their name
on the tip of his tongue but he couldn't remember . . . It was urgently

important that he listen now, because they were saying something very important, almost shouting. *Listen, listen!* But he was too busy analyzing the cut and color of every article of the person's clothing, hypnotically picking each one over in a trancelike state . . .

Jerking awake, Rudolph felt suddenly clammy and frightened, as if a stranger had entered their bedroom without permission. Shadows swirled around the ceiling; his mouth opened in fright. Just a bad dream, he told himself, trying to slow his breathing. Nothing but a bad dream.

He clung to Ingrid, whose black hair lay matted on the pillow. It seemed an oblique reassurance that nothing bad could happen to him, not anymore. She had chosen him—out of all the guys she could've had, like his cousins, she'd chosen him. They were mad about each other, eyes constantly seeking the other's across a room, if only for the silent pleasure of going up and touching the other's shoulder in a volt of electricity. He could see how happiness waited for them, in the distance: it was out there, ready for them to seize it.

Let it happen, let it happen, he begged the universe.

Ingrid had time to read now. She had time to paint, in a pair of old white overalls that grew crusted and chalky with streaks of impasto. Each day, she rode the tube to Green Park. The sweaty clumps of commuters marched forward, still in their relentless rhythm, but she was no longer a part of their masses. In the pitch dark portal of the train, she listened to the low rumble and screech of its thunderous wheels clanging together.

Rudolph watched her with a faint confusion. He would've been bored stiff without a job. One night, noticing her hands dodge in and out of knitting needles over another watermelon-shaped hat in front of the TV, he encouraged her to sell her funny knitted scarves in an online shop, a business. They could even hire a web developer to help her. Her own mother, Rudolph knew, had sold homemade ceramics at craft fairs on the weekends. Tuna sandwich-scented memories. Ingrid got a funny expression whenever she talked about them: a clear nostalgia, but also pride.

At first Ingrid grew excited; then it seemed to fade away.

"I really wanted to paint," she said wistfully. "Not sell knitted things online. I mean, I'm not just some bored housewife, am I?"

He'd looked up sharply. Then, swallowing his surprise, agreed that she wasn't.

"Anyway," she said after a moment. "I still have years and years to figure out what I want to do."

Until she found purpose, planning the honeymoon lent additional structure to her days. In December they'd leave for Southeast Asia— perfect timing, he assured her, since by then he'd be making enough money to afford the luxury, any luxury. A flight to Bangkok first; then they would board the *Alexa*, an Indonesian *phinisi* schooner with billowing scarlet sails outfitted in teak and white linen. They would sail across the Gulf of Thailand and the Strait of Malacca, stopping in Phuket and Jakarta and Surabaya along the way; they would watch the closest ancestors of the dinosaurs crawl across the deserted island where the Komodo dragons lived. At last they'd disembark on the isolated island of Sumba, the closest place to paradise on earth as could be found.

The happy isle, they joked over dinner. Where their happiness would crystallize, its memories carrying them through any hopefully brief dark spots in the next fifty years together.

He tried on his new Huntsman suit in the gilt-edged mirror, inspecting himself carefully in the smoky glass salvaged at auction from the Palace des Tuileries. A subtle green houndstooth in achingly soft cashmere, traditional but not overly studied, casual-cool. A little more English than what he'd have worn in New York, but didn't his first exhibition in London deserve a bit of flair?

He resembled, he thought approvingly as he slid on the false glasses he wore sometimes to look more intellectual, a minor royal caught by the tabloids. Not the ugly inbred English kind like bald mole rats, but the glamorous European pretenders, with supermodel or TV presenter parents.

"I'm about to head out," he called, hearing Ingrid's thin socks slide on the parquet. "Meet me at the gallery at six?"

She emerged from the bedroom, rubbing sleep out of her eyes.

"Did you know Komodo dragons can grow up to ten feet long? They've got a toxic saliva that'll kill you within twenty-four hours—*if* you're lucky enough to escape their serrated teeth."

"That right?" He raised his eyebrows. "Better not veer off-piste, then."

She laughed. Ingrid had been researching the dragons obsessively for days now; she loved morbid little factoids like this, and he liked knowing this about her. Everything felt so fresh between them, so candy-new with possibilities of unexplored knowledge and emotion.

Rudolph danced around the side table, finding his wallet and keys, sliding his stiff fingers into leather driving gloves with a snap. He tightened the cashmere scarf around his throat.

"Okay, then. I'm off." His lips brushed her cheek. "Don't be late."

She mimed slitting her own throat.

"I would never."

The morning hung in river mist, soft and bright as a gray pearl. Rudolph could smell the sharp scent of green leaves in the cool vaporous wind. The world seemed fresh and willing today, open, as if he might spread it apart and take what he wanted. He could feel the channels of blood pumping through his veins, and jogging toward Mayfair with his briefcase in hand he felt both young and ancient, godlike with vigor, excitable as that small torpedo of a boy who'd once swung a backpack through the gates of first grade.

I only want life, he thought as he walked to the river. Life, whole and entire.

Beholden to no one.

The look of the laborer had come back into fashion, and Fergus decided Rudolph's glamorous opening was the ideal occasion to show off the original 1970s street sweeper jacket he'd bought on his gap year to Spain. For fifteen years its fleshless ghost had hung limply in the closet— between charity galas, parliamentary meetings, and shooting weekends, the opportunity hadn't ever quite been right. But tonight, *tonight* was his moment. Examining his reflection in the mirror, he'd thought with satisfaction how authentic it looked. How wonderful to be the kind of chic, endlessly adaptable man who could glide between Whitehall and the coolest opening of the season looking absolutely cracking at both!

"My favorite thing about the new gallery," he told Ingrid, his wet blue eyes swimming with wine, "is the concrete staircase. Sick, isn't it? We salvaged it from a housing estate in East London. When Rudolph first contacted the architect about the space—my family's very close with Francis Ayorinde—I said to him, I said 'Rude, the country's going to the damn dogs. Let's make the space feel functional, right? Let's change the culture.'"

He took a large swig of wine and swept his arm out behind him.

"You know, it's like hunting. How many people do you know who can hunt down an animal and eat it? It's so important to stay in touch with our ancestors, get back to basics. Naked, red-blooded humanity. It's like the way I love to go back up to Northumberland. We'll do a bit of shooting, Marina and I will pick the apples ourselves and make apple crumble—we've had these people working for us on the estate for absolute eons, they're almost like family—"

Ingrid nodded. Where was Rudolph, to handle this conversation smoothly? He would've said something flattering to Fergus, managing to interest Ingrid at the same time, but all night he had been dragged away by the bobbing crowd, stars to his sun. Everyone wanted a word, a smile, a quote, a painting. *Almost all sold,* she heard him explain. *One's just been acquired by Beaux-Arts in Paris—though I may, just may, be able to scrounge something up for you, only as a friend—*

Just then Fergus spotted someone moving across the floor behind her and shouted, "Hullo, Cornelia, how are you?"

Automatically Ingrid stuck out her hand, smiling. Fergus spun her around in his camp jokey way. "Have you met Ingrid? Absolutely gorgeous, isn't she, we love Rudy's new wife—" and *Oh shit.* It was *that* Cornelia. Ingrid shrank away, feeling short and dark and provincial in comparison to this tall, milky blonde drifting toward them in a long black column dress.

"Hi," Ingrid said awkwardly. "Nice to meet you."

The blond girl swiveled her head at Ingrid, still limply holding out her hand. It was one of those instant moments of recognition that feel so awkward to both parties: the girl in the silver jumpsuit, Cornelia, was the girl from the party. Her expression was dumbstruck but poisonous, like a cornered snake. Ingrid immediately saw how hurt she was.

Wrinkling her lips at Ingrid, she muttered something under her breath.

"I don't appreciate being made a fool of," she said loudly to Fergus. "Huh?"

Ingrid looked from her to Fergus, who put up his hands in a defensive gesture. He let his eyes shimmer weakly with artificial sympathy.

"Hey, hey, Cornelia. This isn't a very good time—"

"You don't know anything about him," she said in a low voice to Ingrid, smiling a little, her breath sour with wine. She turned to Fergus:

"Screw you both with your little fucking boys' club. And you can tell him I said that, okay."

Fergus rolled his eyes. He was smiling faintly. Some men, Ingrid thought, liked it when women erupted into tears or small rages. It confirmed something animal and illogical about women in general, the way that a puppy soiling the carpet is cute—forgivable for its lack of control.

"Sorry, she's a real nutter," he said to Ingrid, casting a pitying glance at Cornelia's back. "Known to shout at people at parties. Don't pay her a moment's attention."

And he opened his mouth to say more, but in that second the chatter of voices and laughter rose and then dropped, sharply and completely. It was as if a veil had been tossed over the room. People were looking around through the crowd in confusion, searching for the source of the crackle.

The silence was dense. Loud somehow, sticky and discomfiting as the sound of bees. Suddenly the noise snapped back, a jolt of electricity. Hushed voices now, whispers of unease. Everyone was looking at the alien glow of their cell phones as some shocking piece of news traveled quickly and quietly through the crowd.

"What's going on?"

Ingrid craned her head to look for Rudolph. The chill of excitement was percolating like a storm, growing louder and louder as the voices chattered, spreading the word.

Finally, she saw him. He stood stock-still, trapped, amid a group of five or six collectors. His face was white as a Kabuki doll, utterly robbed of color.

"The *New York Times*," she heard someone murmur.

"Some girl artist—I don't know . . . Simone something. Ever heard of her?"

"Total exposé—a predator—a rapist."

"Could it be a setup?" a sleazy-looking man wondered, and several people cut him savagely with their eyes.

"You think it'll kill his prices?" someone else said with annoyance. "I've got a *Big Nude* up for auction tomorrow. Christie's promised me double the high."

"Are you kidding? Your painting is screwed. He might as well commit seppuku now—they're all going to start coming out of the woodwork."

"Holy fuck," Ingrid said aloud.

A skeleton key turned and clicked into place in her mind.

Her stomach seemed to drop an inch, then another. A sick, writhing feeling, like she had never known how low her dread could go. A single thought pressed at her brain, shunting her downward with its leaden weight: *You should have known.*

"Rudolph!" she tried to shout over the din, but he was too far off and couldn't hear. All she could see was his small and frightened white face, pinned to the buzzing crowd, before he was swept away again by a swarm of locusts.

30

He had to wait out the whole interminable evening before he could let loose.

Of course he noticed, how could he not, everyone whispering over their phones, trading gleeful looks of shock, horror, wry acknowledgment. But no one dared say a word to him. He tried his best to speak normally to clients, panic rising high in his throat. Something was wrong.

Eventually he managed to break away from his conversational partner with a smile and a murmured apology—"Excuse me, sorry, I've got to take this call"—rushing into the bathroom to scream in his fist, blood in his mouth. Then he squatted over the toilet and opened his phone. It took no time at all to find what he was looking for.

DAT'S KAPITAL

Flying coast to coast at your service. Weekly columnist CHARLIE ERROLL serves up the juiciest gossip in the art world.

#MeToo Scandal Hits Iconic Artist

Tonight I was present at what may be remembered as the most memorable private view of the season, though not in the way intended. New York dealer **Rudolph Sullivan** has expanded with an eponymous new gallery on London's Mount Street, and his new exhibition is a remarkable display of paintings by Bill Bowes, brimming with promise. By eight, the Brutalist mansion was positively thrashing with glitterati downing '96 Dom and cold roast beef sandwiches. An afterparty at Loulou's was promised; all signs pointed to an opening with a bang. Well, it sure did.

Another unforgettable exhibition opened last night across the pond: **Simone Machado** at **Paul Bernot New York** in an eagerly awaited follow-up to her first solo show this spring. Machado, whose prices have increased a whopping 500 percent over the past six months, collaged a tapestry over the walls of Paul Bernot, cutting her signature corpse-like women into a string of paper doll–shaped figures from a pair of used jeans. Across the tapestry, she painted a single phrase ten feet high in dripping black letters:

J'ACCUSE BILL BOWES

Tonight, barely an hour into Sullivan's Bowes opening, Machado's exclusive op-ed for the *New York Times* dropped. Machado writes a harrowing tale, claiming Bowes hired her as an assistant, assaulted her in his studio, and fired her in short order. The denim used in the tapestries is allegedly taken from a pair of jeans Bowes allegedly wiped his, er, fluids on–a scrap of which, Machado writes, has been provided to the New York Police Department for further testing.

Now, at nine, Sullivan's carnivorous guests are eagerly examining the Bowes paintings for signs of inappropriate advances, comparing them to Gauguin's infamous portraits of prepubescent Tahitians. Focusing, as it does, almost exclusively on nudes, the exhibition is ripe for analysis. I overhear Lary Schmaltz wondering whether a fleck of white impasto might be a subtle admission of guilt: "A reference to the fallen seed? Genius!"

I ask one high-placed collector if she plans on buying anything. "Fuck no!" she says. "Bowes is dead in the water. I'm getting out of the market right this second."

Mr. Bowes, 76, in New York at the time, has strenuously denied all allegations. "I'm sorry if I made anyone feel uncomfortable, but last time I checked, discomfort is not a major offense. Great art will always push the boundaries of acceptable discourse."

I wonder if the Palais des Beaux-Arts will agree . . .

The fury building up inside Rudolph was so thick and overwhelming that it actually blocked his hearing, like huge balls of cotton wool had been stuffed inside his skull. His muscles seemed to be collapsing. *The pervy old bastard! Well, the nudes—it kind of all makes sense now . . .* As if they'd had a fucking clue! He forced himself to re-enter the room, suppressing a whimper under a taut, false smile. Some clients were beginning to look angry. They'd blame him, he realized unhappily, blame him because they had no other scapegoat to rack and punish for the sin of losing money . . .

"How're you holding up, bro?"

Charlie! It was Charlie, Charlie giving him a look of guilty pity in his red Adidas trackpants and torn Comme des Garçons shirt, Charlie who had been drinking *his* champagne and wandering around *his* gallery even as he managed to knock off the gloating newsletter that was Rudolph's own epitaph. Charlie! Rudolph shrugged him off, anger making his vision go scarlet. You write that from the bathroom, you sick fuck? he wanted to shout.

"I'm sorry, dude," Charlie said apologetically. "I really am. But I'm a journalist at the end of the day." He sighed. "I have editors to report to. It was too good to miss."

"Right," Rudolph said in a monotone, and went back into the crowd. He could hear Charlie shouting behind him.

You understand that, don't you Rudy? Rudy!

You're dead to me, he thought. All fucking dead.

No one could be trusted, not a single one.

For a second he thought about hanging himself from the rafters. At least that would be a glamorous death. But of course, he'd ripped them out of the ultramodern cube commissioned from a leading architect to make his mark on the city.

No choice, then, but to live.

The rest of the evening seemed to go on and on. The rubberneckers wouldn't stop, wouldn't *leave*, it was a never-ending nightmare of which he was the star attraction. Summoning a courage he didn't possess, he straightened his back against the chatter of gossip and grimly forced himself to answer questions.

It was nine-thirty by the time the gallery emptied out, though a few loyal friends hung around to ask if he wanted them to stay. No, no, he assured them with a wry smile. It'll all blow over tomorrow. A lie—he could tell by their pitying faces—but he just wanted to be alone. Except for Ingrid of course, but then a wife was an extension of oneself. Which made the question he needed to ask her all the more unspeakable.

Ingrid was waiting for him outside in a waft of smoke, still as a frightened gazelle. Her eyes were wide and searching, the color of midnight under the streetlamps.

"Let's go," he said abruptly, locking the door behind him with an awful sense of finality.

* * *

At home, he waited a little longer. The 2010 bottle of Opus One he had been saving to celebrate the exhibition was still sitting on the black-veined marble counter, and he could feel Ingrid's watchful gaze on his back as she took a seat at the kitchen island. Rudolph removed a corkscrew from the drawer, twisted the sharp metal prong into the flesh of the cork, and wrenched it out with a violent *pop*.

"Wine?"

Ingrid hesitated. He could tell she wanted to say no, but she gave a reluctant nod. He poured them each a glass of rich cabernet. Took a sip. Then, framing it as a statement:

"Did you know?"

"What?"

Frozen seconds passed between them; he stared at her. The silence was absolute—an expression of guilt, pleading almost, twisted her face. The realization filled him with horror.

"You *fucking* knew!"

"Just wait a minute—"

But he would not be stopped. "You knew? Holy fuck, Ingrid. How could you know? How could you fucking know and not tell me? How could you listen to me talk about this guy like he's the greatest artist of all time, when all along you knew that he was a goddamn rapist and he was about to be exposed—or, or—"

"Stop it! Stop. Look—I knew something happened, okay? I knew she was assaulted, but I swear I didn't know it was him. I mean, there were a lot of visiting professors, all right? And he—honestly, I just didn't know!"

"So you're fucking stupid, is that it? You're a dumb fucking girl in addition to everything else." He was almost screaming. "How could you not ask the most obvious question!"

Silence ruled in the kitchen; his shouts felt deadly. Ingrid was watching him carefully, as carefully as one would observe a wild gorilla raging across an open cage. Her skin appeared waxy, greenish under the steel light.

Not knowing what to do, Rudolph banged his glass hard on the marble countertop, dark liquid sloshing redly over his hands. The noise of glass on cold stone was like a gunshot, startling them; both, he realized, expected the glass to break.

"I didn't want to push—"

"Yeah, yeah, you didn't want to push her, you didn't want to push the precious little snowflake," he sneered, splashing more wine in his glass. "Because that's not what we do, is it? We let people express their trauma, and then it explains everything about them. It's all so facile and fucking reductive, as if people are nothing more than the sum of all the worst things that have happened to them!"

"Rudolph. Come on, that's not fair," she flared. "He chose her carefully, don't you see? Everything was calculated to manipulate how much she admired him as a famous artist, to make her feel like a prude for speaking out. And she couldn't, because of his power. She's fighting back in the only way she can, by forcing the art world to look at her instead of him. Do you know what it's like to be invaded like that? To be hurt. To feel afraid? Because these are basic elements of a woman's experience. But when's it going to be good enough for you? Do you think women's problems are just not that serious enough to include in a major work of art?" He blinked rapidly at the sudden volley of questions. "You know what I think," Ingrid said with bitterness. "I think it's great. Simone's found her voice. I, for one, want to hear it."

"Oh my God, thank you for explaining contemporary feminism to this sad, toothless, deranged man!" he bit back. "You're totally missing the point, as usual. I'm talking about separating the art from the artist."

"Who?"

"Bowes!" Rudolph yelled, and Ingrid blinked. He continued, in a frenetic, high-pitched voice, while pacing around the kitchen counter, "I don't give a shit about Simone. So her paintings are about rape. What I care about—and I'm fundamentally shocked that you didn't get this—is the market of Bowes. Bowes, Bill Bowes. All our assets are parked in that guy, Bowes. Market about to flatten to zero, Bowes. Heard of him?"

"You don't know that—" Ingrid hesitated.

"I know it," Rudolph said, in a low, deliberate voice. "So it affects me. It affects you."

"People are trying to hold him accountable—"

"So what does that look like, honestly? Are we no longer allowed to appreciate great art by flawed people? Because we can only accept people into the pantheon who are morally good by our standards? Because *we* are so much better than them, because *we* are not bad and evil people too?"

He could see her thinking, *He's miserable, he's angry, he's upset and not thinking straight*, but he'd never felt clearer.

"Are you saying that people deserve—"

"Not at all!" he burst out. "What I'm saying is that he should be hauled in front of a court, if there's a case for it. Sent to jail! But art is beyond the artist. It's beyond morality. Let it exist on its own terms! Should we tear everything off the wall because it makes us uncomfortable? Is that what society's become?"

"Look," she said patiently. "I know you don't want to hear this right now, but every era defines the value of things according to trends in opinion. Why is it so bad to want to support women? To protect the integrity of their bodies by casting their abusers out of the history books? Would you want to see Hitler's paintings hung at the Met, even if they were the greatest paintings in the world?"

"Bill Bowes is not FUCKING Hitler!" Rudolph shouted.

To her credit, she didn't flinch. She advanced toward him with her arms outstretched. There was a pity in her eyes that he found hard to look at; he was already backing away, gripping the bottle of wine tight in one hand.

He found himself in the small downstairs study, carefully re-created from a sixteenth-century Scottish hunting lodge he'd once stayed at with Cornelia. Rich with antique tapestries, the lodge had calmed him beyond measure; bespeaking, as it did, of roaring fires that shut out the howling winds. This was the promise of money, wasn't it? Protection from sickness and pain; protection from all the worries and evils of the outer world, which could not be changed. From death.

Oh God, he prayed, make me safe and whole.

But now he looked at the green plaid wallpaper, the hunting landscape by George Stubbs and the Edwardian armchair he'd personally re-covered in white sheepskin, and a sharp nausea rose inside him at the very sight of it. It was all so wrong to think he could stuff an ancient Scottish lodge into a contemporary townhouse! Now he would have to renovate it all anew with a more experienced interior decorator—but he'd be flat broke tomorrow—

Fuck!

In despair he raised the bottle of wine to his lips, hardly noticing Ingrid's presence in the room until he felt a tentative hand flutter over his shoulder like a question.

"I just want to say I'm so sorry."

"You should have asked her," he said in a low voice. The olive and sage and dun-colored stripes on the wall were beginning to blur across his vision.

She sighed.

"Maybe, but I didn't want to pry. To break her trust. Can you not understand that?"

"I can understand it, yeah. It's just dumb, is what it is," he said, but his heart wasn't in it anymore. The wine was flooding his senses, finally, finally. Thank Christ. He staggered into the armchair. Sober and straight-backed, Ingrid sat down in the rocking chair beside him; the chair he'd once imagined children wobbling back and forth in.

"Can you leave me alone, please," he said dully. He wanted the opposite, in fact—he wanted her to wrap him in her arms like a small child—but he couldn't bear her to witness his most sordid humiliation.

"Rudolph," she pleaded.

"Leave me alone, I said."

Her shoulders were hunched forward, he could tell she was trying hard not to cry. But Rudolph had no time for her crocodile tears. He was prepared to pity her—hell, he'd pity them both—but not at this moment. Right at this moment, he wanted to dive straight into this bottle of Opus One and finish it, then go down to the temperature-controlled wine cellar for another.

At last she got up and left the room, leaving him alone, in the ersatz hunting lodge.

The study was dark now, and suffocatingly hot. Rudolph lay motionless on the sofa, watching the dim emerald glow of a Tiffany lamp throw shadows over the wall.

Some exhibitions flopped. Well, you had to be resigned to that. So he'd put about twelve mil into the exhibition, okay. That was one thing. The larger issue was, he had about thirty million dollars' worth of Bowes paintings just sitting in warehouses in Geneva and London and New Jersey, and tomorrow nobody would buy the work. Paintings worth five or ten million today would tumble to zero tomorrow, crushing Rudolph under the huge plodding feet of the market.

How long could he survive the crushing overheads of two enormous galleries, a staff of ten, art fairs, plane tickets, entertaining, shipping at fifty thousand a pop when his entire reputation lay in shreds, his assets worthless?

A few weeks, maybe. No more.

The rosy fingers of dawn were streaking past the window by the time Rudolph finally crept upstairs. Life went on, with or without him.

He understood now that he had one option, only one option, and that was to call Frederick Asaka.

Admittedly the thought made him choke with nausea. What tessellating spiral of Escherian monstrosities could Asaka reveal with a flick of the wrist? The whitewashing of money, offering his storage facilities to unsavory groups for black-market goods . . . Oh God. But he had no choice. He refused to end up penniless, refused to sink into the backwaters from whence he came. It was survival and survival and survival at all costs.

Ingrid must've left some foreign music on before she fell asleep, he realized tiredly as he crawled into bed beside her. Some kind of Southeast Asian thing, probably research for the honeymoon—passive-aggressive, he thought wearily, one more thing I can no longer afford. But he was too drained and exhausted to get up and turn off the speakers.

He lay there quietly with his eyes peeled back, expecting not to sleep. But to his surprise the silvery music washed over him, and its queer metallic sounded like the stirring of a thousand bells. Even in his misery, the melody sounded out some elusive memory in his mind, some echo of a song that time forgot. For what seemed like hours he lay, listening to its strange percussive rhythm ring out and then collapse, in an echo that seemed to comb its way across his brain, until finally that melody of cymbals rocked him into a black and smothering dream.

3I

MONDAY.

By the time he sat down at his desk, Rudolph had already been up for hours, filled with all the verve and ambition he'd ever felt in his life. He would fix things, really fix them this time, not a moment to spare.

Scrubbing himself in the shower, he'd cultivated a warm glow from his inner ribs, a smiling but regretful voice with which to charm Asaka. Asaka was in Paris right now, probably sitting at breakfast with his family in that beautiful house on the Île Saint-Louis—the kind of house, he thought furiously, that should rightfully belong to Rudolph Sullivan.

He wasted no time on the phone, waxing nostalgic about how much he missed Asaka's friendship, his company—their long lunches at Scott's, their cherished vacations in St. Tropez . . . The Bélizaire debacle was, of course, an unfortunate misunderstanding. But he respected Asaka enough to want to make amends.

Through all this he heard Asaka listening quietly, with the muffled noises of the city in the background. At one point, Asaka even said, "That's good to hear."

Rudolph felt reassured by this. He began to grow confident, hopeful enough to plunge into the second part of his spiel.

And while we're on the subject of making amends, he said hesitantly, he'd been reconsidering the scenario Frederick had once presented about working with several of his friends. In retrospect, Rudolph admitted he might have reacted too quickly by saying no. But now—out of respect for Frederick, out of a desire to repair the relationship—he was willing to reconsider. Might the opportunity still be open? Because if it was, Rudolph would be only too glad to help.

There was a long silence.

Rudolph waited. His parched throat ached for coffee, but he didn't dare pick up the cup. Finally, unable to bear it one second longer he broke in eagerly:

"So what do you think about that?"

He could feel his voice, desperate and anxious, *give me a bone*, and he knew it was his death sentence.

And Asaka heard it too. His burst of laughter came out loud and delighted, as if he couldn't possibly hold it in any longer.

"Is that all?" Asaka asked, the smile still in his voice. "No, really, is that all?"

Rudolph heard him get up from the table; a door closed as he left the room.

"Really, Rudolph, it's two things. First of all, you rejected me. *My* offer. When I came to you, I thought you were in control of the situation. Ready to make amends. So now I've got to wonder, *why's this guy running back to me?*"

"I—" Rudolph began excitedly.

"Well, but I know why," Asaka interrupted coldly. "I've been following the Bowes business. Quite the mess you're in, isn't in? And that's exactly what I can't have. Because desperate men, they make mistakes."

Rudolph felt his whole world collapse beneath him. He was trying very hard not to cry.

Asaka waited a minute for him to respond. He even said, "Okay?"

When Rudolph didn't reply, Asaka hung up the phone. He had meetings to get to. This wasn't a fucking charity business.

*　　*　　*

Frozen with shock, Rudolph retreated into the dark cave of the wine cellar. He had already been roundly humiliated once today, but the worst of the afternoon was still to come.

Rudolph crouched on the molding cellar floor. Clutching his laptop in one hand and a bottle of wine in the other, he turned on the online auction. He'd placed four Bill Bowes paintings in the auction weeks ago, thinking that the outcome would be unbeatable.

Loss after loss flickered on the glowing blue screen. Midway through the auction, his phone started ringing. Clients were clamoring to get out of sales, canceling agreements they'd promised weeks ago; the blessed warmth of alcohol was dissipating, he felt cold now. When the auction ended, Rudolph slammed the laptop shut.

He dropped his head into his knees and cried.

In less than two hours, his losses had spiraled from less than five million to over forty. Five was doable—forty wasn't. His business debts alone totaled in the tens of millions, it'd be impossible to get another bank loan, impossible to avoid bankruptcy, impossible without putting him in the same, white-knuckled position he was in today.

He was ruined. Well and truly ruined.

That fucking little bitch, Simone Machado. She'd ruined everything—his life, his livelihood, his status among friends . . . And Bill Bowes, all that time and money wasted on Bowes! The act of rape was as brutish and incomprehensible to Rudolph as murder, an act with no purpose, no forethought or calculation. How stupid could you be? What was it the feminists were always saying—the personal is political! Didn't he understand that?

At least the wine was exquisite. Black cherry, blackberry and cassis, lemony tannins lending structure to a rich coffee-scented bouquet with finishing touches of dark chocolate—God, it was good! How on earth could he ever drink Franzia again?

Swinging the bottle to his lips, he watched a brown rat scurry across the dank stones paving the cellar floor, alone in his awfulness. The urge to blow himself up was too tempting, end up in a haze of weed and pills at some girl's house, ignore the reality of things, God knows he'd done it before—so drunk and crazed with misery that he chipped his own tooth lapping at the bottle. He howled in pain, the frightened rat leaping over his foot before it disappeared into a dark corner, its wiry tail whisking rapidly back and forth before the blackness swallowed it whole.

He *had* to survive. Had to prosper.

Only yesterday the future had loomed so bright before him! His soul cried out at the awful injustice of it. Just because he wasn't like all those other trust fund babies with some daddy's insurance policy . . .

What do I have? he wondered desolately. How can I possibly get myself out of this mess?

Think. Think your way out of this. You might've gambled everything on the wrong guy, the guy who couldn't keep his wet dick in his pants, but you're still the kid who made it out of that chipped, peeling room in the poorest neighborhood in Massachusetts to become the powerful owner of a multimillion-dollar gallery by the ripe old age of thirty-three.

The rat. He thought again of the rat in the hole . . . The germ of an idea was flickering at the edges of his brain, but it disappeared the more he tried to grab hold of it.

He imagined himself alone, ten years from now. Under Ingrid's influence, he had cut down on drinking, but she deserved better. Once he was broke she would see that. A vision of himself, crawling up the stairs to Lyndon's grand house in Hyannis Port, his uncles and cousins and even his mother poking and laughing and stabbing him with sharp sticks, the way you'd stab at an animal who's fallen wounded from the pack.

He felt sick. Shivering and coughing in his mother's old apartment on Jacob Street, he would piss and soil himself in his sleep, feeding and feeding off whatever chump change his mother's family deigned to give him when there was no money for heat. The kind of guy who'd stagger into a Back Bay bar drawling, stammering, *Ya know I used to be kind of a big deal . . . Yeah, used to have a couple big galleries . . .* and people would laugh and raise their eyebrows pityingly and clink their glasses with sympathetic smiles, because it was obvious that he was nothing but a wastrel and a liar and a dead drunk, the kind of broken man who'd be doing everyone a favor if he just went ahead and died already.

The answer slipped into his mouth at 4:00 a.m., dissolving on his tongue like the wafer at Communion. He tasted it, tested it, but like all good ideas it was pure and perfect as the Eucharist itself.

Art.

It was so obvious. He'd been doing it all along, using Peter to pay Paul, juggling the balls of any young business owner. But never in any serious way, never enough to risk his livelihood.

But now he'd wrench the wheel left, where he'd always gone right. What do I have, he thought with growing elation, rolling the idea round and round his head, what do I have in terms of tangible, cash-based assets? Nothing. *Zéro.* I'd have to declare bankruptcy. Shamed out of business, millions in debt, and cringing as everyone laughs at my downfall. Because every cent, every shred of credibility is parked in the very thing that's brought me down.

Art. Warehouses and warehouses full of art.

Other people's art, yes. Belonging to other people. Art chopped up into so many shares you'd hardly know what's what, and that's the genius of it. Because only one person is aware what belongs to whom and why and how, and that person is me. Only one person holds every work in their possession.

Me.

Of course, it'd mean cutting his losses. He considered this seriously a while. No more Society Tom. No, he'd have to ignore every client, put every speck of energy into selling as much as he could. But instead of taking his measly 5 or 8 percent, he'd be taking a hundred. Possible to disappear—he knew this for certain—if you happened to be filthy rich. How rich? Thoughtfully he considered this a moment, tapping his lower lip. Two people, two passports, one destination—oh, say around fifty million dollars or so. Sounds right.

A suicide of sorts. The death of Rudolph Sullivan.

Was there really another option?

Yes. Yes. It all made sense now.

This is what I was born to do.

32

THEIR BEDROOM WAS STILL DIM AND CLOGGED WITH SLEEP BY THE time Ingrid went downstairs. A sand of tears had finally glued her eyes shut, after a night thrashing in bed. How could she have been so stupid, so shortsighted?

Anxious to comfort and be comforted, some vague premonition sent her palms sliding across the sheets. But the counterpane was smooth as glass on his side of the bed.

He's left me, she thought in panic. He's gone.

Her worries were beginning to spill over. After the awful failure of the exhibition on Friday, Rudolph had been locked away in his study all weekend, she could hear him pacing around the floor in a white fury at night. He was drinking too much lately. At three in the morning she'd woken up to a muffled crash in the basement; but some oblique fear stopped her from going downstairs.

Trying to swallow her dread, Ingrid rattled the doorknob of his study. It was locked. He was a classic insomniac; maybe he'd gone outside for a run. He often put his sneakers on when he couldn't bear lying there anymore—but this felt different. She checked the bathrooms, the living room, the garden. In the dark cellar she found only wine stains and shattered glass. She stared at the mess for a second. It sent her into another frantic tailspin of movement: running, running, running through the house.

Rushing into the vast stainless-steel kitchen, she was about to scream his name like a madwoman when she saw him leaning against the fridge, calmly drinking a bottle of green juice. His ivory face, waxen like the gold features of a Machiavellian prince on a coin, looked oddly still in the cold sunlight straining through the windows.

She skidded to a stop, breathing hard, deeply miserable in her heart. His rage on Friday night had overwhelmed her; she braced herself for another argument. But Rudolph looked collected, calm.

"Something wrong?" he asked.

"Didn't you hear me calling? I was looking for you all over. You weren't—"

For a moment he turned away, sliding the bottle of juice back into the refrigerator. She couldn't see his face. Then he turned toward her, smiling, and covered her hand. His beautiful eyes were lawn-green and luminous with love.

"Baby. There's nothing to be worried about. Promise."

"But—you've been avoiding me, and you just seemed so upset the other night, I just wanted to know if I could do anything, and I wanted you to know that I never, never would've hidden this from you, Rudolph, I never—"

She was half-crying now, pathetically afraid he despised her, despising herself for her lies. Some secret part of her heart had buried this knowledge, because maybe he would've convinced her to talk Simone out of it, and maybe Ingrid wanted Bill Bowes to be punished. Or maybe she couldn't face taking a side.

He closed his eyes briefly. Then opened them.

"Let's not talk about it, okay? Hey, hey, don't cry. I'm sorry. I shouldn't have shouted. I shouldn't have said those things."

He came over quietly and allowed her to cling to his cashmere sweater, trying to soften his stiff embrace.

"Look," he said soothingly. "Just don't worry about it, okay? I don't want you to worry about a thing."

They sat in silence as he stroked her hair, the air still tight with some repressed disturbance.

"Hey. Did you leave music on the other night?"

"Huh?"

Blotting away tears, she made an awkward wet blubbing sound; her face was scrunched up in an expression of such comic sadness that they both started to smile. It broke the tension between them. Ingrid was relieved to hear them laugh together, even though it pinched her heart to see Rudolph smirk when she cried. But it was nothing. She was overreacting—as usual, she was overreacting.

"Oh that. I was just doing some research for the trip. That's the gamelan, isn't it beautiful? Traditional Indonesian music." She counted on her hands. "I'm learning all sorts of things. In Bali, you hear the sound of cymbals everywhere. They have these witch doctors, where you can get your future read in the blood of pigs. Apparently they squeal in this horribly human way. And it's one of the only countries without an extradition treaty. Cash is still the main currency. I was watching this documentary the other night about a French serial killer who escaped to Jakarta—"

Behind her, Rudolph's eyes opened.

"—and the Javanese coffee is supposedly great," she continued, shaking beans into the grinder. Her back was to him. "I guess I must've left the music on and fell asleep to it—sorry, did it wake you?"

"Oh, no, no, it was fine," he said absently, still rubbing her shoulder.

He turned away with a light laugh then. Ingrid, not noticing, busied herself with buttering two pieces of toast. The rich dark smell of coffee filled the air, signaling morning, signaling fresh starts, and pouring herself a cup Ingrid felt energized.

In the cool sunshine of the living room, she carried her toast and coffee over to the couch. Every Tuesday, she'd taken up the habit of going to Hatchards, a bookstore on Green Park. Her hands would drift over all the volumes of poetry and art books she still didn't know: the lurid scarlet horrors of Lovecraft, the secret workings of the CIA; she could disappear into a thousand startling dreamworlds and never notice the time passing or fortunes changing at Cheyne Walk.

She opened her book, the Bowes crash faded hazily into the distance. They loved each other, and that was all that mattered. They would get past it; they could get past anything. The future was bright. Today she galloped toward the Holy Grail with the Knights Templar, occasionally licking a spot of butter off her finger as she turned another starched white page.

33

CHARLIE HAD ONCE TOLD RUDOLPH ABOUT A FAMOUS RUSSIAN FILM experiment. A director had edited a short film of a silent movie star with alternating shots of a seductive girl on a divan, a woman in a coffin, and a bowl of soup. He'd shown it to an audience, who raved about the actor's extraordinary skills of expression: his ability to manifest grief, hunger, and desire was so powerful, some audience members had even been moved to tears.

In truth, the actor's face hadn't changed throughout the film. It remained expressionless. The combination of images alone did the trick.

"That's the montage effect," he'd laughed. "Putting things together in the way you want people to see them."

Charlie had been talking about writing. But for Rudolph, it had been a life. He'd slipped into their skins, their clothes and women and houses, hoping to convince his clients that he was a giant among men. Now he realized it had worked too well, he'd gone soft. Even he had been fooled.

Things had really fallen by the wayside since Cortez left, Rudolph thought, nausea worrying at his stomach.

A month ago, firing Cortez had seemed like a no-brainer. Rudolph had once thought it was a good idea, hiring a guy who'd worked in the financial services, but Cortez wasn't used to the spending needed in the art world. He had wanted to slow down; Rudolph had wanted the business to grow. They'd been butting heads for months over their conflicting approaches to the gallery's finances. Eventually, after constant arguments, Cortez had seemed to freeze up. Rudolph knew that when people got that glazed, checked-out look, it was time for them to go. He'd been planning to hire someone else, just hadn't gotten around to it yet.

On Tuesday morning, Rudolph forced himself to go through the ledger. The more he stared at the figures, the more a tight, muscular vein began to pulse behind his left eye. All those debts left unpaid! What the fuck had Cortez been doing for the last six months? Still they kept coming, rivers of numbers, an endless black stream that rushed at him with all the cold indifference of mathematics. The numbers didn't lie, nor did they care. He'd felt the crushing burden on his shoulders, but seeing it all on paper was so, so much worse.

Loans. Unpaid rent, supplier and security and electricity bills, million-dollar shipping invoices Madison had done her very best to clear up or fob off. Hundreds of thousands spent on client entertaining and art fairs and business-class flights—unavoidable expenses!— because you had to get out there, show face to these insular jackals, these wolves. You had to be one of them, or else they would not trust you. Would not buy from you.

Now he was in millions of dollars of debt; how much? Enough to feel the worms wriggling inside his brain. Lyndon's face bubbled up from his subconscious: the look of horror as he flipped through the *New York Post* (he was a dedicated, if secret, reader) over breakfast . . . *Art fraudster escapes with millions!*

Well, fuck him! he thought defiantly. I can live with that.

Except a second effigy rose up: his withered mother, cast out of Lyndon's mansion. Eloise sitting alone at the peeling linoleum table, staring into a cheap bottle of gin in the wretched apartment he'd grown up in, her eyes sunk to sad little pouches. The unbearable crushing guilt of it! Never knowing whether he was dead or alive . . .

For a moment he sank to the floor, overcome by the enormity of what he needed to do.

Calm down, he begged himself. Focus on the task at hand—but the image of his white-faced mother haunted him. Oh God, how could he do it?

Slowly he raised his cup of coffee to his lips.

But hadn't she always, always chosen Lyndon's family over him? He pictured them ringed around the living room, Hunter—that blockhead!— shaking his head and laughing a little: *Dad, didn't I always say he was a loser*—Lyndon allowing himself a soft laugh while pretending disapproval, *Hunter, you shouldn't say that about your cousin. Though I do have to say, don't take the risk if you can't take the consequences*—

Smug white-bread people, stupidly satisfied with their dull materialism, while he, *he* the clever one, *he* the sensitive one, the entrepreneurial one who'd dared to forge unhoped-for bridges between art and trading. Those men whose company he'd fought so long and hard to be included in—as if having ten times the money and power made you ten times the man.

All they would see in his inglorious fall was proof positive the arts were nothing but fool's gold, doomed to be crushed beneath the churning wheel of technology and progress. But truly, his business had been about more than money for him. He had dreamed of a celestial alphabet, of translating the forest of all small mute things.

Gotta get ready to sell, he told Madison. Get me the list of our most valuable works, stat. Clients are asking for it.

Madison didn't question this explanation. She understood the Bowes market had crashed; it was normal that he needed to drum up money as clients withdrew their investments. Rudolph Sullivan Gallery had over two hundred artworks stashed in various non-taxable warehouses: New Jersey, London, Geneva, a wrathful Willem de Kooning, a melancholy Dora Maar Picasso. Many paintings had been bought with the Rathenaus' financing, with the intention of selling later at profit.

Should he go to an auction house or private sale with his loot? A catch-22. He needed to sell off the works as quickly and quietly as possible; but the quickest thing would be to pawn them off in one lightning strike. The biggest auctions of the season attracted the richest and most powerful buyers. Let the auction houses do the work for him: marketing, cataloguing, photography, and finally the sale itself. Every work would flood the market at once, too fast for his clients to realize what was happening. The complicated ownership of each work would confuse them, and by the time they figured it out, he would be gone.

But it was too risky, he knew that. Too exposed. The most subtle thing would be to palm off as many artworks and shares as he could, privately, to his own clients.

"Fergus! I was hoping I'd catch you."

"How was your weekend, Annette? Good time at FIAC?"

"I immediately thought of you—it's been in a private collection for thirty years but the best quality, best of the best . . ."

"Something's just come across my desk that I think you might be interested in, if I know your taste."

The words came pouring out of him like they always had, smooth and honeyed and warm as a fireside chat among good friends. No one ever said he wasn't a good talker.

Four days passed before Rudolph realized the subtler strategy wasn't working fast enough. No way could he sell fifty million dollars' worth of art to his own small circle in a matter of weeks. He needed bigger sharks, bigger money with hungrier appetites, foreign cash, people who wouldn't know him from Adam. The clock was already running against him.

Wednesday morning, Rudolph woke to a friendly voicemail in Christian Rathenau's phlegmy tones.

"Rudolph? Rudolph, I wanted to know whether you are all fine?" Loud indistinct noises in the background, possibly a toilet flushing. "Listen, do you know any graffiti artists? We're creating a new programming incubator in Germany, and Jonas thought of a great angle, absolutely *fantastisch*. Say some cool street artist comes to paint inspirational messages on the wall—things to make people work harder, yes? The jewel of Brandenburg—can you not just picture it?" *Haw, haw, haw.* "Also," he added hurriedly, "Stefan thinks we should put a pause on the financing agreement—just for now . . . in light of the Bowes situation. Er. Call me back."

So. Auction it was.

But which auction house to call? Tough question. Christie's was busy with selling the *Salvator Mundi*, which in 1958 was attributed to one of Leonardo da Vinci's assistants and sold for forty-five pounds at Sotheby's in London, but today was heralded as a long-lost Leonardo.

It was a miracle in the art world, performed—like all miracles—out of thin air. The great rediscovered portrait of Christ—thought lost or destroyed for half a millennium—had somehow turned up in a New Orleans auction house five years ago, painted over and damaged. Two ambitious art dealers—deciding that something in the shape of Jesus's hand convinced—snatched it up for a thousand dollars.

The clever dealers brought it to a talented restorer, who completely repainted around 80 percent of the painting, using the *Mona Lisa* as her source. Now, at last, it looked like a real, wet-off-the-easel da Vinci. Christie's was marketing it as the greatest masterpiece on earth. Flashy posters modeled on *The Da Vinci Code* adorned the streets of major cities. "It's the last Leonardo," a slick advertising firm whispered to people grabbed off the street, before shoving them inside a dark room with a camera. The footage was turned into an advertising film, genius

in its simplicity: frame after frame of awestruck civilians looking at
the painting. People who wouldn't know a Warhol from a beat-up Ford
Escort! It was sheer genius, a real inspiration to Rudolph.

Sotheby's, he mused, would be desperate for the sale. Logically he
knew this was the wisest option. Christie's would be a press junket
with the da Vinci; the last thing he needed was a horde of journalists
buzzing around this particular dung-heap.

And yet. Some gut instinct told him that if he put his loot in the
Christie's sale, the da Vinci might sell for a price so dizzying that even
his eagle-eyed clients would be too dazzled to notice anything else. If
he could somehow squeeze his stolen works into the five minutes after
the da Vinci came up—

Careful, careful, he reminded himself. Be careful, do not act rash,
because any piddling little fuckup could be Asaka-level catastrophic,
only much, much worse. Example: He could sell shares of a work
owned by Jack to Jack's best friend John. Jack and John might run
into each other on the street and decide to smoke a couple of cigars
together at John's club—he looked morosely at his own smoking embers
in the fireplace—and John happens to mention that he's just bought
50 percent of a painting, which Jack quickly realizes *he* owns—Fuck! It
could all go so wrong so quickly!

One missed connection, *one* chance encounter, and the entire
house of cards would collapse, with him trapped inside it.

It was past midnight. Rudolph sat, hunched over on the vintage
Chesterfield sofa in his office, watching the fire die. He had a poker
in his hand. The smell of burning wood filled the room. He watched a
stick of wood crack and bounce into the air with a squeal as the flames
coughed up their last, sputtering sigh. Death must be like that. Strange,
how physics worked this way, how the last flash of spark always came

at the end, as though some burst of energy must accompany the disintegration of an object before it changed into a new form.

After spending a couple of hours getting together a proposal of works, Rudolph called Constanza, his contemporary art contact at Christie's. His client, he explained, was an enigmatic Nigerian businessman going through a ruinously expensive divorce. He didn't want his name involved. A common enough explanation, which she accepted without question.

"Well, it's a great collection of works, Rudy."

He could hear her eagerness to make the sale in the brisk way she tapped at the keyboard. It wasn't often such a mother lode of treasure was dropped in their laps without a fight.

"We'd really like to take them, no question about it."

"I'm so glad you think so," he said sweetly. "Though I do have another offer on the table. Sotheby's, of course."

She paused, meditating a moment on how best to clinch the sale.

"I think . . . we could guarantee the three most valuable works."

He pressed: "But can you take all twelve?"

"All but two, I think," she said regretfully. "We can't take the Monet, I don't think. The wartime connection is too risky, unless you happen to have papers . . ." Her voice drifted off. "If it were restituted, Christie's could be liable. But as to the rest . . ."

"Happy to do it," he assured her. *Happier than you know.* "But, Cos, I do have one condition. I know it's unusual, but my client needs cash, and he wants to be paid the guarantee as soon as the works are delivered to Christie's. In advance of the auction," he clarified.

A moment of hesitation. "We usually need thirty days."

"I'd be just as happy to go to Sotheby's," he reminded her.

"Um, okay. Give me a sec while I talk to my boss."

He was put on hold. Then Constanza was back, clearing her throat with an air of decision.

"Yeah, I checked and it's all fine. We can guarantee the three most valuable works, payment up front. We'll divvy them up between the November evening and day sales happening in a few weeks."

Rudolph was ready to sing a hosanna after that. Things were turning out so perfectly, it seemed like a mark of divine favor. He had been hoping that they would promise the November sales, though Christie's would have to reprint their catalogues. Speed was critical. Even with his best excuses, it would not take long for his clients to start asking questions. Everybody read the same papers, talked to the same dealers. He had weeks, maybe months before they figured it out.

So, ten works. Jittery with coffee he totted up the sums in his head: if every work sold at its low estimate, well . . . that'd be about twenty-two million. And we're off, he thought. The leap of excitement, hot in his throat, was now laced with a green thread of terror.

34

THE REMAINING WEEKS OF OCTOBER BLINKED BY. RUDOLPH WAS enmeshed in the black wheels of a speeding train, its cogs whirling inexorably forward through the blur of falling snow. Some shadowy destination, location unknown.

Meanwhile the Bowes scandal kept rolling onward, crushing the paintings on which he'd staked his life savings in its brutal path. Any initial hopes that the elderly artist might be proved innocent soon darkened at the edges: every woman he'd ever hired or taught, it seemed, was coming out with her own story. J'ACCUSE, SHE SAID, the tabloids screamed. PROTEST ART SPARKS RAPE INVESTIGATION FOR LEGENDARY AMERICAN ARTIST. FAMOUS PAINTER'S HOUSE OF HORRORS.

The Twitter hordes were baying for Bowes's blood. The Palais des Beaux-Arts hastily canceled their retrospective. Market watchers posited Bowes's present-day worth at zero. Scrambling to repair his reputation, his lawyers argued the old man was suffering from dementia, the encounter with Machado was consensual, but nobody believed this. A flimsy excuse, people said angrily. Well, theirs was a culture of remorseless leveling-out, a desire to tear down the old and erect new gods in their place.

Change was in the air. Ingrid followed the story avidly; it had awakened an almost hysterical satisfaction inside her. A groundswell of repressed fury was rumbling to the surface, centuries in the making. Why should Bowes get away with it? We're tired of seeing fatuous white men hang on the walls, people grumbled, tired of hearing their bloated excuses. Tired of listening to men gloat about how they contain multitudes. Why do they get to rape and blather on and express their flaws however they want, while we sit patiently waiting our turn? So you'll understand why we aren't interested in offering second chances. Haven't they already had a millennium of them?

A new star was rising, a great ball of fire hurling at the sky.

On a wet chilly morning in early November, Rudolph snatched *Harper's Bazaar* off the newsstand at Sloane Square and paged rapidly through the glossy four-page center spread. Simone looked cool and serious in a paint-stained couture dress, leaning against her wet unframed paintings like she'd planned this moment for decades.

MEET SIMONE MACHADO, THE #METOO SURVIVOR WITH A SOLD-OUT ART SHOW

"What interested me most about the J'accuse series was the reaction," Simone Machado tells me as I walk into her quirky-chic, refreshingly unstudied Mott Street studio. The light-filled loft is filled with unfinished paintings and camera equipment. A new video project? I ask.

Machado nods, enthused. "Exactly. The J'accuse series—I was proud of helping to expose Bill Bowes for who he is, obviously. But the story felt unfinished—lacking nuance. Because what I also wanted to address is how, to rise as an artist, I needed to sacrifice myself. Being a male artist constitutes a different pressure, but I knew I wasn't going to succeed until I got naked for the culture industry. Basically, people have this sick fascination with female pain, and you're never really allowed to grow out of it. It's like a second rape, a rape of the mind, creating this horrible triangle of complicity between you, the rapist, and the press."

I ask how the camera comes into this. Machado leads me into another room, where a large black wardrobe stands next to an open window littered with cigarette butts and empty Diet Coke cans, for which the twenty-eight-year-old aesthete apologizes with a charming smile.

The doors of the wardrobe have been removed to show a collection of objects glued together: newspaper articles, fragments of denim, and two small, staticky 1980s television screens. Flickering across the screens is a clip of Machado herself in a recent NBC interview played on never-ending loop.

"See, I wanted to go deeper," Machado explains, gesturing at the screen. "So I gave the people what they wanted, I poured everything out. I wanted fame, don't get me wrong. But the heart of the J'accuse series is this. I wanted to create a piece that was like a mirror to the crowd, forcing them to look back at themselves. Why are you so obsessed with cannibalizing the bad things that have happened to me? And am I complicit in giving it to you? What does it say about our culture that the best way a woman can succeed is by performing as this fragile, violated, traumatized virgin? Yes, it simplifies the story. But actually, I'm not that interested in simplicity."

Rudolph crumpled up the magazine and threw it away.

Everything depended on the auction, which would take place in New York in two weeks' time. Rudolph vowed to be there. The da Vinci would suck all the air out of the room—he would sell off his spoils unnoticed, then flee with Ingrid. Either that, or—don't, don't even allow yourself to imagine another possibility, he counseled himself. How often had he heard Lyndon say the words? *To accept failure as an option is to allow yourself to fail.*

Since his fateful decision three weeks ago, Rudolph had managed to sell off a few bits and bobs privately, too. Christian Rathenau's de Kooning *Woman*: a nude figure with pointed nipples turned to gaping eyes, her Chelsea smile leaking tears of blood. That was a cool eleven million right there. But the lion's share of his winnings would come from the auction.

He had a number in his head, the pot of gold he wouldn't mind disappearing into the mist with, and that number was around fifty million. It seemed like a lot, but really it wasn't once you broke it down: the beautiful house, a couple of cars, a small yacht. Enough for two people to live well for the rest of their days.

But sometimes he allows himself to dream, the shadows of a new life taking shape in his tired mind. He is lounging on a shadowed veranda, tanned skin tattooed with a geometric pattern of white-hot sun. Through the fringes of a grass roof, he sees a dark-haired woman diving into crystal-clear waters, the turquoise waters of an infinity pool. As the sun melts down to the keening cicadas, pink bougainvillea and frangipani swirl through rainforest air.

In this dream there is a child.

Children had always been a bit of a blank for Rudolph. But now he tried to imagine a red-haired boy worrying over a board game with Ingrid's curious gaze. Abruptly, the thought broke him out of his reverie. Could he bear to be savagely undressed by those inquisitive black eyes, fifty years alone in their suffocating exile?

A chill settled over his skin. What if she didn't want to come? What if she did, and hated him for the constricted life he caused her to live? A life of immense wealth, yes. Escape. But an escape into eternal isolation, a life spent constantly looking over their shoulders. Never coming home. Unless he figured out a way to hide in plain sight—but he could not think about what that might look like.

He shook off the thought. He would tell her, and she would understand.

Just not at this precise moment.

In a way it was pure lunacy, of course. Rudolph had learned to change his spots from brown to yellow long ago. But Ingrid was different. She had never had to be anything other than a normal middle-class American girl who stuck out like a sore thumb. When they'd gone to Paris, she'd looked around wide-eyed and pointed in awe, slipping, tripping, slamming into doorways, spilling coffee over herself while she laughed at her own clumsiness. There was great privilege in never having to adapt to another country or language, the greatest privilege, though Ingrid was blind to it. But she would have to become a person of secrecy and stealth, a person who could lie and think on her feet, and he worried about that. She was his Achilles' heel.

For days he pored over his laptop in his office, sipping coffee or negronis to calm his fraying nerves. Sketching out a plan.

Fact one: He had a Swiss passport. Rudolph Gris had no connection to Rudolph Sullivan, and he was quite certain that the US government didn't know he possessed a second citizenship. Unless Eloise squealed, and he prayed some long-dormant love for her only child would stop her from betraying him. Beyond her, though, nobody else knew.

Fact two: He still had the Swiss bank account. The Swiss storage container, full of art.

But now he needed to hide the money deeper. Wash it so clean, you'd never see a speck of dirt again.

So. He already had a foundation in Panama, controlled directly through power of attorney. The Panama foundation would need to own several anonymous companies in the Seychelles—trackable only through physical shares that Rudolph would keep in his possession.

The Seychelles accounts would be registered with two bank accounts belonging to the Monaco offices of his Swiss bank. So offshore, you'd have to have multinational police cooperation to even have a hope of finding a single account. But would Müller help him jump through all the hoops required to transfer ten or twenty times as much money? Was the Swiss bank really as sketchy as his clients claimed?

Rudolph explained what he wanted to do to Müller, who lapsed into a long silence. This practice of owning a company through a single physical share was legal only in the Seychelles, and it smelled fishy. Very fishy. For a moment Rudolph panicked: What if Müller balked? Reported him? What the hell was he supposed to do? He'd be up shit's creek without a paddle.

But the Swiss banker replied:

"Monsieur Gris, ça ne sera pas un problème."

Things were beginning to fall into place. Until then, he needed to keep on the phones. Talking, chatting, charming, selling—it all came so easily. For days he could forget the ugly unknown waiting for him at the end of his journey, faceless and opaque.

But two days before his flight to New York, Ingrid threatened to throw a spanner in the works. Insomnia was giving him déjà vu, all this constant packing and unpacking of suitcases to the low soothing monotone of Terry Gross on *NPR*. He was talking to Müller about some nitty-gritty details surrounding access and wealth, cell phone pressed alertly to the whorl of his inner ear.

"You're positive the debit card won't be traceable to the Panama foundation?"

"Not in the slightest," Müller assured him. "It's beyond the reach of the American authorities." Rudolph heard the creak of his chair lean back. *"Vous savez,* our clients are like a family to us. And with every hundred dollars in the world's households, eight are offshore. I wouldn't worry about any unwelcome, ah"—he cleared his throat—"oversight."

"Great, great. I've already sent over the first transfer."

Methodically Rudolph snatched socks from his drawers and tossed them into the suitcase, so concentrated on thoughts of money swirling from country to country that he didn't notice Ingrid hovering in the doorway.

"Hey, I was just thinking—" she began.

"You can't sneak up on people like that!"

Ingrid ruffled her feathers visibly at his sharp tone. *Be nice!* he urged himself. It wasn't her fault that he'd been forced to have a fire sale of other people's paintings and don a new identity, although then again, it sort of *was* . . . Ingrid was waving a newspaper around, going on and on about how Simone's accusation had put her at the vanguard of a movement. "MeToo"—they were calling it MeToo. An expression of solidarity.

"What a stupid name," Rudolph snapped, unable to contain his irritation.

Affronted, she put down the newspaper.

"Why are you yelling at me?" She picked up a fallen sock. "And what are you even packing for?"

"Look, I'm sorry—"

"I have no idea where you're going, I have no idea why you keep hiding in your office, and aren't you forgetting something? We're supposed to spend Wednesday having dinner together and looking at activities for the honeymoon!"

Shit! He swiped a hand over his sweaty forehead; yes, they were supposed to, yes, she had reminded him weeks ago, obviously hoping for a chance to talk. Jesus Christ, this was the last thing he needed.

"And I feel like I haven't even seen you at all . . . you said we were going to . . ."

Rudolph's heart swelled with rage, but he forced himself to grab her shoulders with the penitent expression of a remorseful nun.

"Hey, I'm sorry. Right now I absolutely have to go to the New York auctions—just for a week—I'm sorry, I know we haven't been able to spend much time together lately, but I promise we will. Lots of time. Why don't we do something special once I get back, okay? Just the two of us"—all he could think was, *I do not want to be seen in public right now*—"at home."

She hesitated.

"Is that good?" he pressed. "Good? I know, Ingrid, I *know* I haven't been great lately. It's just—things are a little stressful this week."

"Uh—okay. I guess that sounds good."

"Yeah? Yeah?"

He buried his face in her sweater. The mohair threads were soft against his unshaven cheek, and they felt like forgiveness. A lump rose in his throat. He hugged her tighter. She smelled like cinnamon, mixed in with the tangled curls of her hair. Under his grip her shoulder blades were wriggling slightly, like two trapped birds—with discomfort, he realized—and his heart sank. But he refused to let go. Murmuring quietly, "It's gonna be so fun. Just us two," he kept clutching her soft, warm body to his.

35

"WHEELS UP," A STEWARD SAID IN AN UNDERTONE TO HIS FEMALE colleague. She gave a tight nod, smoothing the lint off her wool skirt, worrying a ladder in her black stockings before making her way down the aisle.

Hi, Mr. Sullivan. I'm Carmen. I'll be helping you this evening, so please let me know if there's anything you need—sure, a Coke? Regular or diet?

Yeah, Carmen. I need a fucking end to my money problems. I need to stay out of jail. Can you do that for me, Carmen? Can you?

But Rudolph only smiled politely, sliding the silk eye mask over his face to indicate that he would not welcome further conversation. He hadn't managed to score a day flight from Heathrow to JFK and he really should be working, but he also hadn't slept more than four hours a night this week. The exhaustion was awful. He could not possibly justify flying private anymore, but he'd forgotten just how icy the air-conditioning on commercial planes was, even in business. God, how did people do this?

In the month since the Bowes scandal broke, thick knots of tension began to break out over Rudolph's skin, his whole body throbbing with their cruel relentless rhythm. Night after night, he paced through the house, raking his hands through his hair in a frenzy. Cop cars, blaring headlines, gleaming silver bars clinking slowly into place.

In reality, he knew, nothing would gleam. It'd be Rikers for him, the floor slick with shit and rotting banana peels. A shadowy figure in an orange jumpsuit haunted his dreams, coming with a shiv fast and hard at him, slitting his throat the way you'd skin a soft white fish until he bled out . . . Oh God, he prayed, save me, I wasn't meant for this life!

"Chicken or pasta, sweetie?" smiled Carmen the stewardess, and he jumped with fright. His heart was beating faster than a cornered rabbit's.

It was the London to New York red-eye, and he could sense the crew members' calm routines, just another city on the whirling multicity trajectory: Paris, Rome, Dubai . . . He watched Carmen burst out laughing at a joke the steward had made, jiggling the cups of sparkling water. Never had he understood how indifferent this world was to his problems until now. The pilot shouted out commands in the cockpit, the plane was preparing for liftoff.

At the hotel, Rudolph felt too anxious to sleep. He lay on the orange bedspread, fingering the Greek key pattern designed to subliminally reassure guests that they, too, were the heirs to Agamemnon and Zeus. His silver suitcases winked cruelly before him.

I will never, he thought despondently, return to this city again.

Could you blame him? When he was two, it was Gordon Gekko for Halloween, Patrick Bateman at fifteen, Jordan Belfort at thirty. He watched Serena and Blair laugh their way through Gucci and Chanel as the *Gossip Girl* narrator obsessively detailed their every purchase on television. Instagram ads for lives you could never buy, internet scams to game the system and score a quick fix, smiling models running across college campus pamphlets for universities that couldn't land you a white-collar job less a hundred thousand dollars in debt. Celebrities laughing from the gold pyramids at Vegas, indifferent tech bros riding the subway with beggars dragging leaking legs. He had grown up in an inexhaustible orgy of wealth and domination. He had grown up inside the country of illusions, a vast pyramid scheme where greed was good.

But now the inexhaustible dream was exhausted, he felt sickened and confused by his own thoughts. Desolately he shivered at the bottom of his bed like a child who has gorged himself on too much cake. Somehow the breathless rose-tinted dream had gone rotten, the icing was crumbling and stale where it should be sweet. His dream was edged with flies, clotted with cobwebs and rot, and when you carved up a slice its heart tasted moldy and sour.

Given his panicky state of mind, scouting out a double cheeseburger and the porn channel suddenly struck Rudolph as a blow for common sense. Pulling on the ubiquitous navy Yankees hat low over his forehead (he'd always said he was a Red Sox fan, but truth was he didn't give a shit; would've sold his shirt to the other side in half a second. But other men were savage and tribal like that, expecting as proof of your humanity some stupid allegiance to an abstract entity beyond yourself. *I've got heart. I care.* Well, he didn't care), Rudolph made his way uptown to J. G. Melon on 72nd and Third, where he finally treated himself to an extra-dry martini.

Fuck it, he'd gotten this far.

With its wood paneling, water-stained bar, and colored plastic flags, J. G. Melon had always reassured him. Rudolph dabbed a hunk of brioche into a pool of bloody ketchup, gazing absentmindedly around at the decor, which reminded him of the old Barnstable Yacht Club he'd once taken sailing lessons at with Lyndon's sons. A motley cocktail of frat stars, aging WASPs, and pink-faced, badly dressed tourists in Madras shorts—it was all so New York, his New York. And now he might never see it again.

He stood on the corner outside the restaurant, watching the torrents of people shove by. But their raw desires felt distant from Rudolph now, who woke up shivering with a parched throat in the night. Lately his pants were growing loose around the waist. He'd thought of himself as the snake, lolling fat and happy on the sun-dappled path; but the snake was already slithering fast ahead of him, and Rudolph was only the skin it left behind.

As a child he had watched adults like this, anxious to figure out how to act and how to live. Trying to understand how to join the rushing stream, avoid the glazed-eyed look of the bruised and matted men on the street. His mother's glassy green eyes swam in his mind; a terrible agony swept through his chest. Some people got lost. Frozen in their separateness.

An odd, sharp, repellant thought, a thought quite unlike him. But he was feeling a little different these days, a little less like Rudolph Sullivan, though that golden boy's wasted promise still twisted in his gut like the dull edges of a serrated knife. No, he was Rudolph Gris now, just another blank, anonymous Swiss businessman, and perhaps Rudolph Gris was an altogether darker, sharper, more repellent person than Rudolph Sullivan had ever been.

36

THE WIND WAS BLOWING THE WRONG WAY.

A cold western storm had gone howling down the Thames that afternoon, careening through the deserted streets. When another wet clump of ash flew in her face, Ingrid finally admitted defeat and shut the window with a bang. She gathered up her watercolors and a sheaf of paper for the attic floor. A room of one's own, wasn't that what she had wanted?

Maybe we only recognize periods of transition in moments of emptiness. Reflection. These days she often woke up feeling comfortably blank, but it was the blankness of an empty jar, filled with a vague unease like mustard gas. She hoped something was coagulating inside of her, gathering its cells together to be born—but if so, it wasn't ready yet.

Certain half-formed thoughts kept nagging at her. In fact, if she was honest, a writhing snake's nest of suspicions had been hissing around her head for days now, weeks even. Her eyes followed Rudolph down the hall as he disappeared into his study each morning, face hidden from sight. At night he'd emerge with bloodshot eyes, responses mechanical, robotic laughter just a second too late.

Is it Bowes? she'd asked, hesitantly, and his shoulders had stiffened. His lips pursed into a thin white line.

No, he had said shortly. It's not.

The attic was warm and quiet, smelling of turpentine and rain. Ingrid got to work almost immediately, adding silvery ink to a Cubist swan's long white throat. The sputtering radiator made soft creaking noises as the storm beat water against the warped old windows, the wavy Victorian glass uneven with age, the room enfolding her like a dark womb in heat. The old, pitched roof was garnished with painted stars.

In September, shortly after she'd arrived in London, Rudolph had gone to a costume party in Notting Hill where everybody dressed up in Stasi-inspired BDSM outfits. Ingrid had declined. She wanted to spend the night working on a painting to hang over the fireplace.

Later that night, Rudolph climbed up to the attic and leaned against the threshold in his silly black latex jumpsuit. Ingrid was curled up in a pile of crumpled newspapers in the dim attic, her face red with fresh tears.

"What's wrong?"

He bent down next to her, encircling her chest with his warm reassuring arms, the scent of whiskey and laundry and Claus Porto soap.

"It's gone," she sobbed. "Look."

Rudolph picked up the discarded landscape, his lips moving silently as he scanned the twisted green and blue shapes like an editor reading a page; Ingrid quivered. By the time he said, "But it's wonderful! It's beautiful, Ingrid, seriously," she had collapsed. It was too late.

"Did I ever really have it?" she cried, burying her face in her hands. "Do you think I ever had a shred of talent?"

"Of course you did, of course you do," he said, trying in vain to soothe her. He kissed her forehead and held her at arm's length, inspecting her fiercely. "You know what I told all my friends tonight? How proud I am of you."

She looked up at him. He hesitated.

"How lucky I feel," he said. "To be with you."

She absorbed his words like a protective warmth.

"Why don't we paint this attic instead?" he suggested. Seizing tubes of paint, he jumped to his feet, the black latex straining ridiculously tight over his groin. "Hey. I think you need to take the pressure off yourself. It's okay to have a day off, isn't it? Look at this shit—the room's so bare and bleak, it could do with a little color, couldn't it?"

His ridiculous outfit made her laugh, despite her tears. It felt so good to laugh that for a moment she almost forgot why she was crying. Rudolph was running around like a little kid, dashing a squiggly-haired green stick figure—"See, that's you"—cajoling her until she joined in. Hours had passed like that. They'd ended up painting a whole indigo mural of constellations across the walls, every surface, until all those stars and suns and moons enclosed the attic in a bath of yellow light.

She'd had an early awareness of death, and now when she experienced peak happiness it was always with a desperate sense of foreboding, the bittersweet taste of her own mortality between her lips. Perhaps the best things would be over too quickly. Perhaps it had always been too good to last.

Their wedding had crystallized a brief but dizzying period of ecstasy in which Ingrid thought she'd finally found the person who would keep her safe. Who would wrap his arms around her when she grew frightened of strange external forces in the night, whispering in her ear, "I'll never leave you." But lately she rolled over in bed to find his body tensed head to toe, stiff as an ironing board in a pool of electric moonlight.

Something felt ragged, grotesque. He was here but his soul had left the building, leaving a hollow man in his place, a stuffed man, a blank-eyed thing. In the hallway, they avoided each other's gaze. She caught herself longing for the dog he had promised, an animal who would love her again.

Sometimes a girl with pale gold hair drifted through her mind. Cornelia. She was nothing to him, he'd assured Ingrid—a tempestuous

post-college relationship that had ended badly. And Ingrid had
believed him at the time. But before he'd left for New York, she
had lingered in the doorway while he packed, listening to him jabber
away on the phone. Mention of a debit card, a transfer. What transfer
is this? Then Rudolph had jerked around, he'd seen her listening, and a
cold and lifeless mask had formed across his marble face. But not fast
enough to conceal the fleeting look of reptilian lust in his eyes, lust
such as she'd never seen directed at herself.

She put down her wet paintbrush.

I need to get into his computer.

In her haste she knocked dirty water all over the wood planks,
running down the stairs two at a time to get to Rudolph's first-floor
office. How pathetic to hunt through her new husband's things—
absolutely pathetic—but for once, she had to know. She was sick of
denial, sick of lying to herself.

Rudolph had painted the door to his study a bright, glossy emerald—
the color of the imagination, he called it. The color of freedom. In
the kitchen he kept a huge color wheel of different oil paints, and at
night he would sometimes flip through it while they watched TV. He
was always searching for the most elusive, impossible-to-find shade,
Maharaja Green—a color he'd seen only once, a long time ago, and had
never been able to find.

Ingrid tried to wrench open the door, but the room was sealed
tight as Bluebeard's castle. Why would he lock the door?

She ransacked the antique dresser in the bedroom, tossing dust-
covered detritus of their domestic life on the blue star-patterned
bedsheets she had ordered online from a Vietnamese mountain
tribe of weavers. So he really did have something to hide. Abandoned
electronics, expired passports, dried-up tubes of hand cream—but no
key. She clattered down to the kitchen and upturned the key bowl,

spilling it on the floor, but it held every key except the one for the door to Rudolph's study.

It felt good to mess things up, wreck a path of dust and chaos in Rudolph's absence: he was always so clean. Night had fallen, black and cold, but Ingrid sat in the kitchen with her head in her hands, possessed by her jealousy and suspicions. She would not sleep tonight, not while adrenaline still coursed through her veins like a miserable current.

Someone to tell her what to do. Tell her she wasn't crazy.

The idea drifted in the back of her mind as she huddled under the portico, a flurry of rain droplets coating the dark streets. Another storm was coming, wind roughing up the trees.

Logical, practical Julia would have been her first choice for advice, but the thought of Julia's resigned *I told you so* sigh . . . No. But Richard had been cheated on, several times in fact. She imagined Richard's calm, reassuring voice, telling her that she was being paranoid, as he turned down the volume on a true crime show.

Ingrid tightened her raincoat. Waiting for Richard to pick up the phone, she paced up the cold and windy street.

"What's up?" Richard demanded. "Haven't heard from you at all lately! I've been texting, haven't you gotten any of my messages?"

"I got a new phone. Look," she said hurriedly, knowing she was being rude but too anxious to care. "I think Rudolph is—well. He's away. I don't know what he's doing, he's acting different. Keeping—secrets."

"Secrets?"

There was a moment of silence. Then Richard exhaled.

"Oh, honey. You need to get into his messages."

Wind tore down the street; the phone line crackled with static.

"I tried that already," she yelled, turning back. "But he keeps his computer in his study, and it's locked. I don't know how to get in."

Richard said something inaudible.

"What?" she shouted. "I can't hear you!"

"I said you need to get in there!"

"I told you, I can't!"

"You live there!" he yelled over the crackling static. "Call a locksmith!"

37

THE DAY OF THE AUCTION BROKE WITH A PRECIPITOUS YELLOW SUN. From his suite at the New York Palace, Rudolph watched the morning sky rise high over the dark maleficent spikes of St. Patrick's Cathedral, lining the streets with horizontal stripes of cherry and celadon and rose. Seven o'clock and already he badly wanted a drink; but he would do no such thing. Steel had stiffened his complacent bones, though his fists kept clenching into tight nervous balls at his sides.

Today is the day.

But the auction wasn't until evening. He dressed with care: a crisp lemon-yellow shirt from Sorrento, a classic suit in deathless navy worsted courtesy of his favorite shop on Savile Row. Except after today, he realized with a sharp bolt of sadness, I'll never be able to return to any of my old haunts. They'll be watching for me now, searching the crowds for my face. Erased! After spending twenty goddamn years making sure *everyone* knew my name. What a waste, what a goddamn waste it all was.

In the bathroom, he combed his hair in the mirror, leaning over the sink to see the hollows in his white face. He'd slept only a lidless sleep, eyes straining against the sterile hotel room as the minutes ticked on till dawn.

At the last second, moving gently in front of the mirror to inspect his appearance, Rudolph decided to stick an antique diamond pin into his belt. Nobody wore belt pins these days, but Rudolph was a rare bird. Subtly ironic, eccentric, and maybe a touch—but only a touch—flash. In the end, he thought he'd brought it off, just.

*   *   *

Eight sharp. Rudolph slunk over to a nosebleed seat at the back of Christie's biggest and grandest auction room, refusing the piss-yellow champagne with a polite demurral.

Black sunglasses lowered, Yankees cap on, he slouched down in his chair so that no one could catch his eye. This was the biggest auction of the year. He didn't stand out—celebrities were milling about, in sunglasses just like his. Constanza stood edgily in the corner, wearing a bubble-pink dress with her long brown hair coiled in a chignon. Spotting Rudolph, she motioned for him to come over, but he merely waved hello and looked down at his phone.

Memorable was the last thing he wanted to be.

The room was brimming with aging silver-haired socialites in black tie and diamonds, their winter furs fresh from the cold-storage vaults at Saks. Then the younger crowd: tech guys or Chinese teenagers or Saudi billionaires' kids, pustular gamers with money to burn on yet another tacky hyped-up sculpture for the penthouse in Knightsbridge or Dubai or Malibu. It was reassuring to be among his own kind again, gratefully dissolved into the powerful muscles of their velvety fold.

Somehow, after lunch, he'd felt inexorably drawn to the Egyptian section at the Met, where the cold-eyed faience sculpture of Isis stood. It was here that Ingrid had first told him that she loved him, and though he'd been loved by other women before, this was the first time he'd believed it. A warm happiness spread through him like butter— in that moment, he felt exactly like Rudolph Sullivan, of Rudolph Sullivan Gallery, the man he so desperately needed to be. Not that ugly little runt, sometimes forced to stand outside of his mother's locked bedroom door for hours, sometimes hesitantly tapping, sometimes giving in to the urge to furiously beat as panic swelled inside his small, bony chest.

Mom, Mom, come out of the room. Please come out of that room.
It was forbidden to knock, of course. It was forbidden. But sometimes he had to, sometimes he had to because of the smell. But she would not come out. She would not come out for anything.

The memory unleashed a brief and terrible pain, a pain so grating he almost choked; a dry rasping noise escaped his throat. People turned to stare. Then he was running, running out of the museum and through the park, sprinting down Midtown, chasing away the bad, dark feeling in his heart.

"The auction has begun!" someone shouted.

Entranced by the roar of the auctioneer, Rudolph leaned forward in his seat. Arranged in high podiums like haughty Roman nobles observing the gladiatorial arena, the specialists were whispering to their Moby Dicks on the phones, exaggeratedly shielding the mouthpieces with their glittering hands for the benefit of their colleagues: *I'm talking to a really, really big fish right now, Claire. Huge. So you can fuck right off.*

I'd have done exactly the same, he thought bleakly.

The audience's complex dermatological routines generally ensured a look of plump-cheeked passivity, redolent of a crystal shrimp dumpling, lying quietly in its basket. But tonight, tension strained at the seams of the viewers' tight Botox. Christie's had taken a great risk here: it'd be either fobbed off at a shitty price as a magnificent failure, or sold for a price no one had ever dreamed of.

"Lot 9B," the auctioneer intoned, and the room inhaled sharply.

"Leonardo da Vinci's *Salvator Mundi*. The masterpiece by Leonardo da Vinci. Previously in the collections of three kings of England."

The ghost of a smile appeared on Rudolph's face. The joke was that the *Salvator Mundi* was being sold in a contemporary auction—a decision aimed at getting sexier press attention and clients, rather than the boring Old Masters crowd—because it *was* a contemporary painting, having been so dramatically restored last year. Then he remembered what he was doing and sagged back into his chair.

"It's happening," someone murmured in a low voice, and the specialists began to jab their hands into the air, fast and then faster, bidding and bidding and bidding.

"One hundred and ten million. I have it at one hundred and twenty. One hundred and fifty million on the left, at one hundred and sixty on the left, at one hundred and ninety is the bid!"

The room was silent with tension but for the shouts of the auctioneer; the specialists leaned toward the auctioneer's gyrating palms, hands white with strain where they gripped the podium. Reporters' fingers were jittering over phones, breaking news, it had already crossed two hundred million. Then it happened.

Rudolph raised his eyes to where the Savior hung.

The *Salvator Mundi* stared out from a veil of brown smoke, one hand grasping a crystal orb in his lapis-blue robes, the other gently crossed in silent blessing. Rudolph's breath caught in his chest; he touched the cross around his throat. He could feel himself staring, staring, unable to look away from the painting. It had survived five centuries to look down at him with soft amber eyes like a living man of flesh and blood, and suddenly Rudolph experienced a strange melting feeling in his head. As if his skull had turned to wax. God was here—in the room with him.

These works of art, so physically fragile and costly to maintain, yet they lived a thousand years longer than their creators. Spiraling past the human memory of those they had owned, their children and children's children and children's children's children, they hurtled into the future with an eternal aliveness, resisting death, resisting the end of spirit and flesh, they rattled down the smoky end of time. It's the immortality we pay for—we want our place in history. We want to live forever.

He had the awful sensation of having finally found the answer that could save his existence, too late.

"Two hundred and fifty million!" the auctioneer thundered.

Rudolph leaned forward, the iron screws in his chair digging into his thumbs. Whispers of disbelief spun into a maelstrom of reluctant awe; the price kept going higher and higher. If it went above three hundred million—but that was impossible—

"At three hundred and thirty million. Would you like five? . . . Three hundred and fifty-five million dollars . . . Three hundred and seventy . . . Four hundred million!"

Shocked whoops from the audience; cries of delight.

"Four hundred million dollars is the bid. And the piece is," he banged the gavel down, hard, "sold!"

Upheaval. Wild cries erupted; Rudolph was blinded by the flash of cameras as he jumped to his feet. It was happening. The da Vinci had dazzled the crowd like a storm of glitter, everybody was turning to each other with expressions of stunned disbelief. A painting of uncertain origins had just been sold for a sum far exceeding anything ever paid for a work of art in the history of mankind.

The distraction was too magnificent to look away, and now he would have an absolute fire sale right under their feet.

The energy in the room was beginning to ebb. The auctioneer shuffled his papers. People were leaving, they were bored now, but Rudolph's fingers curled tighter over the edge of his seat.

Sink or swim, he chanted to himself in a monotone. Sink or swim.

"Next up, the iron scorpion some see as a menacing self-portrait of the sculptor . . ."

It was on. Rudolph's whole body strained forward, his eyes glued to the auctioneer as the man capered around the stage like a monkey, calling bids out of the sky. Four, five. Higher, higher. Six. Go higher. Eight, eight, dear God make it eight.

"Ten!" the auctioneer bellowed, banging down the gavel. Rudolph breathed out sharply. Constanza shot him a pleased smile; she was probably hoping they'd fuck later. Not today, old sport, he thought, leaning back in his chair. Not today.

The only work he owned in the auction was Warner Theilmann's *Blutfleck 103*, a photograph dripping with crimson like the rusty color of blood on Tampax, Cornelia had once joked. They'd bought it together on that crisp jubilant September day he'd turned twenty-five, when Olbrich gave him the gallery to manage, and the world still seemed to hold some bright hopeful core of himself within it.

Gone, now. Everything gone.

Everything felt so stuffy suddenly, claustrophobic. A hot, itchy scarf seemed to be wrapped tight around his throat, choking him— he leaned down and gripped his head with his hands, desperate to breathe. The plan was working. Working so well that he'd have more than enough to run. But he couldn't catch his breath. He was lost, cut off from the herd.

"You okay?" he heard someone ask with mild concern, and with a terrible ache of loneliness he realized that normally he'd be here with a friend.

No more.

Unthinking he rose up to his full height. He dashed out of the room and down to the lobby, where he swept off his baseball cap and craned his neck up to the sober mezzanine. He was desperate to get outside, to gulp down the fresh air of Rockefeller Plaza—

"Hey, you little shit—!"

Rudolph turned very, very slightly. His ears pricked to attention. Reflexively he'd already pasted on his social smile, but a deeper, more ancient voice in his gut was telling him to run.

"You've been avoiding my calls for weeks, hey? And now we see why!"

Rudolph stood rooted still, half-amazed that anyone could scream at him in a place like this. Christian Rathenau was jogging down the mezzanine, his placid German face purple with rage.

"You don't understand," he heard someone say softly, before realizing it was himself. Words were spilling out, *a sales strategy, disappointed our relationship has deteriorated in this way,* but all the while he was walking backward with beads of sweat racing coolly down his spine.

"My *art!*" Rathenau screamed. "I've trusted you for—a *year!* People told me, you know—but I trusted you. And finally I come here, finally I come here, and we see why you've been avoiding the calls! It's all being sold off in front of my eyes!"

A couple of bodyguards turned in astonishment. Vaguely Rudolph registered a burly man coming up behind Rathenau, a thick rod-shaped item pressed tight under his belt.

He's got a gun, he realized hazily—but he couldn't move, he was walking underwater—

"When I get hold of you I am going to drop you off a fucking bridge!" Christian screamed, and Rudolph snapped to. Power came rushing down his arms and legs. Clenching his fists, he turned on his heel and sprinted out.

Fear was hot and thick in his mouth, blocking his ears as he dashed through Rockefeller Plaza. "*Hol ihn dir!*" Christian shrieked at the armed bodyguard. Rudolph didn't speak German, but he knew that was foreign for sic 'em.

He ran like he'd never run before, fighting the snaking blare of cars and traffic as the doglike sound of heavy panting blundered close behind. The bodyguard's sweaty fingertips were pawing at Rudolph's jacket, he tripped—was jerked down. Shoulder hit concrete. Christian Rathenau was yelling somewhere above them in an excited rage as Rudolph struggled on the ground, trying to hit out with blows, he was hurt somewhere.

The world stopped; Rudolph had a moment of doubt. Then the man's battering fist smashed him in the face. A sharp pain burst through his skull; he felt his nose break like a shingle. His eyes jerked back in a black and mottled confusion of sparks. He could feel his tongue moving but no sound, just a heavy rich liquid running down his throat from his broken nose.

The man tensed his fist for another blow. But with the blood came animal terror, animal adrenaline, and Rudolph wriggled under the man's weight, panting and furious. His fingers closed over the diamond belt pin's sharp tip. He threw up his hand, a single urge running blind through his brain. *Kill him.* Needle tore through skin. The man yelped and recoiled and one hand flew to his cheek.

Rudolph lurched to his feet, almost falling in his haste. His nose felt oddly loose as he ran, the cartilage was flapping and clumsy. Dimly one of his eyes was open and he saw the traffic through a bloodied haze and, as he flung himself around the front bumper of a cab, he made out the taxi driver's astonished face.

He'd lost him. Thank Christ, he'd lost him. Still he kept running, dodging and dashing toward the West Side Highway until finally collapsing in darkness, red panic still juddering high in his throat. Something wet and viscous was dripping down his face. Wiping his nose, he saw fresh blood trickling down his shaking wrists, mingling with the soot and the bird shit as if his own spirit were seeping into the dust.

Those dumb fucks, he thought with a sudden flight of rage, rubbing his scraped knuckles on his pants. They're the ones to blame, not me. First of all, they'd ruined the entire world. We thought we'd be getting a whole new, clean planet that was ours for the taking, but turns out *they'd* already plunged their dirty shit-encrusted fingers deep inside of its warm, fresh holes. Soiled it, raped it, and yet they *still* wouldn't fucking die. They just wouldn't *leave!* Eighty, ninety, one hundred years old, they were still making the laws and strangling the boards and the corporations and the whole damn country with their sick, aging bodies like deathless parasites unable to leave the host. Look at the Rathenaus! Profiting off *my* name, *my* talent to evade taxes, hiding their money in Luxembourg and Lichtenstein—when they could personally fund a small foreign nation with all that cash! Choking me! Choking us!

He was almost laughing, sweating, chuckling maniacally, as he jogged past the Mexican restaurants lining Ninth Avenue trying to avoid being seen. *Asshole!* some guy swore at him as he spun into a child's pink toy bicycle, accidentally kicking it over. *That's my kid's tricycle! Can't you watch where you're going?*

They deserve it, he thought furiously. How can I be responsible for playing the game they created? I'm not guilty, no—they are. They are.

They're the guilty ones, guilty as sin.

The sweat had dried cold on his skin; he was shivering now, the bright blaze of restaurants in his bleeding eye strained very far away. Next time a cab rolled by he stuck his hand out, gasping in pain as he wrenched the door open.

"Fiftieth and Madison, please," he said to the cabbie. "And go quick. Please, I just need to go quickly."

38

"BUGGER OF A LOCK, ISN'T IT?" THE LOCKSMITH COMMENTED, GLANCING at Ingrid over his shoulder.

He was a kind-faced, graying man in his early fifties. She flushed red with embarrassment, turning her face to the window—in her obsessive thoughts about getting into the study, she'd already forgotten what he'd said. Instead she watched a lone fox dart behind a mildewed stone angel in the garden below. Its wail pierced the air.

"I thought foxes only howled at night," she remarked.

They both went still, listening.

"Do they cry because they're fighting or mating?" she continued aloud.

The locksmith rolled his eyes behind her back. He hadn't wanted to do this job, was forced to leave his wife's birthday party because no one else was available. Now this silly American girl, in her absurdly expensive house, obviously thought she was charming. A complete lack of reality. He started to wrench at the door with renewed energy.

"There we are!" he exclaimed in satisfaction.

"Is it open? Is it open?"

He jammed his weight against the door and thrust it open with a muffled yelp. Behind him, the American girl was jumping up and down.

It was a hundred pounds more than quoted. But Rudolph would be back tonight, and she had no time to argue. All smiles now, the locksmith called to her in a jovial tone as he walked over to his battered van, "Next time don't lock the key inside!"

For one heart-rending moment Ingrid hung about in the doorway, too frightened by her newfound power to step inside. The overheated room smelled rancid, sickeningly sweet, as if an overripe fruit had been left to rot. Wrinkling her nose at the stench, she stepped over the threshold and opened the windows to let in a gust of wind.

The general impression was of a person in the grip of mania. Papers and pens strewn haphazardly on the floor; uncapped highlighters bled ink on a soiled cashmere blanket. Ingrid picked up a bowl of cut-up pears furred with green mold from the teetering pile of abandoned plates under the coffee table. It seemed somehow obscene that this man, usually so fascistically neat, was living in an atmosphere of panicked derangement right under her nose.

The sullen sky was distorted inward, colored oblongs through the stained-glass windows casting a strange, jeweled light. Rudolph was very proud of these windows, salvaged from the auctioned home of a Tudor merchant beheaded for disloyalty by Henry VIII.

Her eyes moved unwillingly toward the big leather-topped writing desk. An upturned cocktail glass lay in a pool of congealed amber liquid: remnants of a negroni, knocked over as if in a clumsy escape. Setting it down, she allowed her fingers to drift over his laptop. It purred silently on his desk, like a restive cat.

She couldn't believe how easy it was to get inside his computer. His password was the same as his cable streaming account.

She was so intent on finding something suspicious that the cheerful wallpaper of rolling hills surprised her with its ordinariness. His recent documents consisted of provenance documents, press releases, consignment agreements. The files of an overworked businessman, nothing more.

Text messages, then. Luckily his texts were connected to the computer. Within a few short hours she'd burrowed deep into his mind, droplets of inky water beat at the stained-glass windows as morning waned into afternoon, guilt ebbing away as her fingers flew across the keyboard.

She had read every message Rudolph had sent in the past six months and found absolutely nothing, nothing at all. No torrid string of messages to Cornelia. No imprint of abnormality. No tangible proof that might justify her suspicion.

Her paranoia unnerved her.

But the snakes hissed in her head again, louder now: *He might have used his phone for everything* . . . and as if he'd heard them whispering, Rudolph's bright smiling avatar flashed up on her phone. *Boarding the flight now,* he'd written. *Love you. You have no idea how crazy meetings have been.*

She stuffed the phone back in her pocket without replying. Time was running out.

By one o'clock, the rain had started again.

. . . *thought you might be interested in a beautiful Loie Hollowell that's just come across my desk* . . . She examined his messages with Madison for any trace of an affair, but everything seemed appropriately businesslike . . . *Can you please invoice Mr. Mao for the Soulages number 349209* . . . *Need provenance on the Picasso, stat. Can you check whether he sold it to Madame de Neumes in 1959 (Caracas?).* He seemed to be operating at an inhuman speed; the time stamps gave no sign of a man who ever slept, though her own fingers were trembling with nerves.

Take a break, she told herself. Make some tea. Try to calm down.

But returning to his computer, she discovered she'd somehow signed out of his email. Shit, shit, shit. Hurriedly she clicked back to his email server, but to her surprise she saw not one but two accounts presenting themselves for log-in. There was Rudolph's normal email;

then a second account, a meaningless acronym of numbers and letters like a spam address.

Suspicion twinged deep below her ribcage.

Curiously, the second inbox was almost empty. His received messages only went back to April: promotional emails and a few bank notifications. The sent mailbox contained a single thread, addressed to one Yves Müller. Signed Rudolph Gris.

Her palms slowed over the keyboard, stopped.

Rudolph Gris. She tasted the name inside her head. It was an average enough name, a French or German name probably. But why would Rudolph call himself by that name?

She scrolled down to the bank logo. Something felt familiar, but only disconnected snippets appeared in her mind.

Dear Mr. Gris, attaching your October performance report here. As mentioned previously, we have upped your shares in Tesla by 15 percent . . . Signed, Yves Müller, Senior Wealth Advisor. She peered more closely at the signature. *Allard Group.*

A memory floated up from the depths of her consciousness, shimmering to the surface.

Summer in New York. Ingrid had started work at Paul Bernot only the month before, and she was eager to please, sitting up straight at her desk and smiling her big-toothed *I'm new! Please like me!* smile at anyone who walked in the door.

Rita was showing her how to create an interest list, tapping her black nails like chips of onyx at the keyboard. Ingrid was staring at them, half-wondering where Rita had gotten them done, when Paul emerged from his office with another graying client. Pieces of conversation drifted past as they headed out to lunch . . . *Couldn't get the asshole off the phone . . . Great contacts, though—billions in Siberian oil trading. Ceaușescu chased him out of the country . . . Profits meant for the investors, but he liquidated the company. Oh, yeah, it was fine. He just put it through Allard, you know that Swiss bank ... Easy ...*

Voices fading from hearing as they walked down the stairs. *You know how helpful the Swiss can be ...* The door closing softly on their muffled laughter, Ingrid returning to her workday task without another thought.

Oh, Rudolph, she thought with a shiver of unease. What have you been up to?

Allard Group came up immediately online as a private bank based in Lugano, with offices in Guernsey, Geneva, the Bahamas, and Panama. Stray articles by the liberal press passed under her eyes: *Kremlin links to offshore bank accounts. Swiss bank denies holding offshore accounts for 1 percent ...* A theme was becoming clear.

Rudolph was evading taxes. Her shoulders loosened with relief. Well, it wasn't advisable, but she could live with tax evasion. She wasn't born yesterday, and wasn't this common enough for men in his position? Of course they'd have to talk about it, but it appeared that he was faithful.

Except some section of the matrix still felt out of place.

The computer kept drawing her hand unwillingly back, even though she knew she should leave the room, tidy up, and pretend she'd never come in. He had a right to privacy—but her eyes were riveted to the computer's electric glow.

A thin brown hail heckled at the windows. Ingrid got up and closed the curtains.

She typed in the bank website, which Rudolph appeared to have visited just days ago. His password was saved.

The website was chunky and dated-looking, like any small-town bank. Only a long string of numbers identified the owner of the account. The website was in French, which made it difficult to know what to look for, but Ingrid finally navigated over to the current statement.

Her heartbeat skittered in her chest. The account was brimming with cash. Millions and millions and millions in Swiss francs. Could the gallery really be making so much money after the Bowes catastrophe, the crash? Methodically she scrolled through transactions: small deposits sent periodically from six or seven accounts. Jersey or the Seychelles, inscrutable acronyms for names. Every few weeks he'd send another couple thousand dollars; but nothing big, nothing that would flag a tax agency's suspicions.

Going back in time, though, she discovered larger deposits. In April, he'd sent nearly $4 million; another $2.85 million in June. Only two days ago, his modest trail had suddenly spiked upward with a massive $12 million transfer to an account in Panama.

The tiny blue strings of numbers disturbed her. No small company could transfer so much money without someone else noticing eventually. And why did they go into so many different accounts? Why was more and more cash flowing outward, faster and faster, as if something had frightened him—something gone wrong?

Ingrid's eyes kept snagging on one date, one number, like a piece of raw loose skin caught on a rough thread. It itched at her, it wounded, because she knew that number. She could never forget.

$2.85 million . . .

$2.85 million.

Paul will be livid with you if it isn't paid by tomorrow.

She could feel the blood pounding in her throat, threatening to break free from her spinal column. Twisting her hands together, unable to think clearly, she got up from the chair and paced around the room.

Livid. She had always suspected that it was Claudia behind that transfer, Claudia who'd stolen the money for her own ends. But *livid, livid* . . . that wasn't the word Ingrid would have expected Claudia to use. Because she didn't have the best vocabulary—to be honest, Claudia wasn't that smart. She would have said *Honestly, I can't believe this isn't done already*, but *livid—livid* was a word a person of some intelligence would use. Flair, even.

The floor pitched silently under her feet. She felt herself trapped in a vanishing box, unable to say the truth out loud.

Livid. Would a Chinese hacker use that word?

No. The author of that sentence would be sitting at the keyboard, maybe even laughing incredulously that he'd had the balls to craft such a scam. Pleased with his own cleverness. And that was not really like Claudia at all, she realized dizzily, her legs collapsing beneath her feet.

She sat motionless on the sofa. The room was colder now. Her fingers froze where they brushed the velvet cloth, unable to flex her arms or legs. The furniture that Rudolph had bought, the possessions that kept her silent, conscious of her dependence, unwilling to confront unwelcome facts.

She had a sense of a collage coming together, a cracked and fractured scene becoming whole. But still a piece of the puzzle eluded her grasp.

At last she got up from her torpor. Rising to her full height, she shook the pins and needles out of her feet.

Only then did the realization hit her, hard as a blow to the face.

Rudolph Gris was a false identity. He had worn many masks, including Claudia's, because it was he who had deduced just how weak their financial security was, after months of listening to Ingrid complain about how Claudia skirted the rules. It was he who had planned the precise moment when Ingrid would be alone and harried in the office, distracted by a trip he had invited her on.

It was he who had sent the email that had led her to be fired and accused of stealing three million dollars from her boss.

Rudolph Sullivan was a total fraud.

39

THERE WAS AN ANIMAL TRYING TO GET OUT OF HIS STOMACH. "STOP THE car," Rudolph croaked in an uneven voice, and when the car jerked to a halt on the side of the long unbeautiful highway he stumbled out and threw up a thin stream of buff-colored vomit.

Popping an antacid tablet, he wrestled open the bottle of water they'd given him on the plane and splashed it over his pants. In his panicky state of mind, he'd eaten something at the airport that, while claiming to be a pistachio cannoli, had tasted more like a taco filled with semen. And honestly, his stomach had never reacted amazingly to dairy.

The cabbie leaned against the car, watching him. A cheap gold chain jangled off his hairy wrist as he shielded his eyes from the sun.

"You okay there, mate?" he asked doubtfully in a thick Irish accent. "Because if you're ill, I'm sorry, but I can't let you back in my car. I've an insurance policy to report to—"

Just take me home! Rudolph almost screamed.

Swallowing the half-digested remains of his vomit he managed, teeth chattering: "Look, man, I really need to get home. Please. I'll give you a hundred-pound tip, that's twice the price of this ride, all right?"

Indifferently the cabbie shrugged.

"Just—clean yourself up." Glancing at the layer of sweat that coated Rudolph's sallow face: "Best if you pay up front, I think."

Babylike, trembling with effort, Rudolph laid his freckled cheek to the cold window. At the Palace he had washed off the oily sweat and blood from his face, yelping as he disinfected his bruised eye. Now he wheezed painfully out of his fractured nose. No time for a doctor. Lyrics from an old Eminem song circled around his feverish brain.

He wasn't ready to face Ingrid, not even close, despite the clotting pressures closing in on all sides. What he had just done sharply divided him from the rest of the ordinary, law-abiding world, and yet he could not quite comprehend it. Every time he tried to think of the right words to say—*Look, so I've gotten in a little over my head*—he pictured Ingrid's brow furrowing in confusion, and it was so realistic a re-creation of her disillusionment and disappointment that he simply couldn't go further, lost his nerve every time.

Only eighteen hours ago, he'd been hurrying down the wide hurtling gray streets of Midtown, hands buried deep in the pockets of his polo coat. It was dangerous, downright stupid even to return to Rockefeller Center, such a crowded tourist place—the place Rathenau had chased him away from just last night! But he felt sick, sick at heart and burnt out to the soul. Maybe the shining blue and gold lights of the Christmas tree would cheer him up, the marching scarlet and blue nutcrackers with their wide chopping white teeth, the radium blue glow throwing luminescent fox fire to the tangle of shoppers below.

During the holiday season, the city felt saturated with cinnamon-scented nostalgia, a throwback to when Saks was king, real estate was still affordable, and families stayed together despite everything. Before human ingenuity leapt past its creators' wildest dreams, a Frankenstein of artificially designed desires to rip through your small rodent brain with the explosive power of a supercomputer sun.

The Rockefeller Center Christmas tree sang to him like a frosty beacon in the dark, and even though he knew how the city looked and smelled and tasted like a bad cocaine comedown 90 percent of the year, for a minute Rudolph wanted to cry. He would never see this tree again, though he'd planted it, bled for it, watched it grow with the raw mineral grain of his ambition. How could it all mean nothing, this relentless cycle of hopeful people seeking to reinvent themselves in a city of uncontrollable growth? Surely this tree had to mean something. Surely he could not just sink back into the dust.

I have to see the gallery, he thought. I have to see it one last time.

Madison sat at the sleek white reception desk, beige head obediently lowered to her computer. How hardworking she was! Doing such a good job. He hadn't told her what he was doing, of course; not exactly. He'd simply said they needed to sell, pronto.

"Madison!" he said jovially, shutting the frosted door behind him. "How're things?"

Madison lifted her head to greet him, a brief smile of recognition crossing her face.

"Hey," she said, her voice oddly small and tight. Out of his narrowed vision, he saw her eyes widen at his cut nose. "What happened?"

"Got mugged on the subway last night. No big deal."

He was examining the catalogues arranged around her minimal white bookcase, hands automatically drifting to reorganize the titles. How beautiful the gallery was! Maybe things weren't as bad as they seemed, maybe—

"Rudolph."

"You know, I was thinking we should do an exhibition on Rothko," he murmured dreamily, running his hands over the fat pink spine of a Philip Guston book.

"Rudolph, the police are here."

Quickly he looked up. Madison's face was pinched with anxiety.

"They're upstairs," she whispered. "You need to leave. They came here asking questions about a—about a lost artwork." Her pale lips thinned, pressing back the word *stolen*. "There's some confusion, I guess, I don't know—can you talk to your clients about it? I—I think one of them might have gone overboard, because they said there's an investigation of some kind. I don't know, maybe it'd be best to go up and talk to them—?"

Her words began to blur. He could feel the blood beating in his ears. Slowly he stood and raised a finger to his lips, listening intently.

"Whaddaya think of this cat's asshole, huh? Real aesthetic!"

Lumbering through his carefully curated private rooms, guffawing over the Japanese sculpture in their broad amused Queens accents. They were, he noted in some vague far-off way, mispronouncing *aesthetic* as *estetic*, like all true philistines.

Madison was staring at him with growing horror. Something in his rigid expression twigged a reaction; she was realizing her loyalty had been horribly misplaced.

For a moment they stood frozen, with their eyes locked together, as the muffled laughter grew closer and closer, as the police boots started to thud down the polished concrete stairs. *Be quiet*, Rudolph mouthed, willing her to save him, and Madison's eyes widened.

She nodded once, rapidly.

The Guston book was still clutched in his hands. He darted back onto the busy street just as the policemen clattered to the bottom of the stairs.

He sprinted all the way through the ugly sprawl of Penn Station and the sleazy glitz of the Diamond District before he managed to catch his breath, collapsing against his knees to suck in cold air like water. You are utterly fucking insane, he thought, head spinning. You sick, sick puppy. Why would you return to the scene of the crime, like some idiot sentimental serial killer?

Blankly his head whipped this way and that, overwhelmed by the flashing red and green and yellow city lights and the noise and the cars, the smiling advertisements and shrieking trains. It was enough to make him scream.

But, almost as quickly, a cold and calm rationalism slid over the surface of his brain. The voice was steely, absorbed from one of those criminal lawyers from the cop shows he'd seen as a kid. *Ditch your phone*, it whispered. *They could be tracking it. You've got days until the FBI alerts the British police, maybe less.*

In less than two minutes, he'd bought a business class ticket out of JFK and texted Ingrid to let her know he was coming home. Rudolph broke into a light jog, tossing his phone into a garbage can near the hotel. One last look at the place he had dreamed of—now he was gone, sinking back into the stillborn pile of ashes once known as Rudolph Sullivan. The criminal lawyer whispered into his ear, *Time to run.*

40

THE SKY WAS STILL BLUE, A BLUE MIXED WITH CINDERS WHERE RAIN clouds began to thicken and clot by the time Rudolph got out of the car. His legs were shaking so hard with fear and exhaustion that he half-wanted to collapse right there on the wet street. The relief of coming home overwhelmed him. Never had a place looked and smelled so beautiful, like silver and green trees and cool vaporous fog—his front door burned out of the drizzle like a green flame.

"Ingrid? Ingrid?"

Very gingerly, he opened the door and let himself into the hallway. It was empty. He could hear the noise of his suitcase wheels, squeaking too loudly across the limestone tiles, as though he were walking underwater.

"Baby?" he called. His voice sounded strangely high and tight.

The rooms had never seemed so spectrally dark and empty, as if built for some other, larger, richer family who had suddenly fled the house after a terrible disaster. Only his house and his possessions gleamed back at him, cold and shadowed.

"Ingrid, you're scaring me. Where are you?"

But she was not there. She was nowhere.

Now in a panic, he ran through every bedroom, every bathroom, and every closet in that big, big house, searching for her in every place she could possibly be. Finally he collapsed at the kitchen table. Hot tears were beginning to leak down his face. He felt panicked and lost, as if he had just missed a very important appointment without realizing it.

Outside, the sky had darkened to ash. Wind rippled at the branches, tearing the fragile limbs of trees and flinging them into the mud with a chaotic fury. A branch snapped against the glass; startled, Rudolph looked up. To his shock and joy, he saw a thin dark shape sitting motionless in the garden on a mildewed stone bench.

"Ingrid!" he cried.

He ran outside, expecting her to jump up to embrace him. But she didn't move, she did not even look up, and he had a sharp lesion of anxiety.

Her hair hung around her face, lank and unwashed; she was holding something in her hand, something crumpled and white. In the fog he could not quite make it out.

"What are you doing out here? You're going to get sick."

She didn't answer.

"I was worried about you."

"Oh, you were worried, were you?" she inquired blandly.

He swallowed. She was still holding the piece of paper in one curled-up fist.

"Good trip?"

"Oh yes," he said anxiously, and his eyes moved again to the paper. He wanted to pry it out of her hands, to look at it more closely.

"You really should change," she said tonelessly.

"Oh God—"

With a lurch of nausea, he realized the insidious odor of vomit was rising off his trousers and into the sodden rain. Ingrid was studying his bruised face with a cold, unsurprised expression, as if it answered a question someone had only recently explained to her.

Finally he reached over, laughing in a strange, high-pitched way. But even before he had forcibly pried the paper out of her palm and smoothed it flat, a nightmarish resignation had already settled over his skin like a cold sweat.

"Listen, Ingrid. I need to explain something—"

For a moment her whole body stilled as if she were listening to a high-pitched noise just out of reach. Her silence petrified him.

"I just—well." He babbled. "First of all, I want you to remember the good in me. Whatever I've done I know we can get past it, and we'll be happy. Just as happy as we always were."

Her eyes surveyed him like a stranger, cold and black and shining.

"Happy?"

"Yes," he whispered, afraid.

"Happy?" she repeated, and in her laugh he heard a sharp disturbance. "Happy, is that what you think we were?"

She advanced toward him. Her shape was like a huge spider in the rain. Fear seized his body; he backed away, stumbling into a cracked pot of hydrangeas bleeding mud into the weeds.

"Is that why you stole three million dollars? Had me fired?" She jeered with disbelief. "Happy!"

"It wasn't like that—"

"Oh, it wasn't, was it?" she said. "You dirty little asshole. You dirty conniving little asshole. Happy!" She kept saying it over and over again, until he longed to put his hands over her mouth, the words getting higher- and higher-pitched until her piercing voice reached a scream. "Happy! Yes, Rudolph, I've never felt so fucking happy in my life."

"Listen—" he cried, but she swung away into the wet serpentine darkness where the overgrown weeds grew wild. He followed her, fear pulping his heart, groping for words to convince, anything.

"I love you. I love you I love you I really do—"

"And I know all about the clients!"

She was screaming now. Her face was contorted into something he didn't recognize.

"Who is Rudolph Gris? What are you doing with the money?"

For a split second he didn't answer. At this fatal hesitation, she laughed sardonically and wheeled around as if she'd expected nothing less.

"It's me, it's me!" he cried, frantically, but too late; he'd forgotten the cruel etiquette of fights gone this sour. He shouted after her: "My clients—what was I doing that they hadn't done themselves? They're parking cash in my taxes, avoiding taxes, moving their money from one eviscerated company to the next—why them and not me? Why should they get everything and not me?"

He was searching blindly for her, screaming, "Why should anyone feel sorry for them and not me!"

A blur of white flew past his vision. He seized at her like an escaped animal, twisting her forcibly back to face him, but as soon as he saw her eyes he realized his mistake.

"I should've known when you told me about your mother," she said. "You know what I think? You're nothing but a greedy little narcissist, an insane thief. You never cared about me, or anyone. You only wanted me to save you, be your mommy and wipe away your snotty tears— to control me—God, am I glad to be rid of you, am I ever glad! You manipulated me into marrying you, you needy little fucking freak."

He stared at her. Tears sprang to his eyes; he felt as though she'd stuck one fist through his beating heart and rudely wrenched it apart.

"Stop it," he whispered. "Please stop. We don't have time. The police are coming."

She shook her head, uncomprehending.

"What are you talking about?"

"I'm saying I'm about to be arrested."

Her expression froze in shock.

"What?"

The cold rain needled at his skin, soaking his hair to his skull. He began talking quickly, excitedly, documents, passports, he had it all, but already she was turning away, shaking like a person who has just been plunged into a bucket of ice. He was losing her, he realized; unthinkably, he was losing.

"Don't you get this is not a joke anymore?" he screamed. "Come on! I'm so sick of you acting like the world's a big fucking surprise. Yes, I was stealing. Where did you think all this money comes from? Hope in the human goddamn spirit? Open your fucking eyes! You say you loved me, but you knew—"

"I didn't!"

"—that was part of the appeal, wasn't it? But you didn't care, because people like you never want to know," he sneered, his voice swelling with rage now against all the people who could never face up to the truth. "That would ruin the aesthetic, wouldn't it? That would ruin the cookie-cutter aesthetic of your fake progressive ideals. But let me tell you, Ingrid, you don't get anything out of life except by going full throttle. And still I love you—God, do I love you!—but I'm not blind. You've done everything you could to avoid struggle, including marrying me. So I want you to know something, really know it this time, because guess what? The world is fucking dirty. And the people paying for you and your friends to have your beautiful ideals, their money is made from dirt and blood. Like mine."

He tried to force her eyes back to his. But she was shaking her head, already resisting his power, resisting his pull, and now she said slowly, in a voice that was raw with hurt:

"No. No, I can't come with you. Not even if I wanted to. Because the thing about you is that you're warped, Rudolph. You're warped and corrupt and corroded, and if I went with you I'd be all that too."

A sharp rod of agony entered his heart.

"Don't say that," he whispered.

She wrenched away and suddenly he was scrabbling after her he is nothing more than a little boy beating at his mother's door until she flings it open and shouts *What did I tell you about NOT opening my door* and he cannot breathe he is choking with fear can you just look at me he is saying we still have time if we leave now the boat he is trying to tell her *I will be waiting for you outside the . . . but I need you*—but even as he is gabbling like a man on speed she smacks him in the face with a stinging horrible smack and he reels away in the mud with a cry.

Her hand flew to her mouth. Her eyes were frightened, shocked by her own capacity for violence, for a moment a wild hope in him mistook her expression for regret.

"Listen," he cried, struggling to find the only true words in his heart. "I need you. I don't want to be this person. Please—I can be different. You make me different. Please, God, help me, let me try to be good."

But when she looked down at him, pleading in the mud, he realized he had been sorely mistaken. Her gaze swept over him, so hard he shrank away from it. It was a look of the most implacable contempt.

"You've never realized," she said coldly, "that some things can't be bought."

She left then. Rudolph was alone with his miserable self.

The dark ceiling of sky had opened up. Lashes of gray rain rushed downward, the first low percussive notes of an ice storm. For a moment he stood there, lurching hazily back and forth as if he'd been struck.

When he was a boy, he would sometimes wake between unclean sheets, in an atmosphere of absolute silence just like this. At night, his mother's despair would seep like smoke into the squalid bedroom where he lay, listening to the shriek of distant railcars and looking out at the corrugated tin roofs rolling out over the horizon below. It was here that his dream had begun, his dream of opening a bright green door into a bright clean house where he could hold the woman he loved and hear the music of children float up from the lawn. But somehow, as he aged, that dream had grown to astonishing size. He had learned to lust after those cool private rooms hidden from view, he'd wanted to pave his house and his garden and his wife in layer after layer of liquid gold, and somehow the simplicity of the original dream had dissolved through his hands like a million grains of sand.

UNDERGROUND

DAT'S KAPITAL

The Suicide of a Disgraced Gallerist

December 20, 2018

Hello, dearly beloved readers.

Many of you have been following my extended series on my former friend, the disgraced art dealer Rudolph Sullivan, who drowned at sea off the coast of Thailand eight months ago after vanishing in November 2017. His death followed a grueling international manhunt by British and US law enforcement and furious billionaire investors, who accused Sullivan of fleecing the art establishment in an elaborate years-long Ponzi scheme to the tune of $80 million.

I can now exclusively reveal here that Sullivan's reported drowning was, in fact, a suicide. To Sullivan's friends and victims—namely, myself—the news came as a devastating shock, not least because our litigation was jerked to a halt.

As readers of my column know, I loved Rudy from the moment I met him in 2008, then a suave twenty-four-year-old art world prodigy with auburn curls and a patrician Boston lockjaw. Less than two years after joining gallerist Harry Olbrich as an intern, Sullivan was sitting in the front row of auctions as a sales director bidding on multimillion-dollar works. By thirty-three, he had opened galleries in New York's Chelsea and London's Mayfair, regularly advising a roster of high-profile clients.

We were the best of pals, drinking buddies. He was the source for many of my gossip columns. He was charismatic,

funny, and quick-witted—though his meteoric rise did strain
credulity for some. Later I would find out that his apparent
wealth, like so many things he told me about himself,
was a lie. Sources have since told me that his mother was
an alcoholic drifter who had been disinherited from her
wealthy family, and instead he had a clandestine financial
relationship with Olbrich.

Unfortunately, I can't spill too many details before my
upcoming movie on our wild ride through the art world.
Beloved readers, please don't forget that *Rudolph & Me* airs
on streaming platforms worldwide September 3.

Shortly after he opened his New York gallery, I noticed
Rudolph's behavior becoming more erratic than usual. The
market was beginning to shift. Though he never confided in
me about the extent of his $40 million debts, he was drinking
a lot. He had a new girlfriend, Ingrid Groenfeld, who later
became his wife. The FBI considered Groenfeld a suspicious
enough character to warrant a six-month investigation into a
fraudulent transfer she purportedly executed as an assistant
at Paul Bernot Gallery.

After the Bowes market crashed, Rudolph began
planning a sophisticated con involving forged consignment
agreements, works fraudulently sold at auction, and
artworks owned by clients as collateral against bank loans.
I myself was scammed out of an eight-hundred-thousand-
dollar Gunter.

In January 2017, I went looking for him at his London
gallery. The gallery was shut, the walls bare. I peered through
the window: the fridge was open. I saw nothing on its shelves
but a leftover yogurt, gone moldy.

Where had he vanished? I heard rumors of a remote Pacific Island, the Bahamas, Cuba, Australia. Wherever he was hiding, I was sure his wife had the key.

In early 2018, I tracked down Groenfeld to the suburban town of Schaumburg, Illinois, where she was said to be working as a store clerk in a third-rate gallery at the local mall.

I hid in the parking lot until I spotted Groenfeld walking over to a battered ten-year-old Toyota. Wearing a stained polo and wrinkled khakis, she looked almost unrecognizably haggard and thin. When she saw me approaching, she drove off at top speed.

Thankfully, I can now exclusively share new details on my psychopathic friend's mysterious disappearance. On an anonymous tip, I traveled to Phuket to interview the driver of the tourist boat Rudolph reportedly boarded a few weeks after fleeing London. Speaking through a translator, the driver described a well-dressed American, whom he identified as Rudolph Sullivan through a photo I provided. The boat driver alleges that after a night of heavy drinking from a flask, the tourist began to weep and voice suicidal thoughts.

"I am frightened of that man," the driver told me. "He crying about his wife, his job. He jumping and jumping and the boat move up and down. I'm yelling to him stop, stop, but he is crying too hard."

The driver indicated that Rudolph had jumped overboard near shark-infested waters around Racha Island, nearly causing the motorboat to tip over. A diamond pin and an American passport belonging to the deceased conman were later found on board.

One question remains: Where did Rudolph hide his stolen treasure? Most of his ill-begotten gains seem to have disappeared into the ether. "We estimate between fifty and seventy million in cash assets," the lawyer tells me. "Unfortunately, the legal hoops required to jump through make it unlikely we'll ever find all the money. It could be anywhere–nameless accounts in the Caymans, Lichtenstein, Central America–and his computer appears to have disappeared with him. He could have used bearer bonds to physically retain ownership of the accounts without any digital trace. They may resurface years from now."

Next week I'm off to a writer's retreat in Montauk to explore the real-life psychology behind this suicidal American Psycho. Readers, your cash contributions are always appreciated while I mourn the man I thought I knew–along with the $800,000 he stole from me.

Editor's note: All charges against Groenfeld have since been dropped.

ONE

W<small>HEN THE AGENTS FIRST TOLD</small> I<small>NGRID WHAT HAD HAPPENED TO</small> Rudolph, she simply stared at them in disbelief. For months, her life had seemed to be sliding into a grotesque and bizarre derangement, but this, this . . . She had the sensation of hurtling down a broken roller coaster, one she could not—not for the life of her—get off.

Suicide, she'd thought dizzily.

Sharks.

This is not real. Not true.

But they were nodding dourly, these people who knew the facts of her life so very, very well. Who had followed her and hounded her from practically the day Rudolph had disappeared. Who said slyly, *We know all about your time at Paul Bernot. It's unfortunate, but we won't be able to stop the district attorney from filing a case against you. Unless you help us.*

Unless you've got something to trade.

I don't know where he is, she'd insisted over and over and over again. *I don't know where he would have kept the money. We never talked about his business problems. I thought the transfer instructions came from Claudia.*

I don't know anything.

In December, facing her first rounds of questioning by the London police for weeks on end, Ingrid had wandered their Chelsea townhouse, where Rudolph's ghostly presence lingered in every empty space. She had left the half-drunk negroni on his desk, hesitating occasionally in the doorway to glance at it, as though he might walk back in at any moment to finish it. When at last the orange syrup started to rot, to congeal with flies, she'd finally picked up the glass and poured the viscous liquid down the drain.

In January she had dragged her suitcase away from Cheyne Walk, the same little rollie suitcase they had first gone to Paris with. She had turned to give Rudolph's green door one last long look. Sold, by the bankruptcy court, like all their other shared assets, to some faceless LLC to pay Rudolph's angry creditors.

Where should I go now? she wondered in desolation. What can I do?

On the phone to Richard, her sobs came thick and fast. *I don't I don't know where to go from here.* When he invited her to stay in Greenpoint until she found a new job, she had sagged against a stranger's car, weak with relief.

The FBI had gone silent, though at the time she failed to note anything ominous in this. Phone tapping, sifting through internet records, interviewing Paul, Claudia, Madison, the investors. Weaving a new tapestry in which she appeared as predator instead of prey. All these things could pass silently before your unknowing eyes, struggling against the tide of grief and panic.

Except one day there was a dark-haired man, waiting for her, outside Richard's apartment. He wondered if she wouldn't mind coming into the station for a minute. No, rest assured she wasn't the focus of the investigation. They just had a few questions about the operational setup of Rudolph Sullivan Limited, which had paid out a monthly salary to her British checking account between the months of August and December.

The whereabouts of her husband.

The possibility that he'd received help.

It took her a while to understand what they were asking of her. When the gravity of her situation dawned, she had opened her mouth to protest, to speak. Nothing came out. They were staring at her, with that same cold expression she'd seen before, in another institutional room, where every slip, every elision in her halting voice, sounded like an admission of guilt. How had Rudolph sunk her so low? He was a coward.

January. For weeks, her job applications had been mysteriously denied; now, with mounting anxiety, Ingrid watched her interviewer at a New York gallery run his plush blue eyes over her bare résumé. A grimace settled over his features.

Groenfeld? he muttered between his teeth.

Yes, she wanted to say, gripping the sides of her chair. Yes, that's me.

She wanted to get on her knees and beg. Could they refuse if they knew about her draining bank accounts, the student loan payoffs on which she'd fallen behind, the spiraling interest on her credit cards?

But it was all over Google as soon as you searched her name. The salacious story of the disappearing art dealer had gone right up from industry gossip to glossy magazines, national newspapers in a flurry of excitement. "*Disgraced art dealer disappears without a trace,*" the papers blared. "*Suspicious three-million-dollar transfer linked to wife of Ponzi-scheming art dealer.*" At parties, Claudia would tell people, "I always knew that girl was a scammer."

The fact was that Ingrid was untouchable. Every job application looked flimsy, its banal typeset font a thin stopgap against the intolerable reality of Rudolph's absence. She wondered how such an ordinary thing—as unluckiness—could make you hate the world with such a rigid passion.

In May, three weeks after they'd told her that he was dead, she called Eloise. They hadn't spoken since Eloise called Rudolph to congratulate them after the wedding; even now, calling her former mother-in-law wasn't quite as dutiful as it seemed. Ingrid had her own reasons. But when Eloise picked up the phone, Ingrid had instantly regretted it.

"Ingrid, is that you?" Eloise asked, her reedy voice cracking.

Ingrid cradled the phone in her hand.

"Yes. It's me."

They spoke for over half an hour, Ingrid pacing as they talked. Eloise blamed herself. He had always bitten off more than he could chew. She spoke in vague, almost metaphysical terms about "the tragedy," as though it were a terrible accident that had occurred to somebody else.

"Lyndon's going to try to keep it out of the press," she said morosely. "The fact that he—he . . ."

Ingrid stopped pacing. When she spoke, her voice was dry.

"How do you know for sure? How do we know absolutely, one hundred percent sure, that he killed himself? That he's really—?"

"Dead?"

She couldn't say it. Eloise let out a humorless croak that might have been a laugh or a sob.

"Oh, Ingrid. You didn't know?"

"What's to know?" Ingrid interrupted roughly.

Eloise drew in a ragged breath.

"I know what Rudolph thinks—thought. That I could've done better. But he never knew the half of it. We had a bad time, you see. A very bad time."

Ingrid said nothing. Anger was silently rising inside her on Rudolph's behalf. Of course he'd known how bad it was, she thought, living inside that oppressive house every day with you.

"You see, I met a Swiss man—" Eloise inhaled sharply. There was a silence over the phone, so long and quiet that for a moment Ingrid thought the call might have dropped. Then she heard Eloise, speaking in a low and rapid voice, as if she were afraid of being overheard. "I met a Swiss man when I was young. Lyndon gave him a job, and I—I was meant to go to Smith, but then I . . . I realized I was pregnant, and . . . at any rate. Rudolph was born. We decided to leave Boston, we decided to live in Zurich for a while."

Ingrid felt confused.

"What happened?"

Eloise paused. "We came back." Her breathing sounded wet, heavy.

"And then Jorgen saw—he saw something he didn't like."

"What?"

But Eloise did not respond. The silence grew tense, weighted with secrets.

"He always was jealous of us," Eloise said, in a monotone, and Ingrid heard the bright crack of gin on ice. Ice cubes, rattling inside a glass. The dark red threads in Rudolph's hair, his uncle's hair. The rattling noise seemed to stretch out for hours: then a sudden understanding came.

Horror clogged her throat.

"Anyway, what does it matter now? He left the car on. The exhaust."

"But—but Rudolph never told me."

"He found him, see. Rudolph found him in the garage," Eloise said. "Lyndon said we should never speak of it. Just as much for him, you see . . . Rudolph was only five or six at the time . . ." She sounded as if she were arguing with herself. "Lyndon said that if anyone knew, well, it would ruin Rudolph's prospects. Suicide's a disease, that's what he said. So we didn't breathe a word. But I always told Lyndon that we would be punished for what we did. It was—unforgivable. In the eyes of God it was unforgivable. Oh by God I wish we had never done it I wish we had never done it I told Rudolph enough times don't talk bad about your uncle."

Her voice rose maniacally high at the end; Ingrid heard her shudder forcibly down the phone, asphyxiating a lifetime of secrets. Then she let out a dry, bitter chuckle.

"At any rate," she said tonelessly. "It was all so long ago."

"Wait," Ingrid managed, sensing that Eloise was about to hang up. "Hold on. Please—what was his name?"

"Hmm?" Eloise murmured, swallowing.

"The man, the Swiss man. What was his name?"

Eloise giggled. Her voice sounded sour, almost mean, and Ingrid had a brief flash to Rudolph's childhood. It must have felt like this voice sounded, she thought—it came to her as a fact, with a shiver baked inside. Sour and degraded and mean.

"Jorgen, dear. Jorgen Gris. Ugly name, isn't it? I always told him he had the ugliest name."

After she'd hung up the phone, Ingrid sat in shock for several minutes.

My father sort of skived off when I was younger, Rudolph had said on their first date.

What did he see? she wondered now. In their final, furious fight, and afterward, she'd stopped believing in anything he said. Lies were his greatest betrayal, because it felt like their whole life had been built on a fiction, an idea of him, and she was starting to realize how living out an idea that lacked truth—because you fought it off—could poison you. Could poison everything. But, after that phone call, Rudolph had become human to her, which was the worst of all: she could not even live with her hatred. Once again, she'd pictured him as a little boy, chubby and redheaded, wandering into a garage, wanting to play, he'd always wanted to play. There, a body waited.

Enfolding him, she could smell the noxious fumes, which she herself was smothered by.

At night, sometimes, she woke up in the act of searching, hands groping disorientedly along the bed, as if, like one of Pompeii's sleeping figures, he might reappear as a fallen corpse immortalized in lava.

Never before had she realized how beautiful the most passive human gestures could be, as when she imagined his warm living body asleep beside her, a bead of sweat trailing down his forehead during a spell of feverish heat.

Eventually, when Richard apologized to her and said that, unfortunately, he had another friend coming to visit, Ingrid assured him that she'd been meaning to visit home for some time now. Lucky to have family. Lucky to have money for a long-haul bus ticket, just enough. Lucky on a cold March morning to drag her battered suitcase up the icy drive of her stepmother's ugly beige-brown Dutch Colonial.

In the Chicago suburb where they lived, Lina waited at the door. Her arms were folded, her face impassive against the pale sky. Behind her, an empty basketball net fluttered like a dried-out leaf in the wind.

Her father shut the car door. His eyes darted between his daughter and wife.

"It's just temporary," he said nervously.

Lina pursed her lips into a tight little smile.

"Welcome," she said to Ingrid. "Welcome home."

TWO

At 9:00 a.m., the rich chemical scent of salt and butter started pumping from the pretzel stand and swirling through the Schaumberg Mall, forcing an automatic salivation response in customers panting over potential purchases. When she first began working at the mall, Ingrid herself had fallen prey, moving wildly from Bed Bath & Beyond to Nordstrom and back like a confused lab rat, as if there was something she'd forgotten that she really, really needed to buy. You got used to it. But on mornings like this, when the FBI came to call, the smell of butter turned Ingrid's stomach.

Agent Bailey lounged over Ingrid's desk, hands looped in her belt. Behind her, the dusty sign blazing SYMPHONIA GALLERIES cast a sickly light over her blond ponytail, illuminating the orange foundation settling into the creases of her weather-beaten face. Six months ago, when Ingrid had first met her in the interview room—shaking like a child hauled off to a police station—Bailey had offered her that same bright sorority-girl smile. *I'm a Midwesterner, too!*

"—possessions," Bailey was saying, and Ingrid snapped to. She had missed something. It was happening more and more these days.

"What did you say?"

"I said his possessions." Bailey looked at her. "I know you wanted to give his mother the things we recovered from the boat, but if you don't take them, they'll just be destroyed."

Ingrid opened her mouth. She was afraid to cry, afraid of many things.

"His family doesn't want them?"

Bailey paused. She said gently, "They've refused to take them."

Ingrid turned away. Her hands were trembling. She began to sort through the pile of mail for the gallery on her desk to stop herself from saying something she regretted.

"The pin? His special diamond pin?"

Her voice sounded hoarse. Somewhere—last week, last month, last year—she had lost the habit of speaking, the normality of it. Occasionally, desperate for human contact, she tried to speak to customers in the store. But they always turned away, repelled by something mechanical in her face.

"Yes. The pin and the passport."

Ingrid's hands slowed over a credit card bill.

"Yes, I want them. Give them to me."

"All right then."

Bailey looked at her with mild dislike. Of course she'd heard about the girl's slide into bankruptcy, but that was what you got for marrying a con artist. The agency may have made some mistakes here and there, she conceded—in their aggression, in leaking certain unflattering things to the media—but there was no smoke without fire, or such had initially been their impression.

Still, some nagging pity for the wife had dragged her back to this shitty mall. Bailey tried to smile at Ingrid Groenfeld now. But the other woman's expression was so hostile that Bailey turned away in embarrassment to examine a shelf.

"Cute little bunny," Bailey commented, picking up a dusty silver rabbit.

A cold prickle of dislocation crept over Ingrid's skin. The sculpture was a hollow copy of the priceless stainless-steel Jeff Koons that Rudolph had once kept in his apartment—it was a fake, like all the other hallucinogenic purple Marilyns roaring with laughter and goggle-eyed Picassos in this glorified toy shop.

"It's Jeff Koons–inspired," she said flatly, using the word Symphonia employees were required to describe the replicas for legal reasons. "Eighty dollars."

Bailey examined it.

"You know, I got custody of my kid for Christmas. Might make a real good present."

Ingrid ignored her. She sifted through the mail, half-watching the hopeful families looking for holiday gifts in the tinsel-strewn windows as Mariah Carey's "All I Want for Christmas Is You" piped through the speakers.

"Anything good?" Bailey peered at the envelope. "Ooh, must be a wedding invitation. Fancy one."

Ingrid's hands stilled. She glanced down at the bright pile of furniture catalogues and pizza delivery coupons, ads for office clothing. One envelope was different from the rest. It was stiff and cream-colored, like expensive stationery. A hand-glued label bore her name in painstaking black font.

"That'd be nice, huh? Weddings," Bailey said hopefully. "Be nice to get out a little. See some people, have some fun, eh?"

Ingrid stuffed the envelope in her pocket. She couldn't tell Bailey that it had been a long time since she received any form of invitation.

Realizing there was no more small talk to be made, Bailey slid a plastic bag across the plywood desk. The gold foil of an American eagle glinted up from Rudolph's passport.

"Bye," Bailey cried awkwardly, giving Ingrid a stiff half-wave as she shouldered her purse. The bell jingled on her way out, chiming in time with a news alert on Ingrid's phone: Simone had just been nominated to represent the United States at the Venice Biennale.

*   *   *

Night.

Outside, the sky was so overpoweringly opaque that it seemed to devour the stars. Only sharp white pinpricks showed in the darkness, like holes in a sheet.

Ingrid smoked alone on the stone patio, brushing embers over her father's rusted grill. Inside the glass door she could see the reflection of Lina and her father, pretending to follow the blue glare of *Cold Case* from the couch. Their eyes kept flicking worriedly toward her.

Before anyone knew that Ingrid's legal case would devour half their retirement fund, she would sometimes find her parents, looking at sunshine-colored pamphlets on the breakfast table. Oranges, palm trees, condominiums with a pool. Florida. Their eyes had brightened at the prospect of some golden years together, those of rest and relaxation, which her father had worked so many decades to achieve.

One chilly October morning, after the case was finally closed, Ingrid caught her stepmother crying in the laundry room. The lawyers' bills had just been paid. Ingrid had closed the door immediately, and Lina turned away, but not before Ingrid saw her stifling hot, angry tears into one of her half-brother's freshly washed T-shirts.

The condominium pamphlets stopped coming. Their faces grew haggard and gray.

Standing on the patio, Ingrid removed the plastic bag from her purse. Old diamonds glittered out of Rudolph's antique belt pin, the silver tarnished and brown with age. His passport was so crumpled and stained with water you could barely see the photograph: a boy ten years younger, his smile beaming unknowingly up at her.

Her eyes moved back to her phone screen. Simone was getting an award. She smiled radiantly up at Ingrid in a gauzy blue dress, the picture of truth, happiness, and success. *Stand true to what you believe*, chanted the capricious refrain of clichés in her head. *Follow your passion.*

Maybe it could still happen for you.

She stubbed out her cigarette. Her fingers were yellow, she was smoking too much. Sometimes she wanted this, the wrinkling and the rot, the stiffness overtaking her limbs. Sometimes she wanted to feel death inside her body. The patio was shrouded in darkness now; it seemed that no amount of cheerfulness or hopefulness or perseverance could help her find what she had lost in the hour between daytime and night.

A cold gust of wind flew through the kitchen, mingling sharply with the fragrant red-wine smells of Lina's tomato Bolognese. Lina glanced up at the slam of the patio door, but Ingrid was already disappearing down the stairs, into her half-brother's childhood bedroom. She lived in the basement now. She huddled into the navy astronaut duvet for warmth, staring up at the galaxies of green plastic stars that swirled across her brother's ceiling.

The sharp points of the envelope poked into her thigh like a warning.

Someone knocked on the door; startled, she threw the envelope under the bed.

"Hon. You want dinner?"

"I'm fine, Dad, thanks!" she called back, trying in vain to sound calm, trying in vain to slow her rapidly beating heart. When her father's footsteps finally faded away, she seized the envelope and tore it open. The blank side of the postcard revealed a small, unsteady forward scrawl, and her eyes caught a line midway down the paragraph:

*I still love you. I know now I always loved you—more than I
could ever say. I blame myself for everything, I blame myself
for your anxiety and pain. But losing you is crushing my heart,
and I . . .*

Darkness shuttered the sides of her vision. She put her head in her hands, trying to slow her panicked breathing, as if that might stop the frantic joy climbing vine-like through her limbs. He had told her he loved her, he had told her he was still alive. He was alive. It was a dream—for a second she thought she'd imagined it or gone mad. It was as she'd suspected. He had paid off the boat driver or something—she didn't know how he'd done it but he had gotten away.

And she could do nothing about it. The brute pain of this realization almost gagged her, and she made a muffled choking sound. Lina rapped at the door anxiously, saying Ingrid, Ingrid, are you sick? And the truth was that she was, she was.

Rudolph Sullivan had drowned.

But Rudolph Gris was very much alive.

THREE

THREE O'CLOCK IN THE AFTERNOON. INGRID SAT SLOWLY CHEWING A bean-and-cheese Chipotle burrito underneath Symphonia's drained fluorescent lights. Under her desk, her hand kept clenching and unclenching the torn envelope and postcard inside. She needed to throw it away, but her fist kept curling up whenever she tried to drop it in the trash.

A glossy watercolor of an island was printed across the front of the postcard, which, at first, she took for a stock photo. Silver beaches stretched around a mountain of raw jungle; dark leaves shadowed row after row of wood villas shaped like conical straw hats. The Indian Ocean seemed to tremble invisibly like a blue jewel in motion. Carefully, she angled the postcard under the violet lamp; a hurried dash of scarlet caught her eye. She hadn't noticed it before.

In the storeroom she found a magnifying glass and bent to examine the picture more closely. The red speck revealed the billowing sails of a boat, the word *Alexa* outlined in tiny white cursive no bigger than an eyelash. A *phinisi* schooner, she realized with a start. With trepidation, she touched the card, absently noting the dried texture of real paint.

A map.

Her eyes followed the horizon, where sea met sky in a hush of magic stillness. Those dark contours—she recognized them. They used to look at them together. It was an Indonesian island. He must have taken the boat after all. With one finger she traced the silver beach, picturing herself diving into seawater as mellow as a fresh bath. The texture of Rudolph's skin, wet and smooth like a seal as he burst out of the waves to surprise her. The happy isle.

The bell jingled; Ingrid looked up to see a pair of thin young women edging through the door with film equipment, dressed in black leather with their hair braided and shaved on one side. Watching them laugh together, Ingrid experienced a quiet ache of longing.

"It's literally perfect, isn't it?" the blonde was saying. Her accent was English. She waved her camera around excitedly. "It's practically essential for my study of capitalistic decline. See? People are just stuck in these crumbling Rust Belt shitholes right up until they go into a nursing home."

Ingrid's veins flooded with ice. It was Daisy.

Ingrid wanted to melt into the floor. But Daisy was turning around, and as her eyes opened in shock, Ingrid realized, with humiliation, that she had just spilled burrito sauce down her shirt. Its wet lumps trailed shamefully down her faded navy Symphonia polo shirt, as shining and reddish-brown as the red letter *A*.

"Ingrid? Is that you?"

"Daisy," she managed. "Finally doing the movie on suburban malls, I see."

Daisy nodded slowly. She was still gazing at Ingrid in astonishment.

"Yeah. Yeah, well, LA was a little oversaturated for the skincare thing, in the end. Who knew they'd already have three astrological beauty companies floating around?"

Me, Ingrid thought, watching Daisy laugh thinly. She'd lost her patience for Daisy's dizzy manic pixie dream girl persona, her childish careless attitude toward money and jobs and things.

"And you?" Daisy said, avoiding her gaze. "How're you doing with everything?"

Ingrid attempted to smile; mortified, she felt tears coming.

"I'm fine," she insisted, lips jerking upward. "I'm actually really loving it here."

For a second or two, Ingrid hoped Daisy would have mercy and leave. She could even see the twin instincts of compassion and curiosity battling inside Daisy's head. But, in the end, the prospect of filming the wife of a criminal she actually *knew* was too juicy for Daisy to resist. Ingrid felt worn down. So when Daisy asked her if she'd feel comfortable speaking on film, she said yes. She no longer had the strength to say no.

"I just *care* about exposing the misery of corporate consumption," Daisy kept assuring her brightly. "I care about you!"

Ingrid nodded weakly. The camera lights fell heavy on her face.

After Daisy finished the interview, Ingrid knew she should file some invoices, maybe get a start on Symphonia's taxes. Instead, she gazed at the shaky black ink of Rudolph's handwriting on the page. Could it be him? If she stayed here, her misplaced longings would die a long, slow death—choked down, bit by bit, year by year, in her chest. But if she slipped away, told her parents she'd gotten a job in Europe now that law enforcement had let her fall from sight—

Do I dare? she asked herself, afraid of the answer.

She loved him now in a way she never had when they had been together. From London to New York to Chicago she had carried around an ever-more-dwindling bar of his soap. This was a sentimental act that she never told anyone about. But then she never talked about him to anyone, nowadays. Only occasionally did she allow herself to unwrap it, to furtively inhale its secret scent. The soap was disintegrating now. Its flakes were dissolving, under her nails, into an oily powder like gristle the harder she gripped it.

Choose, a voice whispered in her ear.

Slowly, she uncurled her fingers from Daisy's credit card. The pallid fluorescents gleamed over the silver centurion. The idiot hadn't even noticed Ingrid pocket it in their goodbye embrace. Daisy wouldn't pay her own American Express bills; people like Daisy never did.

"Welcome to Batik Air, this is Michael."

He sounded so friendly that Ingrid automatically smiled back. She loved the way people talked to you on the first-class line—so professional, so efficient.

"Well now. I can I see you're calling about a flight to Bali, is that right? Business or pleasure?"

"A little bit of both," she answered truthfully.

"Isn't it always!" he laughed. "And you wanted to add a charter flight to Sumba, didn't you? Could I just get your sixteen-digit card number, please?"

She read out Daisy's sixteen-digit card number to Michael on the phone. The flights were booked; the baggage, added. But something in his voice gave her pause—its kindness, perhaps. Was he an honest man? Ingrid wondered. Would he ever steal from a friend? She imagined him going home to a two-up, two-down suburban house like her parents', kissing a baby in a crib. Accepting the limits of his life, and so could she. Why did she need to want something so very, very much? So much it consumed her?

When she shut her eyes, she could hear the cry of birds across a molten sea of turquoise water. Rudolph smiled at her from a nearing boat. But when he slid down his sunglasses to greet her—she blinked in shock—his eyes were filled with malignant red flames.

Fear crept down her spine.

How would it end? she asked herself, tracing the torn edges of the envelope.

She peered into the silver globe of the rabbit, searching its distorted mirrors for the answer to her own fate. Her face was gray, gray and hollow in the reflection, but the mall behind her—almost as if it had fed itself off her troubles—had fattened and multiplied into a huge silver palace twenty times its size.

For one moment, she thought she saw Rudolph trapped there, within the neon screens. Pleadingly his eyes stared out at her from between the blur of advertisements. She looked below him, at the fountains, but their crystalline waters appeared to have gone murky. The fish were dying in this rotten sediment. Christmas shoppers were shoving past, clambering up the broken escalators, elbowing each other, all to get to the top floor—to a ragged portal in the wall where a paradise should be.

Then she was standing, blinking, alone, in Symphonia.

Ingrid put on her coat. She replaced the metal rabbit carefully on the shelf. From up high, it watched her, blank-eyed but somehow smiling. Then she locked Symphonia's doors and dropped the keys through the metal grille.

Outside, the snow was cold and clear, metallic. There were so many years to get through after you'd realized that none of your dreams would come true. But her days were numbered, they passed like a night's watch, and the blood pumping through her veins was still rich and red, it thirsted for life. Her dream of love, painful and dangerous as it was, still spread out unknown garlands of magnificence before her.

She gazed at the dowdy rows of parked SUVs. Their frosted windshields were starred with new ice. Her car would leave no tracks in the snow to her parents' house, nor to the airport either. A smile spread across her face, tentatively at first, then wider.

A blank canvas. There was nothing more radical in modern art than erasure.

THE END

ACKNOWLEDGMENTS

This book is dedicated to my mother, Deborah Scroggins. Your love and faith have made this book possible at every step of the way.

Thomas, I'm so grateful to you for supporting me through many long nights and lost weekends, as well as pulling me outside into the sun again. For early readers, I'm grateful to Elizabeth Campbell, Colin Campbell, Julia Taylor, Jim Taylor, Lucy Owen-Jones, and Lilia Fetini. Each of you pointed out something helpful and gave me a new perspective on what *The Spectacle* could be.

Above all, thank you to Andrianna deLone at CAA and Barbara Berger at Union Square & Co. Andrianna, your insight and deep belief in *The Spectacle* have encouraged me so much and improved every early draft. Barbara, you took a chance on an unknown author. There will never be enough words to express how grateful I am for your confidence, knowledge, and dedication in championing this book.

I would also like to thank everyone at Union Square & Co. who worked on this book: Kristin Mandaglio, Kevin Ullrich, Sandy Noman, Patrick Sullivan, Erik Jacobsen, and Diane João, who is a fantastic copy editor.

TOPICS AND QUESTIONS FOR DISCUSSION

1. Ingrid is described in passive terms as "floating," "wandering," "relaxed, even physically numb." She observes events from a distance and is frequently depicted in apartments or houses. Rudolph, meanwhile, is constantly on the go: driving cars, flying in planes, or running to meetings. What do the characters gain or lose through action or inaction?

2. Ingrid and Simone have a conflicted relationship, at once loving and competitive. Ingrid reflects that "In many ways they had lived in a cocoon together, a friendship as passionate as a love affair." Discuss the importance of friendship in the book.

3. Throughout *The Spectacle*, art and other possessions are described in religious language. Rudolph's office is "calm and hard and pure like the inside of a chapel, or the nests of certain high-flying birds. . . . He was merely a priest, readying himself to listen to their confession, to their humble little desires." What do expensive objects mean to the characters? What do you think they are searching for in buying these things?

4. *The Spectacle* shows clear delineation between different strata of society: new money and old money, creators and consumers, the powerless and the powerful. How do you interpret the commentary on each of these groups? Is one favored over the other?

5. Throughout the book, Rudolph and other characters frequently take actions that affect Ingrid's life in negative ways. By the end, she feels like a pawn. What are the external pressures Ingrid faces? Could she have done anything to avert them?

6. Discuss the role of love in *The Spectacle*. What do Rudolph and Ingrid represent to each other? What binds them together?

7. Discuss Rudolph's quest for money and power. Does the novel praise or condemn it? What does *The Spectacle* have to say about the condition of the American dream in the 2010s?

8. At the beginning, Ingrid finds a priceless metal rabbit sculpture. By the final chapter, the sculpture has become a factory-made tourist copy at the mall where she works. Discuss the role of reflections and mirrors in *The Spectacle*. How do they reveal or conceal the difference between reality and artifice in the characters' lives?

9. List some of the signs that lead to Ingrid's discovery of Rudolph's fraudulent activities. Would you have seen the red flags that Ingrid misses?

10. In the epilogue, Ingrid considers the difference between living out her present situation and following "her dream of love, painful and dangerous as it was." Why does she find strength "only [in] its extremity"? What do you believe really happened to Rudolph? Do you respect or judge her for her radical final decision?

ABOUT THE AUTHOR

Anna Barrington is a writer who has worked in galleries and auction houses in the art world for over five years. She received an MA from the Courtauld Institute of Art and a BA from the University of St. Andrews in Scotland. Originally from Atlanta, she currently lives in London, where she works at a leading museum. *The Spectacle* is her first novel.